THE MERCILESS

THE MERCILESS II
THE EXORCISM OF SOFIA FLORES

DAN+ELLE VEGA

RAZORBILL

THE MERCILESS

DANIELLE VEGA

RAZORBILL

RAZORBILL

An Imprint of Penguin Random House LLC
Penguin.com

RAZORBILL & colophon is a registered trademark of Penguin Random House LLC.

First published in the United States of America by Razorbill, an imprint of
Penguin Random House LLC, 2014. This omnibus edition published by Razorbill,
an imprint of Penguin Random House LLC, 2018

Copyright © 2014 Alloy Entertainment

Produced by Alloy Entertainment
1325 Avenue of the Americas
New York, NY 10019

ISBN: 9781595147226

This omnibus edition ISBN: 9781984836182

Design by Liz Dresner

Printed in the United States of America

1 3 5 7 9 10 8 6 4 2

THE MERCILESS

CHAPTER ONE

I snag my thumb on the lunch tray's metal edge, and a crescent of blood appears beneath my cuticle. It oozes into the cracks surrounding my nail, then spills over to one side, forming a perfect red droplet, almost like a tear.

I swear under my breath. The cut stings, but at least I didn't smear blood across my T-shirt. Nothing says "be my friend" like serial-killer stains on the first day of school. A stack of napkins sits next to the bin of plastic silverware, but the guy in the food line in front of me is blocking it.

"Excuse me," I say, and the guy turns around. He's good-looking in that athletic, future-frat-boy way where he doesn't really have to try. His brown hair sticks up all over, and he wears a loose, wrinkled shirt, as if he's just rolled out of bed.

Years of being the new girl have helped me perfect my shy half smile. It's as close as I ever come to flirting. I motion to my bleeding finger. "Can you hand me a napkin?"

"Ouch," the guy says, grabbing a few napkins from the stack. His smile beats mine by a few watts, and I blush.

"Hey, do you need a Band-Aid?" asks a girl behind me, and I turn. She has platinum-blond hair cut short, like a boy's. Oversize black glasses without any lenses sit on her nose, and she wears a neon-pink tank top stretched so thin I can see her black bra through the material. A man's golden ring dangles from a chain around her neck.

"Yeah, thanks," I say. Next to her, my standard first-day uniform of a gray T-shirt and dark jeans looks comically plain. A few schools ago, I tried layering rubber bracelets around my wrists and coloring on my Converse sneakers with Sharpies, but today my wrists are bare, my sneakers brand-new. It's time for a change.

"Hey, Brooklyn, what's up?" The boy nods at her. They don't seem like the kind of people who'd be friends, but his tone is nice enough. Brooklyn slides her tattered backpack off one shoulder and reaches into the front pocket.

"Hiya, Charlie," she says to him. "Your brother miss me yet?"

The name *Charlie* fits the cute, athletic guy, and it makes me like him more than if his name were Zack or Chad. A Charlie helps you find your algebra class when you can't figure out your new class schedule. Chad burps the alphabet.

Charlie runs a hand through his hair, leaving it even messier than before. "*Miss* isn't the word I'd use. . . ."

"Ex-boyfriend?" I interrupt to keep from being left out of the conversation. Asking a million questions is New Girl 101. People love talking about themselves. Brooklyn pulls her hand out of her bag and hands me a clear bandage decorated with a tiny picture of a mustache.

"Ex-boss," she says. "But he'll be begging for me to come back any day now. Hey, cool tat."

She points to the crook of my hand, where I sketched a serpent wearing a headdress made of feathers. It's called Quetzalcoatl. When I was little and my mom and I still visited the tiny town where she grew up in Mexico, my grandmother told stories about Quetzalcoatl. Grandmother's too sick to tell the stories anymore, but I sketch the serpent in my journal sometimes. And on my hand, apparently.

"It's not a real tattoo," I admit, rubbing at the drawing with the palm of my other hand. I'll have to wash it off before my mom sees it. She's never liked Grandmother's religious stories. My mom got her US citizenship five years ago, and she says Grandmother's spooky Mexican folktales remind her of all the reasons she'd wanted to move away. "Just Sharpie."

"Oh." Brooklyn sounds disappointed, but Charlie raises an eyebrow and nods in approval.

"You drew that? Nice," he says.

Before I can respond, a dark-haired girl stops in the middle of the cafeteria and clears her throat. The talking, laughing students around us fall silent, as if they've been placed under a spell.

"Can I have your attention, everyone?" she asks, even though everyone's already looking at her. A group of six or seven people crowd behind her, all holding bags and cardboard boxes.

"Jesus." Brooklyn grimaces, pushing her fake glasses up her nose. Her tone is completely different than it was a second ago, when she offered me the Band-Aid. "Is it time for this shit again?"

"I'm Riley, as most of you know," the dark-haired girl continues in a clear, peppy voice. "And it's time for the annual school food drive for the St. Michael's Soup Kitchen. I hope this year you'll all help me do God's work and bring in food for the homeless. Last year alone, we collected over five hundred cans!"

Students around us start to clap. It takes me by surprise, and I join a beat too late. The only time kids at my last school clapped for people was when they tripped and dropped their lunch trays.

Behind me, Brooklyn makes a gagging sound.

"Come on," Charlie mutters. He'd been clapping with the others, but he breaks off to nudge Brooklyn with his elbow. I bite back a smile. I was wrong; he doesn't really seem like a frat boy after all.

Brooklyn makes a gun with her hand and points it at Riley's head, narrowing her eyes.

"*Pew,*" she whispers, shooting an imaginary bullet. She blows smoke from the tips of her fingers.

I raise an eyebrow as I reach past her for a carton of milk. I've hung out with girls like her before, the girls who skip third period to smoke cloves in the bathroom and pierce their ears with safety pins. It's always exciting for a while, but they never become real friends. I usually spend most of my time trying to prove I'm cool enough to hang with them.

Still, beggars can't be choosers. So when Brooklyn winks at me and says "Later," I smile and wave back.

Charlie shakes his head as Brooklyn walks away, and a few strands of floppy brown hair fall over his eyes.

His arm brushes against mine as he leans over the food counter to grab a fork and napkin.

"Don't take Brooklyn seriously," he says, flashing me a half smile. A dimple appears in his cheek. "It's not so bad here, I promise. See you around?"

My heart does a little flip inside my chest as he walks away. I've been bouncing around long enough to know my crushes never turn out the way I want them to, but I still manage to fall in love every time I meet a new guy with a great smile. I should have learned by now that high school romance isn't in the cards for me. My mom's been a medical technician for the army since moving to the States. I'm at a new school every six months, like clockwork.

This time it's Adams High School, in the tiny army town of Friend, Mississippi. Friend feels like the inside of an oven. The grass is brown, I hear insects buzzing wherever I go, and there are more churches in my neighborhood than grocery stores. I've lived in nicer places, but in the end it always comes down to the people. I hesitate near the cafeteria doors and glance back over my shoulder at Charlie. Heat creeps up my neck. This place has potential.

The students at Adams eat lunch outside, so I take my tray through the side door and head toward the bleachers. Adams High is a one-story-high building made of cream-colored brick with mud-brown siding. The classrooms are all outdated, with peeling linoleum floors and rickety desks. In fact, the only impressive part of the whole school is its football field, a deep-green stretch of Astroturf surrounded by shiny silver bleachers. Above the bleachers hangs a blue-and-white sign that reads ADAMS HIGH SPARTANS. A Mississippi flag billows in the air next to it.

As I look around for a place to sit, a gasp of hot wind blows my curls into my face. I lift a hand to push them away, immediately noticing the smell. It's like milk gone bad, or moldy cheese.

I take a step toward the bleachers, and the smell gets worse. Now it's chicken that's been in the garbage all night, fish left out in the heat. I pull my T-shirt over my nose and make my way under the bleachers.

That's when I see it.

It's a cat. A dead cat. Skin's been peeled away from the cat's body in strips. Flies buzz around its head and inside its mouth, crawling over its tongue and teeth. Red paint clings to the stiff grass beneath the cat's body, and candles surround it, cemented to the ground in pools of black wax. It takes a minute for me to see that the paint is in the shape of a star, with a black candle at each point—like a ritual.

I don't notice that I've started picking at the skin along my cuticles until I feel a sharp stab of pain and

look down to see blood pooling around another fingernail. The cat's clouded gray eyes watch me, and the flies'
constant buzz fills my ears.

"What are you doing?"

I whirl around, immediately spotting the dark-haired
girl from the cafeteria—Riley. Her brown curls pool
around her shoulders in perfect spirals, and her eyebrows
start wide and taper to needle-thin points, as if they were
drawn with a calligraphy pen. There isn't a single crease
in her blue dress. It looks like she never sits down.

Riley looks past me, her pale blue eyes finding the
skinned body of the cat. One of her eyebrows lifts, but
her face remains otherwise unchanged.

"Gross." There's no inflection in her voice. She could
be talking about the lasagna they served at lunch. I
take a step away from the cat, nearly tripping over my
sneakers.

"I didn't . . . I mean, that wasn't me. I didn't do that."

Riley turns her eyes on me. They're so pale they
change her entire face, making her dark hair and brows
seem severe. If I were going to paint her I'd have to use
watercolors—only a drop of cerulean for her eyes, keeping them as light as possible.

"Of course you didn't." She glances down at the cat
and shudders. "You're new, right? Sofia?"

"Yeah," I say, surprised she knows my name.

"Riley." She points to herself and her eyes grow several degrees warmer. "This is disgusting. I'm impressed you didn't hurl."

"Me, too." I wrinkle my nose. "Though I'm not sure I'm past the hurling stage yet."

"Right. Let's get out of here." Riley slides her arm around my shoulder and turns me away from the cat. "Come sit with me and my friends today."

She pulls me out from under the bleachers without waiting for an answer, which is probably a good thing because for once I don't know what to say. Girls I've known who look like Riley don't make friends with the new kid. It's a law of nature—Earth revolves around the sun, summer follows spring, and pretty, popular girls form cliques that are harder to break into than a bank vault. If attending seven schools in five years has taught me anything, that's it.

But Riley seemed genuine when she made her charity announcement in the cafeteria. Maybe she's different. Maybe Friend will live up to its name.

"We have the best spot for lunch," Riley explains. A few people smile and wave as we climb past them, and though Riley smiles back, she makes no move to stop and sit. "You can see everything that happens."

"Cool," I say. Riley steers us over to where only two other girls are sitting.

"Girls, this is Sofia. Sofia, this is Alexis." Riley points to a girl wearing all white—white skirt, white tank top, white sweater. Her pale blond hair is long enough for her to sit on, and she has a full, round face and wide eyes.

"Hey there," Alexis says, her voice carrying the hint of a Southern accent.

"And this is Grace." Riley motions to a girl with velvety chocolate skin and braided hair that she's twisted into a complicated-looking bun at the nape of her neck.

"Nice tie," I say, pointing to the polka-dot bow tie Grace is wearing as a necklace. Grace's lips part in a smile that's all teeth.

"Thanks! They're all the rage in Chicago."

"Grace is bringing culture to Mississippi," Alexis adds.

"Are you from Chicago?" I ask, sitting down on the bleachers next to them.

"My dad was transferred here two years ago," Grace says. "You ever been?"

I shake my head as Riley sits next to me and places her hands on her knees. Even her nails are perfect—trimmed and clean. I curl my hands into fists so she won't see my ragged cuticles.

"You'll never guess what Sof and I found under the bleachers."

Sof. The way Riley says my name is so personal and

friendly that I have to bite back a smile. Alexis and Grace lean forward, and Riley grins, a conspiratorial look on her face. She speaks in a whisper.

"A skinned dead cat."

"That's a joke, right?" Alexis asks, fumbling with the lace at the edge of her skirt. With her long hair and wide eyes, she looks like a Disney princess come to life.

Riley makes a cross over her heart. "Honest. I bet this is grounds for expulsion."

Grace shudders, nervously tapping a red Converse sneaker against the back of the bleacher in front of her. "They've got to at least suspend her. That's *disgusting.*"

"Wait." I frown. "You know who killed that cat?"

Grace, Alexis, and Riley share a look I can't interpret. It's like they're trying to figure out if I can be trusted.

"You know that girl you were talking to in the cafeteria?" Riley asks, smoothing a curl behind one ear.

"Brooklyn?" I ask, surprised. I didn't realize Riley saw me talking to Brooklyn.

"Right. Brooklyn. She can be a little strange."

"Strange how?" I ask when Riley doesn't specify. Skinning a cat isn't strange. It's criminal.

Alexis scoots forward, and one of her knees bumps against mine. "There are rumors about Brooklyn," she says. "And since you're going to this school, you should probably know about them. They're intense."

"Rumors?"

"Last year she did a séance in the girls' locker room," Alexis continues. Her Southern accent gets heavier as she tells the story, and I get the feeling she's playing it up for effect. "I was in there the next day. The floor was all black—like it'd been burned—and the entire place smelled like sage."

"Or *something*," Grace adds, and Riley giggles.

"And earlier this year, a bunch of girls heard her chanting in the back of algebra class," Alexis finishes. "It's weird."

"Weird," I repeat. But that doesn't seem to cover it. Maybe the stories Alexis is telling are just rumors— but that cat was very real. And very dead. I shiver. In slightly different circumstances, I could be eating with Brooklyn right now, probably listening to terrible stories about Riley and her friends. I don't believe the same girl who offered me a Band-Aid would also kill a cat.

"And there's what happened last year," Riley adds, "with Mr. Willis . . ."

Before she can finish, a scream rolls off the football field. I jump up, jerking my head around to search for the screamer, but then the sound dissolves into laughter and fades away.

Just someone messing around. I sit back down, feeling stupid.

Grace leans forward and puts a hand on my knee. Her bow-tie necklace swings forward like a pendulum. "Guys, stop. We're scaring her."

"Sorry," Alexis says, wrinkling her nose. I look down at my hand. I've never liked scary stories. Even my grandmother's stories about Quetzalcoatl gave me nightmares. Absently, I rub the sketch of Quetzalcoatl, leaving behind a smudge of red. Blood from my thumb.

I look up and catch Riley watching me. Her eyes follow my finger as I run it over the lines of the serpent sketch on my hand. There's an odd look on her face, the same cold expression she wore when she first saw the dead cat behind the bleachers.

"It's just a stupid sketch." I lick one finger and try to rub it away, but I just smear the ink and blood into my skin. Riley shifts her eyes back to my face, her lips lifting at the corners. The effect isn't the same as it was behind the bleachers, when her smile made her face warmer. This smile doesn't reach Riley's eyes at all. They stay empty.

"Of course," she says.

CHAPTER TWO

My classmates linger by the school doors after the last bell, waiting for rides from parents. You could walk down every street in Friend in an hour flat, but everyone still drives shiny black SUVs that leak air-conditioning and pop music from their open windows.

I see a flash of white out of the corner of my eye and turn in time to watch Alexis and Riley climb into a car. Grace waves at them from the sidewalk, surrounded by a circle of boys wearing sports jerseys and girls with shampoo-commercial hair. No matter the school, no matter the city, the popular group is always made of the same mix of athletes and the unfairly beautiful.

Everything in their lives is just a little shinier, richer—better. Of course I'd want that. Anyone would.

I slip past pockets of kids giggling and talking and start to walk home. I live so close that I can see my neighborhood from the school parking lot. The land here is all flat and dry, and the summers are so hot that I'm already sweating. It's the end of September and I'm still waiting for the last of the ninety-degree days to cool into autumn.

My neighborhood's entrance is marked by a four-foot-tall sign with the words HILL HOLLOW HOMES written in scrolling white letters. There's a fake waterfall and pond, though both are dry now, with weeds and dandelions growing through cracks in the sun-bleached rocks. Past that, the subdivision is a ghost town. The few dozen houses scattered across acres of bulldozed land are mostly empty.

I stare at the toes of my sneakers as I walk past three vacant lots and two identical houses, each with the same blue siding, white porch, and red front door as mine. Whoever chose the color scheme for our neighborhood was very patriotic.

Our place is the lone house on its block. It's a split-level with a narrow porch, a bay window, and a backyard that stretches for half an acre before the grass gives way to dirt and open land. The shed at the top of the driveway looks like a miniature version of the house itself, matching in color and style. Aside from the Uncle Sam paint job, it looks like every other house I've ever lived in.

I climb the rickety wooden steps to the door and let myself in, slipping on a brochure someone wedged under the front door. It's another advertisement for the Baptist church down the street. We've gotten two or three every day since we moved in. Mom hates the brochures so much she actually called the church to complain. She's always been a little touchy about religion. She never told me the whole story, just that Grandmother didn't take her getting pregnant out of wedlock very well.

I'm not a fan of anything that says I'm a mistake, either, but sometimes I wish she hadn't cut religion out of our lives so completely. Grandmother got over the unmarried thing by the time I was born, and I've always thought her dedication to Catholicism was beautiful. I stare down at the creepy bleeding heart on the front of the brochure. I should save them and make a collage of bleeding hearts for my wall. Mom would love that.

I drop my backpack on the kitchen table and grab a glass from the perfectly organized cupboard above the sink. We've only lived here a couple weeks, but almost all the boxes are already unpacked, our things carefully stored in cabinets and drawers. Sergeant Nina Flores handles everything with military precision.

I fill the glass with water and carry it to my grandmother's room down the hall. I knock softly before easing her door open.

"*Hola, Abuela*," I greet her as I push her door closed with my elbow, blinking in the dark. Light hurts Grandmother's eyes, so we hung heavy curtains over the windows to block the sun and draped a scarf over her floor lamp to keep her room dim. The scarf turns the room red, and it takes a moment for my eyes to adjust.

I carefully make my way over to her bedside table and dig out the plastic container of her pills. Grandmother is sitting upright in bed, rosary beads clutched in her shaking hands. She stares ahead, lips moving wordlessly as she pushes the beads through her fingers.

She used to be beautiful, but it's hard to see that now. A few years ago, a stroke ruined the muscles on the right side of her body. Skin hangs from the bones in her face like melting wax, and her cheek droops so low that I can see the foggy white bottom half of her eye and the blood-red part inside her eyelid. The right side of her mouth is frozen in a twisted frown that doesn't match up with the smiling, laughing grandmother I remember.

I force myself to slip the pills past her cracked lips, then lift the water glass so she can take a drink. She's still the grandmother who sent me funny little poems written in Spanish on my birthday, I remind myself.

Water dribbles out of the right side of her mouth. I wipe it away with my sleeve, then squeeze her papery, soft hand. Her raspy breath interrupts the silence in the room, followed by the *click click* of the wooden rosary beads against the table attached to her hospital bed. She hasn't spoken a word since the stroke.

"Okay, exercise time," I say, setting the water glass down on her bedside table. I move her blanket and carefully stretch her right leg, then ease it upward to bend her knee so her muscles don't atrophy. I do this three times, just like her last nurse showed me. We haven't been able to find a nurse for her in Friend yet.

"You would love it here, you know," I say, putting her leg down. I slide the blanket back over it and move to the other leg. "They sell statues of the Virgin at the gas station."

Grandmother's rosary beads click against the table, like the second hand on a clock. She never really notices when I do her exercises. I'm not sure she can feel her legs anymore.

"And it's *hot* here." I grab her ankle and pull her left leg into a gentle stretch. "Do you remember that summer back in Mexico when it was so hot we tried to bake cookies on your windowsill?"

The *click*s of Grandmother's rosary beads are my only answer. I bite back the rest of my story, letting the question linger, unanswered, in the air between us. I picture Grandmother standing at the window, watching the cookies bubble in the heat. That was before the stroke, back when she was strong and beautiful. When she leaned forward, the thick gold cross she used to wear swung into the cookies and got covered in gooey batter. She gave me the cross and let me lick it off, like a spoon.

Now I slide her left leg back onto the bed and cover it with her blanket. Grandmother always said she'd give me that cross some day. She hasn't worn it since before her stroke.

I flip open the cardboard box on top of the stack next to her bed, which my mom marked CLOTHING & JEWELRY, and dig through piles of sundresses until I find Grandmother's jewelry box buried underneath. I open it to find a tangled ball of pearls and beads and thin silver chains. I pick through them, carefully separating the chunky gold cross.

"Beautiful," I murmur, slipping the cross over my head. "What do you think, Grandmother? You like?"

A line of drool spills from Grandmother's mouth. I drop my arm and wipe it away with my sleeve, cringing. Downstairs, the front door opens and closes. Footsteps creak in the foyer.

"Sofia?" my mom calls.

"See you later, *Abuela*," I whisper to Grandmother before slipping into the hall.

Mom stands in the kitchen with her back to me, a bag of groceries sitting on the counter next to her.

"My class was canceled, so I ran to the supermarket," she says when I walk in, putting a carton of milk in the fridge. Her green camo scrubs hang limply from her thin frame, and tiny spots of sweat dot the small of her back. "Do you know they sell Bibles next to the tabloids at the cash register?"

"The nerve," I say, playing along. Mom doesn't notice my sarcasm. She shakes her head and pushes the refrigerator door shut. I clear my throat. "So my first day was fine."

"What?" she asks, blinking at me. Her short black ponytail pulls at the skin around her face, making her confused expression seem more severe. Then her face relaxes as she remembers. "Right, your new school. Did you make any friends?"

She says this in such an upbeat, positive way that you'd think I meet dozens of friends every time we move to a new place. In reality, I'm lucky to find one or two people to hang out with for the few months we're there.

I study Mom's face for a moment to figure out if she's trying to be upbeat or if she's just oblivious. "Oh yeah. Hundreds," I say. "They're actually calling today Sofia Flores Day. Tomorrow I get a parade."

Mom opens her mouth—probably to tell me to watch my tone—but then her eyes drop to my neck. She points to the cross I'm still wearing.

"What's that?" she asks. Without waiting for me to explain, she holds out her hand.

There's no use arguing with her, so I slip the necklace over my head and place the cross in her open palm. "I thought it was pretty."

"It's not meant to be pretty." She sighs and puts the necklace in her pocket.

I press my lips together. Sometimes I wonder how it's possible that she and Grandmother are even related.

I head back to the kitchen table, unpacking my textbooks while Mom goes upstairs to return Grandmother's cross to her jewelry box. I finish my homework in silence.

But later that night, when I'm sure my mom's asleep, I sneak from my bed and creep, barefoot, into Grandmother's room. I slip the cross from the cardboard box. Grandmother stares ahead, unblinking, while I shove it into my backpack. Half of her mouth moves in the same slow, wordless prayer while the other half remains twisted, frozen.

The only sound I hear as I pull her bedroom door shut behind me is the *click click click* of her rosary beads echoing in the dark.

CHAPTER THREE

The next day I wedge myself into one of the narrow green stalls in the girls' restroom between third and fourth periods. Black and silver Sharpie scrawls cover the door, telling me that Erika is a slut and that love that has been lost was never mine to begin with. A roll of toilet paper stretches across the black-and-white tile. As soon as I slide the lock into place, I hear the bathroom door creak open.

"Sofia?" The voice startles me, and I stand too fast, smacking my elbow on the plastic toilet paper holder. "Come out, come out, wherever you are."

"Riley?" My voice echoes off the bathroom walls. I

hadn't even looked for Riley and her friends this morning, assuming lunch was a one-time thing. They took pity on me and wanted to show me that Adams High wasn't all animal mutilation and satanic rituals. Still, I fumble with the lock and push the door open.

Riley leans over one of the sinks, adjusting the silk scarf tied around her neck. She looks like Audrey Hepburn in her sleeveless button-up shirt and high-waisted pants. The fluorescent light flickers overhead.

"Love the necklace," Riley says, catching my eye in the mirror as she pushes a perfect brown curl behind one ear. I touch the cross hanging from my neck.

"Thanks."

"We saw you come in," Alexis explains. She sets her white leather purse next to the dingy porcelain sink and digs out a tube of peach-colored lipstick. Her wispy blond hair trails over the counter as she paints her lips. "Thought we'd say hi."

Grace shuts the door, and Riley slides off one of her leather ballet flats and wedges it beneath the frame. She tests the door, but it doesn't budge.

"There. Now no one can surprise us."

I open my mouth to ask who's going to surprise us, then think of Brooklyn and the dead cat and close it again. Grace leans against the avocado-green counter. Today she's tucked her black braids behind a leopard-print headband, and she's wearing gold platform sandals that add an extra five inches to her height.

Riley puts her hands on my shoulders. "Sof, do you know how pretty you are?" she asks. "Guys, isn't Sofia pretty?"

"You're *so* pretty," Alexis purrs, capping her lipstick.

"Thanks," I say, studying their reflections in the mirror. Are they messing with me? My hair is shiny, and my skin can sometimes look golden in the sun, but these girls are perfect. Their skin looks dewy and fresh and completely poreless, even under the bathroom's harsh fluorescent lights, which are scientifically designed to make everyone look like a zombie.

I smile, shaking my head. Clearly they're just being nice.

Riley slides the hair tie off my ponytail and finger-combs my curls.

"Look how much better it is down," she says. She's right—it is better down, but I've been pulling it back so the Mississippi heat doesn't make it frizz. Already, a thin line of sweat forms on the back of my neck.

Alexis puts her lipstick back into her purse and removes a flask. I've never described a flask as cute before, but hers is tiny and silver, with flowers and vines engraved around the sides. She takes a swig and hands the flask to Grace.

"You guys drink?" I ask.

"We're taking Communion," Grace says. She closes her eyes and lifts the flask to her lips.

"Don't you go to church, Sof?" Riley frowns at my reflection, her fingers still tangled in my hair.

"My mom doesn't like church," I say. "But my grand-mother's Catholic, so I know about Communion."

Alexis giggles and holds out her flask to me, but Grace snatches it from her hand before I can reach for it.

"Wait," she says. "Sofia can't have any. Remember? You two wouldn't even let me touch that flask until I was 'baptized in the blood of the lamb.'"

She says the last part with a thick Mississippi drawl. Alexis throws a wadded-up ball of toilet paper at her. "I don't sound like that," she says.

"Grace is right. You can't have Communion until you accept Jesus Christ as your personal Lord and Savior." Riley's voice is light, but there's a chill in her eyes. She wrinkles her nose at me.

"Right, my grandmother told me that," I say. Mom never let me get baptized, but I used to go to church with Grandmother all the time. When it was time to get Communion, the priest put his hand on my head and prayed for me instead of feeding me the host and wine.

When I look up again, Riley's staring at my reflection in the mirror. "You know, we could do it now, if you want. Baptize you."

I release a short laugh, positive she's joking. But Riley's face stays serious.

"You want to baptize me *here*?" I blurt out. "In the bathroom?"

"We have a sink," Riley says, shrugging. "And, Alexis, you know what to say, right?" Before Alexis can answer, Riley turns on the faucet and plugs up one of the sinks. Water pours into the stained white porcelain.

"But don't we need a priest for it to be real?" I ask.

Riley runs a finger along one of my curls. "It'll be real to us," she says. "Like becoming blood sisters. It's how we'll all know you're in the group."

I scratch at the skin along my cuticles and pretend to think this over. I had exactly one friend at my last school, and the coolest thing we ever did together was stay up late to watch reruns of *Saved by the Bell*.

"Let's do it," I say. Behind Riley, the sink fills. Water dribbles over the side and onto the tile floor. Grace leans past her and turns the faucet off.

"Careful," she says, but Riley doesn't seem to hear her. She grins at me, looking so giddy that I find myself smiling, too.

"Okay, cross your arms like this." Riley raises her arms in an *X* over her chest, Alexis's flask still gripped in one hand. I do the same. "Good," she says. "Now crouch down so you're over the sink. Alexis, you have to anoint her head with holy water."

"That's not holy water," Grace says. Riley tips Alexis's flask of wine over the water. A stream of red spills onto the surface, spreading like blood.

"The wine's been blessed," Riley says. "Same thing."

I let out a nervous giggle as Alexis dips a finger into the water. A blond eyelash clings to her cheek, making a tiny golden half-moon against her skin.

"Sofia, I baptize you in the name of the Father, the Son, and the Holy Spirit." She touches her finger to my forehead, chest, and both shoulders.

"Amen," Riley says. She places one hand at the base of my neck and the other over my crossed arms. I close my eyes and consider praying.

Before I can decide, Riley pushes my head into the sink.

The water hits my face like a slap. My eyes fly open, and on instinct I inhale, immediately flooding my lungs. I choke, releasing deep, hacking coughs that fill the water with bubbles and cloud my vision. I blink furiously, staring at the plugged-up drain at the bottom of the sink.

I try to lift my head, but Riley's hand is like a weight. I press my fingers into the edges of the sink. The bubbles in front of me turn spotty as my vision goes black. My fingers slacken as I start to lose consciousness when, finally, Riley removes her hand. I whip my head out of the water and gasp and cough. My hair hangs in front of my eyes in sopping-wet clumps.

Someone mops the hair out of my face. I blink and Riley's in front of me, her clear, pale eyes bright with excitement.

"Oh, Sof, are you okay? You did so well!"

"I think I survived," I gasp. Bursts of light still dot my periphery, but Riley's smile is sweet, genuine. She leans forward, kissing me on the cheek.

"Now you're one of us," she says. Her words spark something warm inside me. It flickers like a match. I'm one of them.

"Now you're saved," Riley says.

CHAPTER FOUR

"**B**oo!" I jump at the sudden voice, sending the pen I'd been sketching with sailing to the ground. Grace leaps up from behind the wooden bench I'm sitting on and doubles over in a fit of giggles.

"You're so easy to scare," she teases.

"Maybe you're just scary." I pick up my pen from the ground and throw it at her. When it bounces off her shoulder, Grace raises her hands in surrender.

"Hey! I come in peace. Riley asked me to find you."

"Oh, yeah?" Mom took Grandmother to a doctor's appointment today, so I don't have to race home right after school. All that's waiting for me are last night's leftovers. And Grace has a wicked glint in her eye. "What for?"

Grace straightens her leopard-print headband and perches on the bench next to me, staring at the basketball hoops in front of us. The outdoor basketball court is far less impressive than the football field. The concrete is all cracked and grungy, and there aren't even nets hanging from the hoops. The only other kids around the court are clichéd loiterers, sneaking cigarettes and passing around a gallon jug of generic-brand iced tea.

"We're headed to the house," Grace says. "Want to come?" Her fingernails are painted an electric blue that looks neon against her dark skin.

"Whose house?" I ask.

"Don't get your panties in a twist. You'll see." Grace winks. "And you'll *love* it."

I gather my pen and sketchbook and follow Grace away from school and through row after row of perfect suburban houses with Mississippi flags hanging from their porches. The extra-high platform sandals strapped to her already long, skinny legs make Grace move like a gazelle.

"This is what I love about small towns," she says as we walk. "Look at how safe and boring this whole neighborhood is. Back in Chicago, my dad would've called the police if I didn't come home right after school. But here?" Grace spreads her arms and spins in the street. "No one thinks we could get into trouble here. Can you taste the freedom, Sof?"

"Oh yeah," I say. "It tastes like—"

"Red wine," Grace interrupts. "And chocolate."

I laugh, jogging to keep up with her long strides. "I lived in DC for a couple of months freshman year. My friends and I skipped class once—just *one time*—and my teacher thought we'd been abducted." I decide not to mention that this was during my very brief Goth phase, and we skipped class to get fake IDs so we could see a band at a place called Club Trash. "The principal called the cops and everything."

"Nice!" Grace says, laughing. "You move around a lot, then? Are your parents military?"

"Army."

"Me, too," Grace says. "My dad's a combat engineer. We moved every two years of my life until he decided I needed an 'authentic high school experience.' Whatever that means."

I kick a rock with my sneaker and watch it skitter over the dusty sidewalk.

"And you like it here? The whole safe-and-boring thing never gets old?"

"Not if you're creative about it," Grace says with

another wicked smile. "Honestly, I didn't expect to like it here. When we first moved, some racist assholes at school used to make fun of my hair. But then I started hanging with Riley, and she made it clear that anyone who messed with me would pay." Grace shakes her head, like she still can't believe it. "When someone talked shit at my old school, you just kept quiet and hoped it stopped, you know?"

"Yeah," I say. I'm instantly hit with a memory from my last school of Lila Frank's high-pitched jackal laugh. "My old school was like that, too."

"Well, Riley doesn't stand for it. I'd walk through fire for that girl."

"What about Alexis?" I ask.

"She's a sweetheart. Practically Riley's double, though." Grace rolls her eyes. "It's kind of adorable, actually—you'll see."

Grace crosses a packed-dirt lot and ducks through a pocket of trees. A patchwork quilt of land unfolds around us. It's disturbingly empty, nothing but flattened dirt and twisting paved roads, all leading nowhere. The land is flat enough that I can see across the entire development, all the way to a far stretch of bare trees that were never cleared by the bulldozers.

I follow Grace down a block of vacant land and old construction sites. Two houses stand side by side where the road dead-ends. The first is unpainted, with heavy plastic tacked up where the windows and doors should be. When the wind blows, the plastic billows and collapses.

The second could be a completed house, except for the unfinished wood peeking through streaky white paint. Grace walks up the steps like she belongs there.

"Riley's dad's company owns this whole subdivision," she explains. "The land, the construction equipment—everything. Apparently, these houses never sold after the economy tanked, so now they just sit here taking up space. Since they technically belong to Riley's family, we borrow them from time to time."

I grin as I follow her up the stairs. An abandoned house surrounded by empty land definitely has the potential to be not boring. "I hear other teenagers have to hang out in their bedrooms."

"Poor teenagers," Grace says. She hesitates on the porch. "Almost forgot. Don't mention Josh unless Riley brings him up."

I frown, suddenly lost. "Wait, who?"

Grace pauses, her hand pressed against the door. "Josh is Riley's boyfriend. They got into this huge fight after lunch, and now Riley's all pissed at him. That's why we're doing this. Ri needed a girls' night."

"Got it—no Josh," I say.

Grace pushes the door open, and we make our way into the shadowy living room together. Afternoon light filters through the windows, but the cloudy blue plastic hanging over the glass keeps it dark. My eyes blur and I have to blink a few times before I can see. I hear fumbling and giggling in the darkness, then the sound of gas hissing to life, and the room fills with golden light. Alexis picks up a blue lantern and carries it over to us.

"Hey, Sof." She slips an arm around my shoulders to pull me into a hug. The sleeves of her lacy white shift dress scratch against my neck. "Ooh, I've been dying to get my hands on your hair," she says as she pulls away.

"Do *not* let her touch you!" Grace says. "Her idea of beauty is back-combing and Aqua Net."

Alexis pouts. "You make me sound trashy. Not all of us can pull off the color-blind diva look you've got going on."

"Hey, no need to take a swing at the ensemble," Grace says. I see Alexis's point. If anyone else tried on Grace's blue sequined skirt, leather jacket, and leopard-print headband they'd look like they got dressed in the dark. But Grace looks fierce.

"Where's Riley?" I ask, turning in place. Sleeping bags and pillows are scattered across the living room, and an upside-down milk crate acts as a side table, holding a Bible and an empty wine bottle. Cutouts of boys from magazines and postcards of old European churches cover the walls, along with hundreds of pictures of Riley, Alexis, and Grace.

I pull back the corner of a poster torn from a magazine and find a photograph of Riley and Alexis as little girls with long, skinny legs and goofy bows in their hair. They're dressed identically.

"Lexie and I have been friends forever," Riley says. I jump and whirl around—I didn't hear her come up behind me. She's barefoot and wearing a silky, kimono-style dress, her curls wild around her shoulders. It's like she got dressed up just for us. "You like our wall?"

"It's great," I say, my eyes moving over the pictures. Robert Pattinson's face peeks out from behind photo-booth snapshots, movie tickets, and stickers. I snicker. "*What* is this?"

"Grace had this huge crush on him for, like, a day," Alexis explains, stretching out on the floor. "But now she only has eyes for *Tom*."

"Shut *up*," Grace says, launching a pillow at Alexis. Alexis catches it and wedges it beneath her head.

"Ooh, who's Tom?" I ask, and Grace's cheeks redden.

"He's my boyfriend's older brother," Riley explains. "We all met when we were, like, seven."

Grace clears her throat.

"Excuse me," Riley says. "Everyone except for Grace.

The rest of us have been hanging at the lake since we were kids. See?"

Riley leans past me to smooth out a creased photograph of her and Alexis with two other guys all lounging in front of a huge house. It's a gray modern-looking house with steel-toned siding and gigantic floor-to-ceiling windows. Everything about the house looks sleek and intentional, from the Mercedes SUV parked out front to the perfectly trimmed leafy trees dotting the lawn and the long wooden dock artfully jutting out into a clear, still blue lake.

"This was at my family's house at Lake Whitney," she explains.

I lean in to look at the photograph. Alexis and Riley recline on the grass, tanned and gorgeous in their skimpy bikinis, their hair dried into beachy waves around their shoulders. Sitting between them is the cute boy from the cafeteria.

"Hey, I know him," I say, pointing to Charlie. He's wearing a damp white T-shirt over his swim trunks, and his messy hair is slicked away from his face, as if he just got out of the lake.

I turn back to Riley, but she isn't looking at Charlie. Her eyes are locked on the preppy boy next to him with a cleft chin and hair that hangs shaggily around his neck and forehead. The infamous Josh, I'm guessing.

Riley purses her lips and presses her finger over Josh's face, so I can only see his polo shirt.

"Big fight?" I ask. I know Grace told me not to mention it, but isn't that what tonight's about?

"Big enough that I either have to dump the jerk or somehow forget how pissed I am at him." Riley crosses the room, grabbing a half-full bottle of wine from behind a rolled-up sleeping bag. She waves it at me. "Guess which I chose."

"Forgetting by way of wine? I approve," I say.

"You know we've been together for three years?" she says. Riley yanks the cork out of the bottle. With her sexy dress and wild curls, she makes heartache look romantic. "We used to be so in love. Like Romeo and Juliet."

"Romeo and Juliet died at the end of that play, Ri," Grace points out. She crouches next to the milk crate and pulls out a bag of caramel corn and a plastic jar of Nutella. "Not a great sign."

"Whatever." Riley lifts the wine bottle to her mouth and drinks, deep. "This is just a blip. Josh and I are forever."

Grace hands me a spoon. "You eat it like this," she says. She unscrews the jar and dumps the caramel corn inside, then stirs the mixture with a spoon. "It tastes like heaven. Seriously."

I take a tentative bite. It's salty and sweet and crunchy at the same time. I dig another spoonful out of the jar. The corner of Riley's mouth hitches into a grin.

"So what's going on with you and Charlie?"

"What?" I stick another spoonful of Nutella and caramel corn in my mouth to cover my embarrassment. "There's no me and Charlie," I say, swallowing.

"Oh please. I saw the way you undressed his photo with your eyes." Riley collapses onto a pile of pillows and lifts the wine bottle to her mouth again. "You *want* him."

"Does Sofia have a crush already?" Alexis asks.

"It's not a crush," I insist, heat creeping up my neck with every word. "I just . . .like his arms."

Alexis falls back onto the pillows, laughing, and Grace makes kissy noises at me as I hand over the spoon and Nutella.

"My, what fabulous taste you have. Charlie's a ten." Riley smoothes her dress down over her thighs. "I could probably make that happen for you. If you wanted."

"Make that happen?" I say. "We're not dogs. You can't throw us in a room and hope we mate."

"Can't I?" Riley fixes those pale blue eyes on me, and I immediately realize how wrong I am. Riley clearly gets whatever she wants, no matter how insane it sounds.

"Wait a second," Grace says. "How come I never got this offer with Tom?"

"Tom doesn't know what the hell he wants, Gray. You could do so much better. But Charlie . . . Charlie I could work with."

Riley pushes herself to her knees and leans forward, brushing the back of her hand against my cheek. "And just look at Sofia. Isn't she completely gorgeous? She was made to have someone fall insanely in love with her."

My skin tingles where Riley touches it. Her words spark something inside me. I picture Charlie sliding an arm around my shoulders and pulling me close. I feel the heat of his lips against mine, and my body tightens with want. My past boyfriends have always been more of the fumble-around-in-the-dark variety. There was never any talk of love.

I shake my head, suddenly embarrassed. "I'm confused—I thought Charlie was friends with Brooklyn."

Riley frowns, staring at me over the top of the wine bottle. "Why would you think that?"

"No reason, really. He just said hi to her in the lunch line yesterday."

Alexis's lips move as she counts the kernels of popcorn in her hand. "That boy is too nice for his own good," she mutters.

"We all used to be friends, you know," Riley says. "Brooklyn, too."

"I would once again like to point out that this was

BG," Grace says. "Before Grace. Otherwise known as the Dark Ages."

"It's also before Brooklyn started dressing like an Urban Outfitters catalog," Riley adds, fingering the hem of her dress. "She used to be really sweet, but once we started high school, she just . . . changed."

I think of the way Brooklyn narrowed her eyes at Riley in the cafeteria, aiming an imaginary gun at her head. "Why?"

"No one knows." Riley spins the wine bottle with her fingertips, leaving a red ring behind on the floor. She picks it up and passes it to Alexis. "Sometimes I wonder if it's a cry for help. Like maybe God wants us to save her. But we've all tried to talk to her, and she won't listen. I think there's too much history between us."

"She was even horrible to Grace," Alexis says, passing me the wine bottle. "And she barely knows her."

"She was okay to me," I say. I let the wine roll over my tongue, holding it in my mouth.

"Really?" Grace asks.

I shrug. "I mean, we didn't paint each other's nails or anything, but she gave me a Band-Aid."

Alexis snickers. "Can you imagine doing your nails with Brooklyn? I bet every bottle of polish she owns is black."

Alexis giggles even harder, but Riley suddenly sits up straight.

"Wait a second. Maybe you *should*," she says. There's a manic, excited light in her pale eyes—and she's aiming them right at me. "Hang out with Brooklyn, I mean. I don't think she's seen you with us yet. You can find out why she's such a bitch now."

"You want me to spy on her?" I ask.

"Come on, Ri, don't ask her to do that." Grace throws a piece of popcorn at Riley. "It's weird."

"I guess it does sound like spying." Riley's shoulders slump. "Sorry, Sof, I didn't mean it like that. I was just thinking it'd be cool if we could help her."

"Right, of course," I say, but the idea sticks in my head. I chose Riley and her friends over Brooklyn, and I definitely prefer Nutella and red wine over animal mutilation and locker room séances. Still, I wonder what Brooklyn's really like.

Suddenly, Alexis sits up, dropping the rest of her caramel corn on the floor.

"Guys, let's do something else," she says, wiping the popcorn dust coating her fingers onto one of the sleeping bags. "Sofia's going to think that all we do is sit around and gossip about Brooklyn."

"Speak for yourself," Grace says. "I barely even knew that psycho."

"Hand me that." Alexis points to the wine bottle I'm still holding, and I pass it to her. She takes a deep drink.

"Okay, so this is a game Ri and I used to play all the time when we were kids. It's called *concentration*."

"Ugh! No." Riley groans, making a face. "That game is so stupid, Lexie."

"Shut up. It's perfect," Alexis says. "Come on, Grace. I'll do you first."

Grace crawls over to Alexis and sits in front of her, clenching her eyes shut. Alexis knocks on the top of her head, then slides her fingers over the back of her neck and shoulders. Grace snickers.

"After I finish speaking, you will be put into a trance," Alexis continues, walking her fingers up and down Grace's spine. "This trance will allow you to see the most important moment of your life, past or present."

"Oh, god," I groan. Riley laughs through her clenched lips.

"Shut up," Alexis says. "This is totally scientific."

"Ignore them. I'm ready," Grace says.

"Good. Now concentrate," Alexis whispers. She knife-chops her hands against Grace's back and kneads her fingers against her neck and shoulders. Grace's head drops in relaxation, and her eyes close. "What do you see?"

"I see . . ." Grace sways back in forth. Her eyelids flicker, and her lips part in a faint smile. "I see a beach. It's long and white. Stretched out in front of it is the most beautiful, sparkling blue ocean."

"Good," Alexis whispers. "What else?"

Grace's smile fades. "I'm not alone," she says. There's a chill in her voice now. I shiver. "There's someone there. Someone I can't see."

"Turn around," Alexis says. Grace nods. She stops swaying, and her whole body goes rigid. "Look at who's standing behind you, Grace. Now . . . describe him to me."

Grace's eyes shoot open.

"It's Tom," she says, wiggling her eyebrows. "He's spread out across a beach towel, shirtless. He wants to help rub suntan lotion on my back."

Alexis smacks Grace on the arm, and Grace snorts with laughter. "Loser," Alexis says, smiling. "Okay, who's next? Riley?"

Riley takes another drink of wine, shaking her head. "No way. I'm protesting."

Alexis rolls her eyes. "Sofia, then. Come on."

"Fine," I say, cracking a smile. I slide over to Alexis, and she sits up on her knees, putting her hands on my arms. She digs her knuckles into my shoulders, then drags her fingers down my back.

"Concentrate," she whispers as I close my eyes. "Listen to the sound of my voice. . . ."

With my eyes closed, I notice how warm it is in this room. Heat hovers around my skin and presses against my arms. I sway a little, then release a bubbling giggle.

I'm a lightweight—the wine has already made me drunk.

Alexis's fingers dig into my back, and I try not to laugh again. It tickles. The other girls have gone silent. I want to open my eyes and see what they're doing, but my eyelids are so heavy. My mind spins. Jesus, how much wine did I have? I'm starting to feel dizzy. . . .

"Concentrate," Alexis repeats, and to my surprise something does flicker against my eyelids. It's a memory from my old school.

"Tell me what you see," Alexis says.

A sharp elbow jams into my side, and I stumble into a row of puke-green lockers. My books fall from my arms and slap against the floor.

Whoever elbowed me snickers as he continues down the hallway. I drop to my knees to gather my things, not bothering to lift my head.

"Let me help you." Karen kneels to pick up my books. Karen is barely five feet tall, with bobbed blond hair and freckles— the kind of cute-pretty that makes her less likely to be a total bitch, unlike all the other cheerleaders at this school. Even so, I'm sure she wouldn't talk to me at all if we weren't lab partners in biology.

She hands me my textbook. "You excited?" she asks as we walk into class and slide onto the rickety wooden stools next to our lab table. "The big experiment is today."

I roll my eyes. All week, our bio teacher, Mr. Baer, has been talking about our class "experiment" like it's this huge event. Really, we'll just be swiping the countertops and trash cans with Q-tips to see if we can collect some germs to grow in a petri dish. "Oh yeah. I'm so excited."

Karen laughs. "Where do you think we'll find the most germs?" she asks. She narrows her eyes as she looks around the room, settling on Mr. Baer. "How about the gap between Mr. Baer's teeth?"

"Ew! You're probably right. His coffee breath is bad enough to take out a village."

Lila swivels around on her stool, leaning her back against the lab table directly in front of us. Karen chokes back the rest of her laughter.

"What are you laughing at, Greasy?" Lila asks. Lila's a senior, a varsity cheerleader, and so far out of my social circle that the only time I see her outside of class is when she's on top of the human pyramid at pep rallies.

My cheeks burn and I duck my head, letting my hair swing forward to cover my blushing face. I got the nickname Greasy a couple of months ago, when some JV cheerleader in my English class said it looked like I never washed my hair. I wash my hair every day, but my mom's been on this all-natural kick lately. The shampoo she buys is made from avocados, and it weighs my hair down, making it look shiny and clumpy.

"Careful, Karen," Lila's lab partner, Erin, says without

turning around on her stool. She brushes her own perfect brunette waves back behind one ear. "Get close enough to Greasy and you're going to catch whatever she has."

"Right," Karen says, but when Lila turns back around she glances back at me. "Ignore them," she whispers. She says it quietly, though, and she shoots a glance at Lila and Erin, obviously hoping they don't hear.

"Sof? Sofia, can you hear us?"

I open my eyes. Riley, Alexis, and Grace are all staring at me. My cheeks burn with embarrassment and I blink, trying to remember the last thing Alexis said.

"Well?" Grace asks. "What did you see?"

I roll my lower lip between my teeth, the memory still fresh in my head.

Riley gives me a quizzical look. "Are you okay, Sof?" she asks. "Did you really see something?"

"Yes," I say. Then I grab a stray piece of popcorn from the floor and throw it at Grace. "I saw Tom. He said you should apply your own sunscreen."

Alexis hoots with laughter. Riley takes the Nutella from her and licks the back of the spoon. She catches my eye and winks. "Looks like Sofia fits in better than we thought."

CHAPTER FIVE

"How did you all like *The Divine Comedy*?" Ms. Carey asks our English lit class the next day. I stare down at my notebook, doodling in the margins. I hate class discussions, and being tired and a little hungover from last night doesn't help. It feels as if someone's pressing my eyes closed—I have to fight to keep them open.

"Isn't this book about Satan?" asks some blond girl I've never talked to before. "Should we be reading about Satan at school?"

I deepen the familiar lines of Quetzalcoatl's feathered tail with my pen. That sounds like something Riley would say. Ms. Carey nods.

"That's a good point, Angela. Can anyone tell me why we'd read *The Divine Comedy* in high school?"

No one answers. Ms. Carey taps a leather loafer on the floor.

"Come on, guys, there are no wrong answers here. What do you think? Why are we reading *this* book?"

"Because high school is hell."

I stop sketching and glance over my shoulder. Brooklyn sits in the back corner next to the windows. Usually she spends class with her head on her desk, but today she's staring at Ms. Carey, defiant. She stretches the chain that hangs from her neck between two fingers, and the gold ring swings from side to side, like a pendulum.

"If we have to live it, we may as well read about it," she adds.

"Well, that was more colorfully put than I'd have liked," Ms. Carey says as the students around us snicker. I stop doodling and my pen bleeds ink onto the page.

In the back row, Brooklyn flicks her own paperback copy of the book with one finger, sending it sliding over her desk and onto the floor. I shake my head, a little impressed. She really doesn't care what anyone around her thinks. Must be nice.

Before Ms. Carey can comment further, the bell rings and the rest of the students start gathering their things.

Brooklyn winds her way through the chairs and desks. She walks past me without a word.

Making a quick decision, I shove my notebook into my bag and drop behind her as she makes her way down the hall. Riley didn't mention the spying thing again, and by this morning I'm pretty sure everyone forgot about it. But I keep wondering about Brooklyn, if she's really into séances and chanting and animal mutilation, or if it's all just rumors. And my biggest question: If she really was friends with Riley, why would she throw that away?

"Hey," I say. When Brooklyn doesn't turn around, I jog up next to her. "That was funny—what you said about high school being like hell."

"Was it?" Brooklyn shuffles through her bag, pulling out a pack of cigarettes. The entire box is covered in black Sharpie scribbles, so you can't even see the brand name. Brooklyn slides a cigarette from the pack and puts it in her mouth, unlit. We aren't even out of school yet.

"Are you doing anything now?" My lame attempt at being laid-back makes me cringe. Brooklyn stops walking in the middle of the hallway, forcing the kids behind us to move around her.

"Aren't you one of Riley's?"

"What does that mean?"

"That she's collected you." Brooklyn fumbles with the gold ring at her neck, sliding it on and off one of her fingers. "Riley likes new girls. She takes it upon herself to 'befriend the friendless.'"

"I can't hang out with both of you?" I ask.

Brooklyn shrugs and starts walking again. "Do what you want."

It isn't exactly an invitation, but I follow her out the school doors and over to the bike rack anyway.

"What's with the ring?" I ask, nodding at her necklace. Brooklyn grins.

"Souvenir from one of my lovers." She holds the ring up to the light so I see the engraving on the inside: CARLTON & JULIANNA 1979.

I wrinkle my nose. "That's sick," I say. Brooklyn just laughs.

Even before we reach the bike rack, I can tell which is hers—the vintage eighties one with the handlebars that curl around the rider's hands. Brooklyn painted it bright pink with flecks of black, so it looks like a watermelon, and the handlebars and seat are covered in peeling green duct tape.

I stand awkwardly next to her while she unlocks her bike, then loops the thick chain around her arm and starts to push it away.

"I've got an appointment," Brooklyn says. The cigarette, still unlit, dangles from her lips. "Tag along if you like."

I hesitate, but curiosity gets the better of me. "Sure."
I pull my bag over my shoulder and trail after her as
she wheels her bike through the parking lot, toward
a sidewalk that leads in the direction opposite my
neighborhood. When she isn't looking, I pull my cell
phone out to check the time. Grandmother will be fine
if I'm a half an hour late.

Brooklyn takes me to an old service road past the
main street into town. We pass a dive bar and an alley
leading to an empty parking lot. Brooklyn stops at a tiny
tattoo parlor and starts to lock up her bike.

"This is where your appointment is?" I squint through
the dirty windows. I can just make out the hazy shapes
of a counter and plastic chairs.

"'Appointment' might be stretching it." Brooklyn
takes the cigarette she never did get around to smoking out of her mouth and sticks it behind one ear. Then
she leans against the door of the tattoo parlor to push
it open. It smells like smoke inside, and some sort of
lemon-scented disinfectant. Brooklyn walks up to the
counter and slides her elbows over the dingy vinyl.

"Ollie! You here?" she shouts. She leans over the
counter like she's trying to see into the back room. I take
the rest of the shop in. The walls are covered with hand-
drawn illustrations of rose and skull tattoos, with nude
Playboy centerfolds taped between them. Classy.

"Hey, new girl!"

The voice comes from behind me and I jump, nearly tripping over my own feet as I spin around. Charlie is sitting cross-legged on the cracked plastic couch, a textbook propped open on his knees. In his rumpled polo and faded jeans, he looks as out of place here as I do.

"It's Sofia, actually." A blush creeps up my neck. "What are you doing here?"

"Homework." He motions to the textbook on his lap and smiles. A dimple appears in his cheek, and for a second I can't help but stare. His eyes shift behind me.

"Hey, Brooklyn," he says with a nod.

"Charlie-boy," Brooklyn says. "Your brother around?"

"Yeah. Don't think he's going to be happy to see you, though. He's got a customer at four."

"We'll see about that." Brooklyn shifts her weight to her arms, hoists herself onto the counter, and scoots across.

"Hey." Charlie pushes aside his textbook and stands as Brooklyn slides off the other side of the counter. "You know we have a door, right?"

"Doors are for suckers." Brooklyn sticks out her tongue and disappears into the back of the shop. I hesitate, not sure if I should follow her.

"Here." Charlie unlatches a gate in the display case, swinging it open for me. "See? We're not all heathens."

"Thanks," I say. Giving him one last shy smile, I make my way to the back to find Brooklyn.

The tattoo parlor is cleaner than I expected. The green-and-white vinyl floors are cracked and peeling, but it looks as if they've been mopped recently. The entire room has a worn-in, laid-back vibe that actually feels kind of homey. Like a familiar booth at your favorite cheesy diner.

Red plastic chairs are scattered across the room, all covered in duct tape, with metal trays set up next to them. Brooklyn leans against one of the chairs, talking to an older version of Charlie—a guy who's tall and thin, with dark eyes. A thorny rose tattoo stretches across his neck, and three thick metal piercings jut out from his each of his ears like nails.

"Come on, Ollie," Brooklyn's saying as I approach. Ollie shakes his head.

"Look, I don't have time today."

Brooklyn peels a strip of duct tape off the chair. "Santos isn't here. You can just let me use his equipment. I think I could do it myself."

"You kidding? You're sixteen."

Brooklyn smiles, so wide I could count all her teeth if I wanted to. "That never stopped you before."

The bell above the door out front jingles. I glance over my shoulder as a college girl in a jean skirt and Uggs walks in, her hair pulled into a high ponytail. Out front, Charlie says something to her about Ollie being out in a minute.

Ollie's considering Brooklyn now, like he's trying to decide if she'll cause more trouble out front with his customer or back with his needles. He comes to the same conclusion I do.

"Just wait for me back here," he says. "I'll try to fit you in later."

Brooklyn folds her hands over her chest, fluttering her eyelashes. "My hero." Ollie groans and heads back out front while Brooklyn leans against a chair half hidden by a curtain off to the left. Dozens of identical black stickers cover the chair, the words SANTOS AND THE RAISONETTES printed on all of them.

"Santos's band," Brooklyn says, nodding at the stickers. "Isn't that the worst band name you ever heard?"

"How do you even know these people?" I ask, sitting down in the chair. Brooklyn grabs a bar stool and pulls it up next to me.

"I used to work here," she says. "I had a fake license, and Ollie let me apprentice with him until Charlie ratted me out and told him I was only sixteen."

"You've given people tattoos?"

"Nah, I did mostly piercings. See this one?" Brooklyn pushes back her hair to show me a large safety pin running from her cartilage to her earlobe.

"Did that myself," she says proudly. "You got anything pierced?" I shake my head. Brooklyn's mouth drops open. "Not even ears?"

"My mom doesn't like piercings," I say.

"And you . . . what? Just let her make those decisions for you?"

"What are you going to get tattooed?" I ask to change the subject.

"Dunno yet," Brooklyn says. "I was thinking of that snake thing you had on your hand a couple of days ago. That was pretty cool."

"Quetzalcoatl?"

"Is that what it's called?" Brooklyn asks. "You think you could draw it for Ollie?"

"Sure. If you want me to." I'm flattered, and my fingers itch to reach for my pen. Brooklyn narrows her eyes at me.

"You know, you'd look wicked cool with an eyebrow ring."

"You think so?" Almost unconsciously, I lift a finger to my eyebrow. Then, thinking of my mom's reaction, I push the thought away. There was a time I would have done it just to get a reaction from her, but it's not worth it now, not when things are going so well.

"Is it because of your little friends?" Brooklyn snickers, staring down at the tray next to her. It's covered in needles, tiny hoop earrings, ointments, and, inexplicably, a cucumber-melon-scented candle from Bath & Body Works. "I bet they think piercings are a *sin*. God, I don't know how you can stand the holier-than-thou crew."

"I thought you all used to be friends," I say. Brooklyn slides a needle off the metal table and holds it between two fingers.

"You've been talking about me?" she asks. I shift my eyes away from the needle. It's thick—thicker than I expected it to be.

"They just said you used to hang out with them, and that you changed," I say.

Brooklyn shrugs, turning the needle in her fingers. "Let's just say that after years of worshipping at the altar of Riley, I decided I wanted to have some *fun*." The fluorescent light buzzes overhead, casting a flickering yellow glow across the needle's surface. "Be honest now, Sofia. Do you really want to spend high school praying? Because you look like someone who knows how to have fun."

I think of my Goth friends showing their fake IDs to the bouncer at Club Trash, or my last boyfriend—if you could even call him that—who was more interested in his bong than in me. Last night, with Riley, Grace, and Alexis, I finally felt like I belonged.

Still, sitting here with Brooklyn fits, too. The duct-tape-covered vinyl and indie rock blasting from the iPod in the corner remind me of dozens of nights in smoky basements. I lift my eyes to meet Brooklyn's, and a rush of adrenaline spreads through me, like warmth uncurling beneath my skin. I can't help imagining her threading that needle through my eyebrow, the bright pain as it tears through my skin.

"Come on," she urges, touching the needle to my eyebrow. "I dare you."

"No." I shake my head. "I really can't."

"It wouldn't be forever," Brooklyn says. "You can take the ring out whenever you want, and your mom wouldn't even know you had it."

I stare down at the rings, imagining how cool it'd be to have a secret piercing, to get away with this right under my mom's nose. I could even hide it from Riley and the others, if I wanted. I begin to smile.

"Jesus." Brooklyn hops on her stool, then curls a hand beneath the seat, like she's forcing herself to stay put. "You *have* to."

I laugh, and her voice echoes in my head. *I dare you.* I lean forward, and the soaring, whooping feeling of adrenaline rises in my chest. I don't want it to go away.

"Fine. Do it," I say.

Brooklyn grins, the same wolfish grin that shows all her teeth. She sets the needle back down on the tray and picks up a cotton swab and a bottle without a label.

"Eyebrow, right?" she asks, squirting clear liquid onto the swab. I nod, and she leans forward and dabs at my face. "This is just antiseptic. It'll keep you from getting an infection."

"Okay," I say. Brooklyn tosses the cotton aside and picks up the needle again.

"Keep still or it'll be crooked."

I take a deep breath and hold it, digging my teeth into my lower lip. Brooklyn moves in close to me, and I stare at her eyes to keep from looking at the needle. They're dark brown, almost black. I can barely see the outline of her pupil.

I swear I feel the needle a second before Brooklyn slides it through my skin. It's nothing like the sharp, sudden prick I'd been imagining. This pain is slow. Nausea floods my stomach, and I have to close my eyes to keep from feeling dizzy.

"*Shit*," I hiss, letting out my breath in a rush. There's a pop, and I feel the needle slide through the other side of my eyebrow.

I wrap my hand around the chair's armrest and force myself to breathe as the room around me spins. I feel strangely hot. It's so hot that I'm sweating, and now the floor is rising and falling beneath me. I blink, and it's as if I'm looking through a camera's fish-eye lens. Brooklyn is close, but everything around her is distorted and far away.

"Are you okay?" Brooklyn's forehead creases in concern. I stare at my knees, trying to focus on breathing.

When I look up again, Brooklyn straddles her stool and we're sitting so close that our knees touch. She holds the needle in front of her, and my blood winds down the side. The overhead light flickers—it's reflected in Brooklyn's black eyes and in the red droplet of my blood.

"Sofia," Brooklyn says. She slides the needle into her mouth, smearing her lips with red blood. "Now you're reborn," she says, her voice distorted, like I'm hearing it underwater. The light flickers again, and everything goes black.

* * *

The next thing I'm aware of is a weight pressing against my eyelids. My throat is dry and scratchy, and I try to speak, but the sound that escapes my mouth is strangled, like a gasp. I force my eyes open, and light fractures and breaks in front of me, making me squint.

"Hey, Sleeping Beauty. How you feeling?"

"Brooklyn?" I blink and, slowly, my vision clears. I'm not in the tattoo parlor chair anymore. I'm lying in some sort of office area, and Brooklyn is perched on the edge of a desk in front of me. Her shirtsleeve is rolled up, exposing a freshly bandaged shoulder. She removes a cigarette from her mouth and blows out a plume of smoke that curls around her.

"You passed out," she explains. "My cousin's like that—he'd pass out from a paper cut. Charlie and Ollie moved you so you wouldn't freak out the other customers."

"Charlie moved me?" I ask, feeling an immediate pang of embarrassment. Brooklyn nods. There's no blood on her mouth. No strange glinting light in her black eyes or manic smile. It was a dream. Or a hallucination, maybe.

"What time is it?"

Brooklyn pulls a cell phone out of her pocket and squints down at it. "Quarter after six."

"Crap." I sit up, trying to ignore the headache beating at my temples. The office door opens, and Charlie appears, holding a bottle of water. I grab my backpack and stand. The room spins, and I hold on to the desk to steady myself.

"Feeling better?" he asks. He smiles, and the spinning immediately gets worse.

"Where's the fire?" Brooklyn asks, lifting the cigarette back to her mouth.

"I just need to get home. Thanks for the—" I motion to my eyebrow, then duck past Charlie and out of the office, cheeks burning in embarrassment.

As soon as I'm outside, I start to run. My backpack digs painfully into my shoulder and slaps against my hip as I move. If my mom gets home before I do and finds out I left Grandmother alone, I'm screwed. I try to do the math in my head—it takes me about five minutes to walk home from school, and Brooklyn and I walked for maybe ten minutes to get to the tattoo parlor. Tonight my mom's class ends at six thirty, and she'll be home by six forty-five. As long as I don't get lost, I should be fine.

My chest burns, and my breath escapes in ragged gasps. I barely notice the buildings and houses as I race past them, working and reworking the math in my head. I'm almost home. I'm fine. I'll be fine.

I tear up the driveway to our house and fit my key into the lock, glancing at the clock in the hallway once I'm inside: 6:40. I close my eyes, lean against the front door, and breathe. I made it.

Kicking off my shoes, I head down the hall and duck into the bathroom across from Grandmother's bedroom. Her door is open, and the red-tinted lamplight spills into the hall. I hear her wheezing breaths and the rosary beads clicking against her table as I walk past.

"You okay, *Abuela*?" I call to her as I shrug off my backpack and set it on the toilet seat. Then I catch sight of myself in the mirror over the sink.

The tiny gold hoop circles the narrowest part of my eyebrow, looking foreign and wrong against my dark skin. I lean in to touch it, cringing when my finger brushes against the purple bruise spreading across my skin.

I glance over my shoulder into Grandmother's room. She's sitting up in bed, her dark eyes staring out at me from the shadows of her red-tinted room. Her lips mouth wordless prayers as she counts the beads on her rosary.

My breath is shallow, fast. I turn back around, wrapping my fingers around the cold porcelain sink to try to calm myself down. My reflection stares back at me, the tiny golden hoop twinkling above my right eye.

Mom's car rumbles into the driveway, and the engine cuts. In the quiet that follows, I swear I hear my heart beating against my chest. I don't think. I lean in close to the mirror, so close I could count the number of lashes on my eyelid. I hold the tiny golden hoop steady with two fingers and twist the bead off. Then I rock the hoop back and forth, ignoring the blistering pain as I ease it out of my skin. Blood bubbles beneath my fingers.

Grandmother watches me from her bedroom. The front door opens and slams closed. Footsteps thud in the foyer.

"Sofia?"

I let the golden hoop fall from my fingers, and it clinks against the sink, landing a half an inch from the drain. I switch on the faucet and it swirls down the drain in a whirlpool of pink, bloodstained water. Only once it's gone do I allow myself to breathe again.

"I'm in the bathroom, Mom," I call. I rinse my hands and look back up at the mirror. The blood is still leaking from the hole in my eyebrow. It's smudged across my forehead and cheek, crusted into my eyelashes. I unwind a length of toilet paper from the roll and bunch it up into a ball, holding it to my face.

Beneath my fingers, the blood blossoms like a flower. Within seconds, the entire tissue is stained red.

CHAPTER SIX

"I still don't understand why it would bleed so much." Mom wraps up the chicken we just had for dinner in tinfoil while I fill the sink with soapy water and start the dishes. I shrug, staring at a folded dishtowel next to the sink. It's red and white with a picture of a rooster on it.

"It was a really big zit," I say. I cleaned the blood from my face and covered the piercing with a Band-Aid before my mom saw it, but I've had to change the Band-Aid twice since she's been home. Already the new one is red with blood.

Mom puts the chicken in the fridge, frowning as she closes the door. Our phone rings, and Mom leans over the counter and picks it up. "Flores residence," she answers. A tinny-sounding voice echoes from the other end of the receiver, and Mom smiles. "One moment. It's your friend Riley," she says, handing me the phone. "She says she has a homework question. Just don't take too long."

I slip out the back door with the phone and curl up in the wooden chair on our patio. Our backyard stretches forever, without any streetlights or nearby houses to break it up. It's unnerving, like being walled in on all sides with empty space. Insects buzz restlessly, like white noise. I tuck my legs beneath me.

"Riley?" I say into the phone.

"Sof? I saw you with Brooklyn!" My stomach twists, but Riley continues talking before I can worry about whether she changed her mind about the spying. "Why didn't you tell me? What did you find out?"

"Nothing, really. She took me with her to get a tattoo." I run a finger along the edge of the bandage on my forehead but decide to keep the details of my piercing to myself.

"That's it?" Riley sounds disappointed. I lower my hand, quiet for a second as I try to work out what I want to say.

"What did you expect me to find?" My voice comes out sharper than I intend, but I don't apologize for it.

Riley said she was trying to help Brooklyn, but it sounds like she just wanted her to screw up.

"She skinned a cat and left it outside our school." Riley's voice has an edge to it. "Or did you forget?"

I press my lips together to keep myself from arguing. Riley *thinks* Brooklyn skinned that cat. Tattoos and cigarettes aren't in the same league as animal mutilation.

Riley clears her throat.

"Are you okay, Sof? She didn't hurt you, did she? Or manipulate you in some way?" The concern in Riley's voice is real, and suddenly I feel terrible. *Riley's* been a real friend to me since I got here, not Brooklyn. I exhale and shake my head, pulling at a piece of loose skin near my fingernail.

"No, it was nothing like that. She was . . ." *Cool.* The word pops into my head uninvited. "She was weird," I finish instead.

As the word leaves my mouth I realize it's just as true. Brooklyn was cool, but I get what Riley means—something about her did feel off. I think of her slender fingers on Santos's needles, her wolfish grin, and how she persuaded me so effortlessly to get a piercing. She made it too easy to be bad.

"Maybe I'll find something better tomorrow," I mumble. There's a beat of silence. I clear my throat. "How are things between you and Josh?"

"Oh, didn't you hear? We're all better now," Riley says. "He sent flowers to my class third period. Roses."

"Wow. That's great."

"Listen," Riley says before I can continue. "I just want to say I'm sorry if I made you uncomfortable when I asked you to hang out with Brooklyn."

"Riley, you didn't," I insist. "Really."

"It's just that I think she really needs help. I have this feeling like she's standing on the edge of a cliff and she's about to go over. Like she'll fall if we don't help her."

I run my thumb over a cuticle in slow circles. I try to picture Brooklyn at the edge of a cliff, her combat boots sending rocks off the edge, but it just doesn't fit with the girl I hung out with this afternoon. Brooklyn was having fun, not crying out for help. "You really think it's that bad?"

"I *really* do. Did she tell you she's having a party tomorrow?"

"She didn't mention it."

"Well, I heard some kids talking about it at school. It's supposed to be intense. You should go."

I run my tongue over my lips, which are dry now from the cold creeping over the yard. The last party I went to was in a house in the woods, next to the train tracks that ran through town. A bunch of football players stood just inside the door, loudly rating every girl who walked past, and every time a train rolled through, the whole house shook and everyone took a shot.

When I don't answer right away, Riley starts to plead. "Come on, Sofia! There's a reason I picked you for this. Some people have evil inside them, but *that's* what God is for, to fix them when they can't fix themselves. We can still fix Brooklyn."

The insects in the yard have gone still, but wind sweeps over the grass and pounds against the windows. I shiver and pull my arms around my chest. Grandmother used to pray for people in her neighborhood when she thought they needed strength. This isn't any different, I guess. Riley's just a little more active with her faith. Grams would probably like her.

"Sof? Are you still there?"

"Yeah," I say. "I'll do it. Promise."

* * *

I shiver as I make my way to Brooklyn's for the party the next night. An owl hoots in a nearby tree. I pull my sweatshirt tighter around my shoulders and lower my face. Wind sweeps through the tree branches, rattling them like bones. A man with a sagging gut and pock-marked face winks at me.

"How you doing, cutie?" he mumbles. His breath smells like whiskey and beef jerky. I hurry past him as he stumbles toward a dimly lit bar.

Brooklyn lives on the first floor of a cheap apartment complex. It's set up to look like a motel. All the apartment doors face an open-air hallway protected only by the cheap, painted aluminum guardrail. Just beyond the edge of the property, I can see the service road that leads to the tattoo parlor.

A sound like a gunshot echoes down the dark alley near her street. I freeze, every muscle in my body tensing to run. Then a car engine sputters on, and an old Buick pulls away from the curb. Not a gunshot—a car backfiring. I exhale and keep moving. The sooner I make it to Brooklyn's place, the better.

Even if she hadn't slipped me the address in English lit class, I wouldn't have trouble finding Brooklyn's party. The music's so loud it vibrates through the parking lot, and the apartment door hangs open. Girls in short skirts and pierced, tattooed guys lounge against the wall, drinking from red Solo cups and smoking cigarettes that smell like pine needles. Green paint bubbles up around where they stubbed the butts out on the walls. Either they're all over twenty-one, or this isn't the kind of neighborhood that calls the cops for underage drinking.

"Hey, little girl!" someone calls, startling me. I turn just as a large bald guy approaches. He towers above me, and he has to weigh at least two hundred pounds. He wears all black, and a white-and-black skull tattoo covers his face and bald head. It looks like he doesn't have any skin.

I start to turn back around, hoping he's not talking to me. He grabs my arm.

"Don't be like that. I'm talking to you," he says. Deep black lines shadow his eyes, and tattoos of teeth stretch down over his lips. "I've got a question."

"Shoot," I say, struggling to keep my voice steady. The man's lips part, but I can't tell if he's smiling at me or grimacing.

"My friends and I are taking a poll." He nods to a group of people standing by the apartment door. They're all pierced and tattooed, but next to Skull Guy they look like members of a church group. "If you could choose how you were going to die, would you rather be beaten to death with a shovel or have your face eaten off?"

I swallow, trying to keep my nerves from showing on my face. The guy might be freaky looking, but he just wants to get a reaction out of me. It's all just part of his game.

"I'd go for the face," I say, meeting his gaze. "I'd want to look my killer in the eye."

This time I'm sure Skull Guy smiles at me. The white-and-black cheekbone tattoos stretch across his face when his lips part. "Solid," he says, bumping my fist.

I nod at a couple more people as I walk past, trying to look like I belong. The music pounds around me, an insistent *bomp bomp bomp*. Once inside, I push my sweat-shirt hood back and glance around the room. It's smoky and dark. Bodies crowd around me, packed so tightly I can't move without bumping someone's arm or back. The floor is sticky, littered with empty beer cans.

I can't believe I worried this would be anything like my last party. It's a completely different world. I've never heard the music before, and I don't think any of the people here actually go to our school. A girl with long, white-blond hair and glassy eyes passes a tiny bag of powder to another girl in a leather jacket, then walks away without glancing at her. I weave through the crowd to a table covered in booze and beer. I grab the single can of off-brand soda sitting next to a case of PBR, just so I have something to do with my hands.

A voice rises above the music, startling me. "Sofia!"

I turn and, through the sea of people pushing in on me, spot Charlie waving his hands above his head like he's signaling planes. If I were a cartoon character, my mouth would drop to the floor and exclamation points would shoot out of my eyes—that's how excited I am to see him standing there, wearing a worn T-shirt with some faded sports logo on it and a dark gray zip-up sweatshirt. He moves around a crowd of guys to stand in front of me and says something I can't hear over the noise. I smile so wide the corners of my mouth threaten to split.

"What?" I shout.

He grins back at me, and even in the dark I notice the dimple in his cheek. Pushing the hair from my neck, he leans in close enough that his breath warms my skin.

"It's loud," he says. "Wanna go outside?"

"Sure."

Charlie takes my hand, and we head for the back of the apartment to a smudged sliding glass door. I crack open my soda as Charlie pushes through the door and we slip outside. Cold air rushes to greet me, and I shiver, almost glad the can is warm, even if the soda tastes terrible.

"You seem to be the only other person here not trying to get completely hammered," Charlie says once we've left the pounding music behind.

"I'm not a big drinker," I say. Charlie nods.

"Me neither." He smiles at me again, that dimple appearing in his cheek. My stomach flips.

"I'm glad you're here. I don't really know anyone else." Charlie glances around at the kids sprawled on lawn chairs and hovering near the apartment door. At first I don't recognize any of them, either, but then I spot Tom wearing a backward baseball cap. He leans forward, passing his cigarette to a cute girl with black dreadlocks and thick glasses. The girl giggles at something he says, then leans in to kiss him. I cringe. Grace would be devastated.

Charlie sees him, too. "I know Tom, I guess. But he's been preoccupied. Josh said he was coming, but I haven't seen him. And now I know you."

"Josh is coming to this party?" I didn't think this was Josh's scene—he seems so preppy, like Riley. Charlie shrugs.

I glance around at the patchy grass and dirty white lawn chairs. Beyond them, I see the outlines of a slide, a swing set, and what I assume is a pool surrounded by high wooden fencing. Despite the cold weather, I hear giggling and splashing.

A smile creeps across my face. I pull on Charlie's sleeve. "Come on. I have a plan."

"Are we going swimming?" Charlie asks when I start to lead him toward the pool.

"It's, like, fifty degrees out!" I pull my sweatshirt tighter around my shoulders. "Besides, I don't have a suit."

"Why should that stop you?"

I groan and push him toward the slide instead. The playground equipment is made of that old steel that isn't used at schools anymore, because people are afraid kids will impale themselves on the sharp metal while play-ing. I approach the slide hesitantly and test the bottom ladder rung to make sure it'll hold my weight.

"Are you serious?" Charlie says. I raise an eyebrow in challenge.

"It's either the slide with me, or you go back to the party to hang out with people who don't even remember their names. Your choice."

Charlie purses his lips, pretending to think this over. "Which people, exactly?"

I pick up a rock and threaten to throw it at him, and he raises his hands in surrender, laughing. "Kidding, kidding." He jogs to the bottom of the slide and crouches down. "Okay, go. I'll catch you."

"I don't need you to catch me," I say. I set my soda down on the ground and climb up the ladder, perching on top of the slide. Charlie grins.

"Of course you do." He grabs the sides of the slide with both hands and shakes, causing the entire thing to rattle. "This thing is a death trap."

Despite the coolness of the night, the metal is warm beneath my hands. I push myself down, and as I start to gather speed, I shriek. Charlie grabs my shoulders before I hit the dirt and holds me steady.

"You okay?" he asks. He actually looks concerned. "I can't believe they let kids on that thing."

"Your turn," I say, pushing myself back to my feet.

Charlie grins and races around to the ladder. The entire slide rocks as he climbs, the metal creaking so badly I'm convinced it's about to fall apart.

"Shit," Charlie says as he settles at the top. "Now I have so much more respect for you for going first."

"Well, I'm a rebel."

"Here goes nothing." Charlie pushes off and shoots down the slide. Somewhere along the way he goes into warp speed, and then he's not sliding anymore—he's flying—and I can't move out of the way before he tumbles into me. We both roll backward, hitting the dirt in a tangle of limbs.

"I'm so sorry," he says, pushing himself onto an elbow. He doesn't roll off me right away. "Did I break you?"

"No." I keep my arms still because I don't trust myself not to grab his sweatshirt and pull him even closer. I clear my throat. "You're . . . fine."

Charlie tilts his head, and I wonder if he can tell what I'm thinking. "I'm really glad you're here, Sofia," he says.

"Yeah, well, I did break your fall," I say. He still doesn't move away from me. He brushes a curl off my forehead and shakes his head like I'm missing something.

"It's not just that. I'm glad to see *you*."

The night instantly grows ten degrees warmer. "Why?"

"You're joking, right?" Charlie eyes lose focus. He's about to kiss me. I inhale, hoping the warm soda hasn't made my mouth taste gross. But he just runs his thumb along my jaw, tracing from my ear to my chin, like he's memorizing my face.

"I like you, okay? You're different from girls around here." He leans toward me again, his eyes closing. This time he hesitates an inch away from me.

"Is this okay?" he asks.

"Yeah." I've barely spoken when he presses his mouth to mine—tentative first, then harder, hungrier. He parts my lips with his tongue and slides his fingers into my hair, pulling me closer, until there's not an inch of his body that isn't pressed against mine. I stop thinking and just react, letting my hips and chest rise and fall with his. One hand is tangled in my hair and another tugging at the waistband of my jeans. He slips his fingers through my curls as he moves his hand down to trace the skin from my neck to my collarbone, sending shivers through my entire body. Decades pass before Charlie pulls away. His hair sticks out from his head in all angles, and I itch to reach for it again, to smooth it back behind his ears. All the blood in his head seems to have rushed to his lips, because they're bright red and swollen from kissing me.

His nose brushes against mine. "You taste minty," he says into my mouth, leaning in to kiss me again.

The giggling in the swimming pool rises in a shriek of laughter and then cuts off abruptly. Charlie hesitates and reluctantly pulls his lips away from mine.

"What do you think they're doing?" I ask. "Should we find out?"

Charlie pushes himself to his feet, then leans over to give me his hand. "Only if it'll help convince you that swimsuits are optional."

"Unlikely," I say, but I follow him toward the pool anyway. There are gaps in the fence, each about one inch wide. I squint into the gaps, but I can't make out entire people—just jumbled shapes. Charlie comes up behind me. Circling my waist with his arms, he starts to kiss my neck.

"I thought we were spying," I whisper.

"Spies do this."

Just beyond the fence a girl says something, but the wind snatches away her words. I lean in closer, pressing my eye against the largest gap.

Brooklyn stands at the top of the plastic staircase leading into a hot tub, holding the stub of a cigarette between two fingers. Black swimsuit bottoms hang low on her hips, and she has a white tank top knotted above her waist. The tank top is wet and pasted to her skin in patches, making it easy to see she's not wearing a bra.

"What are they doing?" Charlie whispers. I shush

him, lifting a finger to my mouth. There's a boy in the hot tub, too, his brown hair slicked up in wet spikes. Thin lines of steam rise from the tub, mingling with the smoke from Brooklyn's cigarette.

"Ever done it in a hot tub?" Brooklyn asks, her mouth curling. She's wearing dark red lipstick that smudges across her cigarette. The boy stands, water dripping from his faded navy boxers. He grabs Brooklyn and spins her around.

I immediately recognize the light brown eyes, the cleft chin. Josh. *Riley's* Josh.

I press my face closer to the fence. Josh sets Brooklyn back down and pulls her to his chest. She drops her cigarette into the water behind her, then lifts her face up to his. They kiss long and deep, and I blush even harder.

Brooklyn looks up, and her eyes find the exact spot in the fence where I'm watching. It's like someone has touched an icy finger to the lowest part of my back and runs it up the length of my spine. She wraps her arms around Josh's neck and kisses him again, possessively, her red-painted mouth mashing against his teeth as she pulls him closer. The whole time, she never takes her eyes away from the fence. From me.

It's like a dare. A challenge. I pull away from the fence and turn back to Charlie, feeling as though I've had the wind knocked out of me.

"Sofia, what's wrong?" Charlie asks. I shake my head. "I've got to go," I say.

* * *

I make my way to Riley's house, following a long, curved road that dead-ends onto Riley's street. Gnarly trees line the sidewalks. The houses sit back far from the street, their windows dark. Overhanging branches send skeletal shadows over their yards.

A bird squawks above me, rustling the tree branches as it flies away.

"Crap," I mutter, trying to still my rapidly beating heart. I ran most of the way here, not because I wanted to get to Riley, but because I didn't want to spend any more time in Brooklyn's neighborhood. In fact, now that I'm here I wish the trip had taken longer.

I pass a few more towering houses before I locate Riley's. Her house is a mini-mansion. A wide white porch wraps around front, and Greek-style pillars stand on either side of the double doors. I ring the bell, and a tinny *ding-dong* echoes inside.

A tiny green garden snake slivers across the wooden porch, its body undulating over the concrete. I cringe and cross my arms over my chest. A second later it disappears behind a heavy clay flowerpot.

Footsteps sound just inside the house, then the door swings open.

"Sofia?" Riley leans a cheek against the edge of the door, considering me. "Are you okay?"

"I'm sorry, I tried to call." I try to catch my breath. "Can I come in?"

The corner of Riley's mouth twitches upward, and her face grows several degrees warmer. "Of course. You want something to drink?"

"Um, sure."

Riley steps back, opening the door into a foyer with high ceilings and real marble floors. I step inside, momentarily distracted. Beautifully posed photographs of Riley sandwiched between her parents cover the walls, all three wearing matching preppy-chic. I gape at them, amazed at how perfect everyone looks, like they're posing for a catalog.

"Your parents look nice." I stop in front of one of the photographs. Riley's family is dressed entirely in white and they're sitting on a bench in front their lake house. Despite what I saw at Brooklyn's party, I find myself wishing I could step into Riley's life for a day or two, just to see what it's like. It must be nice to have the perfect family, the perfect house, the perfect friends.

Riley stops next to me, staring at the photographs without blinking. "Come on," she says.

"The kitchen's this way."

I follow her down a white-carpeted hallway and

into a huge kitchen with stainless steel appliances and cabinets made of deep, dark wood. Gray tile covers the floors, and the only light comes from the window over the sink, where moonlight filters in through gauzy curtains. Riley motions for me to sit on one of the bar stools at an island in the middle of the room.

"Is something wrong?" She opens the fridge and pulls out a pitcher of water. I see just enough of the inside of her fridge to notice most of the shelves are bare. I clear my throat. I spent the entire walk trying to come up with something to say, but every time words formed in my head I was hit by a sudden, overwhelming feeling of guilt—like I'd been the one making out with Josh instead of Brooklyn.

Riley puts the pitcher on the counter, considering me. In the dim light her blue eyes look gray.

"Sweetie, what is it?" Her forehead wrinkles in confusion. I look down at my sneakers, unable to meet her eyes. If I'd found Brooklyn as soon as I got to the party instead of rolling around on the ground with Charlie, none of this would have happened.

"I . . ." I shift on my bar stool. Footsteps sound in the other room, cutting me off. Riley's head jerks up as a woman wearing a silky white robe comes into the kitchen. Her glass is empty except for a few ice cubes.

"Hi, girls," she says with a weak smile. She must be

Riley's mother—Mrs. Howard—but she looks nothing like the person from the photographs in the hall. Her hair falls above her shoulders; it looks like a trendy cut that's grown out. Her face is strange, too—there's something about her features that don't match up with where I expect them to be. Her cheeks have a hollow look, like they're going to cave in.

She crosses the kitchen, the ice in her glass clinking. She pulls a bottle of something clear out of the freezer, and when she bends over, her robe gapes open and I have to avert my eyes to keep from seeing her bare chest.

"You girls having fun?" Mrs. Howard asks.

"A blast," Riley deadpans. "Come on, Sofia. We'll have more privacy in my room."

"Nice to meet you," I mutter, then follow Riley upstairs, wondering if her father is behind one of the heavy doors lining the hallway. The thickly carpeted floor quiets our footsteps.

Riley pushes open a door at the end of the hallway, revealing a bedroom larger than the master suite at my house. Old-fashioned floral wallpaper covers the walls, and heavy velvet curtains hang over the windows. It's so dark I have to squint to see the edges of the furniture. An ornate wooden cross hangs above her door.

"Make yourself at home." Riley crosses the room to turn on a light and settles herself in the faded pink armchair in front of a vintage vanity table. Glass bottles of makeup cover the table, along with half-burned candles and lacy fabric that looks like a scarf. Alexis's and Grace's pictures crowd the mirror, leaving only a tiny circle in the center uncovered. I stop in front of the vanity, smoothing a dog-eared snapshot. If I weren't here for such an awful reason, I'd make Riley tell me the story behind every photograph. I'd take pictures of the two of us on my phone, hoping I'd make it to the mirror, too.

To the left of the mirror stands an old porcelain doll with a cracked face and brown curls like Riley's. The doll's cloudy glass eyes follow me as I perch on the edge of Riley's bed.

I open my mouth and try to speak, but I can't say the words out loud. *Your boyfriend is cheating on you.*

"Sof?" Riley leans forward, putting a hand on my knee. "What is it?" Something passes over her eyes, and she leans away, her back ruler-straight. She speaks in a whisper, "Did something happen at the party?"

I take a deep breath. "Riley, you have to break up with Josh," I blurt out.

A crease forms between Riley's eyes. "What?"

"I *saw* him," I say, quickly so I don't lose my nerve. "With Brooklyn just now."

Understanding passes over Riley's face, and the

crease disappears from between her eyes. She opens her mouth, then closes it again.

"You saw them together," she says, her voice steady. She squeezes her eyes shut, and I expect her to start crying, but her eyes are dry when she blinks them open again. "Were they having sex?"

"No. Just kissing." Brooklyn's words echo in my head as soon as I say this. *Ever done it in a hot tub?*

Riley nods. She pushes herself out of her chair and starts pacing the length of her room. She stops in front of the door and presses a hand against the wood, closing her eyes. I push myself to my feet to give her a hug when her lips start to move silently. She's not crying—she's praying.

"Amen," she whispers, and her eyes flicker open. She stares at her door without saying a word.

"Riley, I'm so sorry." My shoulders tighten, and I stand a little straighter. "I came right here after I saw them. I just thought you should know."

"Sof, it's okay," Riley says. "I prayed, and I think it's obvious what we need to do. Brooklyn is lost. We have to help her."

"You want to *help* Brooklyn?" I gape at Riley, confused. "But what about Josh? Aren't you pissed?"

"Josh strayed from God," Riley says. "Yeah, it hurts, but I believe he'll find his way back to the Lord. But

Brooklyn . . . don't you get it, Sofia? This just *proves* she needs our help. Brooklyn has to be fixed."

A smile flutters across Riley's face. It reminds me of when I first met her, when her smile never seemed to spread past her lips, leaving her eyes cold and empty. Now, though, her eyes are bright with a kind of manic energy. When she talks again, her words tumble into one another, like they're racing to get out of her mouth.

"We thought Brooklyn was rebelling, but this is worse. Some people have evil inside them, Sofia. Brooklyn needs us."

The word *evil* still seems too strong to me, but I can't argue with Riley after what I saw. If this is what she needs to get over Josh, I can be there for her. I squeeze her arm. "How do we do that?"

"Don't worry." Riley places her hand over mine and squeezes back. "You don't have to do anything. I have a plan."

CHAPTER SEVEN

A floorboard creaks somewhere in the house, jerking me from sleep. I force my eyes open, not sure if what I heard was real or an echo from a dream.

A heavy footstep thuds against the floor downstairs. Then silence.

I sit up, my comforter falling to my lap. My heart pounds in my ears. It could be Mom going downstairs for a glass of water. But that's unlikely. Most nights she takes insanely strong sleeping pills and is out like the dead till morning.

I push back the rest of my blankets and slip from the bed. The floor freezes my bare feet, and I shiver as I stumble for the door. There's no moon tonight, leaving my room so dark I can't see my arms stretched in front of me.

The house falls silent. I'm being silly. Even if it wasn't Mom, that sound could have been a million things: the house settling or wind pounding at the windows. Still, I hold my breath until I find the door with my fingers. I press my ear to the wood, listening for a sound in the hallway.

The top stair groans: another footstep. Someone's out there.

I stumble backward and crash into my desk. There's another creak, this one outside my door.

"Who's there?" I whisper. I step away from my desk, forcing myself toward the door. Louder, I ask, "Mom? Is that you?"

It's too dark to see, but I hear my door latch click and feel the air move as the door swings open. A fingernails-on-sandpaper scratch cuts through the silence, and I smell sulfur. Blue-orange light flickers to life.

I blink against the sudden brightness, and, as my eyes focus, I make out a lit match and a face. Light dances in Riley's eyes. She puts a finger to her lips. *Quiet.*

"You scared me to death!" I take a deep breath to get rid of the last of my fear and lean against my desk, my heart still thudding like crazy. "How did you get in?"

She doesn't answer, but her eyebrow twitches higher. Her eyes are manic, wide and dark, her pupils dilated in twin black pools. An emotion I can't place flickers across her face, and my question changes from *how* she got in to *why*.

"Hurry," she whispers. The match burns down to her fingertips, and she shakes it out. A silver curl of smoke stretches to the ceiling. "I want to show you something."

This has to be about Josh. I bet the others are waiting at the house for us, and we'll spend the night eating ice cream and complaining to one another about what jerks guys are. My fear flips into relief.

I grab my sneakers, then push my bedroom door open. Riley follows silently. Once in the hallway I hesitate, glancing at my mom's door. I motion for Riley to keep quiet as we start down the stairs.

We hurry out of my house, stopping for Riley to grab a pair of gray sneakers she'd hidden behind the potted plant on our front porch. She slides them onto her bare feet without untying them first, and we head down the street.

The wind slices through the sleeves of my sweater and coaxes goose bumps from my skin. I press my lips together to keep my teeth from chattering and pull my sweater over my hands. Despite Riley's bare legs, she doesn't shiver.

I notice a shadow crouched on the porch steps as we near the abandoned house: Grace. She looks plainer than I've ever seen her, in a black T-shirt, jeans, and faded sneakers. The hood of her giraffe-print sweatshirt hides her hair.

"Hey, Grace," I say as I pass her on the steps.

"Hey," she echoes hollowly. Her eyes don't quite focus, and she doesn't acknowledge Riley at all. You'd think she was the one whose boyfriend just cheated on her.

"Is she okay?" I ask. Riley pushes the front door open, and the two of us slip inside.

"Grace? Probably just tired. Come on—it's this way."

I ease the door shut behind me and realize a doorknob has been added where there wasn't one before. Riley notices my confusion and pulls a key out of the pocket of her jeans. "Can never be too careful," she says, as if that answers everything.

We walk past the living room, where the sleeping bags are rolled and stacked next to the pillows in a corner. None of the tea lights are lit, and it makes this place feel emptier than before. I realize how alone we are out here, with nothing but dirt and the skeletons of half-built houses surrounding us. Wind rattles the plastic at the windows. I imagine it rolling over miles of empty land to press against this house, and suddenly it seems strong enough to rip off walls.

"We're going to the basement," Riley says, opening a door I thought was a closet. I peer down the stairs, but I can't see past the concrete wall below. The rest of the basement is dark.

"What's down there?"

"A surprise," Riley says. The first step creaks beneath her bare foot. She takes me by the arm. "Don't be scared."

I start down the stairs with her, focused on placing one foot in front of the other. Cold air creeps in through the concrete walls and floor, holding a damp scent of dust and something I can't place. I wrinkle my nose as we make our way down. It smells metallic, like pennies.

There's a muffled whimper deep in the basement, like someone crying into a pillow. I freeze on the bottom step.

"Riley . . ." I still can't see past the concrete wall, and I suddenly want to keep it that way. But Riley tugs on my arm, her fingernails pricking the skin on my wrist. My feet move forward on their own.

"It's okay, Sof," she says, and I let her lead me around the corner.

The blue oil lamp from upstairs sits on a table near the far wall, casting a wedge of flickering light over the concrete. Alexis crouches over the lamp, messing with a lever on the side. There's a flicker of movement, like an arm reaching out of the shadows behind her. I jerk my head around to stare, praying it was just a trick of the light.

The lamp's tiny flame dances higher, illuminating Brooklyn's crumpled body. Duct tape winds around her mouth and cheeks, plastering her short, sweaty hair to her head. She's tied to a wooden pillar in the middle of the room, her arms pressed against her sides, and her legs trapped beneath her.

Fear rises in my chest, but I push it back down. This is a joke. They must've set it up to mess with me. I laugh nervously, but then Brooklyn raises her head and shakes the matted hair from her eyes. Her gaze shifts to mine, and it's like I've been plunged in cold water. The fear in Brooklyn's eyes is real.

"Riley." My voice is hoarse, a whisper. "What did you do?"

"What did I *do*?" Riley's voice hits the concrete like a slap. Brooklyn jerks at the sound, but her red eyes stay fixed on me. "We talked about this, Sofia." Riley crosses the room to Alexis and picks up a black backpack. She reaches inside and pulls out a butcher knife. Brooklyn breathes in through her nose with a shaky sob, and I throw a hand over my mouth.

"Shit! Riley, why do you have that?"

"I'm going to get the evil out of her." Riley turns the knife to catch the glare of the lamp. I glance back at Brooklyn. The ropes rubbed the skin around her wrists raw, and her hair's drenched with sweat, but otherwise she's unhurt. She mostly just looks scared. I exhale. There's still time to fix this.

"Riley, give me the knife," I say, holding out my hand. The blade distorts my reflection, making my forehead too long, my eyes beady pricks of black. I look like a monster.

"Don't be silly, Sofia." Riley pulls the knife to her side and wraps her fingers around it possessively. "We talked about this. You said we're in this together."

Riley's delusional. We talked about helping her, not *kidnapping* her. Brooklyn hasn't taken her eyes off the knife. Her face twists in fear, crinkling the edges of the duct tape. I start to cross the basement, but Alexis steps in front of me, blocking my way.

"Let me through," I demand. Alexis crosses her arms over her chest and glances at Riley over my shoulder. Brooklyn shifts on the concrete behind her. The ropes binding her wrists tighten with a groan as she moves. "Alexis, we have to untie her!"

"This is for her own good, Sofia." Riley steps up behind me and places a hand on my shoulder to prevent me from moving any closer to Brooklyn. A chill spreads from the tips of my fingers to the small of my back. "Alexis, did you pack everything?" Riley shifts the back-pack in her arms, grimacing under its weight.

"I think so." Alexis watches Riley from beneath the

veil of her own pale white-blond hair. I can't tell if she's as freaked out as I am, but it's obvious she's not going to do anything to stop this.

"What's in there?" I ask, eyeing the backpack.

"Very important supplies." Riley unzips the bag and removes jars of water and salt, three bottles of wine, and a heavy, leather-bound Bible. She sets the items on the floor and reaches into the bag again. I expect more knives, but Riley pulls out a wooden cross.

Suddenly something clicks. "This is an exorcism."

"Lexie taught me how to perform one," Riley says. She sets the knife down on the floor and picks up the bottle of wine, yanking out the cork.

"We're going to draw the demon out of Brooklyn," Alexis explains. "Most priests use holy water or a cross, sometimes blessed salt."

I decide to skip over the "demon" comment and move to the most obvious flaw in their plan. "But none of us is a priest."

"We don't need to be," Alexis says. "That's what I was telling Riley. Anyone can perform an exorcism as long as they're filled with the Holy Spirit. And the more true believers you have with you the stronger you are. With you and Grace, we have four."

"Don't be scared, Sof," Riley says, taking a drink of wine. "This'll be fun."

I nod woodenly. None of their supplies are too terrible, aside from the knife. Maybe they'll just throw some water at Brooklyn and chant for a while. They probably only brought the knife to freak her out—punishment for screwing around with Josh. I breathe in deeply, trying to calm my nerves. This could still be okay.

But then I glance up, meeting Brooklyn's red-rimmed eyes. Her shoulders rise and fall in silent sobs and sweat, and tears mingle with her eyeliner, sending thick black lines streaming down her face. This isn't a prank. Riley didn't say she wanted to punish Brooklyn—she said she wanted to *save* her, and for some reason that involves a knife and holding a girl prisoner in the basement.

"I can't do this," I say. I ease my foot off the floor and move it behind me, slowly backing toward the staircase. My legs are so numb I worry I might collapse. "I have to go."

I turn and stumble toward the staircase without waiting for Riley to answer. When I reach the concrete wall, I break into a run, my shoes slipping against the steps. My brain is moving too quickly, telling me I'm overreacting, that nothing's wrong. At the same time my palms start to sweat and my knees shake. My body wants to get as far away from here as possible.

Once I'm through the basement door, time speeds up. My heart pounds in my ears, making it impossible to think. I tear through the kitchen, moving so quickly I smack an arm against the doorframe and stumble into the hall, landing *hard* on my knees. Pain shoots up my legs. But I grit my teeth and push myself to my feet and run.

The shadows in the living room seem to reach for me as I race past. I glance outside when I get to the front door, but Grace isn't on the porch anymore. I don't stop to think about where she might've gone. My hands tremble so badly the doorknob rattles as I work the lock, but, finally, my fingers manage to twist the deadbolt. I turn the knob and pull.

The door doesn't budge. I pull harder. The knob turns easily, but the door itself stays firmly shut. Finally, I glance up. There's a lock screwed into the doorframe, held shut with a heavy, metal padlock.

"Shit." My voice is barely a whisper, but it seems to boom around me. I think of what Riley said when I saw the new doorknob. *Can never be too careful.*

I stumble back down the hall, pulling open the first door I see. It's a bedroom, with two windows on the far wall. I race across the room and feel for the edge of the window with my fingers. My hand brushes against metal. My heart sinks.

Nails line the window frame, sealing it shut. Some are driven deep into the wood, and some are long and crooked, jutting awkwardly out of the frame. A single bent nail lies on the sill, next to a wobbly sketch of a heart that someone etched into the wood.

For a long moment I just stare at the nails, trying to keep myself from hyperventilating or dissolving into tears. Riley isn't crazy enough to lock us all in here, to nail the windows shut so we can't leave. But even as this thought occurs to me, I know it's exactly what she's done. I'm trapped here with her—we all are.

My legs shake as I move backward. I start opening doors at random, desperately searching for an exit Riley might have missed. My breathing gets more ragged as I run from one empty room to another. I claw at the nails in the windowsills until my fingers bleed, but they don't budge. Riley must've used a nail gun.

Finally I stumble into a bathroom. There's only one window here, the kind you crank with a lever to open. There aren't nails sticking out of the frame. I release a shaky, desperate sob.

I grip the lever with both hands. The plastic notch digs into my skin as I yank it around and around. The window jerks and starts, opening at an angle and letting cold air seep into the bathroom. Clouds hide the moon, leaving the night perfectly dark. Cicadas buzz in the grass.

I stop cranking once there's a gap wide enough for me to climb through. The cicadas sound louder, but maybe that's just because my heartbeat has slowed. I'm going to make it. I'm going to get out of here, and I'm going to call the cops. Wiping my sweaty hands on my jeans, I lean forward, knuckles white as I wrap my fingers around the sill.

A hand slaps the outside of the glass, slamming the window shut on my fingers.

Bright, hot pain rips through my hands. I cry out and try to pull away, but the window pins my fingers in place. The clouds move, bathing Riley in moonlight.

She studies me with those gray eyes, then leans into the window with her shoulder, pressing it against my fingers.

"Can't let you leave now, Sof." Riley moves away from the glass, and the window swings open. I snatch my hands away, my breathing ragged. Blood oozes around my knuckles and drips down my wrist, staining the sleeves of my cardigan.

"Clean yourself up," Riley says. "We're just getting started."

CHAPTER EIGHT

I drop to my knees on the cold bathroom floor and fumble for the roll of toilet paper next to the toilet, clumsily mopping up the blood dripping from my fingers. I open my hand, then close it again, testing. Nothing's broken.

Someone pounds at the door. "Hurry up, Sof." The wood muffles Riley's voice. "We're waiting."

I take two deep breaths. My lungs burn and my head feels dizzy. It's just Riley. Riley, who gossiped with me about boys while drinking red wine. Riley, who insisted I eat with her after finding that dead cat. She's not crazy—she just snapped. The real Riley's still in there.

Besides, I can't stay in the bathroom forever. I lick my thumb and wipe the blood from my knuckles. Then I push the door open.

The moonlight from the bathroom window illuminates Riley's narrow shoulders and long, skinny arms. She cocks her head, and her dark curls pool on one shoulder. She looks just like a doll.

"Go back to the basement," she says. "I need to take care of that."

She nods at the bathroom. She's holding a nail gun. She pushes past me to nail the last remaining exit in this house shut.

"Riley, think about this," I say. Riley turns. She doesn't smile, but the creases around her eyes and mouth soften. She takes my hand, squeezing just above my wrist.

"I know you're scared, Sofia," she says. "I know that's why you tried to run. But if you're not with me, you're against me."

She tightens her grip, just enough to pinch the skin at my wrist. I cringe and pull my arm away.

"I'm with you," I say, glancing down at the nail gun.

"Good," Riley says. "Now go."

Shadows stretch across the hallway, making it hard to see where I'm going. I find a light switch in the kitchen and flip it on and then off, but nothing happens. Cursing, I push the basement door open, gripping for the banister in the dark. I feel for the top step with the toe of my sneaker.

Grace peeks around the concrete wall, hovering at the bottom of the stairs. "Are you coming down?"

"Grace," I say, relieved. Shadows hide her face, so I picture the hollow, unfocused expression she wore on the porch. Alexis will side with Riley no matter what, but Grace is different. She can't think what's going on down there is okay. "I think Riley . . ."

The basement door opens behind me, cutting me off. I turn.

Riley steps onto the staircase. Only the outline of her narrow body is visible in the dim light. She pulls the door shut, and something metallic thumps against the wood. I shift my eyes to the door, noticing a thick padlock attached to the frame.

"What is that?"

"Riley put it up," Grace says.

"We don't want anyone sneaking in on us," Riley adds.

I blink against the darkness. She clicks the lock closed, then slips the key into her pocket. She's not locking everyone else out; she's locking us in.

"Hurry up, girls," Riley says, starting down the stairs. "We have work to do."

Grace shuffles farther into the basement without

a word. I follow, but every time I place my foot on a creaky step a new image flashes through my head: first the backpack filled with wine and holy water, then the windows nailed shut, and now the brand-new padlock attached to the door. It must've taken days to do all this, weeks maybe. I picture Riley nailing the upstairs window shut seconds before we all arrived at the house to drink wine and gossip about Josh, Riley stopping at the hardware store to buy a new padlock on the afternoon I walked to the tattoo parlor with Brooklyn. I wipe my sweaty palms on my jeans.

Alexis is crouched next to Brooklyn, whispering. She glances up as the three of us approach and pushes her wispy hair behind one ear. She's surrounded Brooklyn with flickering candles. She motions to the one she's still holding.

"I read that demons are afraid of fire," she says, blinking her wide eyes.

"Good plan, Lexie," Riley coos. "It's like we're surrounding her with a circle of light, to pull her away from the darkness."

Riley squeezes my shoulder. "Yeah, good thinking," I add, and she beams at me.

Alexis puts the last candle down on the floor and stands. "We're all here now. We should get started."

She reaches for my hand while Riley takes the other

one. Together with Grace we form a semicircle around Brooklyn. I don't want to look at her, but I don't have a choice, so I lift my eyes.

A sweaty strand of white-blond hair hangs over Brooklyn's face, fluttering around her nose every time she exhales. Thick black eyeliner runs down her cheeks like tears. I tighten my grip on Riley's hand. We just have to get through the exorcism. This could still be okay.

"We have to be right with God before we can begin," Alexis explains. Brooklyn shifts her combat boot—covered foot. The sole screeches over the concrete floor. "If we want him to drive the demon away, we have to confess our own sins and ask for his forgiveness."

An uneasy silence stretches between us, broken only by the flames licking the candlewicks. I'm not sure I want to know their sins.

"I guess I'll go first," Grace says, fumbling with her sweatshirt zipper. She stares at her sneakers while she speaks, like she's telling her story to them instead of us. "I need a scholarship in order to afford a good college, so I have to get perfect grades. Calculus has been kicking my butt, though, and last week I stole some of my little brother's Ritalin. He has ADD, and the pills are supposed to help him concentrate. I figured they'd be good for studying."

"Oh, Grace," Riley says. "Why didn't you tell us you were struggling?"

"I was embarrassed," she says, dropping her hand from her zipper. "It was just once. They helped get me through the test, but I felt woozy the whole time. I'm never taking them again."

Riley matches Grace's gaze as she lifts her head. "Good."

Wind presses against the tiny, rectangular window near the basement ceiling, making the glass groan. Yesterday Grace's confession might have shocked me, but in light of everything else, pill popping is pretty tame.

"Your turn," Riley says, nodding at Alexis.

Alexis drops Grace's hand and weaves a strand of her long, blond hair around a finger. She turns to me as she begins, "Riley and Grace already know this, but my older sister, Carly, has been in the hospital for the past several months. What should be her best year as a senior she's spending in a coma, all because she accidentally ate one little peanut." Alexis's accent deepens as she speaks, and she pauses in all the right places, as if she's told this story many times before. She whispers the word *coma* like it's too painful to say out loud.

Riley clears her throat. "That isn't your fault, Lexie," she says.

Alexis winds the blond curl tighter and tighter around her finger. "It's not that. I should be sad all the time, but I'm just . . . not." The candlelight flickers, reflecting in Alexis's wide, dark eyes. "Things have been easier with her gone," she continues. "I don't have to compete with her, and we don't fight anymore. There are days I wish she'd never wake up."

"But she's your sister," Grace says.

"I know," Alexis says. I can tell Alexis feels tortured by the way her voice has started to shake. But still, there's something that feels off about her confession. "I pray for forgiveness every day. God knows I want Carly to be okay."

Grace nods, but her mouth twists in disgust. What kind of person wishes her own sister would stay in a coma?

"We forgive you, Lexie," Riley assures her. "Carly will wake up before you know it, and you'll be happy to have her back. I'm sure of it."

The wind rises to a howl. Grace gives Alexis an uneasy smile, and Alexis exhales in relief.

"I'll go next," Riley says. She squares her shoulders and deliberately softens her eyes. "I always told you Josh and I were waiting for marriage, but, well, this summer at the lake house things got a little out of control."

"Seriously?" Grace's eyes widen. "Why didn't you tell us?"

"Yeah, how out of control?" Alexis adds.

"We didn't go all the way, but we got close. I stopped

him before we went too far. But sometimes, I wonder what would have happened if I didn't. It's probably my fault that . . ." Her voice cracks and she shakes her head, unable to finish her sentence. She lifts the bottle of wine to her lips, closing her eyes as she takes a drink. Lowering it, she whispers, "Forgive me, Lord."

Another silence stretches between us, this one charged. Alexis squeezes my hand so tightly my fingers go numb, and Grace glares at her sneakers, refusing to meet anyone's eyes. Riley nudges me. "Sof? Your turn now. You can tell us anything."

I stare at the floor as their eyes settle on me. I'd been so distracted by their stories I almost forgot I had to share my own. My skin prickles, and the memory unfolds in my head before I can say a word.

I slide onto my bar stool in biology class and slip a Q-tip into a sandwich bag, writing the label with a Sharpie. I'm hunched over the table when something pokes me in the head.

"Hey!" I say, turning around. Erin stands behind me, a Q-tip in her hand. She's wearing a leather tank top with a V-neck so low it's impossible for her to wear a bra.

"Lila and I have a bet going on what the germiest thing in the classroom's going to be," Erin says, dropping the Q-tip into a sandwich bag. "My money's on your greasy-ass hair."

She doesn't laugh, but the students behind her giggle and

snicker into their hands. I glance at Karen, who's standing across the room with Lila. She doesn't look as amused as everyone else, but she stares at her shoes and doesn't say a word.

Tears prick the corners of my eyes, but I know the worst thing I can do is cry. Instead I push back my stool and walk, quickly, from the room. By the time I get to the hallway my shoulders shake, and it's all I can do to hold back the sobs. I hear them laughing behind me. The sound echoes in my head.

"Sof?" Riley's voice brings me back to the present, and my eyes flicker open.

Alexis touches my arm. "It's okay, we're here for you."

I swallow, shaking the memory away. Almost without realizing it, I start picking at the skin around my cuticles.

"I didn't fit in at my last school. There were these girls in my science class who always made fun of me. And . . ." I bite off the end of my sentence, not sure how to finish. Riley nudges me with her shoulder.

"And what?"

I pull at the skin around my thumbnail. "I got into a fight with one of them," I lie. "She had to go to the hospital."

I wish that was what happened, and I remember Grandmother telling me you can sin with your thoughts—that thinking something is almost as bad as actually doing it. If that's true, I've sinned as badly as the rest of them. I really wanted to punch Erin.

"Oh, Sofia." Riley steps in front of me, grabbing my shoulders. She pulls me into a hug, running a hand along the back of my head. "You must've felt so alone," she says, quietly enough that I'm sure I'm the only one who can hear her. "But you're with us now," Riley continues. "Right where you're supposed to be."

For a second it's easy to forget the real reason we're here and that Brooklyn is tied up in the corner. Then Riley squeezes me, and her embrace is just tight enough that I can't tell whether it's meant to be comforting—or a warning. When she pulls away she doesn't look at me again. Instead she turns to Brooklyn, her eyes narrowed.

"We've all humbled ourselves before God," she says, taking a few steps forward. She kneels on the floor again, this time so close that her knees press against Brooklyn's frayed jeans.

"What about you?" Riley grabs the duct tape covering Brooklyn's mouth and tears it away. Brooklyn gasps, and her head lolls down to her chest. I cringe at the angry red stripe left across her face.

Riley grabs Brooklyn's chin, forcing her to meet her eyes. Some of Brooklyn's smudged eyeliner comes off on Riley's fingers. She takes a ragged, raspy breath that sounds so painful my entire chest aches.

"Are you ready to confess?" Riley asks.

For a long moment Brooklyn won't lift her eyes from the floor. She blinks rapidly, like she's fighting back tears. This is it, I realize. This is all Riley wanted. Maybe she isn't going to perform the exorcism at all—she just wants Brooklyn to admit what she did.

Finally, Brooklyn looks up at Riley. Lips trembling, she opens her mouth.

And spits in Riley's face.

"Go to hell," she says.

CHAPTER NINE

Riley wipes Brooklyn's spit from her cheek with the back of her hand. I expect her face to twist in fury, but she just stares ahead with glassy eyes, her mouth a thin, hard line. I don't see any sign of the girl I thought I knew—this Riley seems to be missing some key ingredient to make her human. She drinks from the wine bottle, then runs her tongue over her lips.

"How does it feel, bitch?" Brooklyn throws herself against her ropes, making the pillar she's tied to groan. She spits again, this time spraying Riley's foot. "I should baptize you in the name of *Satan*."

Riley cocks her head to the side, reminding me of a

hawk eyeing a mouse. "Well then. We have our work cut out for us. Alexis, what's next?"

"We must pray for Brooklyn's soul. I have the passage," Alexis says. I chew on the inside of my cheek as she slips a faded sheet of paper from her Bible's pages. Even now, in the middle of all this, she looks flawless in a white cardigan covered in silver hearts and jean shorts. I take that as a good sign. She wouldn't have dressed nicely if she thought things were going to get violent.

"Then I'll draw the demon forth." Riley picks up the bottle of holy water.

"Sofia, I need you." Riley holds her free hand out to me. When I don't immediately take it, she grabs my hand and weaves her fingers through mine, pulling me closer. "We can face the demon together. Your strength will be my strength."

I try to meet Riley's eyes, looking for some flicker of the Riley I like, the Riley I thought was my friend. Because of the position of the lamp, her eyes are in shadow and it's her smile that's illuminated. It twists into a smirk.

"Have some faith," she says to me. She grabs Grace's hand and brings her closer into the circle.

Alexis begins to read. "We exorcise you, impure one, you satanic power." Her clear, steady voice fills the cold corners of the basement. I want to pull my hand away from Riley's, but when I move, she squeezes tighter.

"Be humble under the powerful hand of God," Alexis says. I shift my attention back to her, wondering where she found the ridiculous passage she's reading. It sounds like something from a bad horror movie.

Alexis's voice grows louder. "Tremble and flee!" She glances up from the Bible and studies Brooklyn's face, like she's expecting her to start writhing on the floor or for smoke to pour out of her mouth.

But Brooklyn just lifts an eyebrow. "Did you find that on Wikipedia?" she asks, snickering.

"Yeah, where did you get that, Lexie?" Grace asks, frowning.

"It's the official prayer for a ritual exorcism," Alexis says.

Brooklyn laughs even harder. "I don't know why I was worried," she says. "Clearly you all are pros."

"Stop it," Riley snaps. "It doesn't matter where the passage came from. What we say isn't as important as what we believe."

Riley tips the bottle of holy water over Brooklyn's head. The water dribbles from the bottle, and Brooklyn flinches when it hits her, then blinks and stares at Riley.

She tilts her head so the remaining water pours over her face. She shakes her hair out, like a dog.

"Is this so I'll be ready for the wet T-shirt portion of the night?" she asks. Riley tightens her grip on the bottle, her smile hardening.

"She's making fun of us," Riley says. "Sof, hand me the salt."

I don't move. Riley glares at me.

"The sooner you help, the sooner all this can be over."

"Fine." I pull my fingers from Riley's grip. Brooklyn's right. Riley's not a professional—she's just a pissed-off teenage girl. Locking us in here was messed up, but this is just a hazing ritual, something to show Brooklyn who the alpha bitch is. I grab the jar of salt from the floor, thrusting it into Riley's hands. Most girls would just start a burn book.

Water drips from Brooklyn's hair.

"Keep going," Riley urges, and Alexis clears her throat.

"From the snares of the devil, free us, Lord," she continues, a little less enthusiastically than before.

Riley pours the salt in her hand and throws it. I flinch when the salt hits Brooklyn's face, but she squeezes her eyes shut and turns, so it mostly hits her hair. A few tiny white crystals cling to her wet cheeks and the corner of her mouth. Brooklyn runs her tongue along her lips.

"Next time get me some tequila and a lime to go with that," she says. I bite back a smile.

"Heathen," Riley hisses. She pours another handful of salt into her palm and whips it into Brooklyn's face. This time it catches her in the nose and mouth. Brooklyn swears under her breath, trying to blink the salt from her eyes. Riley throws another handful at her, and then another. When the jar is almost empty, she drops to the floor, her knees inches from Brooklyn's.

"This isn't enough for you, is it?" Riley wraps her fingers in Brooklyn's hair and yanks her head back, forcing her to look up. The corners of Brooklyn's eyes crinkle.

"Riley." I take a step toward her. This isn't funny anymore. Even Alexis stops reading.

"This isn't how we're supposed to do it," Alexis says, her voice wavering for the first time. The defiance fades from Brooklyn's eyes.

"Can't you see what she's doing?" Riley says. "She's laughing at us."

Riley releases Brooklyn's hair roughly and stands. Her eyes dart to the cross hanging from Alexis's neck. I'm the only one watching Brooklyn, and I see her square her shoulders and jerk her hands apart to loosen the ropes. I want to help her, but when I take a step toward her, Brooklyn moves her head back and forth, then looks pointedly at the staircase. I frown, but I understand what she's trying to tell me. We're locked down here and it's three against one. I can't afford to challenge the others yet.

"We need something stronger," Riley says, leveling her gaze on Alexis's necklace. "*That*. Alexis, let me borrow your cross."

Alexis hands me her Bible without a word. She finds the chain at her neck and fumbles with the clasp. The cross drops into her hand. She holds it out for Riley.

Riley lifts the cross by its chain. "Thanks, Lexie," she says. Riley lets the cross swing, pendulum-like, before Brooklyn's eyes.

"I exorcize you in the name of the Father, the Son, and the Holy Spirit," she says. They're almost the same words she used to baptize me.

Brooklyn watches the cross sway. Her angry red eyes flick back to Riley. Riley's expression tightens. She pulls back her arm and whips the cross over Brooklyn's face. The chain flashes through the air, landing with a smack. The cross cut deep into Brooklyn's cheek, leaving a thin red line across her skin. A single drop of blood oozes down her face, like a tear.

I take a step back. "God," I say under my breath. Any hope I had that this might not get violent drains away. We have to get out of here. Now.

"Let's try this again," Riley says.

Suddenly Brooklyn shifts her weight to the side and whips her bound legs out from under her, ramming a combat boot into Riley's shin. Riley slams into the concrete, her wrist twisting beneath her body when she hits the floor. The cross clatters out of her hand.

"Bitch!" Riley sweeps the hair from her face and

pushes herself onto all fours, wincing as she eases weight onto her wrist. Grace moves to help, but Brooklyn slams her feet into Riley again, this time striking her in the ribs. Riley collapses into Alexis, and the two of them stumble to the floor, knocking over a tea candle. The flame sputters and dies.

If it weren't for the lock on the basement door, this would be the perfect time to run. The muscles in my legs tense, but I hold myself still. By the time I think of tackling Riley and stealing the key, she's already standing again.

Brooklyn's sharp laughter fills the basement. Her eyes flicker with red light, and even though it must be the reflection of the candlelight, they look like they're glowing. "Riley, I think it's working!" she shouts. "I think I'm saved!"

"Oh my god." Grace bunches her hands near her mouth. "Alexis, your sweater!"

A curl of smoke twists away from Alexis's back, growing thicker as it drifts toward the ceiling. Orange and blue flames lick at the tiny white hearts along her sweater's hem.

"Shit, Lexie, you're on fire!" I say.

Alexis twists around, screaming when the fire catches on her sleeve. She tries to pull the sweater off, but her hands shake so badly she can't seem to work the buttons.

I grab her arm and yank at the cardigan, not caring when the buttons pop off and clatter to the ground. Alexis flings it away from her body as the fire climbs up the sleeve. The sweater lands on another candle a few feet away, still crackling. The flames eat at a tiny pearl button, and the smoke around it fills the basement with a hazy gray cloud.

Grace mutters a string of curses under her breath. She pulls her sweatshirt up over her mouth and stomps the fire out with her sneaker. The fire dies, but the smoke remains. Grace wraps her arms around Alexis's shoulders, pulling her into a hug.

"Shh, you're fine," Grace whispers.

Brooklyn leans against the pillar and takes a shaky breath. "I needed a cigarette, but I guess this will do."

Riley's cheeks are flushed red and her hair is more disheveled than I've ever seen it before. She approaches Brooklyn slowly. I dig my teeth into my lower lip, wanting so badly for Brooklyn to kick Riley again, for her to go down long enough for me to steal the key and get out of here. But Riley stops when she reaches Brooklyn's combat boots.

"You look scared, Ri," Brooklyn says. "I thought demons were supposed to cower before your God, not the other way around."

I take a deep breath and calmly search the room for

something I could use to pick the padlock at the top of the stairs—or even a weapon. I'm past pretending to be on Riley's side, past letting this play out and hoping no one gets hurt. This stops now.

"Alexis, get me the knife," Riley says, and I freeze. Nothing down here is strong enough to use against the knife. Alexis slides it off the floor. The sound of metal dragging over concrete cuts through the basement.

Riley grabs the knife from Alexis. She runs a perfectly manicured nail along the length of the blade. When she reaches the tip, she presses the flesh of her finger into it, drawing a tiny bead of blood. The blood winds around her finger.

"Good," she says, taking a step closer to Brooklyn. "It's sharp."

"Holding a big knife doesn't make you scary," Brooklyn says. A smile tugs at her lips. "I have to believe you've got the balls to use it."

"You don't believe I'll use this?" Riley asks. Brooklyn starts to shift her legs, but Riley drops onto them before she can lift them off the ground. She slams the knife handle into the side of Brooklyn's knee, just below the cap.

Brooklyn's mouth forms a perfect O, and her skin turns white. Her face crumples, and she lets out a strangled cry.

Alexis walks behind Brooklyn and yanks her head back, exposing the pale, fragile skin at her neck. Riley lifts the knife and pushes the tip of the blade to Brooklyn's neck. She turns it as she speaks, twisting the sharp point farther into Brooklyn's skin. Brooklyn cringes and tries to pull away, but the pillar behind her head blocks her in.

"Tell me: Are you scared yet?" Riley asks.

CHAPTER TEN

Riley pushes the knife closer to Brooklyn's throat. I try not to think about how easily she could rip it open. She'll draw blood if either of them moves. I can practically feel the hate radiating off Riley's skin. Maybe she does want to help Brooklyn, but that's not all she wants. She wants her to pay.

"Wait!" The word flies from my mouth before I can think about what I'm doing. Silence follows, and now they're all looking at me, expecting an explanation. I clear my throat and take a hesitant step toward Riley. "Let me try."

I know Brooklyn's sin. Maybe I can get her to

admit it without hurting her. Riley considers me with an icy expression, almost as if she can see past my skin and bones, to all the parts I want to keep hidden from her. Then, as though she flipped a switch, her face lights up.

"Of course," she says. "You should be the one to get her to confess."

She pushes the knife to my palm, and I wrap my fingers around it. My skin tingles where it touches the wooden handle. Riley takes me by the shoulders and pulls me close, kissing me on the cheek.

"Make us proud," she says. Her lips leave behind a damp spot that burns into my skin like acid, but I don't wipe it away. Maybe it's sick, but I *do* want to make Riley proud, even after everything.

"Brooklyn," I say, forcing myself to meet Brooklyn's gaze, "I know what you did at the party. I saw you. If you just admit it, we can all go home."

"What did I do, Sofia?" Brooklyn asks. She blinks at me, her dark eyes filled with hate. "Enlighten me."

"You were in the hot tub with Josh," I say. "You were . . ." I don't want to describe the possessive way she mashed her mouth against Josh's and wrapped her arms around his neck, so I let the rest of my sentence trail off, hoping the others can fill in the blanks.

"Ri, why didn't you tell us?" Grace says.

"I don't think I wanted to admit it," Riley whispers. "I . . ."

"Wait," Brooklyn interrupts. "You think I screwed your boyfriend?" She pulls her battered leg closer to her body, and her boots scrape against the floor. "I never touched that preppy asshole."

"Brooklyn, I'm trying to . . ." *Help you,* I'd wanted to say. But I press my lips together, cutting myself off.

Riley touches my arm. "She just wants to piss us off," she says. "But I have ways of finding the truth."

She pulls a cell phone out of her back pocket. It's covered in duct tape, and someone drew a tiny picture of a kitten with vampire teeth on the back in thick black Sharpie.

"What are you doing with my phone?" Brooklyn asks. "Did you think me and Josh were sending each other dirty text messages?"

"If you were, you deleted them," Riley answers. Her eyes have that glow to them again, the same glow they had when she first brought me here to see Brooklyn tied up. "I guess I'll just have to write some new ones. If you're not going to admit you've been screwing my boyfriend, I'll get him to do it for you."

I stare at the phone, wanting to grab it from Riley's hands and call the police.

"What are you doing?" Riley reads as she types the message. *"I'm lonely."*

She hesitates for a beat, then taps the screen with her thumb. "Send," she says. She slides the phone back into her pocket and crouches in front of Brooklyn again.

"Now, what should we do while we wait for a response?" she asks, unbending a finger from Brooklyn's fist. She takes the knife from my hands before I can stop her and slides the tip of it beneath Brooklyn's fingernail. A phantom pain shoots through all my fingers at once. "How about we play a game? Either you admit your sins, or I do your nails."

Brooklyn glances down at the knife, then back up at Riley.

"Go to hell," she says through clenched teeth.

"That didn't sound like a sin to me," Riley says, and she drives the knife beneath Brooklyn's fingernail.

Brooklyn throws her head against the pillar and releases a desperate, animalistic scream. I close my eyes, and, again, I see Riley wedge the knife beneath Brooklyn's fingernail and shove it forward; I hear the sick pop of the nail separating from Brooklyn's finger. I start to heave, but I force it down. I can't fall apart now. I have to get Brooklyn out of here.

I open my eyes in time to see Brooklyn's tiny black fingernail fall from Riley's knife and drop to the floor. Brooklyn's screams dissolve into shaky sobs, her chest rising and falling rapidly. I stare at the bloody clump on the concrete as Riley unpeels another finger from Brooklyn's fist and slides the tip of her knife just beneath the nail.

"Riley, let's air this place out," I interrupt before Riley pushes the knife any farther under Brooklyn's fingernail. The smoke is thick enough to agitate the back of my throat. Riley's shoulders stiffen and I freeze, certain she heard the fear in my voice. Any second she'll turn the knife on me.

Then her shoulders sag, and she wipes the sweat from her forehead with the back of her hand. "Yeah," she says. "Let's go upstairs."

Grace and Alexis crowd around Riley as they make their way to the door. I let them walk ahead of me, hesitating at the bottom of the stairs.

Now that she's alone, Brooklyn collapses against the wooden pillar and her chest rises and falls in quick succession, like she's going to start hyperventilating. She moves her leg and a spasm of pain shoots across her face.

Riley digs the dead bolt key out of her pocket, her hair covering her face like a veil. Grace and Alexis huddle behind her, whispering in hushed, sympathetic voices. It sounds like they're talking about Josh, but I'm not really listening.

I could untie Brooklyn, and then it would be three

against two. Brooklyn's hurt, but we might still be able to get past them.

I step back from the stairs, rolling my foot from the ball to the heel so the soles of my sneakers don't squeak against the floor.

Alexis pats Riley on the shoulder. "It's better this way," she says. I try to breathe normally, but every time I inhale, my mouth fills with smoke and I have to struggle not to cough. "At least now you know what kind of guy he is."

I duck around the concrete wall and race across the basement to kneel next to Brooklyn. She stares straight ahead, like she can't see me.

"What are you doing?" she hisses, her voice barely a whisper. I grab the rope binding her to the pillar and try to pull the knot apart with my fingers.

"I'm getting you out of here." I say the words directly into her ear so they don't echo across the basement.

"Riley's ruthless. If she catches you, she'll tie you up, too," Brooklyn whispers. The ropes slip in my fingers. Shaking now, I search the basement for something I can use to help pull them apart.

"I was lucky Sofia saw them," Riley says, her voice drifting down the staircase. I ignore her, grabbing a ballpoint pen sticking from the pages of Alexis's Bible. I try to jerk Brooklyn's knots loose.

"Sofia?" Riley calls. There's a moment of silence, and my body goes cold, my fingers frozen on the ropes. The stairs creak as Riley starts down.

"Damn it," I whisper, digging the pen deeper into the knots. Brooklyn twists around to face me.

"Go," she says. "Our only chance is if she thinks she can trust you. Otherwise we're both screwed."

"Sof, what are you doing?" Riley calls down the stairs. There's another groan of wood, and I hear Alexis and Grace whispering as they head back down to the basement with her. I'm so close. The knots will give at any moment. I twist the pen against the ropes, and it slips from my sweaty fingers, clattering to the floor.

"Shit," I hiss.

The footsteps hesitate, and someone mutters, "What was that?"

Brooklyn glances at the staircase, and a muscle in her jaw tightens.

"Stab me." Her eyes shift down to the pen on the floor. *"What?"*

"Sofia, she *has* to trust you," Brooklyn insists. "It's our only way out." I wipe my hands on my pants and pick up the pen. My fingers tremble as I lift the pen to Brooklyn's leg. There's no way I can do this. Riley's feet slap against the basement floor—any second she'll turn the corner and see me.

"Do it!" Brooklyn says. A candle sparks behind me, turning Brooklyn's eyes red. They look like they're glowing again. I nervously drop the pen, and it clatters to the floor again, rolling next to Brooklyn's fingers. I reach for it, but Brooklyn grabs it first.

Without hesitating, she wraps her fingers around the pen and drives it into her leg.

"Shit!" Brooklyn screams. A dark circle of blood appears on her jean shorts. Tears spring to her eyes, and she throws her head back against the pillar, sobbing. She pushes the pen into my hand, and I immediately wrap my fingers around it, trying not to feel ill. I can't bring myself to look down at the blood staining the pen's tip.

"Oh my god!" Riley shouts. She's at my side now and watches the blood spread across Brooklyn's leg, her eyes bright—proud.

"She tried to escape," I lie. "As soon as you went for the staircase, she started pulling at her ropes."

Riley presses her lips into a thin line and squeezes my shoulder. It simultaneously comforts and disgusts me. "I knew we could count on you."

CHAPTER ELEVEN

My grandmother told me about an exorcism she went to once. She was very young, at a small country church in Mexico. A five-year-old boy was brought before the congregation. He'd cut the skin on his arms to ribbons using a straight pin he found in his mother's sewing kit, and he spoke in a language no one knew. The priest spent the entire day dousing the boy with holy water and saying prayer after prayer for his salvation. The day grew late, and most of the congregation left. But my grandmother and her mother stayed and prayed over their rosaries to give the priest and the boy strength.

My grandmother's voice—strong and deep before she got sick—always got quiet when she told the next part of the story:

"The boy, he *tembla*—trembles—and he cries in pain," she'd say in her shaky English, grabbing and motioning with her hands as she spoke, like she was trying to pull the story from the air. "His eyes glow red, and he falls to the ground, and he screams. When he opened his eyes, *mija*, they don't glow anymore. We knew he was saved. Free."

I turn my grandmother's words over in my head while Brooklyn howls in pain. I think of how her leg gave way beneath the pen's sharp tip and my hands quiver. Footsteps echo across the floor.

"Oh my god. What happened?" Alexis asks. Grace hovers behind her, keeping to the farthest corner of the basement.

"Brooklyn almost got away, but Sofia stopped her," Riley explains. "We can't stop now, not when she's weakening. Let's pray."

Alexis reaches for Riley's hand, but Riley takes mine instead. "Alexis, can you pray over Brooklyn? I want Sof next to me."

Jealousy flashes across Alexis's face, but it's gone in an instant. "Of course," she says. "Whatever you think is best."

Riley tightens her hand around mine. She sees me as

one of them now. Brooklyn whimpers, and I glance up, meeting her eyes. Even now her pupils seem to glow red.

Grandmother's low, gravelly voice echoes through my head.

"The boy, his eyes glow red, and he falls to the ground, and he screams. . . ."

Cringing, I look away. It's just the candles, nothing more.

Alexis closes her eyes and starts speaking in another language. *"Pater noster, qui es in caelis,"* she whispers, swaying. The Latin sounds strange when spoken in her Southern accent.

Brooklyn writhes on the floor below her. Her eyelids flicker open, but she rolls her pupils so far back that all I see are the whites. I'm reminded, again, of the boy who shook and trembled while my grandmother and her mother recited the Lord's Prayer in that empty church. Then Brooklyn snickers, breaking the spell.

"She's screwing with us," Riley says. She grabs the backpack and pulls out a pack of matches. A cold finger of fear traces down my spine.

"What are you going to do?" I ask.

"Trust me," she says. She strikes a match, and for a moment we're all quiet. The sulfur lights, shooting blue sparks from the tip before the fire deepens to a flickering red-orange. Riley turns the match in her fingers, and its flame reflects in her dark eyes.

She throws it at Brooklyn.

The match lands on Brooklyn's bare leg, just below her frayed cutoff shorts. All at once her face seems to fold in on itself. She sucks in a sharp breath, shaking her leg wildly to get the match off her skin. It falls to the concrete and dies, leaving only the smell of burning pennies.

"Your turn." Riley takes my hand and places the pack of matches on my palm. I hesitate. The cardboard box seems heavy, even though I know it's practically weightless. "Is there a problem?"

"No," I say too quickly. I slowly remove a single match from the pack and light it against the sulfur strip on the bottom of the lid. I run through every option I can think of, trying to figure a way around this, an excuse, a distraction—anything. I search every dusty corner, but there's nothing. No plan, no other options.

The match's flame flickers, first blue then orange.

I have to get out of here, I tell myself, but the words don't have much power. Riley's testing me, and I have to pass if I stand a chance.

The flame creeps slowly down the match. My fingers tremble so badly it almost goes out. I lift my hand and toss the match into the air. Luckily, my shaking fingers cause the match to land on the concrete next to Brooklyn instead of on her bare skin.

"So close, Sof," Riley says, but she isn't watching anymore. She picks the knife up off the ground.

Alexis starts chanting again. *"Sanctificetur nomen tuum . . ."*

Next to me, Grace closes her eyes and lifts her hands to the ceiling in prayer.

"Again, Sofia," Riley says as she kneels before Brooklyn. This time, when I light the match, I let the flame burn down until it's almost to my fingers. It dies in midair before hitting Brooklyn's skin, and I feel an instant rush of relief.

Brooklyn barely notices when the blackened match drops on her leg. Her eyes are on Riley's knife.

"More threats?" she asks in a choked voice. "That's getting old."

Riley turns the knife so its blade catches the candlelight. "I read about this method of exorcism called bleeding," she explains. "If you harm the host body enough, it scares the demon away."

Riley presses the knife into Brooklyn's exposed thigh and pulls the blade toward her knee. She moves the knife so slowly that I hear the skin rip seconds before a thin red line of blood appears on Brooklyn's leg.

Brooklyn presses her eyes closed and her jaw clenches, but she doesn't scream. Blood bubbles up just above her knee and winds around her leg.

"Riley," I say. Another match burns to life, but I'm so distracted that it dies in my hand, stinging my fingers. I drop it with a start.

"Don't worry, the cuts aren't deep," Riley says. "We don't want to kill her—we just want the demon scared."

Riley pulls the knife across Brooklyn's opposite thigh, just as slowly. I imagine the knife biting the flesh on my thighs, tearing my skin. It stings.

Brooklyn's mouth falls open in a wordless sob. Her chest rises and falls rapidly, and tears cut down her face, leaving behind murky gray trails of eyeliner. Next, Riley drags the blade over Brooklyn's shins—first the left, then the right. Blood drips to the floor.

Alexis falls to her knees, chanting louder. *"Adveniat regnum tuum!"*

Riley stands, the bloody knife still clenched in one hand. She brushes the hair from her forehead, leaving a smudge of red above her eyebrow.

"Sof, could you hand me the salt?" Riley asks, wiping her bloody fingers on her jeans. "I don't want to get blood everywhere."

My body moves before I tell it to, like someone else has control of my arms and legs. Grace is still swaying, her arms in the air above her, her eyes clenched shut. I walk past her and crouch next to the faded backpack lying against the wall, finding a bag of salt in the front pocket.

When I turn back around, the pool of blood beneath Brooklyn has oozed beneath Riley's bare feet. She doesn't notice, and when she walks toward me, her toes leave bloody prints on the concrete.

"Thanks," she says, taking the salt from my hands. Riley pushes a lock of my hair back behind one ear. I feel something wet and warm against my cheek. Brooklyn's blood.

Riley opens the bag of salt and pours a handful into her palm. I want to close my eyes, like Grace, so I don't have to see what she's about to do. But fear keeps me from turning my head or pressing my eyes shut. It's the same fear that keeps me from telling Riley to stop or trying to wrestle her knife away. I don't want to be next.

Riley crouches in front of Brooklyn again. Blood soaks through her jeans where she kneels. She takes Brooklyn by the chin and forces the salt past her clenched lips.

Brooklyn's eyes fly open. She tries to pull her head away, but Alexis comes up behind her and grabs her by the hair to hold her steady. Riley covers Brooklyn's mouth with both her hands.

Brooklyn whips her head to one side, then the other. Alexis tightens her grip on her hair, and Riley pushes her hands up against her face, until Brooklyn can't move at all.

"I'll let go when you admit your sins," Riley says. Brooklyn goes still. Her eyelids flutter, but they don't close.

"Are you ready to submit before the Lord?"

Brooklyn nods, and, slowly, Riley leans back. Alexis pulls her hands out of Brooklyn's hair, a few spiky bleached-blond strands still clenched between her fingers.

Brooklyn heaves forward, vomiting the salt onto the floor. Still bent over, she lets out a low sob, then spits to get all the salt out of her mouth.

"Well?" Riley says. Brooklyn shakes her head and mutters something too quietly for the rest of us to hear. Riley grabs her by the hair and pulls her head up.

"I didn't hear you."

Brooklyn inhales shakily. Riley leans in closer.

A tense, hushed silence stretches between us. Wind presses in against the window. The fabric on Grace's sweatshirt rustles as she moves her arms. A brief, faint hope sparks in my chest.

Please. Please just let this be over.

Brooklyn lifts her dark, hate-filled eyes to Riley and parts her lips. Blood spatters her nose and drips down over her teeth.

She lunges forward, grabbing a chunk of Riley's face between her teeth.

Riley's horrified scream cuts the silence. Brooklyn's lips are coated with red when she pulls away. She spits, and a blood-covered chunk of skin slides across the concrete floor.

CHAPTER TWELVE

"**Y**ou fucking bitch!" Riley stumbles away from Brooklyn, clutching her face with both hands. Blood appears in the cracks between her fingers.

"Riley, oh my god!" Alexis tries to pry Riley's bunched fist from her face, but Riley shoves her away.

"Get me a bandage!" she screams. Behind her, Brooklyn licks the blood from her lips. Her eyes shift to the staircase, but this time I don't need her to tell me what to do.

"We have to get to a bathroom," I say. I go to Riley's side and gently pry her fingers from her face. She moves her hand just long enough for me to see the mangled, bloody skin beneath. Brooklyn's teeth left a perfect indentation on her cheek. "It'll get infected if you don't wash it."

Riley's fingers tremble. She nods, letting me steer her toward the staircase.

"I think I saw Band-Aids in the kitchen," Grace adds.

Alexis tightens Brooklyn's ropes. "These should hold this time," she says, then follows us up the stairs.

I keep my expression emotionless as Riley slips her free hand into her pocket and pulls out the key to the basement door, hoping she can't read in my face how badly I want to rip it from her fingers. After she unlocks the dead bolt, Riley grabs my hand and squeezes.

"Once we clean off the blood you won't see a thing," I lie. I wouldn't be surprised if she had a scar on her face for the rest of her life. Alexis narrows her eyes at me but says nothing.

Once upstairs, I let Alexis take Riley's arm as Grace leads the way to the bathroom. I hold the door open while they all filter inside.

"I'll find the Band-Aids," I say. Riley nods, but the bathroom mirror distracts her. She mutters a curse and leans over the sink, gingerly patting the tender skin around her wound. For the first time since getting here, nobody's watching me.

I slip down the hall, into the kitchen. Dust coats

the countertops and cobwebs stretch across the ceiling. No back door like I'd been hoping, but there's a single window on the far wall. I lean over the sink to reach it, but another row of crooked nails jutting out of the sill keeps me from trying to pry it open.

A long, colorful string of curse words flies through my head. Riley must've nailed every single window shut. I lean back again and wipe the dust from the window ledge on the seat of my pants, then start opening cupboards and drawers. There might be a spare key around here, or at least something I could use as a weapon.

But the cupboards are mostly empty, with cobwebs stretching across the corners. There's a wineglass on the highest shelf. Standing on my tiptoes, I pull it down. It's plastic, not glass—no use as a weapon. Bright red lipstick, like the kind Brooklyn wears, smudges around the lip, and the bottom is stained red from wine that never got rinsed out. I set the glass back inside the cupboard and close the door. Kneeling, I open the cupboard below, but all I find is half a loaf of bread and a plastic jar of peanut butter.

"Sofia, we found the Band-Aids," Grace yells from the bathroom, startling me. "They were in here, under the sink."

If they're bandaging Riley up already, then they're almost done. Sighing, I stare through the dirty glass in the window above the sink. There's no yard behind the house, just a long stretch of upturned dirt bordered by thick trees, their leaves already turning orange and brown.

I wonder what's on the other side of those trees. More abandoned houses and empty lots? Or could there be a road, businesses—civilization?

Something moves in the yard beyond the dirty glass.

I see it from the corner of my eye and glance up. It's a man—homeless from the looks of it. He wears a black T-shirt and sweatpants, tattered and at least three sizes too big, and he's holding a bottle concealed by a brown paper bag.

He stumbles through the trees. Any second he'll disappear. I lean over the sink, lifting a hand to bang on the glass. My voice catches in my throat as I smack my fist against the window. The man cocks his head toward the house. I open my mouth to yell.

"Sofia?"

I clench my mouth shut and whirl around. Riley's right behind me. She glances at the window.

"There was a bug," I lie, lowering my hand. "A cockroach."

Riley wrinkles her nose. "Gross. Didn't you hear us? We found the Band-Aids."

She motions to the flesh-colored bandages on her

face. They make an X over her left cheek. I want to turn back to the window and see if the homeless man is still there, but I can't do that with Riley standing in front of me. Riley crosses the kitchen and leans against the sink.

"I know you feel uneasy about what we're doing," she says. She makes it sound like I'm nervous about sneaking out at night or going skinny-dipping.

"I wanted to show you this to help you understand." Riley pulls a folded piece of paper from her pocket and hands it to me.

It's a newspaper clipping. I unfold it and read the headline. BELOVED TEACHER KILLED IN ACCIDENT. Just below is a photograph of an older man with thick white hair and dark, deeply lined skin.

I frown, scanning the first lines of the article.

Adams High School geography teacher and drama coach Carlton Willis died at 8 PM last night when he fell from a ladder in the school gymnasium. He leaves behind his wife, Julianna Willis . . .

Something familiar tugs at my brain, but I can't figure out what it is. "What does this have to do with Brooklyn?"

"Mr. Willis used to lead a Bible study after school." Riley wraps her fingers around the edge of the sink. "Grace and Brooklyn were in his last period geography together last year. Grace says Brooklyn *hated* Mr. Willis.

One day, Brooklyn was chanting in the back of his class. It was really creepy and disruptive, and Mr. Willis kicked her out. But before she left she threw her textbook at him. Grace says she broke a window. Mr. Willis swore he was going to have her expelled—maybe even arrested."

Despite myself, I'm curious. "So what happened next?"

"Nothing. That was the night Mr. Willis had his accident."

"Accident . . ." I glance back down at the black-and-white photograph on the clipping. Something on Mr. Willis's hand catches my eye: a thick, gold wedding ring. I move my eyes back over the obituary, and once again I stop at the last line in the first paragraph: *He leaves behind wife, Julianna Willis . . .*

CARLTON & JULIANNA 1979.

"His ring," I say, pointing at the picture. "Brooklyn . . ."

"Brooklyn wears it around her neck," Riley finishes for me. She brushes a strand of hair off her forehead. "Like a trophy."

I shake my head. This is insane. "But *why?*"

"Because she's the one who killed him," Riley said. "Because she's evil. That's why we have to stop her."

* * *

I consider Riley's story as we make our way back down the stairs. First there was the skinned cat beneath the bleachers, and now a teacher. Could Riley be spreading more lies? Or is Brooklyn actually dangerous?

Brooklyn's eyes are closed when we get down to the basement, but they flicker open at the sound of our footsteps.

"Back for more?" she asks.

Riley's expression hardens. She lifts a hand to the bandages on her cheek. "Don't we have any more wine?" she says.

Grace pulls a new bottle out of the backpack and hands it to her. I expect Riley to smash it against the wall and attack Brooklyn with the broken glass. But she just twists off the screw top and drinks, watching Brooklyn over the mouth of the bottle.

The cell phone in her back pocket vibrates, and Riley lowers the bottle of wine. All at once it's like the air in the basement thickens. Riley pulls out the phone and taps the screen. She shifts her eyes up to Brooklyn.

"It's from Josh," she says. "He wrote . . ." Riley hesitates, and every muscle in her body tenses. *"Need some company?"*

Any hope I had that this might be over vanishes. Riley tosses Brooklyn's cell phone, and it skitters across the floor. She drops to her knees, straddling Brooklyn's bound legs.

"Whore," she spits, and whips a hand across Brooklyn's

face. Brooklyn's head smacks against the wooden pillar behind her. I cringe and look away, my gaze falling on the butcher knife half wedged beneath the backpack at Grace's feet. No one else seems to remember that it's there.

"Admit it!" Riley screams. I shift my feet to the left, edging slowly closer to the knife.

"Fine!" Brooklyn shouts. She spits blood onto the concrete and stretches out her jaw. "You want me to admit my fucking sins? I did it, okay? I slept with your boyfriend. And you know what the best part is? We'd come here, to this house, and we'd drink your wine, and he'd screw me on your sleeping bag."

Riley's face is empty, expressionless, like she didn't hear a word of Brooklyn's confession. Without even blinking, she slaps her again. I drop to a crouch next to the knife and slide it out from beneath the backpack. Riley stands and starts to pace.

"Give me that," she says, stopping directly in front of me. Before I can say a word, Riley rips the butcher knife from my hand.

"Riley." I stand, no longer thinking about what's smart or what will convince Riley I'm on her side. If Josh is what sent Riley off the rails in the first place, who knows what she'll do now. I reach for the knife, but Riley holds it close to her side possessively. "Come on. She admitted her sin, there's nothing left for us to do."

Riley shakes her head. "That wasn't her only sin." She crouches near Brooklyn again, this time grabbing her hand. "Hand me the Bible, Lexie," she says.

Alexis doesn't answer her. Her glassy eyes are fixed on the far wall.

"Lexie!" Riley yells, and Alexis flinches. "Hand me the Bible."

Alexis takes the Bible out of the backpack and passes it to Riley. "Dirty sinner," she mutters as Riley slides the Bible beneath Brooklyn's hand, then spreads her fingers out flat on its cover.

Brooklyn lifts her face. Black eyeliner seeps into the corners of her eyes and smudges around her nose. Her mouth is rimmed in blood. She tries to pull her hand away, but Riley holds it tight, pressing Brooklyn's fingers down flat with her palm. She positions the knife over the tip of Brooklyn's pinkie.

"You fucking psycho!" Brooklyn screams. She kicks and squirms, fighting against the ropes binding her in place. "Just let me go!"

"Guys, help me hold her down," Riley says. Alexis immediately moves behind Brooklyn and grabs her shoulders so she can't throw herself against the ropes anymore. Grace hesitates, then crouches beside Riley and grabs Brooklyn's wrist.

Riley moves both hands to the knife.

"Okay, okay!" Brooklyn shouts, fear slurring her words. "I killed the cat beneath the bleachers. It was wandering around my apartment complex, so I drowned it in my bathtub. Then I skinned it with this pocketknife I stole from a kid at school. Is that what you want to hear?"

"I don't care what depraved thing you did with that cat." Riley rocks the knife over Brooklyn's finger and Brooklyn cringes from the sting of the blade. "Tell me about Mr. Willis."

Brooklyn shakes her head. "He had an accident. What do you want me to say?"

Riley presses down on the knife. There's a crunch as the blade slices through skin and nail and digs into the leather cover of the Bible beneath Brooklyn's fingers. My breath catches in my throat, and I clench my eyes shut so I don't see the tip of Brooklyn's pinkie roll off the Bible and land on the floor with a sticky thud.

Brooklyn's screaming vibrates through the basement and echoes off the walls. When I open my eyes again, Riley has another finger stretched across the Bible. Blood drips onto the floor, leaking from Brooklyn's bloody pinkie. Riley didn't cut off that much skin. She slid her knife right below the nail, taking only a millimeter of Brooklyn's finger at most. Still, I can't stop staring at the bloody stump she left behind.

I back up until I feel the cold concrete wall behind me. Sweat drenches my entire body. I don't know what's worse—the stories Brooklyn's telling or what Riley's doing to get her to admit to them.

"Tell me about Mr. Willis," Riley says again.

"I killed him, too!" Brooklyn yells, struggling to pull her hand away. "I waited for him in the auditorium. I wanted it to look like an accident, so when he got out the ladder and started climbing, I . . . I . . ."

"You pushed him?" Riley finishes for her. Brooklyn presses her lips together and nods.

"Yes. Yes, I pushed him," Brooklyn screams. "Are you happy now, you psycho?"

I taste sour bile at the back of my throat. I try to swallow, but the sharp, metallic scent of blood and the lingering smoke fill my nostrils. My stomach cramps and restricts, and acid rises in my throat. I drop to my knees and my entire body heaves, splattering vomit onto the concrete.

I look up and Brooklyn catches my eye. She slowly shakes her head and her eyes turn desperate, pained. She's lying, I realize. She's just trying to survive. I exhale in relief.

"Yes, actually, I am happy," Riley says, her lips twisting into a sneer. "Now you just have to be baptized."

CHAPTER THIRTEEN

I work my fingers through the tangled knots binding Brooklyn to the pillar. She barely moves now, having passed out from blood loss or pain, I'm not sure. The stiff ropes scratch my skin, but they finally come loose and pull apart. *We're getting out of here*, I want to tell Brooklyn. The baptism will be easy compared with what she's already been through.

Brooklyn's eyelids flicker but stay closed. Grace wraps a wad of toilet paper around the remaining stub of her finger and secures it with a few Band-Aids. I avoid looking at the bloody tissues while she works.

"Make sure to tie up her arms and legs again." Riley

sticks a heavy wooden cross and the remaining salt and holy water into the backpack. "We're going all the way up to the second floor. Don't want her to get loose."

"Isn't there a bathroom on the first floor?" I ask. Alexis crawls around me, toward Brooklyn's legs, and starts retying the bindings at her ankles.

"Only the bathrooms on the second floor have bathtubs," Riley says.

"Why do we need a tub?"

"You'll see." Riley's words chill me, but I say nothing. I tie the ropes at Brooklyn's wrists, leaving them loose intentionally—just in case. Alexis finishes the knot at Brooklyn's ankles and starts to giggle.

"What's so funny?" I ask her. Alexis glances up, but her eyes don't quite focus on my face.

"It's like she's not even real," she says, poking Brooklyn's limp leg. "She's like a doll."

I try not to think too hard about what she means. Riley sets the backpack down next to the wall and grabs Brooklyn's arms while Alexis and Grace take her legs. Even with the three of them lifting together, they're only able to get her a few feet off the ground. They crouch as they walk, moving slowly toward the staircase. Alexis's breathing grows heavier with every move, and Grace already looks like she might pass out. Sweat lines her forehead, and a few fuzzy strands of hair come loose from her ponytail. They stick out of her head at odd angles.

"Sof, can you blow out the candles?" Riley asks, groaning as she shifts Brooklyn's weight. One of her arms is looped around Brooklyn's torso, while Grace now holds her bound arms and shoulders. Riley's face tightens every time she takes a step back. "And grab the backpack?"

"Okay." I quickly blow out the candles on the far side of the basement and move to grab the backpack still leaning against the wall. I kneel next to it and start shoving the knife and rosary inside. Then my hand brushes against something hard and plastic. I freeze.

Brooklyn's cell phone sits next to the backpack, wedged between the strap and the wall. It must've landed back here after Riley threw it.

Nerves race up my spine. I glance over my shoulder. Riley and the others are still dragging Brooklyn up the stairs. I pick up the phone and press the power button. The screen lights up. Any fear I had that Riley might see me vanishes. Brooklyn lost a *finger*. She needs to get to the hospital.

I move my thumbs over the screen.

911, I type. When I press send the screen flashes a warning: 2% POWER.

I swear under my breath. Maybe a text will go through. I press the message icon, and Josh's last text pops up.

Need company? Josh wrote. I think of what Brooklyn said—that this is where they used to go together.

Yeah, come to the house, I type, praying he'll remember which house is the right one. I press send, but before I can see whether the text goes through, the screen goes black.

"Sof?" Riley calls.

"Coming." I stick the cell phone in the backpack and pull the bag over one shoulder. Riley and the others are halfway up the stairs now. I slip past them and help Riley with Brooklyn's shoulders. Relief washes over her face as I take on some of the weight.

"Maybe Grace can get the door?" I say. Riley nods.

"The key is in my side pocket."

Grace slips her hand into Riley's pocket and removes the key. She unlocks the dead bolt and pushes the door open. I focus on the text message and the possibility that Josh might be on his way now.

He's coming, I think. One way or another, we're getting out of here.

I breathe deeply, trying to get a better grip on Brooklyn's torso by repositioning my arms beneath her shoulder. My back aches from hunching over, and pain shoots up my calves as we shuffle across the living room and into the main hall, where a shadowy staircase leads to the second floor.

Grace helps Alexis by taking one of Brooklyn's legs, but still it's a struggle as we half pull, half carry her up the stairs. Blue veins run along Brooklyn's closed eyelids, and her skin is pale as milk. If I didn't feel her breath on the back of my arm, I'd worry she was already dead.

We pause on the staircase landing to catch our breath. Long fingers of moonlight reach through the arched window next to us and stretch over the polished wood floor. Gasping, Riley leans against the wall, holding a hand over her chest. I glance out the window next to her, hoping to see Josh's car driving toward the house. But the street is empty.

"Come on," she says, readjusting Brooklyn's weight. "We're almost there."

The second floor is less developed than the first. Cloudy plastic hangs from the ceiling, blocking off sections of unfinished wall. A paint can sits next to one of the bedroom doors, surrounded by a few empty Bud Light bottles.

The master bedroom is directly across from the staircase. Moonlight pours through the windows as we slide Brooklyn across the dark gray tile floors, leaving behind bloody smudges. It's past midnight. Soon, the moon will dip behind the far hills and the whole house will grow even darker than it is now.

The bathroom is huge. White marble stretches out

across one wall, and the largest Jacuzzi tub I've ever seen is tucked in the corner, beneath a window covered in cloudy plastic. A thin film of dust coats the porcelain double sink.

When she reaches the tub, Riley sets Brooklyn down and leans against the counter, panting. I let go of her shoulder, too, and try to set her down gently on the tile. Brooklyn groans and curls into a fetal position. Slow, shaky breaths escape her mouth.

"Sof, you have the holy water, right?" Riley leans over the tub and turns on the faucet. Nothing happens. She swears under her breath and turns the faucet off and then on again, but nothing comes out.

"Maybe we can just sprinkle Brooklyn with holy water, or . . ." I start. A churning, gurgling sound echoes below the tub, cutting me off. Thick brown water spurts from the faucet. Riley squeals and plugs the drain.

"Perfect," she says, watching the dirty brown water fill the tub.

Grace makes a face and covers her nose with her hand. "Gross."

"All things are made pure in the eyes of God," Alexis says. She stares down at the muddy brown water and giggles again. "Dirty, dirty, dirty," she whispers.

Her voice makes my skin crawl. Grace cringes as the tub fills and finally turns away—unable to watch.

On the floor, Brooklyn releases a low moan. Riley kneels next to her and pushes a sweaty strand of hair off her forehead.

"Hush, now," she says. "This will all be over soon."

Brooklyn presses her lips together and nods. Even I can't help but be comforted by Riley's words. *This will all be over soon.* Alexis leans past Riley and shuts off the faucet.

"Tub's full," she says. "Do you need help lifting her?"

Riley's eyes shift to me. "The holy water?"

"Oh, right." I pull open the backpack and dig out the now half-full bottle of holy water. I hand it to Riley, and she pours a few drops into the dirty brown sludge. She sets the bottle on the counter, then hauls Brooklyn up by the shoulders. Alexis grabs Brooklyn's arms to hold her steady.

"I baptize you in the name of the Father, the Son, and the Holy Spirit," Riley says, and shoves her face-first into the bathtub. Water drips down the side of the tub.

I hold my breath as Brooklyn struggles in the tub. I remember my own baptism, and my lungs burn all over again.

"Let her up," I say. "That's enough."

But Riley tightens her grip, shoving Brooklyn farther below the water. "Just a few more seconds," she says.

Brooklyn pushes against Riley's hand, but Riley grits

her teeth and holds her down. Bubbles float to the surface of the murky water. I push past Grace and kneel next to the bathtub.

"Riley, stop." I grab Riley by the arm, but she pushes me away. Alexis snickers when I stumble to the floor.

"Are you okay?" Grace offers me her hand, but I ignore her, crawling back over to Riley. Brooklyn's not moving. The water's up to her shoulders now, and Brooklyn's bent so far over the tub that her knees no longer touch the floor. She doesn't struggle.

"Riley!" I shove my hands into the water, groping for Brooklyn's arm. But the tub is deep. My fingers brush something that feels like hair when Riley grabs me by the shoulders and pulls me back. I hit my elbow on the floor and pain shoots up my arm.

"Calm down," Riley says. "I was just about to let her up."

Riley finally releases Brooklyn's head and leans back on her heels. Her arms are stained brown from the water. Brooklyn stays still. I move closer. Just as I'm about to reach out for her again, Riley grabs Brooklyn by the legs and flips her into the tub. Murky water sloshes onto the marble floor, spraying our feet as Brooklyn's body disappears below the surface. I struggle back onto my knees, but Riley elbows me out of the way before I reach into the bathtub again.

"You're crowding her." Riley narrows her cold eyes as she looks down at me.

"She's *drowning*." I hiss.

"Maybe," Riley says. "If that's God's will." Riley tightens her grip on my arm and starts to pull me out of the bathroom.

"Riley, no!" I try to yank my arm away, but Riley holds on tight. "She's going to die!"

"Lexie, get the door," Riley says.

"No!" I scream. Alexis and Grace follow us out of the bathroom. Even Alexis seems uncertain of Riley's orders, but she still closes the door behind her. I listen for the sound of splashing or screaming—anything to tell me Brooklyn's still alive on the other side of the door. But all I hear is silence.

I pull away from Riley, but she digs her nails into my skin and forces me out of the bedroom and into the hall. While Alexis grabs my arms, Riley slips the tiny key out of her pocket again. There's a silver lock nailed to the doorframe, just like in the basement and at the front door.

Riley planned this—this exact moment. She never meant to baptize Brooklyn. From the beginning, she's been planning to lock her in that bathroom to die.

While Riley is fumbling with the key, I twist my arm away from Alexis, then swing it back, hitting her just below the ribs. Swearing, she doubles over, and I slip out of her grip. I barrel into Riley shoulder first, shoving her aside before she can click the lock shut.

"Sofia, *stop!*" Riley yells. I don't listen. I push the bedroom door open and race for the bathroom. My feet slip over the slick wooden floor, still wet from blood and the dirty tub water.

Riley catches up to me as I reach the bathroom. I try to open the door, but she slaps it shut again.

"You don't know what you're doing," she says, panting. "The devil . . ."

I force the door open, pushing her aside. She slips on a puddle of water near the bathroom door and nearly falls, grabbing hold of the wall to catch herself. The water's surface looks as still as glass. I run to the tub and drop to my knees, thrusting a hand through the brown water. Grace and Alexis crowd behind Riley in the doorway, their footsteps echoing against the marble floors. They hurry over to me, but they're too late. We all are. I stand, pulling my trembling arm out of the water.

"Oh my god," I say, lifting my hands to my mouth.

The bathtub is empty. Brooklyn isn't dead—she's gone.

CHAPTER FOURTEEN

Brooklyn's gone. I back into Riley and her body stiff-ens. Her fingers enclose my wrists.

"Where is she?" Riley asks.

"I don't know."

Riley drops my arm. Her eyes widen, and she scans the bathroom, edging her way toward the door. Every muscle in her body tenses, as if she expects Brooklyn to jump out of the walls.

I replay the situation in my head again and again, like it's a math problem that doesn't add up. I wrap my arms around my chest and search the bathroom. Grace clutches the doorframe, her knuckles going white. Alexis hovers next to her. The corner of her lips twists into something between a smile and a grimace.

"We should have known she would get away," she says. I ignore her and start throwing open the cabinets and closet and shower doors. Empty, all of them. Brooklyn really isn't here.

"Where the *fuck* is she?" Riley slams her open palm against the counter next to the sink.

"Riley—"

"No!" Riley snaps, cutting me off. "We have to find her. Now!"

The weird smile stays painted on Alexis's face. She wraps a long blond strand of hair around one finger. "Don't you get it? She's going to find *us*, and then she's going to kill us."

"No!" Riley jerks her head back and forth. "No. She's too weak. That's not going to happen. Grace, search the basement. The rest of us will look for her on the main floors."

"Why would we look for her inside?" Grace is talking so fast that her words slur together. "She probably went right for the front door, Ri."

"No," Riley insists. "There's no way out, I made sure of it. She's still in the house. We just have to find here."

Grace looks like she might say something else, but instead she presses her lips together and nods.

"You check the bedrooms," Riley says to Alexis. "Sofia and I will look downstairs."

Alexis's smile fades. "You want me to go alone?"

"Just do it." Riley grabs my arm and pulls me from the room into the hall.

Shadows pool in the corners. The plastic hanging from the ceiling rustles in phantom wind. Every second that ticks past pounds at the inside of my skull. I *want* Brooklyn to get away from here. I should be trying to mess Riley up—every moment we waste could be the moment Brooklyn finds an open window or a door without a lock on it.

But as much as I want this to be over and for Brooklyn to be safe, I still don't know what she's capable of. She could be hiding around every corner, waiting on the other side of every wall. She could be anywhere.

A floorboard groans. I jump and spin around, but it's just Grace. She slips down the stairs without a word.

Riley lifts the worn black backpack from the floor where I dropped it. She pulls it open and removes the butcher knife. Her bare feet are practically silent as she moves down the hallway, her back to the wall to keep the floorboards from creaking. I picture the rows of nails wedged into the window frames. There's no way Brooklyn could pull them out of the wood before we reach the first floor. I have to stall Riley.

"Hurry," Riley hisses. She starts down the stairs, and when she reaches the landing, she pauses and cocks her head.

I hear it, too—laughing. At first it's faint, but then it bubbles into a giggle and cuts off abruptly. I turn to look for Alexis, but the hallway behind me is empty. She must've already gone into another room.

"Check on Lexie," Riley says. The top of her head disappears from view as she makes her way to the first floor.

I drag my feet down the hall until I'm standing in front of the window at the end of the hall, next to the cloudy sheet of plastic hanging from the ceiling. Out of the corner of my eye I see something dart across the floor, and I spin around. A knotted rope hangs from the ceiling, casting a shadow that sweeps over the floor as it sways back and forth, back and forth. I reach out to steady it, then tilt my head, following the rope to a door directly above me. The attic.

The plastic sheet rustles, even though there's no wind.

"Brooklyn?" I turn, listening for breathing, but I only hear my own heart hammering in my chest. The blurry shadows between the plastic and the unfinished wall look large enough to be a person. I step closer, my sneakers squeaking against the floor. I lift a shaking hand and wrap my fingers around the plastic.

Someone laughs. I turn so quickly I lose my balance and stumble into the window behind me. The pane shudders, and for a second I'm certain it'll crack. But it holds. The glass feels cold against my bare arms.

There's silence in the empty hallway, then the laughter rises again. It's breathless at first. Then gasping—hysterical. It's coming from the bedroom across from me. I creep forward and push open the door.

Alexis is alone in the empty room, her wide, vacant eyes fixed on some point on the wall in front of her. She balances on the sides of her feet, curling her bare toes inward, like claws. Blood stains the skin along the bottoms of her feet.

Giggling quietly to herself, she twists a long strand of blond hair around her finger. Tighter and tighter she winds it, until her fingertip turns blue.

Then she yanks—pulling the hair right out of her head.

I gasp, covering my mouth with my hands to muffle the sound. Alexis turns her head slowly, like she just realized I was there.

"Don't you think it's funny?" She spreads her fingers and the lock flutters out of her hand, landing on a pile of hair at her feet. Curly strands cover the floor like tiny blond question marks.

"What's funny, Alexis?" I swallow, forcing my eyes away from the hair.

"We're all going to die here," she says in a raspy voice. "We're going to die screaming."

A chill runs down my spine. The door behind me slams open and hits the wall with a crack. I take a deep breath as I turn around, so I don't look as terrified as I feel.

Riley stands in the hallway, one hand curled around the doorframe while the other rests next to her leg, clutching the butcher knife. Brown crusty blood clings to the hems of her jeans. She glances at the hair piled beside Alexis's bare feet but says nothing.

"Find Brooklyn yet?" Alexis asks. Riley taps the knife against her leg.

"She's not downstairs." Riley lowers her hand from the doorframe and steps into the hallway to glance out the window. "Grace thinks—"

A ceiling beam groans above us.

"What was that?" I whisper.

"She's on the roof." Alexis puts a cold hand on my arm. Blond hair clings to her fingertips. "How did she get on the roof?"

The attic door falls open with a crack. Riley jumps and her knife clatters to the floor, its handle sliding beneath the plastic sheet behind her.

I swear under my breath and stumble into Alexis. She releases a string of half-crazy giggles and winds another bunch of blond hair around her finger. The attic door swings back and forth, its hinges creaking.

"No one's there," Riley gasps, relief flooding her face. She kneels, fumbling along the floor with shaking hands. She stares at the dark hole in the ceiling that leads to the attic while she gropes for the knife. I watch the door, too, picturing Brooklyn dropping down on us. Every hair on the back of my neck stands on end.

Out of the corner of my eye, I see a figure appear behind the plastic sheet covering the walls.

Before I can react, Brooklyn tears the sheet from the ceiling and brings it down over Riley's face. Riley screams, and Brooklyn tightens the plastic around her head, pulling her to the floor. She pins Riley's arm to the floor with her shoulder and tightens the plastic around her face.

"Help!" Riley yells, sucking the plastic to her lips. Her fingers find the butcher knife, and she waves it around wildly.

Brooklyn pulls her hand back and slams it into Riley's face. She tries to tear the knife out of her hand, but Riley's gripping it tight as she stabs at the air, blinded from the cloudy plastic covering her face. Gritting her teeth, Brooklyn slams her elbow into Riley's fist. Riley swears, and her fingers go slack around the knife handle. Brooklyn yanks at the knife again, and this time she tugs it free.

"Get away from her!" Alexis races toward them just as Brooklyn struggles to her feet, holding the knife in front of her. Alexis freezes, then takes a step backward.

"Don't you fucking touch me!" Brooklyn shouts. Now that's she's not tumbling around on the ground with Riley, I see just how thrashed she looks. Her clothes are soaked and bloodied, and her hair sticks up in damp spikes. The toilet paper around her destroyed pinkie is gone, revealing the red stub where the tip of her finger used to be. The dirty tub water washed the blood from her skin, but that only makes it easier to see the deep, ugly cuts twisting across her face and legs and arms. Angry purple bruises blossom on her cheeks like flowers.

I lift both arms in surrender and try to catch Brooklyn's eyes. They're shifty and nervous, like a wild animal's. But she holds the knife steady.

"Brooklyn." I take a step toward her and she jabs the knife at me. This is the moment I've been hoping for since Riley first locked us in the basement. The power has shifted. We can finally escape. "Brooklyn, please. I . . ."

Riley pulls the plastic sheet away from her face and pushes herself to her elbow, kicking Brooklyn's legs out from under her. Brooklyn falls backward and slams into the wall. She loses her grip on the knife, and it clatters to the floor. Riley leaps to her feet and rushes her, throwing a shoulder into Brooklyn's gut. Brooklyn regains her footing, and the two girls stumble to the edge of the staircase. Brooklyn starts to fall backward down the stairs and Riley tries to pull away from her, but Brooklyn grabs her by the hair, and they hit the floor together. They teeter at the top of the stairs before rolling over the edge, crashing downward in a tangle of arms and legs.

I race to the top of the staircase, Alexis right behind me. They hit the landing together, and Riley manages to pull herself away from Brooklyn. Brooklyn tries to stand, but Riley kicks her in the chest, sending her plummeting down the rest of the stairs alone. I race after her, but before I reach the landing, Brooklyn rolls onto the floor. She lays there, unmoving.

Riley pushes herself onto her elbow, her breathing ragged. Her hair is slicked back with sweat, and there's a new bruise forming at her jawline. Alexis kneels next to her.

"Does that hurt?" she asks. She tries to touch Riley's bruise, but Riley swats her hand away, glaring at her. I move around them and start down the steps.

Brooklyn's arm is wrenched behind her, her legs curled beneath her body at strange, unnatural angles. The bottom steps are streaked with blood. I hold on to the railing as I make my way to the first floor. Riley says something, but her words blur before they reach my ears. I'm focused entirely on Brooklyn. I watch her eyes, praying for them to flicker open. But they're still.

Halfway down the stairs, I notice Grace hovering next to the wall. It's so dark that her sweatshirt and blue jeans blend into the shadows, and I can't quite make out her expression. She must hear me walking down the stairs because she glances up from Brooklyn's body.

"I think she's dead," Grace says.

CHAPTER FIFTEEN

"She's not dead." Riley pushes herself to her feet and limps across the landing. "Grace, help me carry her."

Grace stares at Brooklyn's body. Her lower lip trembles. "I . . . I don't . . ."

"We should call the police," I interrupt. "Or an ambulance. She could be . . ." I falter, not wanting to say the word *dead* out loud. "She could be seriously hurt."

Riley winces as she puts weight on her left leg and starts down the stairs, leaning heavily on the banister. She hesitates next to me and lowers her voice so the other girls don't hear.

"What would we tell the police? That the girl we've been torturing accidentally fell down the stairs?"

She says this so bluntly that it takes a moment for her words to sink in. I smell the wine on Riley's breath, but I don't meet her eyes.

"You were here, too, Sofia," Riley continues. "You think *anyone* is going to believe you're innocent just because you tried not hit her when you threw matches on her bare legs?"

"You saw that?" I ask.

"I see everything. Go splash some water on your face. Alexis, Grace, and I will get Brooklyn upstairs."

The thought of using that sludgy brown water on my face makes my stomach churn, but I head up the stairs anyway. I need to be away from Riley.

I pass Alexis on my way up the stairs. She tilts her head to the side, like she's listening to something I can't hear. There's a raw red spot behind her ear where she pulled out her hair.

I creep past her without a word and head for the master bedroom, but when I put a hand on the doorknob, I change my mind. I don't want to go inside the bathroom where Brooklyn almost drowned. Instead, I make my way farther down the hall, opening doors until I find another bathroom. I slip inside and close the door. Then I lock it, turning the knob as quietly as possible so there's no chance Riley will hear it on the first floor.

With a locked door separating me from Riley, I feel safer than I have in hours. I clench my eyes shut and lean my head against the wood, and I have to dig my teeth into my lower lip to keep from sobbing out loud. All the fear and nerves and anxiety bubble up inside me, and I curl my hands into fists. This pulls the mangled skin on my knuckles and makes the torn cuticles around my fingernails sting, reminding me why I'm here in the first place. I lower my hands and take two shaky breaths.

There isn't a mirror hanging on the wall over the sink, just empty white space. It's probably better, I think, as I switch the faucet on and off. I don't want to know what I look like after spending the night in a bloody, smoky basement. I check over my shoulder again and again to make sure the bathtub behind me stays empty. With my back to it, I find myself picturing Brooklyn sitting inside, blood and muddy water streaming from her hair.

It takes a while for water to spurt out of the faucet, and this time it's not muddy and thick, just a little brown. I run the water over my hands, cringing when it hits the skin at my knuckles and around my fingernails.

There's a hair tie next to the faucet, a pink one with a strand of brown hair curled around it. I flick it to the floor, wondering if there's a single room in this house Riley hasn't been. I put my hands back below the water, and, after a moment, it actually feels good. I close my eyes, keeping my hands below the stream until the cold turns them numb.

I turn the faucet off and open my eyes again, glancing back down at the sink just as a cicada pokes its head from the drain. I choke down a scream and stumble back so quickly that my feet bang against the tub and I have to grab hold of the wall to keep myself from falling inside. The cicada crawls out of the drain and into the sink, wings spreading.

Someone bangs on the door. "Sofia! Hurry, we need your help."

Straightening, I unlock the door and pull it open, one eye on the cicada inching across the counter as I slip into the hallway. My skin tingles when I pull the door shut behind me.

"Watch your head," Alexis says, and I duck out of the way as she slides a ladder from the door in the ceiling. Behind her, Grace and Riley drag Brooklyn down the hallway by her arms. I watch her for signs that she's starting to wake, but she doesn't move.

Riley stops at the foot of the ladder. She lets go of Brooklyn's arm, and there's a sick thud as it drops to the floor.

"Sof, you'll have to hold her around her chest and go up backward," Riley says, nodding toward the attic. "Then Grace and I can each take a leg."

"You want to take her to the attic?" I ask. The attic is dark—darker than the basement or the hall next to the kitchen. I doubt there are any windows.

"The basement was getting too smoky," Riley says, wrinkling her nose. "And the attic has a good lock, so there's no chance she'll get away again. Lexie, why don't you run downstairs and get the candles? It'll give us some light."

Obedient as ever, Alexis nods. Her bare feet slap against the floor as she heads down the hallway. Riley takes one of Brooklyn's legs and Grace shuffles forward, doing the same.

"Sof," Riley says, nodding at Brooklyn's chest. "We need your help."

Reluctantly, I slide my arms around Brooklyn's torso and lift her off the ground. My hands tighten around her chest, and I feel the faint *thump thump* of her heartbeat just below her rib cage. Relief floods through me. She's alive.

The three of us slowly make our way up the stairs, stopping every few seconds to redistribute Brooklyn's weight among us. The attic stairs are too steep to go up backward without holding on to anything, so I keep one arm wrapped around Brooklyn's chest and the other hooked over the rickety railing attached to the ladder. Brooklyn isn't heavy, but her body still threatens to slip from my grip.

Finally, we make it into the attic. Raw wooden beams and pink insulation form the walls, and the ceiling angles sharply upward. Stacks of faded *Vogue* magazines sit in the corners, next to Ziploc bags filled with nail polish bottles and an old hair straightener. Empty beer and wine bottles line an entire wall of the attic, arranged by height.

"What is all this?" I ask, panting as we drag Brooklyn off the ladder and onto the unfinished attic floor. Riley glances up and shrugs.

"I come here on my own sometimes," she says. "Just to get away from home."

From the look of things, she comes here all the time. I keep my head ducked until we get Brooklyn to the center of the room, where a thick wooden beam juts up from the floor. Then I lean against another wooden beam, exhausted from my climb up the stairs. The tiny circular window on the far wall looks out over the main street.

I steal a glance out the window, still hoping Josh got my text message and he's on his way now. But the street is empty, and steely black clouds cover the moon, bathing everything in darkness.

"Grace, get me that rope," Riley says, pointing to a metal toolbox next to the wall. Next to the toolbox is the bright yellow nail gun she used to nail the bathroom window shut earlier. I stare down at it, wondering when she brought it up here.

Riley positions Brooklyn against the beam, and when Grace hands her the rope, she begins winding it around Brooklyn's body until there's a thick layer of rope binding

Brooklyn in place. Her head lolls forward, and her chin rests against her chest.

"There," Riley says, knotting the rope behind Brooklyn. "That should hold her."

"We left the backpack downstairs," Grace says. She hovers near the ladder, one hand still gripping the wooden railing. "I'll get it."

Grace climbs down the ladder. Once her head is out of view, Riley turns to me, but before she can say a word, a sharp, clear ringing cuts through the house. The doorbell. Riley's face hardens. My heart jumps in my chest—Josh.

Riley races to the ladder and starts to the second floor, going so fast the rickety wood creaks and groans beneath her weight. I head for the ladder to follow her, but Riley jumps the rest of the way down. She grabs the bottom of the ladder and starts sliding it back into place.

"Watch her," she yells up at me.

"Wait!" I cry out as Riley pushes the ladder up. The door closes, and there's a clicking sound as it locks into place. "Riley!" I shout, banging on the floor. I work the lever to get the ladder to release, but it holds, tight. The doorbell rings again. Heavy footsteps race down the stairs.

Shit, I think to myself. She did this on purpose. I push myself to my feet and run across the attic to the window. I press my face up to the glass and squint out onto the street. A bright red pickup is parked by the side of the road. Someone's in the front seat, his arm resting on the open window.

I recognize the rumpled shirt immediately.

"Charlie!" I slam my hand against the window hard, hoping the glass will shatter. "Charlie!" My voice starts to go hoarse, but I don't care—I shout anyway. "Look up! Look up!"

The front door swings open downstairs, and low voices sound just below me. If Charlie hears me at all he doesn't show it. He glances down at the watch on his wrist, then motions impatiently to Josh at the front door. The voices downstairs get louder—it sounds like he and Riley are arguing. I curl my hand into a fist and bang it against the window. The glass shudders, but it doesn't break.

"Sofia?" The voice is weak and raspy. I stop pounding on the glass and turn around. Brooklyn lifts her head and her eyelids flutter open.

"You're awake!" I crouch next to Brooklyn, studying her face. She cringes and tries to move her arm, but the rope holds her tight.

"Fuck," she says, pulling against the rope. "Where am I?"

"Attic." I crawl over to her and try to pull the ropes away with my hands, but they're knotted, tightly, behind her back. "We're locked up here together." Outside, a car engine roars to life.

"No." I stand and turn around to face the window. A flash of white cuts across the street as the truck lights turn on. I press my face to the glass just in time to watch the pickup pull away from the house.

"No!" I slam my fist against the wall. Desperate, frustrated tears sting my eyes. "No!" I shout again. "Come back!"

"Sofia?" Brooklyn shifts on the floor, making the rope binding her groan. Too numb to answer her, I slide to the ground, choking back tears.

"Josh and Charlie were here," I explain. "But they're gone now."

Brooklyn turns her head to the side. Her eyes sweep across the room, studying the old bottles and dog-eared magazines. She wrinkles her nose. "And Riley and the others? Where are they?"

"Downstairs."

Brooklyn's eyes widen. "So we're alone?"

I nod toward the door behind her. "Yeah, but we're locked in."

"Attic doors like that lock automatically, but there's a trick to get them to release." Brooklyn motions to the ropes with her chin. "Untie me and I'll show you."

I study Riley's old things as I cross the attic toward Brooklyn. Riley's porcelain doll sits next to an ancient pink plastic CD player. A new crack cuts between the doll's eyes, like a scar. I shiver, thoroughly creeped out.

I crouch next to Brooklyn and start working on the knots binding her to the pillar. Behind me, something clicks.

"Shout to the . . . Shout to the . . . Shout to the . . ." The words fill each nook and cranny of the attic, echoing off the exposed beams.

I stand and stumble backward. "What the hell is that?"

"It's that CD player." Brooklyn says, studying something behind me. "You must have kicked it."

"Shout . . . shout . . . shout—"

I turn and grab the CD player, hitting the power button. As soon as the music cuts off I hear something else—scratching. It's coming from the corner.

"Do you hear that?" I ask, moving toward the noise. It goes silent.

"It's probably just rats," Brooklyn says, shifting on the floor. "Sof, come on, you have to untie me."

"Right." I shake my head and hurry back over to Brooklyn. "Downstairs," I say as I pull at her ropes. "In the basement, you said you pushed that teacher off a ladder."

"Lies," Brooklyn insists. "Everything I 'confessed' was a lie. I thought Riley would let me go if I played her game."

"I knew it," I say, and a wave of relief washes over me. I work my fingers around the knot, but I can't manage to pull it free. Frustrated, I sit back on my heels.

"I need scissors or a knife or . . ." I spot the toolbox under the window and get an idea. I race over to it, and dig around inside for one of the long, slightly crooked nails. "This might work."

I crouch next to Brooklyn again and try to work the nail through the knot. I manage to loosen it a little before the sweaty nail slips from my fingers. I swear under my breath and fumble along the floor with my fingers.

The scratching sounds in the corner. They're louder this time. Brooklyn tenses beneath her ropes.

"Pretty big rat," she whispers. The shuffling cuts off, and the attic goes silent.

I find the nail and stand, inching toward the noise. It came from the far corner of the attic, directly above the empty room where Alexis pulled out her own hair. The floor over there is bare, empty. It's kind of strange— Riley's magazines and cosmetics pack every corner of the attic. Except that one.

I kneel on the floor next to the wall.

"Is something there?" Brooklyn hisses. I hold a finger to my lips, quieting her. There is something, but it's quiet enough that I couldn't hear it across the room. The noise sounds familiar now. It's a low, rasping sound that I can't quite place.

I lean into the wall and press my ear against the wood. I recognize the noise now.

Breathing.

I yank my face away from the wall and dart back, an animalistic survival instinct kicking in. My entire body tenses to run.

Then my brain catches up. Someone's hiding back there, watching us. I narrow my eyes, and I lift a hand to the wall. It's too dark up here to see, but I feel a shift in the wood. A door.

"Sofia, what the hell?" Brooklyn hisses. I wedge the crooked nail into the narrow opening. The door creaks open, revealing a shadowy, cramped crawl space. Two eyes blink in the darkness. I startle as Grace moves into the dim attic light, her skin ashen. Sweat gathers beneath her hairline.

"Grace, you scared me half to death!" I say.

"Riley made me," she whispers before I get the chance to ask her what she's doing. "She wanted to see what you would do when you were alone."

My throat goes dry. "Why?" I ask. The sound of the attic door falling open interrupts us, and Riley appears at the top of the ladder. She glances at Brooklyn's ropes and the crooked nail in my hands.

"Why do you think?" Riley says.

CHAPTER SIXTEEN

I back away from Grace's crawl space, dropping the nail. It hits the floor with a soft ping, then rolls to a stop next to Brooklyn's knee. Riley follows it with her eyes.

"What were you doing, Sofia?" she asks. Grace crawls out of her hiding space and inches along the back wall to the alcove by the door.

Brooklyn collapses against the beam, and her face slackens. The hope drains out of it, leaving her cheeks sunken. Her hair forms stiff blond spikes that stick out from her head like thorns.

"Just let me go," she whispers, digging her fingernails into the wooden floor. "Please."

Riley ignores her pleading. "You were going to untie her," she says to me, taking a step closer. Brooklyn gasps, releasing jagged bursts of air that make her chest heave. A tear crawls down her cheek.

The dark of the attic paints Riley's face black and gray. Her cheeks and eyes look hollow, her skin ashen. I step away from her, but the wall with the window is directly behind me. I press my hands flat against the cold glass. Outside, the wind howls.

"Riley, I . . ."

"You were going to let her go!" Riley slaps me across the face. I gasp, and pain spreads through my cheeks. Grace cringes, staring at the floor. She won't meet my eyes.

"What did you think would happen?" Riley continues. "That you and Brooklyn would race downstairs and run off with your boyfriends?"

"Please," Brooklyn begs, and in that second I hate her. *I* want to cry and beg and fall apart. But instead I stare into Riley's icy, empty eyes and try to be strong. Brooklyn inhales and mouths the word without making a sound. *Please.*

Riley slaps me again. I cringe against the sting of her hand.

"Do you think I didn't know you texted them? That I didn't hear you fumbling with the phone in the basement? I know everything, Sofia!"

How? I want to ask. *How do you see everything, know everything?* I wonder briefly if she installed security cameras when she nailed all the windows shut, but even that doesn't explain how she seems to see inside my head, how she knows what I'm thinking and feeling.

"Riley," I gasp, lifting a hand to my cheek. "I'm . . ."

"Shut up! Don't you see? God wanted this to happen. He wanted you to fail so you'd understand that the only way out of this house is through *him*."

Riley's face crumples and she sinks to her knees. "I knew this would happen," she says, her hands trembling as she lifts them to her face. "I tried so hard to keep us all strong, but I knew, I *knew* one of us would fall! Now it's up to me to bring you back. "

I watch Riley for a long moment before I realize she's crying. Brooklyn stares at Riley's shaking shoulders, her eyes reflecting the same anger I felt moments ago. Riley doesn't deserve to cry. She hasn't earned it.

A warm yellow glow appears at the door in the floor. The ladder creaks, and the glow comes closer. Riley straightens and wipes her eyes. Alexis appears at the ladder holding a thick white candle.

"Where's the knife?" Riley asks, her voice steady. The skin around her eyes is slightly red, but otherwise there's no sign she was crying.

"Downstairs, in the backpack." Alexis puts the candle

on the floor to the left of the ladder and starts to climb into the attic. The flickering light fills the room with shadows.

"Go get it," Riley snaps, pushing herself back to her feet. She starts to pace, and her stiff, bloodstained jeans sound scratchy, like dried paper dragging across the floor. She shoots a look at Grace. "Both of you. I need a moment alone with Sofia."

"Don't go," I say. As soon as the words leave my mouth, I know I've made a mistake. Riley stops pacing and levels a glare on me that could burn through skin.

"What's going on?" Alexis asks, hovering near the ladder. She shifts her gaze from me to Riley to Grace.

"Please," I say, but I'm watching Riley now. I realize Riley could never feel pain. Riley doesn't feel anything.

"Get the knife," Riley says again. Alexis frowns but heads back down the ladder anyway. Grace shuffles after her. I don't realize I'm reaching for them until they're already gone. My hand hovers in the air, grasping at nothing.

"You're letting the devil manipulate you." Riley turns away from me, talking to herself now. "That's why you texted Josh, why you were going to let Brooklyn go. That's the only explanation."

"Riley . . ." I start, but she cuts me off.

"The devil feeds on your weakness, Sofia! Don't you

see how Brooklyn's working you? How she's using you? This is what the devil does!"

Riley's voice rises to a hysterical scream. It bounces off the walls of the attic. She stops walking and lifts her hands to her head, running her fingers through her hair. The hair comes loose from her ponytail and frizzes around her face.

"Riley," I say, edging toward the ladder. I try to make my voice as soothing as possible. "Riley, I'm not possessed. You have to calm down."

"Calm down?" Riley stumbles over Brooklyn's leg to dart in front of me, blocking my path to the door. Brooklyn doesn't even flinch but watches us with wide, curious eyes. "How am I supposed to calm down, Sofia? We tried everything. Everything! None of it has worked. And you were just going to let her *go*."

The ladder creaks, and Alexis climbs into the attic again, Grace behind her. She's carrying a box of granola bars, the black backpack looped over one shoulder.

"Give me that." Riley yanks the backpack from Grace's arm and rips it open violently. The silver zipper pops off and clatters to the floor. Grace backs away from Riley, rubbing her shoulder. Riley pulls the butcher knife out and lets the bag drop. Hand shaking, she holds the knife in front of her. The blade trembles in her grip.

"Sofia betrayed us." Her eyes meet mine, and cold

dread creeps up over my bones. She takes a step closer, gesturing with the knife while she speaks. "She tried to let Brooklyn go."

"Riley, wait." I raise my hands in front of my chest, stumbling back against the wall. I can't tear my eyes away from the knife. It looks different somehow, like it's watching me. It's the same knife Riley used to cut off Brooklyn's finger, the one that sliced open her skin and spilled her blood onto the floor. It has a taste for blood now.

"What are you doing?" Grace whispers. Riley pushes the point of the blade to my chest. I picture her thrusting it into my body, and my head spins. I place a hand flat against the wall behind me to steady myself.

"I don't know. What do we do to sinners?"

The knife winks at me, or maybe it's just the light reflecting off its blade. I squeeze my eyes shut. I'm just scared, imagining things. But then I open my eyes and Brooklyn is staring me, her eyes glowing red. She runs her tongue over her lips, smearing blood across her mouth. Her voice echoes in my head: *Now you're reborn.*

I blink and Brooklyn's eyes are normal again; there's no blood on her mouth. Her lower lip trembles as she watches me.

Riley lowers the knife from my chest and places it just below my wrist. "In the Old Testament, when God's people sinned, they'd cut off the part of their body that failed him," she says. "This is the hand that failed your God. Would you sacrifice it, if it's what the Lord commanded?"

The blade pricks my skin. Brooklyn clenches her hand into a fist, but all I see is the bloody stub where her finger should be. Fear bubbles inside me.

"Riley, no. *Please.*" I squeeze my eyes shut, and tears leak onto my cheeks. I remember Brooklyn screaming in the basement and the sick sound of flesh dropping to the floor. I try to breathe, but it's as if someone's hands are wrapped around my lungs, squeezing them. I struggle to inhale, and my tears quickly become ugly sobs. "Don't, please, don't."

Suddenly the cold blade is no longer pressed against my wrist. Something clatters to the floor, and then Riley's arms are around my neck, pulling me close to her. She rubs her hand in circles on my back.

"Shh, Sofia, it's okay," she whispers, hugging me tight. "It's okay, I won't hurt you."

I wrap my arms around Riley without thinking and lower my head to her shoulder. Relief spreads through my body like a salve, calming the hysteria in my head, erasing the crazy things I thought I saw. Riley moves her hand to the back of my head and pats down my hair.

"You have to fight the power of Satan," she begs. "I need you with me on this. We can still help her, Sofia."

"How?" I say into her neck. I pull away from her and wipe the tears from my cheek with the back of my hand.

For a moment no one says a word. I look from Riley to Grace to Alexis, but their faces are all blank.

"You didn't humble yourselves," Brooklyn's voice cuts through the silence. Riley turns, and Brooklyn smiles at her wickedly. I picture her glowing red eyes, her mouth dark with blood, but force the image away. That wasn't real, just a trick my fear played on me.

Alexis takes a step away from the ladder. "What are you talking about?" she asks.

"Your sins," Brooklyn says. She leans forward, pulling at the ropes binding her to the beam. "None of you told the truth about your sins, did you?"

CHAPTER SEVENTEEN

"No one lied," Riley says, too quickly. Heat climbs over my face, and I shift my eyes to the floor. *I* lied, but I can't admit that now. Riley nearly cut off my hand for trying to untie Brooklyn. I can't imagine what she'd cut off if she found out I lied to God.

"Guys, *tell* her," Riley hisses. Alexis stares at her feet to keep from meeting our eyes. Grace backs up all the way to the wall, pulling her sweatshirt sleeves down over her wrists.

"They're not the only ones who lied, Riley." Brooklyn's face stays blank, but her voice seems almost amused.

Riley's face hardens. "*I* didn't lie," she insists.

"You didn't tell the whole truth, though," Alexis says. She clenches her hands in front of her, and the tips of her hair brush against her fingers. "None of us told the whole truth."

"Does that mean you want to start?" Brooklyn asks. Alexis winds a strand of hair around one finger, saying nothing. "How about you, Riley?"

"Shut up," Riley says, staring down at her knife on the ground. But she doesn't move toward it or threaten Brooklyn. "I told the truth," she insists again.

"What about Grace?" Brooklyn searches the shadows in the corner for Grace. "Did you admit the whole truth about your little addiction?"

Grace's eyes shift first to Alexis, then to Riley, and finally to me. She hunches up her shoulders, nearly disappearing into her oversize sweatshirt. "I told you I had a problem with drugs and I did," she says.

"Ritalin," Brooklyn corrects her. "Is that all you've ever tried?"

"No." Grace's voice breaks. She picks up the backpack off the floor where Riley dropped it and pulls out a bottle of wine. She yanks out the cork and swigs it back.

"What else have you tried?" Alexis asks. Grace takes another drink of wine.

"It was only Ritalin at first," Grace admits. "I was only going to take a few to study, just like I said. But the high felt so good. It was like my brain went still, like everything fell away except for the thing I was doing. Everything just got so . . . easy."

Grace pauses for a beat and shifts her eyes back down. Brooklyn taps her combat boot against the floor.

"Well?" Brooklyn says. "Don't stop now. You were just getting to the good part."

Grace weaves her hands around the wine bottle nervously. Her electric-blue nails stand out against the dark glass. I stare at them, remembering when I first met Grace, when she seemed impossibly exotic and cool. Now she's vulnerable, naked.

"You don't have to tell us this, Grace," I say.

"We all have to come clean before God," Riley murmurs. She stares blankly at the wall ahead of her. "She does have to tell."

"You all do." Brooklyn looks at me when she says this, and now I'm sure I hear amusement in her voice. Her eyes seem to peel away my skin and see directly into my brain, to the things I'm most ashamed of. I turn back to the wine bottle, focusing my attention on Grace's chipped blue nails again.

"I should've stuck with Ritalin," Grace says, almost to herself. "But I found Xanax in my mom's bathroom one morning. That was even better. After that, I tried my dad's Ambien and some X from a girl at school."

"Grace, the Lord forgives you," Riley says in a hushed voice. She takes the bottle of wine from Grace's hands and drinks. "We all fall. All of us."

Grace smiles through her tears. The candlelight flickers, reflecting the lines they made down her face. From behind her, Brooklyn starts to cackle.

"Are you kidding me?" she says. She leans her head against the pillar, laughing harder. "You're *still* lying!"

"Grace, just tell her. Let's get this over with," Alexis says. Grace grabs the bottle back from Riley and raises it to her lips. This time, she drinks deeply. A red drip oozes out from the side of her mouth and dribbles down over her chin.

Gasping for breath as she lowers the bottle, Grace continues. "When my brother broke his leg this summer, he left his Oxy pills in the bathroom like they were *nothing*. I had to stare at them every morning while I was brushing my teeth." Grace hiccups and takes another drink of wine. "What would you have done?"

Alexis takes the wine bottle out of Grace's hands. "It's okay," she starts, but Grace shakes her head.

"It's not okay!" she yells. Tears fall down her cheeks, faster and faster. She hiccups again. "I want to be cured. I want to be better. But . . . but I . . ." She can't talk now—she's crying too hard. She lowers her face to her hands, sinking to her knees. "I want to be better," she sobs.

Alexis crouches next to Grace, wrapping her arms around her shoulders. "It's okay," she murmurs into her ear. Even Riley crosses the attic to kneel next to her. She closes her eyes, and her lips move in a silent prayer.

I move toward Grace, but Brooklyn lifts her head before I can crouch next to her. Her eyes widen, and she leans her head toward Grace. She's trying to tell me something.

All at once, it clicks. Grace is an addict—addicts have drugs.

No wonder Brooklyn was egging Grace on. Drugs mean freedom—escape. If Grace has pills with her, I can find them and put them in the wine they've all been drinking. If I add enough, they'll pass out.

Riley whispers "Amen," and her eyes flicker open. She picks up the wine and takes a deep drink, staring at me over the top of the bottle.

I twist my face into what I hope is a sympathetic expression and stoop beside her, looping one arm over her shoulder and the other over Grace's.

"Amen," I whisper.

CHAPTER EIGHTEEN

"**W**ho's next?" Brooklyn asks. She's trying to distract them. *If they keep admitting their sins, they won't pay attention to me. And I'll have enough time to find Grace's pills.*

"How do you know all this?" Grace wipes her tears away with her palm as she turns to Brooklyn. Alexis pulls away from her, pushing her hair back behind one ear.

Brooklyn smirks. *A wild thought flies through my head—maybe she reads minds. Maybe Brooklyn already knows everything we've done.*

"Grace stares at the floor when she lies," Riley says before Brooklyn can answer. "Anyone can see that."

Grace blushes and pushes herself to her feet. She backs into an alcove just off the main area in the attic and presses her body against the wall, like she's trying to disappear into the wood.

Brooklyn's eyes linger on her. "It's almost worth the fire, the drowning, and the brutal torture to hear about how shitty you all are," she says.

"Do we need to gag you again?" Riley motions to the duct tape on the floor, but she leans over to pick up the wine bottle instead.

"What's the matter, Riley?" Brooklyn groans, struggling to move beneath the layers of rope binding her in place. "Afraid what your friends will think when you *really* admit your sins?"

"I already admitted them," Riley insists. She pushes a sweaty lock of hair off her forehead with the back of her hand, then drinks deeply from the wine bottle.

I scan the attic while Riley drinks, wondering where Grace stowed her pills. But Brooklyn's words stay with me. *Afraid what your friends will think when you* really *admit your sins?*

I push the question away, and my eyes fall on the black backpack sitting by the stairs. Grace was the one who brought the bag up here. It would've been easy for her to slip a bottle inside.

"Or maybe you should go next, Lexie." Brooklyn

shifts her eyes to Alexis. "You could tell everyone why your sister's really in a coma."

"You don't know what you're talking about," Alexis hisses.

"I know more than you think." Brooklyn's wolf grin deepens.

Riley lowers the wine bottle. "What's she talking about?"

Alexis leans back on her heels and grabs a lock of hair, winding it roughly around her finger. I think of the way she looked standing in that empty room with wispy locks of white-blond curls piled at her feet, like a fairy-tale princess stuck in a horror story.

"She's just making things up," Alexis says. The skin around her fingernail starts to turn blue, but still she winds the hair tighter.

I edge my way closer to the staircase and the back-pack. Nerves pull at my skin like tiny, pinching fingers and my heart jackhammers in my chest. I move slowly toward Grace, inching my feet across the floorboards. She hums a pop song under her breath, her eyes fixated on her shoes.

"You said you hoped she'd never wake up." Brooklyn allows each word to hang in the air for a beat before she continues. "That's not the first time you wanted her dead, is it?"

Alexis shakes her head. "I never wanted that!" There's a faint sound, almost a rip, and the hair drifts away from her fingers. Alexis pushes herself clumsily to her feet, nearly stumbling into me as I inch along the wall behind her. Before she reaches for another lock of hair, Riley takes her hand.

"Just tell us what happened, Lex." Still holding Alexis's hand, she drinks from the wine bottle again. Her words slur a little when she says, "We all have to admit our sins before God."

Grace hums louder. The song tugs at my memory, just out of reach. She takes a step toward the stairs and lifts the faded black backpack from the floor, hugging it to her chest like a teddy bear. I drive my teeth into my lower lip. *Damnit!*

"Are you nervous?" Grace asks me. I'm so distracted by the backpack I almost don't hear her.

"What?"

"About telling your sin." Grace hums another line from the song, and now I remember where I heard it before. It was at that party I went to, the one at the house by the train tracks, where the jocks rated every girl who walked through the front door. Karen invited me to that party.

"No," I say, but I *am* nervous. Not because I don't want to tell my sin, but because I don't want to relive it.

Grace starts humming again, and now it's too late. I'm there, at the party. The entire house trembles as a train rolls past. . . .

I nervously make my way through the crowd of kids inside, stopping in the kitchen to get a soda. When I turn around, Lila's behind me. Her black hair hangs down over her narrow shoulders in a perfect, glossy sheet. Her red-painted lips curl up in a cruel smile.

"Wait." Lila frowns, and her eyes shift to my hair. "You have something caught in your hair."

Lila reaches forward and plucks something from my hair. The curl of her lips hardens as she pulls her hand away.

She's holding a Q-tip.

Some of the kids behind her start to snicker, but Lila manages to keep a straight face as she asks, "Now, where did this come from, Greasy?"

More laughter. It bubbles up around me until I can't tell who it's coming from anymore. Cheeks burning, I push past Lila.

Everybody at the party is staring at me, laughing behind their hands and into their beer cups. I try to move forward, but the kids in front of me crowd together, blocking my path.

"Where are you going, Greasy?" a girl with frizzy red hair asks. She tosses a Q-tip at me, and it gets caught on my sweater.

Another Q-tip soars across the room and hits me in the cheek. A third flies past my arm. Before I know it, everyone's throwing Q-tips and laughing. Horrified, I cover my face with my hands, but still they catch in my hair and on my clothes. I finally find a break in the crowd and force my way through the people—and run right into Karen.

She's standing next to Erin, holding a beer.

"Come on, Sofia," she says, breaking out into a grin. "Take a joke."

I stare, dumbfounded, as she lifts her hand and tosses a Q-tip right at me. It bounces off my chest and drops to the floor.

"Sofia, are you okay?" Grace loosens her hold on the backpack. I could take it from her now, but instead I lean against the wall. Sweat forms on the back of my neck.

With my eyes closed I smell the stale beer that coated the floors in that house, I hear the cruel laughter and the distant roar of the train. After that night I promised myself I'd never go to another party, never again be friends with girls who laughed at other people's pain. Now I'm trapped in an attic, and the only way I'm getting out is by reliving the worst night of my life.

"I'm fine," I say, easing my eyes back open. Grace nods sympathetically, but I don't meet her eyes—I'm staring at the backpack. I was wrong; there is another way out of here. I just have to find those pills.

Alexis's voice rises into a yell. "It's not like Brooklyn's

saying it was!" Alexis looks from Brooklyn to Riley, and her lower lip begins to tremble. "Riley, you know how Carly is," she pleads.

Riley swirls the wine in the bottle, watching liquid slosh up against the sides of the glass. "I know you guys are really competitive."

"Exactly," Alexis says. "But it's not even a competition, because Carly *always* wins. Carly got into Stanford, and Carly's boyfriend is perfect. Do you have any idea what it's like hearing about how wonderful she is all the time?"

Alexis sobs and lowers her head to her hands. Her hair sweeps over her face like a curtain.

"Come on, Alexis," Riley says. She takes another swig from the bottle, then wipes the wine off her top lip with the back of her hand. "Finish the story. Tell us what happened next."

Sniffling, Alexis pushes the hair from her face. "It was an accident, like I said. Carly has a really bad peanut allergy. She has to carry an EpiPen wherever she goes. Last year she and my mom went on a juice cleanse to get ready for the annual charity gala my mom runs, and the only things they could eat were these gross smoothies made from spinach and lemon juice. One day I just . . . I snuck a peanut into Carly's smoothie. Just one."

Alexis's admission shocks me so much that I

forget about the night of the party and Grace's pills—everything but what she just said.

"You poisoned your sister on purpose?" I ask. I think about what my grandmother always said about confession as Alexis studies our faces, looking for sympathy.

"Words, they have power, mija. *When you say your sin out loud, you admit it to yourself as well as to God."*

If I were Alexis, I'd have taken that secret to the grave, no matter what Riley or Brooklyn said.

"She was supposed to have her EpiPen with her!" Alexis continues. "Once she took her shot she'd have been fine. My parents would have made her stay home to rest like they always did when she had a reaction. I could have gone to the gala in her place. But she didn't take her EpiPen that day, because it didn't fit into the stupid designer bag she wanted to carry. So instead of getting sick, she . . ."

"She went into a coma," Grace says.

Alexis grabs for another strand of her hair, but Riley slaps her hand away. "You're sick," she says.

"Stop it!" Alexis yells. "You're drunk!"

"Don't you dare turn this around on me." Riley's eyes are red-rimmed, but I can't tell if it's from the wine or the shock of what Alexis just admitted.

"Why not?" Alexis's voice trembles. "I'm not the only one who's sinned."

Riley slaps her. Alexis's head snaps to the side, and her hands fly to her face. When she turns back to Riley, her mouth hangs open in shock.

"I don't have anything to hide," Riley says. "Whatever I am, whatever I've done, it's *nothing* compared with trying to kill your own flesh and blood."

"You're lying." Alexis sways back and forth, her weight on the balls of her feet, like a ballerina's. There's a light in her eyes that I don't quite understand. It's manic, unhinged. "You're lying, but I know the truth. I know *everything* you've done."

CHAPTER NINETEEN

I pull my arms close to my chest, staring through the open attic door to the ladder descending to the shadowy hallway below. I imagine prying the nails out of a windowsill with my bare hands. My fingertips sting just thinking about it, but I shift toward the door anyway.

"You pretend you're so much better than the rest of us," Alexis shouts. "But you're a *slut*. Every word out of your mouth is a lie."

"Like anyone would believe you after what you've done," Riley spits out.

Grace hiccups again. She's crouched in the alcove next to the door, hugging the backpack. The attic is small—maybe only ten feet long and five feet wide—but because of the angle of the ceiling and walls I can't see what she's doing. Still, she's the only one between me and the door. She'd catch me before I made it to the stairs.

"I'd believe her," Brooklyn says. A strand of hair falls over her eyes. She blows at it, and it flutters back over her forehead. "Whatever happened to coming clean before the Lord, Riley?"

Alexis laughs and shakes her head so violently her neck cracks. "Why are we even here? Because Brooklyn screwed around with your *boyfriend*, right?"

"Shut up." Riley's voice trembles.

"But that's not really true, is it?" Alexis says. "Because he's not your boyfriend. Not anymore. He dumped you two weeks ago."

"I told you to shut up!" Riley screams. Her hands fly to her head, covering her ears.

"And you know what the best part is?" Alexis yells back. "He dumped you because you're a *slut*. He found out what you did with Tom. Why don't you tell that to your precious God, Riley?"

Riley squeezes her eyes shut, shaking her head. I hadn't been paying attention, but now I turn toward Riley.

"Tom?" I repeat. "Wait, Josh's brother Tom? The one Grace . . ."

Grace steps out of the alcove. "What did you do with him?" she asks, her voice cracking.

Riley's red-rimmed eyes widen. "Grace, I . . ."

Grace drops the backpack and steps forward, grabbing Riley's arm. "I've had a crush on Tom since I moved here!" she says, but I'm no longer listening. All I see is the backpack abandoned in the alcove.

"I know," Riley says. "But . . ."

"Did you sleep with him?" Grace interrupts. Riley hesitates, and Grace yells, "Tell the truth!"

"It was just one time. It didn't mean anything!" Riley says. She turns back to Alexis. "You bitch. That was a secret."

"Isn't that the point?" Alexis hisses. "We're all sharing our secrets. You don't get to judge me if you're not willing to own up to yours."

Riley shouts something back at Alexis and their voices grow louder, until they're both screaming at each other and I can't make out what they're actually saying. Brooklyn kicks my ankle lightly with her combat boot, and I look over at her. *Pills*, she mouths, nodding at the backpack.

Grace buries her face in her hands. I creep behind her, sliding into the alcove, where I'm hidden from everyone but Brooklyn. Star-shaped Christmas lights hang from the ceiling above me, and Riley pinned three dead butterflies into the wood with tiny pink pushpins. Their tissue-thin wings look brittle enough to break.

My sneaker brushes up against the bag and I crouch down, pulling it onto my lap. Grace lifts the bottle of wine to her lips again and again, trying to drown all the things she just heard with booze. As long as she doesn't turn around, I'm safe.

I unzip the backpack and thrust my hand inside, digging for the pill bottle. Riley's and Alexis's shadows stretch over the floor. If either of them takes a single step to the left they'll see right into the alcove. My fingers bump up against the wooden cross, but that's it—there's nothing else inside the backpack. Frustrated, I rip open the front pocket.

"I came here to help you, you ungrateful bitch!" Alexis yells. "But now I don't know why I bothered. You obviously don't care about anyone but yourself."

Alexis's footsteps pound against the floor. I glance up as she steps directly in front of the alcove. *Shit.* I drop the backpack and stand, but her back is to me. I don't think she saw anything.

"Alexis, don't," Riley says. Over Grace's shoulder I watch Riley grab Alexis's arm, dragging her back to the center of the room. My heart thuds against my chest. Grace takes another swig of wine, watching the fight unfold like it is a movie.

"You leave when I tell you to leave," Riley says. Her fingers grip Alexis's arm so tightly her skin starts to turn red.

Alexis tries to yank her arm away. "Let go," she says. But Riley holds on tight.

Heart hammering against my chest, I kneel and pull the backpack to my side. I grope against the fabric inside until my fingers enclose a plastic cylinder. I pull it out and quickly turn it in my hand to see the label.

AMBIEN, it reads. My heart thuds against my rib cage. This is it. This is finally *it*.

A floorboard creaks. A chill streaks down my spine, and I look up. Grace's dark eyes are turned toward me, watching me.

Time freezes. My mind moves at hyper-speed, trying to come up with some excuse, some reason to be digging through the bag for the pills. But I can't think of a single reason, and all I can do is wait for Grace to call out to the others and tell them what I'm doing.

Grace considers me for a moment. Then she lifts a finger to her mouth, shooting a look over her shoulder at Riley and Alexis. Neither has noticed us. Yet.

Satisfied they aren't watching, Grace sets the wine bottle on the floor next to me, then turns back around, as if she didn't see me with the pills at all.

CHAPTER TWENTY

I ease the bottle open and pour the pills into my hand. Ten white pills tumble onto my palm. I don't know anything about drugs, but ten seems like a lot—definitely enough to take out a teenage girl. I pry open one of the capsules and dump the fine white powder into the wine bottle.

Riley's jeans scratch against the floor as she paces around the room. Grace is angled in front of me to keep Riley from seeing what I'm doing, but I still freeze, certain I'm about to be discovered. The powder from the pills sticks to my fingers and the mouth of the bottle. I swear under my breath and try to brush it all into the wine.

"I thought you two were so close," Brooklyn says, her voice dripping with fake sympathy. If either Alexis or Riley notices she's making fun of them, they don't show it. They only seem to see each other.

"You were always a shitty friend," Alexis yells, her voice cracking. She wraps a long blond strand of hair around one finger and gives it a sudden, violent tug. "The only reason we even hang out is because you can't stand to be alone."

"I think you have that backward, Lexie." Riley's voice is quiet and even, barely above a whisper. Alexis stands in the middle of the attic while Riley moves around her, an animal circling her prey. "The only reason we're friends is because you need someone to obsess over. You've been pretending to be me since you were eight years old. I just can't get rid of you."

The quieter Riley speaks, the more outraged Alexis grows. "Why not? Because *God* wouldn't want you to?" Alexis shouts. "You hide behind God so no one will see how screwed up you really are."

"I'm not ashamed of anything I've done," Riley continues, rounding back on Alexis. "But you have everything to be ashamed of. You tried to kill your sister! How can any of us ever trust you again?"

Alexis's breathing gets heavier, and she starts to cry. Grace stiffens in front of me. Alexis must've pulled another clump of hair out of her head, but I refuse to look up and watch her. My fingers feel thick and clumsy as I work them around the pills.

"You're wrong," Alexis says.

"Am I?" Riley's voice takes on a cruel, almost gleeful edge. I recognize that tone by now—it means she knows something the rest of us don't.

"If I'm so wrong, why are you still hiding?" Riley continues. "You're keeping secrets from all of us."

The floorboards creak as Alexis takes a step back.

"Stop it," she says. I have the final pill pinned between two fingers, but I peer around the corner to see what's happening.

Riley has Alexis backed against the wall. I can't see Riley's face, but Alexis looks broken. Her eyes are red-rimmed, and she releases a choked, gasping sob. She shakes her head and covers her hair with her hands.

"No," she whispers. "Riley, *please*."

Riley slaps Alexis's hands away and pulls her forward by the head, brushing her long, beautiful hair back with one hand. Beneath the top layer of perfect blond locks, Alexis's entire scalp is red and raw, spotted with still-bleeding scabs.

Alexis pulls away from Riley and tries, desperately, to smooth her hair back in place. Her face crumples, and she drops to her knees, her shoulders shaking with silent sobs. She lifts her hand to the hair just behind her left ear and starts compulsively winding a lock around her finger—tighter and tighter—until it comes off in her hands. Blood spots the skin at her scalp.

"You're disgusting. Soon you won't have any hair left."

Brooklyn releases a slightly hysterical-sounding laugh at the exact second the pill hits the floor. Frowning, Riley pivots to face her.

"What's so funny?" she hisses.

"Hurry," Grace mutters under her breath. I refocus my attention on the pills. I wedge my thumbnail into the last capsule and pull it apart. The white powder dissolves into the wine.

"Your little catfight is just adorable," Brooklyn says. "Which of your friends are you going to turn on next?"

"Shut up," Riley spits out. She crosses the attic and kicks Brooklyn in the shin. Brooklyn makes a big show of squeezing her eyes shut and yelling out in pain, but I know she said those things for me, to distract Riley from what I'm doing.

Grabbing the wine bottle, I stand and slip out of the alcove, placing a hand on Riley's shoulder.

"She's messing with you," I say, squeezing Riley's arm. I lift the wine bottle to my mouth and tip it back, but I keep my lips tight to keep from drinking the drugged wine. I pretend to swallow as I lower the bottle. "She wants you and Alexis to tear each other apart."

"Give me that." Riley's face is blank as she rips the bottle from my hands. She stares down at it for a long moment. Across from us, Alexis sinks to the floor. She sobs quietly, her hands curled into fists around her hair.

"You're right." Riley smiles as she turns the wine bottle in her hand, watching the liquid slosh up against the sides. "We have to trust each other."

"Exactly," I say. "We can't let Brooklyn come between us."

Riley's smile immediately disappears. "We can't let *Brooklyn* come between us," she repeats. She lingers on Brooklyn's name and tightens her grip around the bottle.

Grace weaves her fingers together. She glances at me nervously, but I won't look at her. I can't tear my eyes away from Riley.

Riley shifts her eyes back up to me. They're the eyes of a predator: dead and calculating.

"Didn't realize you were a big drinker," she says, lifting the bottle.

"What?" I swallow, waiting, but Riley holds the wine just below her mouth. The glass brushes against her lower lip.

"The wine," she says. "You seem more interested in it all of the sudden."

"I guess I'm just thirsty," I say.

Riley inhales the scent of the wine, closing her eyes. "Me, too," she murmurs. She tips the bottle back and the wine slides forward. I hold my breath, but the second seems to stretch for an eternity. Sweat breaks out along my palms.

Just before she drinks, Riley's eyes flicker back open.

"Do you think I'm stupid?" she whispers. My throat goes dry.

"Of course not."

Riley lowers the bottle. "What did you put in here?"

Dread creeps into my gut. "I . . ."

Riley heaves the wine bottle across the room. It shatters against the wall just a few feet from where Alexis is crouched, spraying the floor with glass. Alexis flinches, throwing her hands over her face. The thick liquid oozes down the boards behind her head, but the wood drinks the wine before it slides to the floor, leaving behind a deep red stain.

"You tell me you want me to trust you, but you're lying to me!" Riley screams.

"Riley, I didn't . . . ," I say.

"Shut up!" Riley says. Alexis releases another loud sob, and Riley's face twists. She whirls around to face her.

"None of us feel sorry for you!" she yells. "You deserve to suffer. You're a *monster*."

Something in Alexis snaps when Riley screams that last word at her. The light drains from her eyes, leaving her skin hollow and pale. The final sob dies on her lips, and her mouth hangs open—shocked.

"Lexie." Grace takes a step toward her, but Alexis pushes herself to her feet and races from the room. The rickety ladder shakes and moans as she climbs to the second floor.

"You bitch, I told you not to leave." Riley pushes past Grace and tears down the ladder after Alexis. Alexis's sobs echo below us. Her bare feet slap against the floor as she drops from the ladder and starts to run.

"Should we go after them?" Grace asks.

As an answer, I head for the ladder. I shouldn't be so worried. Alexis has been almost as bad as Riley this whole time. She put her sister in a coma. I should leave the two of them together—they deserve each other.

Still, I can't get Alexis's broken expression out of my mind.

Riley drops to the floor, causing the ladder to shake. I grip the banister to keep from falling.

"You're as bad as Brooklyn!" Riley shouts, tearing down the hallway. "Maybe we should exorcise you next."

My heart thuds in my chest as my shoe slips on a blood-coated rung. I smack my chin on the ladder before managing to catch myself. Black stars blossom before my eyes.

"Get back here, psycho!" Riley trips over a beer bottle and falls, hitting the ground on her knees. Alexis races into the master bedroom. Riley pushes herself back to her feet.

"Riley, wait!" Stomach turning, I jump to the second floor. The shock jolts through my legs, but I don't pause long enough to notice. I reach for Riley's shoulder, but she whips around on me.

"This has nothing to do with you," she spits out, pushing me. I slam against the wall.

"Riley," I groan, but she follows Alexis into the master bedroom and shuts the door in my face. I grab the doorknob, but it won't turn. Grace runs up behind me, breathless.

"Locked," I say. "From the inside."

Grace wiggles the doorknob, but it holds tight. She swears under her breath, then pounds against the door with her open hand.

"Riley! Let us in."

No one answers. I picture Riley pushing Brooklyn below the water in the bathtub, Riley peeling away Brooklyn's fingernail and letting it fall to the floor in the basement.

"Riley wouldn't hurt Alexis, right?" I ask.

Grace swallows and presses her lips together. "I don't know what Riley would do."

I press my face against the door to the bedroom. Muffled voices sound inside—more arguing, but I can't hear what they're saying. Cursing, I pull away.

"We have to get inside," I say to Grace. "Can you think of anything?"

Grace's face lights up. "Riley kept a key in a drawer in the kitchen. I don't know if it's the master, but . . ."

"It's worth a try," I finish. "Come on." I grab Grace's arm and we start down the stairs.

I take them two at a time, nervous for every second I'm not in the bedroom with Riley and Alexis. I see that desperate, broken expression every time I close my eyes and urge my feet to move faster.

Alexis releases a shrill scream. "Riley, no!"

I jump to the landing as a shadow falls past the arched window overlooking the staircase. Something crashes into the bushes next to the house, sending a shudder through the floor. A thousand pins prick the back of my neck. I freeze on the landing.

"Oh, god." Grace's body stiffens behind me.

"What was that?" I whisper, terrified I already know. I don't want to look, but I turn toward the window anyway and lean into the glass.

Alexis's body lies crumpled in the dirt. Her

white-blond hair glows in the dim moonlight, and a halo of blood pools around her head. I lift a trembling finger to the window, my breath misting the glass.

"Move," I whisper to her broken body. But she doesn't. She stares at the sky with milky, lifeless eyes. Her arm twists above her head, and her fingers curl toward her palm, almost like she tried to grab onto something as she fell. Her cracked lips hang open in a silent scream. Her final words echo through my head. *Riley, no!*

The door above us creaks open, and footsteps pad across the floor. I lift my head as Riley stops at the top of the stairs, her face white as death.

"Alexis jumped," she says.

CHAPTER TWENTY-ONE

Riley wraps her fingers around the banister at the top of the staircase, her eyes unfocused.

"Our Father who art in heaven," she whispers, barely loud enough to hear. A tear slips over her cheek. "Hallowed be thy name . . ."

"Don't." I step away from the window, hands trembling at my sides. "He's not listening."

"Sofia," Grace murmurs. She tries to touch my arm, but I shake her hand away. I can't stop thinking about Alexis's cloudy eyes, her broken body, the way her fingers curled toward her palm. I don't want to be comforted.

Riley considers me for a long moment, until the anger burning through my chest cools, just a little. "You're grieving," she says finally. "I get that. But we have to pray for the Lord to forgive Alexis's sin."

"No!" I shout. The word is a death sentence, but I don't care. Maybe I want Riley to kill me next. "You're wrong about everything. God's not helping us. He's not fixing Brooklyn, and he can't forgive Alexis, not anymore."

Riley's feet pad down the stairs soundlessly. She crouches in front of me.

"You don't know that, Sof," she says, wiping a tear from her cheek with the back of her hand. "Come back up to the attic. We have to finish what we started."

"The attic?" My voice sounds so shrill I hardly recognize it as my own. I swallow, trying to steady it. "We have to call the police. Alexis is *dead*."

The word sounds so final as it echoes through the house.

Grace sobs into her hands. "Don't say that," she hisses through her fingers. "Maybe she's just . . . just . . ."

"Stop it! Alexis is *dead*, Grace! She committed suicide." Riley's voice caresses that word. *Suicide*. It's like she's trying it out on us, seeing how the story sounds when she says it out loud.

"Think about it," she continues. "What would happen

if we brought the cops here now? What do you think they'll do when they see Brooklyn? They'll think we're *monsters*. I don't want to spend the rest of my life in jail. Do you?"

Grace shakes her head. "Shit," she whispers. She hangs her head and starts to cry, her movements already slow and clumsy from the wine.

Every emotion I've forced down since entering this house explodes out of me. I try to speak, but the most I can do is release a gasping, ugly sob. My chest tightens, and I cry like I'm five years old again, like it's something I just discovered I could do.

"Sofia." Riley grabs me by the shoulder and squeezes. "Sofia, you need to calm down."

I can't stop. I realize, for the first time, that none of us is ever going home. Even if I somehow get out of this house alive, I never get to return to my old life. Tears race down my cheeks as I heave and choke for breath. My head starts to feel fuzzy.

"Sofia, look at me." Suddenly Riley's voice is soft and even. My eyes flutter open, and I focus on her face, my lips trembling as I struggle to breathe.

Riley presses her lips together, considering me. The deep shadows under her eyes make her look older, wise even. She's given up on the ponytail, and now her hair falls limply around her thin, angular face. It hides the bite mark on her cheek, so she looks almost normal. She squeezes my shoulders again.

"I know you don't realize it now, but everything that's happened is Brooklyn's fault," she explains. "The devil compelled Alexis to jump out that window. There's nothing we can do for her now, but you need to be strong—you need to keep the devil from taking control of you, too."

Keep the devil from taking control of me, too. The words echo in my head, meaningless, but I still feel my breathing begin to steady.

"There's my girl," she whispers. "Now, don't worry. As soon as we beat this, we can all go home."

"How?" I whisper. Riley wipes a tear from my cheek with her thumb. My skin burns where she touches it, but I try not to let my disgust show on my face. The only way out of here is through Riley. I have to be strong.

"We'll figure it out. Some exorcisms are just trickier than others." Riley stands, smoothing her bloodstained tank top. "Take a moment to catch your breath, then come back to the attic. All three of us need to be united if this is going to work. We might have to resort to extreme measures to defeat the demon."

I nod numbly as Riley turns and walks back up the stairs and down the hallway. Grace crouches near the wall, so still she looks like a shadow.

"Are you ready?" Grace asks. I don't think I'll ever be ready to go back up there, but I push myself to my feet and take a step toward her. She wraps a hand around my arm, and we walk down the hall together.

"What do you think Riley meant when she said extreme measures?" I ask before we reach the stairs to the attic. Grace blinks at me blearily. Her eyes are clouded over, and she can barely walk straight. When she speaks, her voice is raspy, almost a whisper.

"She meant that sometimes the host has to die."

CHAPTER TWENTY-TWO

"Jesus, Sofia, *go*." Grace pinches my leg, and the jolt of pain gets me moving. I climb up the last three ladder rungs, then pull myself into the attic. The room itself feels evil, like something twisted crawled into the spaces Alexis left behind.

Riley stares out the window at the far end of the room, one arm angled in front of her. Rope coils around her feet. I peer around the beam. Brooklyn lies, twisted, on the floor, her arms and legs untied. Her spiky blond hair is slicked with blood.

The attic door slams shut behind me. I whirl around in time to see Grace stand and wipe her dusty hands on her jeans.

"What's going on?" I ask. Grace shifts her eyes to the floor.

Moonlight streams through the window, leaving the attic thick with shadows. I don't see what Riley's holding until she steps forward and candlelight illuminates her hands.

The nail gun.

Sometimes the host has to die. Just a few hours ago I'd have done anything to stop this. But now I hesitate, curling my fingers into fists. It's Brooklyn's life or mine. By helping her, I make myself Riley's next target.

Brooklyn whimpers and tries to sit up.

"Almost done," Riley says. She shifts the nail gun to one hand, then drops to her knees and rolls Brooklyn onto her back.

"Don't, please!" Brooklyn writhes and kicks beneath Riley's legs. Riley lowers the nail gun.

I can't do this. I can't stand by and watch someone die, even if it means saving myself.

"Get off of her!" I throw my whole body into Riley, using every ounce of strength I have left. "You psycho bitch!"

We tumble to the floor next to Brooklyn. Riley regains her balance first and whips an elbow into my face. I slam back down, pain exploding across my cheek.

"Grace, take care of her," Riley snarls. Brooklyn tries to move, but Riley straddles her chest and pins her arm to the floor with one hand. I push myself up and try to crawl toward them, but Grace grabs me from behind.

"Let go!" I claw at Grace's arms, but she just tightens her grip around my chest and drags me away. Splinters jutting out from the unfinished wooden floor scrape the backs of my legs.

An eerie silence fills the attic. Riley lowers the gun. The nail shoots into Brooklyn's hand with a dull blast, breaking the quiet.

Brooklyn roars with pain, so loud I swear I feel the floorboards tremble beneath my feet. Riley moves to the next arm, pinning it beneath her knee as she positions the nail gun over Brooklyn's hand. It sticks straight out from her body, like a cross.

"You're crucifying her," I whisper, horrified. A thick line of blood oozes over the side of Brooklyn's hand and pools on the floor.

She aims the gun at Brooklyn's other palm and pulls the trigger. Metal crunches through skin and bone.

"I wanted to hang her from the beams," Riley explains, motioning to the ceiling with the nail gun. "But I didn't think we could lift her that high." She curls her toes into the floor and pivots around to face me.

"Now, what should we do with you?" she says, almost to herself. She raises an eyebrow, and suddenly it's as if all the air in the room has been sucked away.

"No, please," I beg. Grace tightens her grip around my arms, and I can't move.

"It's for your own good," Riley says, gathering the ropes she'd used to tie up Brooklyn. "First you texted Josh, and then you played that little trick with the wine. Now this. I just don't trust you anymore."

"Please," I whisper again, trying to pull out of Grace's grip. "I can cooperate. I can help."

Riley untangles a length of rope as she moves toward me. She lifts a finger to her lips.

"This'll be easier if you don't struggle," she says. As Grace holds me in place, Riley binds my arms and legs in thick knots. The ropes pinch the skin around my wrists, and they're so tight they cut off circulation in my hands. When she's done, Riley pushes the hair out of my face and leans in to kiss me on the cheek.

"When we're done with Brooklyn, we'll help you. Okay?" She taps my nose with her finger. "It's almost dawn. Grace and I need to do something with Alexis's body before the sun comes up."

I turn to the window and see that Riley's right. The black sky has faded to a deep blue. I think of my mother crawling out of bed at seven in the morning as always and finding my room empty. A spark of hope flickers through my chest—if she calls the police, then maybe . . . but no. Even if she called 911 as soon as she found me missing, they'd never find me here. Not in time to stop Riley.

Grace pushes my shoulders down, and I awkwardly sit. "Riley," I try one last time. "Please don't leave me here like this."

Riley ignores my pleas as she opens the attic door and starts down the ladder.

Grace hesitates at the door. "It's easier this way," she says. Without another word she follows Riley down to the second floor.

I release my breath in a rush of air. *It's easier.* Karen said that to me once, after watching Lila and Erin torture me in biology class. *It's just easier to let them do what they want.* What bullshit.

I struggle to keep myself calm, but as reality sets in, each breath feels more ragged. I squeeze my eyes closed, and the situation comes into clearer focus. Riley knows I'm not on her side, that I can't be trusted. Alexis is dead. Soon, Brooklyn will be, too. Maybe Riley will decide I'm possessed, too. Maybe I'll be the next person nailed to the floor.

Tears stream down my cheeks. I'm crying for Alexis and for Brooklyn, but also for myself—for fear of what's going to happen next. I release another sob, no longer trying to keep my pain under control. My shoulders shake, and my chest aches as my breathing gets heavier and heavier. Tears cloud my eyes until I can barely see.

"Stop!" Brooklyn screams. Her voice startles me so much that I dig my teeth into my lower lip, sniffling. Brooklyn groans in pain, and there's a shuffling sound as she tries to readjust her position on the floor. "This isn't the time to cry. We need to figure out how to escape."

"Escape? I've been trying to escape since we first got here!" I press my lips together to keep from sobbing again. "There *is* no escape."

"Bullshit. We've just been thinking about this wrong." Brooklyn pauses, and for a moment the only sound in the attic is her low, steady breathing. "What's Riley been saying this whole time?"

"That . . . that you're evil." I stutter. "That you're possessed by the devil."

"Right. And what would the devil do in this situation?"

The words flash into my head, and I say them without thinking. "Fight fire with fire."

There's a beat of silence. Then Brooklyn says, "Exactly."

CHAPTER TWENTY-THREE

The words repeat in my head: *Fight fire with fire*. It's not exactly a solution. My arms and legs are bound so tightly I can hardly move, and Brooklyn is nailed to the floor. There's no way for us to fight. It's over.

Still, I keep replaying those words, like something about that sentence can unlock the secret to escape. Brooklyn is oddly quiet, and I wonder if she's doing the same thing. Or maybe she's already figured out a plan of her own.

Wind presses against the far window, and the glass groans. There's only one candle still lit—the thick white one Alexis brought up here. Its flame flickers, like it's mocking me.

Giggles echo through the floor below us, then the ladder creaks. I shoot a fearful look at the door. Riley and Grace are back.

"Brooklyn," I whisper.

"I hear them." Brooklyn groans, and the rough soles of her boots scratch the floor as she moves her legs. "It's okay. We have a plan, remember?"

"Fight fire with fire," I whisper. The words echo through my head, meaning nothing to me. *Fight fire with fire. Fight fire with fire.*

The attic door shudders and falls open with a slap that makes the floor tremble. Still burning, the last candle topples over and rolls to the wall, coming to a stop against a bit of exposed pink insulation. I watch it happen as if it's a dream.

The flame leaps to the wall and licks the raw wood hungrily.

"Brooklyn, did you see that?" I can't see Brooklyn's face, just the blood-coated soles of her boots. She taps them together, like Dorothy. Time to go home.

"All part of our plan," she says.

What plan? I want to scream at her. All we had were words—words that definitely don't have the power to knock over a candle.

But as the fire spreads, it burns the question from my mind. The very small, very *wooden* attic I'm trapped in is going up in flames. I yank against the ropes binding me in place. Smoke seeps into my mouth and presses against the back of my throat.

Riley appears at the attic door as smoke clouds the far corner and rises to the ceiling, thick and dark. She grimaces and waves a hand in front of her face.

"What the hell?" she mutters.

Brooklyn snickers, her laughter bouncing off the burning walls. I stare at her boots, shocked. She's lost her mind.

Riley hovers on the ladder, the flames reflected in her eyes. Grace's hysterical voice echoes below, but I can't make out what she's saying. Footsteps slam against the floor as Grace runs away.

"Riley!" I shout. "You have to untie me!" The ropes rub away the top layer of skin around my wrists as I twist and pull against them. I hardly even notice the pain. A flicker of orange appears in my peripheral vision, eating its way closer to me. I take shaky breath after shaky breath, ignoring the smoke coating my mouth and tongue. "Riley, you have to let us out. Riley!"

Riley presses herself against the attic door, searching the floor for something to suffocate the fire. But there's nothing up here except for the discarded toolbox. Even the bottle of holy water is empty.

"Help! Help us, please!"

Riley's shoulders tense. She shifts her eyes to me.

"Don't," I beg her. All around me, the fire presses in. It takes every ounce of willpower I have not to imagine it crawling over my skin, eating away my hair and my fingernails until there's nothing left. "Don't leave me. *Please.*"

But Riley's eyes glaze over, until it no longer seems like she sees me. "The exorcism . . ." she says.

"It doesn't matter anymore," I say. Blue tendrils stretch over the wood, reaching for us like fingers. I tug my legs apart, trying to loosen the ropes at my ankles. But they hold tight.

"You can't leave us here!" I shout. Of all the ways I thought I might die in this house, burning alive is the most cruel. "You can't!"

Riley hesitates. There's a loud crack, and a ceiling beam splits in half and swings to the floor, spraying sparks as it falls. The tiny embers land on my arms and legs and eat through my jeans, stinging my skin.

"Oh, god," I beg, squeezing my eyes shut. "You can't leave us here."

Riley's face turns white, and her lower lip trembles. "Lord, forgive me," she whispers. Her head disappears as she ducks out of the attic, the ladder creaking beneath her weight.

"No! *No!*" I scream for so long that my voice goes

hoarse. Smoke fills my lungs, and my sobs dissolve in a fit of coughing. The air around us thickens. It clouds my head when I breathe it in, making me feel dizzy and sick to my stomach. We're never getting out of here. We're going to burn to death. We're going to die screaming as flames eat away our faces.

Fire crackles, and another wooden beam drops to the floor. It crashes in the corner, lighting more of Riley's tower of *Vogue* magazines on fire as it sparks. I cough and cough, unable to catch my breath as I watch the flames grow and move.

"Sofia," Brooklyn says, her voice eerily steady, "we can get out of here, but you need to help me."

I choke back my sobs, but I can't slow my rapidly beating heart. "How?" I ask, my voice shaking.

"Can you walk?"

I clumsily try to stand, but my legs are angled in front of me, and without using my arms I can't keep my balance. "No."

"Then crawl if you have to," Brooklyn insists. "Crawl to me. Hurry!"

Crawl. I breathe in and then out, focusing on that one word. The fire is so close that I can feel its heat flickering at my ankle, but Brooklyn's not far away. I can make it to her before the fire reaches me. I push past the fears growing in the back of my head. I can crawl. I *will* crawl.

I rock my weight to the left and bite back a groan when my shoulder crashes into the floor. Now I'm lying on my side, my legs curled next to me. Brooklyn's boots are two or three feet away. With my arms still tied behind my back, I can't use them to pull myself, so I dig my heels into the floorboards and scoot across the attic. The fire reaches Riley's nail polish and the bottles explode in a burst of colorful glass, showering me with sparks.

My shoulder aches as I push it over the floor, past Brooklyn's combat boots and blood-and-soot-covered legs. I push myself farther, and then I'm beside her arm.

"What do I do?" I gasp when I'm close enough to see her face. She turns her head so she can look at me. In the crackling orange light, her eyes glow red.

"You need to get the nails out." Brooklyn cringes, and the skin around her eyes crinkles. "You'll have to use your teeth."

Teeth. If I stop and think about what I'm about to do, there's no way I'll go through with it. So I don't think. I rock my body to the side until I roll onto my chest. I pull my knees up, using my forehead to balance my weight against the floor. Brooklyn steadies me with one leg, and I pull myself up to a crouch. I edge myself closer to Brooklyn's hand.

The nail is wedged deep into her palm, and

everything—her skin, her fingernails, the nail itself—is coated in a thick layer of blood. I lower my face to her hand and work my mouth around the nail head. Brooklyn gasps as my teeth scrape over her skin. I bite down on the nail and pull.

The nail digs into my teeth and gums, but it doesn't move. Blood fills my mouth, and it tastes sharp, metallic. I don't know whether it's mine or Brooklyn's. Probably both. I try not to breathe it in as I pull again. The nail bites into the enamel of my teeth, and blood trickles down my throat. I start to gag.

"Sofia, come on," Brooklyn says. "You've got this."

I bite down again, this time wiggling the nail head with my teeth before I pull. It comes loose in my mouth, and I rock backward, nearly losing my balance. Brooklyn releases a strangled cry and hugs her now free hand to her chest. Before I can even spit the nail from my mouth, she reaches to her other hand and digs the nail out herself. It clatters to the floor when she pulls it loose.

"Jesus. Fuck!" she screams, sitting. Fire crackles around us, and the smoke is so thick I can barely make out Brooklyn's face. "Come here," she says to me. "Hurry!"

I move toward her so she can untie the ropes at my wrists. The fire grows around us. Between Brooklyn's bloody hands and the heat of the fire making us sweat, the rope is slick and hard for her to handle. Twice, it slips through Brooklyn's fingers.

Fear beats at my skull. *We're not going to make it*, I think. But then Brooklyn tugs the knots around my wrists loose, and I'm free.

I help her untie the ropes around my ankles, then stumble to my feet, not entirely sure how long the floor will hold. Fire moves over the walls and eats the wood. My eyes sting. I blink, but I can't clear the smoke away. Tears stream down my cheeks. My terror hardens into determination. I'm not dying here. I refuse to die here.

We make it to the next floor seconds before the fire leaps to the top rung of the ladder. Brooklyn doubles over, coughing so hard I worry she'll vomit.

"You can't stop." I grab her arm and pull her toward the stairs. My heart beats in my ears, counting every second that passes. The fire is traveling too fast. It's chasing at our heels, blocking every exit. I'm not sure how much time we have left.

Smoke billows around us, filling my lungs. I pull my shirt over my face, but it doesn't help. My chest aches for air, but every breath I take is toxic. I start to choke, and then I can't stop. My entire body shakes with coughing. Brooklyn straightens and pushes herself down the steps. I slide her arm over my shoulder to help her.

We make our way to the first floor and down the hall.

When we turn the corner, relief floods my body. The door hangs open. I start to run.

The stairs cave in with a crash like thunder, and the smoke is so thick I can barely see. I tighten my arm around Brooklyn and push myself forward. We cross the front porch and make our way down the stairs.

I drop to my knees on the ground, and Brooklyn collapses next to me. For a moment I just rest my forehead against the cool grass, gulping down fresh air. Behind us, the fire licks and crackles and spits. Listening to it, I sit back up and look around.

The sidewalk and road are empty. Riley and Grace are long gone. I swallow the bile that rises in my throat as I picture them stumbling out of the house, ignoring my screams. But I can't think of that now. We don't have a lot of time. This part of the neighborhood might be abandoned, but eventually the smoke will stretch high enough that someone will see and call the police. And then . . .

I turn to Brooklyn, surprised to see she's already watching me. Her black eyes reflect the light of the fire. She pushes herself to her feet and offers me her hand. Once I'm standing, she pulls me close to her and leans in to whisper in my ear.

"Tell no one." Her breath smells like blood and smoke. She steps away from me, then nods once. Without another word, she starts to limp away.

For a long moment I stand there, watching the house burn. I laugh out loud, and the sound is so shocking and wonderful that my eyes well with tears. I didn't die. It's over. I'm free.

The fire moves through the house like a living thing—wild and desperate and hungry. By the time it's done, all the evidence of last night will be destroyed. I think about what Brooklyn said—*tell no one*. If we go to the cops, it'll be her word against Riley's.

I swallow and turn away from the fire. Then I head down the sidewalk, toward home.

CHAPTER TWENTY-FOUR

My front door creaks open, and I step into the hallway, listening. Silence. Mom isn't out of bed yet. I hold the knob to keep it from clicking and ease the door closed without a sound. I slip my sneakers off and carry them up the stairs so she won't hear my footsteps on the carpet.

I spent the entire walk home debating what I would tell my mom. I want to blurt out the whole story, but Brooklyn's words echo through my head, warning me. *Tell no one.* Besides, if I tell her, she'll just call the cops, and they'll ask questions I'm not sure how to answer. Best to just pretend nothing happened.

I make my way to the bathroom and turn the shower on as hot as it will go. I strip down, and my clothes fall to the floor in a heap of blood and smoke and sweat. I shiver as I stare down at the faded pockets of my jeans, then kick them away from me. I should burn them.

Turning this thought over in my head, I step into the shower—gasping when the hot water hits me. It's painful at first, but as the water runs over my skin, I start to relax. It stings the raw patches of my arms where the ropes rubbed my wrists, and the mangled cuts around my knuckles burn as water soaks the dead skin, washing away clotted blood and dirt. I tilt my head back and fill my mouth with water, then spit it out to get the blood off my teeth and tongue. The water circling the drain is stained a deep, muddy red. I watch it slip away, feeling the horrors of the night disappearing down the drain with it.

Nothing happened, I remind myself. It was a nightmare, that's all.

Somewhere in the house a door opens, then shuts. I freeze. I wrap my fingers around the shower curtain, trying to remember whether I locked the front door.

"Sofia?" my mom calls. "Are you up already?"

I shut off the shower and hurriedly dry myself off. I don't remember ever feeling so relieved to hear my mother's voice.

"Just taking a shower." I duck out of the bathroom and into my bedroom, where I quickly change into fresh clothes. I grab a plain white T-shirt, jeans, and my faded gray hooded sweatshirt. Since burning them isn't really an option, I roll my dirty clothes into a ball and shove them all the way to the bottom of the trash can beneath my desk.

I step into the hallway, tugging my sleeves down over my hands so Mom won't see the raw skin at my knuckles. Mom is easing Grandmother's door shut. She glances over her shoulder at me, lifting a finger to her mouth to tell me to keep quiet.

"She's still sleeping," she says. I cross my arms over my chest, cringing when my torn fingers brush against the fabric of my sweatshirt. My mom cocks her head, considering me.

"Are you okay?" she asks. "It's so early. I'm surprised you're awake."

I nod. "I'm fine," I say, but the word cracks in my mouth. Tears pool in my eyes. I try to blink them away, but they spill onto my cheeks. So much for pretending nothing happened.

"Sofia?" My mom crosses the hall and folds me into a hug. For a moment I just let her hold me. The tears come faster, until I'm crying so hard my shoulders shake. Mom smoothes the still damp hair off my forehead.

"Shh," she says. "Shh, it's okay. Tell me what happened."

"I . . ." I choke back my sobs and pull away from her, drying my tears with the sleeves of my sweatshirt. "I just heard that a friend of mine committed suicide." I stare at my bare feet, certain Mom will know I'm lying if I meet her eyes.

"Oh, Sofia." Mom pulls me to her chest again, resting her chin on top of my head. She rubs a hand over my back in slow, comforting circles. "Honey, I'm so sorry."

I close my eyes, allowing myself to relax into her. For the first time in days, I feel safe.

* * *

Fifteen minutes later I'm perched on a stool in the kitchen, the heavy smell of French toast filling the air. I actually smile as I breathe it in. Mom's never been the best cook, but she's perfected her French toast over the years. She uses only the thickest, crustiest bread and always mixes brown sugar and a pinch of cinnamon into the batter. She takes the frying pan off the stove and slides the toast onto a plate.

"I know it's been hard to make friends," she says, pulling the maple syrup and butter from the fridge. "And after what happened at your last school . . ." She shakes her head, and under her breath, she mutters, "Such a needless tragedy."

I shift uncomfortably on my stool and push the French toast around on my plate. I don't want to think about what happened at my last school, not when my wrists are still raw from Riley's ropes. But now that Mom's brought it up, I can't help seeing the similarities. Both times I thought I knew someone, I thought she was my friend, and in the end I was wrong.

Maybe there's a reason these things keep happening to me. Maybe I'm defective.

Mom sets the pan in the sink and crosses over to me, brushing one of my damp curls aside. "But you can't give up, *mija*. I believe in you," she says. "I know you'll find your way."

It's the exact right thing to say at the exact right moment, and I blink furiously to keep from crying. Mom places the plate on the counter in front of me, and I cover the toast in a thick stream of syrup. I can't give up.

* * *

I stay awake for as long as I can, but by noon my eyes are so heavy I can barely keep them open. I tell Mom I'm not feeling well and crawl into bed, falling asleep as soon as I pull the comforter up over my shoulders. While I sleep, I dream.

Riley and I are sitting on the train tracks, passing a bottle of red wine back and forth. Red-and-orange light bleeds into the sky. Clouds race above us, their shadows flickering over Riley's face. Her skin turns dark, then light again. The ground below us trembles—a train's coming.

"Truth or dare," Riley says. She looks perfect, like she did the first day I met her. Her hair pools around her shoulders in flawless spirals, her eyebrows arch high above her eyes. Her cheeks burn pink, so glossy she doesn't look real. The strange light makes everything about her glow. She takes a drink, and a thick drop of wine oozes out of the bottle and over her chin.

"Dare," I say. Riley lowers the bottle, but it's not Riley anymore—it's Brooklyn. Black liner surrounds her eyes, making them look too large for her head. The wine running over her chin thickens. Not wine—blood.

"Why not truth?" she ask. The train's headlight flickers through the trees behind her.

"We have to go." I stand, reaching for Brooklyn's arm. The train flashes its lights. "Brooklyn!"

I grab her hand, but it's not Brooklyn—it's Karen. Blood drips from her mouth and coats her teeth.

"Why can't you tell the truth?" she asks. The train's horn blares. It sounds like a scream.

The screaming horn echoes in my head, and I jerk awake. Outside, the only sounds are the wind pushing against the glass in my windows and the low buzz of the cicadas in the grass.

It was just the dream, I tell myself. A nightmare. My eyelids grow heavy, and I'm just about to drift back to sleep when I hear it again—a shrill, terrified scream.

I sit straight up in bed. Hands shaking, I reach over to my bedside table and flip on the lamp. It's getting dark outside. I must have slept all day.

I force one leg out of bed, then the other. I jerk at every shadow, certain it's Riley. But the halls are empty. Downstairs, the front door is closed tight. Everything is still, quiet. Unnerving.

"Hello?" I whisper, but there's no answer. I step forward and open the front door.

Fluorescent red and orange light streaks across the sky. It's that eerie in-between light, neither night nor day. Just like in my dream. I hesitate near the door, wondering if I'm still asleep. Heat presses on my arms and gathers beneath my thick hair. A bead of sweat trickles down the back of my neck. This is too real to be a dream.

"Mom?" I say, stepping onto the porch. She should still be awake. It's probably only seven thirty or eight o'clock. But the street in front of our house is eerily quiet—deserted. After what happened last night, I'm more aware of the emptiness. There's no one here to see where I'm going, no one to hear my screams.

I step, barefoot, onto the dry grass. It crunches beneath my weight, poking the soles of my feet.

"Mom?" I call again, making my way around the side of our house. Our driveway curves off the main street and back behind our house, to an old shed. The sun-warmed pavement burns the bottoms of my feet. Insects buzz in the yard, but the sound is so familiar to me that I almost don't notice it.

The red-lit sky casts shadows over the driveway. I move slowly, easing around Mom's giant black SUV.

A shadow streaks across the driveway and I freeze, biting back a scream. Then my eyes focus, and I make out a squirrel crouched beneath a bush. I breathe a sigh of relief.

The smell reaches me first, the same heavy, sick scent I noticed beneath the bleachers on my first day of school. Chicken after a night in the garbage. Fish left in the heat. I picture the skinned cat, and my skin prickles. Trembling, I walk around the car.

There's another sound now, a dripping. My skin pricks, warning me. I should run. Instead, I move closer.

Thick white candles line the sides of the driveway, their wicks flickering in the twilight. A hastily painted black pentagram stretches across the driveway beneath them, and in the middle of the star lies a dark black pool.

Drip. Drip. Drip.

I look up.

A human body hangs from the shed, its arms stretched out to either side and tied to the roof gutters with thick rope. The body doesn't look remotely human anymore. Its skin has been peeled back in strips, revealing the pink muscle and blood and tissue beneath.

The only parts of the body that are still intact are its hands and its feet. My eyes hover at its feet. From the feet hang Grace's gold platform sandals.

I gasp and throw my hands over my mouth. Grace's head lolls forward unnaturally, and her lifeless, cloudy eyes stare at the ground. Someone shaved off her hair, leaving behind a bloody scalp. Her arms stretch to either side, like she's been crucified. Blood drips from her body.

"Grace!" I shriek. There's not a person on earth who could survive what her body's been through, but I stumble toward her anyway. "Oh my god, Grace! Grace, no!"

I trip over one of the candles and fall, hard. The driveway peels back the top layer of skin on my knee. I cringe and try to push myself to my feet. The candle sputters out as it topples onto the asphalt.

In the candle's last glimmer of light, I see movement below Grace's body. I freeze. Brooklyn crouches in the shadows, her head ducked so that, at first, all I see is her spiky blond hair. She stands slowly, her eyes leveled on me. She steps into the circle of candlelight.

"Fun fact," she says. "We're not really afraid of fire."

She smiles, a pocketknife clenched in her hand. The candlelight surrounding her flickers, making the knife's blade glint.

"Brooklyn," I start, but the words I want to say get caught in my throat. I picture Grace jumping out from behind my bench to scare me on my second day of school. Grace, who wore leopard-print headbands and sequin skirts and got so excited about her crush on Tom. She must've felt the same relief I did when she ran out of the house this morning. She must've thought that whole terrible night was finally behind her. And now she's dead.

Not just dead—mutilated. Tortured. Bile rises in my throat. I clench my eyes shut, but Grace's body stays painted on the insides of my lids. Her skin curling away from her limbs. Her scalp, bald and bloody.

I open my eyes again. Brooklyn crouches and lowers her finger to the pool of Grace's blood, then lifts it to her mouth. Her grin widens as she runs her tongue up the side of her finger, licking the blood away. She stands, tightening her grip on the knife. My fear sharpens, and I stumble backward, banging into the back door to the house.

Behind me, the door creaks open. I whirl around as my mom steps outside.

"Sofia?" she says, groggily. "What's going on? I heard noises."

I glance over my shoulder, but Brooklyn's gone. My voice freezes in my throat.

"Mom," I start. "I . . ."

Before I can think of what to say, my mom's eyes shift to the body hanging from the shed. The blood drains from her face, and she screams.

CHAPTER TWENTY-FIVE

"**M**om?" A tremor begins in my hand, then spreads up my arm until my whole body shakes. I did this. I trusted Brooklyn, I let her out. The sharp, metallic taste of her blood still lingers on my tongue. Riley told me she was evil, but I didn't listen. What happened to Grace happened because of me.

I put a hand on my mom's arm and she stiffens, finally dropping her hands from her mouth.

"Get inside. Lock all the doors and call the police." Her voice is quiet, but there's steel behind her words. She's Sergeant Nina Flores now, medical technician for the armed forces, and this is just another fallen soldier.

She rolls up her sleeves and starts down the porch steps. "I'll get her . . . I'll get it down."

I hesitate. I don't want to leave my mother outside alone. Brooklyn could be lurking behind a bush or parked car.

"Sofia, now!" Mom's tone leaves no room for argument. I cast one last look at Grace's broken body, then race back inside and stumble upstairs for my cell phone. My hands are sweating when I reach my bedroom, and I mess up the three-digit number twice and have to start over.

Finally, "Nine-one-one, what's your emergency?" a robotic voice asks on the other end of the line.

"I . . ." I swallow. "My friend's been . . ." I don't know what to say. Mutilated? Tortured? Skinned? I swallow. "My friend's been killed. Please come."

I give them my address, then hang up the phone. For a long moment I stare down at it, stunned. Riley was right. The reality of that hits me, and I almost can't breathe. She was right all along—Brooklyn's possessed. She killed Mr. Willis. And now she's killed Grace. If my mother hadn't come along, she would have killed me.

Maybe she should have killed me. Maybe I deserve that.

"*Diablo.*"

I freeze, shocked to hear my grandmother's voice for the first time in years.

Diablo—devil.

I walk to my bedroom door, my cell phone clenched in my hand. The thick carpet in the hallway muffles my footsteps, and the red-tinted lamp from Grandmother's bedroom casts the only light. A violent, hacking cough rattles behind her door. It sounds like death.

I ease one foot into the hallway, searching the shadows around me for the outline of a body. I can't blink without picturing Brooklyn holding that pocketknife, Brooklyn dipping her finger into the pool of Grace's blood—then licking it off. *Your fault*, my brain whispers to me. *Your fault*.

I push the images and accusations away. The shadows seem to move around me, but I know it's just my imagination. Brooklyn isn't here.

Grandmother's face looks like a melting candle. Her skin droops so badly that it's difficult to pick out her features. Her rosary beads click against her table. She releases a rough, raw-sounding cough.

"Grandmother?" I hover near her door, almost afraid to go inside. Grandmother inhales. The sound is like a crumpling paper bag. She moves her thumb along the row of beads.

"Are you okay?"

Grandmother turns her head very slowly. The rosary beads shake in her fragile, trembling hands.

"*Diablo*," she whispers. A shiver creeps down my spine. She hasn't spoken since her stroke. The doctors weren't even sure she *could* speak anymore.

She focuses her cloudy eyes on me. It's like she's looking through me.

"*Diablo*," she says.

"It was an accident," I hiss.

"*Diablo*," Grandmother says, like a prayer.

"It wasn't my fault. It was an accident, just like last time." The words rush out of my mouth before I can think about them.

"*Diablo!*"

I look past Grandmother, to the Virgin statuette on her windowsill. It glows white in the red-tinted room. Grandmother used to tell me confession absolved you of guilt. By admitting our sins before God, we are no longer held responsible for them. God takes the blame from us. He makes us pure again.

More than anything in the world right now, I want to be pure. My dream echoes through my head. I hear the roaring train race down the tracks, and Karen's distant voice. *Why can't you tell the truth?*

I drop to my knees next to Grandmother's bed and fold my hands in prayer.

"Blessed Mary, mother of God," I whisper. "Forgive me for I have sinned."

I close my eyes, and I'm at the party with Karen, humiliated and crying.

I stagger when I push my way out of the party and reach the porch. I almost expect the other kids to chase after me, throwing more Q-tips. But they don't. They're probably too drunk.

I'm not entirely sure where to go next. I don't want to go home—it'd be too humiliating seeing my mom and grandmother after this. Tears prick my eyes and spill onto my cheeks.

Then the high-pitched sound of the train horn blares through the night, followed by the distant roar of an engine. I stumble down the porch steps and into the backyard. It's dark, but the train's headlight flickers through the trees. I start to run.

The sound calms me. It's so loud, so all encompassing that I can't think of anything else. I step out of the trees and into the clearing just before the train tracks. Adrenaline fills my blood, making me reckless. The laugher and the Q-tips are far away now, almost like they happened to someone else. Like they were a dream.

The train's headlight shines through the trees as it curves around. Without thinking, I step onto the tracks. They shudder and quake beneath my sneakers. I close my eyes, and the world fades away. It's just me, the shaking earth, and the thunderous noise.

"Sofia!" My eyes snap open, and I turn to see Karen stumble through the trees. She's still holding her beer. As she runs toward me, the foamy liquid sloshes over the side and spills to the ground. "What are you doing?"

"What does it look like?" My eyes linger on Karen's face long enough to see the blood drain from her skin, and her eyes widen with shock. Good. After what she did, she deserves to be afraid. I turn back around. I want to face the train head on. The light moves closer.

Karen stops a few feet away from the tracks. "Jesus! It was just a joke."

"A joke?" I say. "How funny do you think it'll be when they find my body tomorrow and everyone blames you?"

The tracks tremble violently beneath my feet. It's almost hard to keep my balance, like I'm standing on the high dive and peering over the side, preparing to jump. The train honks again, and a wave of doubt crashes over me. What am I doing? I don't want to die.

Karen's face crumples. She drops her beer and grabs my arm. "Sofia, get off the tracks!"

Her cold fingers tighten around my wrist, disgusting me. Maybe I don't want to die, but the alternative—letting Karen save me, going back to the party where I was humiliated—is even worse.

I blink into the headlight, frozen. It's close enough now that I can't look at it directly. . . .

"Karen jumped in front of the train," I whisper in Grandmother's red-tinted bedroom. "She pushed me off the tracks. She . . . she saved my life." I sniff and reach for Grandmother's hand. "And it killed her."

Lights flash from the window, painting the Virgin red and blue. I cross Grandmother's room and push the curtains aside. An ambulance pulls up to the curb. Paramedics leap out and race for Grace's lifeless body.

I step back, and the curtain slides back into place. Grandmother stares at me with those glassy eyes and slowly raises a finger.

"*Diablo . . .*" she croaks. My skin prickles with horror, not at what she's saying, but at the rasping emptiness of her voice. It's not my grandmother speaking anymore. The voice doesn't even sound human.

"*Diablo . . .*" she says, pointing at me. I back away from her bed.

"Grandmother, no," I say. But she's right. I let Brooklyn go, so Grace's death is my fault, just as much as Karen's is. If Brooklyn gets to Riley, I'll be responsible for that, too.

I feel like I'm standing on the tracks again, blinking into the headlight of the oncoming train. But this time I know exactly what to do. I can't be responsible for another girl's death, even if it's Riley's. I have to find her before Brooklyn does, and I have to save her life. It's the only way I'll ever be able to forgive myself for the blood already on my hands. It's the only way God will ever forgive me.

I turn, stumbling as I race from the room. Grandmother's whispery voice follows me down the stairs.

"Diablo . . . Diablo!"

CHAPTER TWENTY-SIX

I slip out the back door so Mom doesn't see me leave. I don't have time to explain this to her, not when Riley's in danger. I ease the door shut and hurry, barefoot, across the yard. The dewy grass chills my feet, so I stop at the garage and pull on my mom's gardening boots. Then I start to run.

I call Riley three times, but she doesn't answer. I'm out of breath when I reach her driveway.

Riley's palatial house towers over me, its windows dark. I imagine the worst: Riley's body crumpled and broken inside the house. Brooklyn standing above her, blood dripping from the pocketknife clenched in her fingers. The horrors cycle through my head as I walk up to the house.

Perfectly trimmed bushes line her driveway. The garden hose is tied up neatly, not a kink in sight. A handmade WELCOME sign hangs on the front door. This is all wrong. Riley's family doesn't deserve this. Brooklyn can't destroy their picturesque life.

A curtain in one of the windows moves. My heart leaps in my chest.

"Riley?" I stumble up the steps to her porch. I lift my hand and knock on the door. It creaks open beneath my fist.

My whole body tenses. I should run, pretend I was never here. But the second I consider leaving, my grandmother's raspy voice whispers in my ear. *Diablo, Diablo.*

"Riley?" I step into the dark hallway and run my hand along the wall. My fingers find the light switch, and the chandelier hanging from the ceiling blinks on.

A bloody handprint stretches across the wall, like someone dragged their fingers over the paint. Deep gouges scratch into the wood, and the framed photographs lining the foyer hang crooked. Several have fallen to the floor, the glass in their frames spider-webbed with cracks. I take a step closer, narrowing my eyes at them. Someone's drawn bloody smiley faces over the photographs. It looks like a child's finger-painting. In the corner of one, I see the same pentagram symbol that had been drawn on my driveway under Grace's mutilated remains.

Brooklyn's been here.

A dull, buzzing noise echoes in my ears as I walk down the hallway. It's the cicadas outside, just like always. But they sound louder now, closer. The floor beneath my feet seems to tremble, like on the train tracks the night of the party. Any second, my world could come crashing down around me.

"Riley?" I call again. I make my way into the living room, where I find overturned furniture scattered across the floor, a shattered television set, and pillows slashed open. A layer of downy feathers covers the carpet. I kick them up with my boots as I cross the room, studying the damage. The wispy white feathers stick to my jeans and my hands and my hair. They tickle my skin, sending shivers up my arms.

Something drops onto the floor behind me with a thud. I spin around, heart hammering in my chest.

It's just a book. Books have been pulled from all the shelves lining all the walls, their pages ripped from the covers, crumpled and tossed around the destruction like confetti. Brooklyn dragged her knife through the curtains, shredding them. She smashed through windows. Shattered glass glints from the carpet, and warm, sticky air moves what's left of the curtains. Eerie red twilight spills onto the floor, painting the entire room the color of blood and fire.

"Riley?" I leave the living room and head to the staircase. "Riley, are you there?"

I wrap my trembling fingers around the banister. As I climb each stair, they creak beneath my rubber boots. Brooklyn could be hiding inside any of these rooms, carving up Riley's body with her pocketknife like she did Grace. Waiting for me.

My hands shake. I stop in front of the first door and wrap my fingers around the doorknob. *I'm allowed to be afraid*, I remind myself, taking a deep breath of the hot, stale hallway air. I'm just not allowed to run away.

I push the door open.

It's just a coat closet, empty and dark. My shoulders slump, relieved. I reach forward and tug on the metal chain hanging from the ceiling.

The light switches on, glinting off the fresh, bloody handprints covering the walls. The porcelain doll from the attic hangs from the ceiling, a thick rope knotted around its neck. Fire blackened most of her face and burned off her hair. Stuffing pokes through the ripped seams at her arms. Her eye sockets are empty, the cloudy glass eyes long gone.

"Shout to the . . . Shout to the . . . Shout to the . . ."

The music blares to life, startling me. I choke back a scream, searching the closet until I see the pink CD player on the top shelf. I stand on tiptoes and yank it down, letting it crash to the floor. Dropping to my knees, I rip open the deck and pull out the CD, flinging it back into the closet. I stand and slam the door shut again, heart racing. I squeeze my eyes closed, collapsing against the wall behind me. It's just a CD player, I tell myself.

I make my way down the hallway one room at a time. I open every single door, steeling myself for what I'll find behind it. I'm greeted with more destruction: a bathroom filled with shredded toilet paper, a guest bedroom empty except for a few broken pieces of furniture.

I save Riley's bedroom for last.

I approach it slowly, like I'd approach a rabid dog or wild animal. I turn the knob all the way around, so the lock won't click when I open it. Then I lean my head against the wood, listening. Silence. At first. Then I hear whispering.

"Riley?" My voice shakes. I push the door all the way open and stumble into the room, preparing myself for what Brooklyn's done.

But Riley's room is perfect: no broken furniture or shattered windows, no blood on the walls. I cross to her vanity table and flick on her lamp. Golden light spills over the scarves and glass bottles lining her vanity table, sending broken fragments of colored light flickering over the wood. It illuminates Riley's porcelain doll's glassy, lifeless eyes and the collage of photographs covering Riley's mirror.

I pause in front of the mirror, running a finger along a photograph's edge. It's a picture of Riley, Grace, and Alexis at the lake house, all of them carefree and happy. When Riley first invited me into her room, I remember wanting my photograph to make it to her mirror collage, wedged between snapshots of Grace and Riley. Now that doesn't seem possible.

I unpeel the picture from the mirror, studying Grace's and Alexis's faces. There's something hideous about their smiles, especially when I think of how they ended up. It's like the world played a cruel joke on them. Still, I slip the photograph into my pocket. Better to remember them like this, the way they were.

I hear it again—whispering.

I slide the photograph into my back pocket and start to turn. Out of the corner of my eye I see Riley's bed reflected in her mirror. I freeze. Someone's there, lying beneath the comforter.

"Riley?" The tension building in my chest suddenly releases. I exhale and race across the room. "Jesus, Riley, I've been yelling for you. Are you okay?"

I fumble for the blanket's edge and pull it back.

Alexis's dead body flops onto its side. The few remaining wispy blond strands of hair attached to her skull flutter away from her face. Blackened flesh bubbles like tar around the hole where her nose is supposed to be, and crispy red flecks of skin stick to the pillowcase. Skin peels away from her cheeks, letting bone and muscle poke through.

Bile rises in my throat, but I can't look away. Alexis's teeth remain intact, but blackened, and fire ate away her lips, leaving her mouth in a permanent snarl. Even her eyes are gone. All that's left are two sunken, empty sockets.

The sound starts again. It's not whispering, not exactly. It sounds more like dull clicking, like fingernails snapping. I freeze, and my stomach turns.

Alexis's mouth drops open.

"Holy shit." I stumble backward, staring. Something moves deep in Alexis's throat. It twitches in the darkness, and a tiny, hairy leg stretches over her teeth.

The cockroach crawls across Alexis's tongue and spills onto her chest. A second clings to the roof of her mouth, antennae twitching. It watches me with glassy black eyes.

Dozens of cockroaches pour out of her mouth and scurry down her body. They nestle into the charred remains of her clothes and dig into her blond hair. A few burrow into her ears. They crawl on top of one another, gushing out of Alexis's nose and mouth and cracks in her skull. An antenna appears in the tissue of her cheek as a cockroach digs through the remaining rotten, weak flesh on her face.

The clicking grows until it's too loud for me to hear anything else. A cockroach creeps over Alexis's burned stub of a chin and hisses. Tissue-thin wings unfold from its back.

I scream until my throat goes raw. I back away from Alexis, trip over a pillow, and drop to my knees. The cockroaches multiply, blanketing the bed. They drip onto the floor in a brown scaly mass. I try to push myself away, but I'm too late. Cockroaches skitter up my fingers and legs. Their tiny legs dig into my arms. They plow into my hair and slip below my clothes. One crawls along the neck of my T-shirt, then falls into my bra, antennae twitching against my skin. Another creeps along the side of my face and hisses in my ear.

I push myself to my feet and race for the door. The floor lamp flickers, sending two-foot-long shadows of cockroaches over the walls. I glance over my shoulder. The insects climb over the lampshade, wings fluttering. They're everywhere now: crawling up the walls and covering the floor. A thick layer of roaches swarms the window, blocking out the moonlight.

I rip the door open and race into the hallway, slamming it behind me. Cockroaches click and hiss behind the wood, and I see their flickering shadows in the inch of space between the door and the carpet. I back up against the opposite wall. My skin itches. I feel them crawling over my body, slipping down my T-shirt, clinging to the back of my neck. I swat at my arms and legs, but my hands come away clean. I close my eyes, exhaling, and collapse against the wall.

Something drips onto my nose. My eyes shoot back open.

The ceiling swells with blood. Thick, tacky drops trickle down on me, coating my hair and shoulders, speckling my face. I push myself away from the wall, and my boots slip on the blood splattered across the hallway as I run for the stairs. I grab the banister to steady myself. A cockroach crawls over my fingers and I scream, shaking it off.

The air moves behind me, and the clicking, hissing cockroaches fall silent. All the hair on the back of my neck sticks straight up.

Someone's there, in the hallway. I can feel her. I imagine Alexis climbing out of Riley's bed, sooty, ashy skin crumbling from her face with every step she takes.

I don't look back over my shoulder. I don't want to know if I'm right.

I take the steps to the first floor two at a time. The ceiling rains blood, and swarms of cockroaches crawl over my rubber boots. The weight of the staircase shifts beneath my feet. I feel that thing behind me, feel it closing in, reaching its raw, burning red hands out to grab me.

I leap down the last three steps and stumble into the foyer, landing on all fours. Glass shards wedge into my knees and bite the palms of my hands. I push myself back to my feet and scramble out the front door, onto the porch.

The sky still burns with eerie light, like it's on fire. It's demon light. The devil's light.

I don't stop running until I reach the curb, and then I collapse against Riley's mailbox, panting for breath. I glance back at the house, steeling myself for what's about to burst through the front door.

But the house just sits there silently, its windows dark. Blood doesn't ooze beneath the front door; cockroaches don't swarm the porch. The perfectly trimmed bushes rustle in the stale air, then go still.

As I run from the house, the curtain at Riley's window flutters, like it's saying goodbye.

CHAPTER TWENTY-SEVEN

I stumble through Riley's neighborhood, lost as to what to do next. Every towering house lining the street looks exactly like the one next to it, and I picture that each one is filled with the same horrors. I wrap my arms around my chest, trying not to shiver. I still have to find Riley. If that's what Brooklyn did to her house, I can't imagine what she has in mind for Riley herself.

Helplessness washes over me. I crouch on the street curb and lower my chin to my hands, trying to keep myself calm. I don't know Riley well enough to know where she'd go instead of home. To Josh's place, maybe? But no, Alexis said they broke up. My throat tightens as

I realize that all of Riley's other friends are dead.

I lean forward, and something in my pocket crunches. I cringe, thinking of the cockroaches. I reach into my pocket and pull out a crumpled piece of paper.

It's the photograph of Riley and her friends at the lake house. I consider it for a long moment. Alexis wears a white bikini, her smooth, perfect skin tanned to a deep golden brown. Riley sits next to her, her hair tied back with a silk scarf. They all look so perfect. Like people from a magazine.

Riley said she went to the lake house when she wanted to be alone. It's near Lake Whitney, half an hour away by car. Too far to walk. I need a ride.

I consider trying to take Mom's car, then dismiss the idea almost immediately. With the paramedics and Grace's body, our driveway is probably still a mob scene.

I slip my cell phone out of my sweatshirt pocket, quickly pulling up Charlie's number. I picture Charlie's bright red truck, and my thumb hovers nervously over the screen.

Finally, I work up the nerve to send him a text: *can u pick me up? its an emergency.*

I give him Riley's address and hit send. Then I wait. Less than a minute later, the phone vibrates in my hand. *Be there in 10.*

I weave my hands together anxiously. Every passing

second feels like the difference between saving Riley's life and letting her die.

"Hurry," I whisper under my breath. I slip the phone into my pocket and walk to the porch. I tug my sweatshirt over my hands and crouch on the top step, drawing my knees up to my chest.

Luckily, it doesn't take ten minutes for Charlie's red truck to roll down the street and slow to a stop in front of Riley's house. Charlie throws the door open and jumps out without cutting the engine. He's wearing faded jeans and a sweatshirt, and his hair sticks up in all directions.

"Sofia? What is it? Are you okay?" He stops in front of me and reaches for my shoulder, but I immediately pull away. I feel dirty, like all the horrors of this weekend are streaked across my face. Like he'll know what I've done just by looking at me.

"I need to borrow your car."

"What?" Charlie frowns, and the dimple disappears from his cheek.

"It's a long story. But I need to go somewhere. Now."

He leans in and kisses me on the forehead. Just a couple of days ago this would have made my stomach flip, but now it feels like something I've stolen. I don't deserve a guy like Charlie.

"You can tell me the long story on the drive," he says. "I'll take you wherever you need to go."

I start to shake my head before he's even finished speaking. Hurt flashes across his face.

"Look," I say. "You can't come. I can't explain why right now, but you just . . . you can't."

Charlie's frown deepens. "Sofia, if you're in some kind of trouble, I want to help."

"You *can't*." This comes out sounding more frantic than I intend for it to, but I can't help it. I'm running out of time. "Charlie, you're a really nice guy, but you're better off without me."

Charlie laughs and reaches for me again. "That's not true."

I lean away from him, pressing against his truck. "It is true," I say, slipping my fingers into the door latch. "I've done terrible things. You'd hate me if you knew. You'll probably hate me for this, too, but it's for the best."

Charlie shakes his head. "What are you talking about?"

I don't answer. Instead, I open the car door behind my back and slip into the front seat, pulling the door closed. Before he can reach for the latch himself, I hit the lock.

"Sorry!" I yell. Charlie bangs against the glass, and the muffled *fwump fwump* echoes through the truck.

"Sofia!" he shouts, but his voice sounds far away. I shift the truck into drive. If I see how betrayed he looks,

I know I won't be able to do this. I close my eyes when I hit the gas and keep them closed when the truck lurches forward.

By the time I open them again, my vision is clouded with tears, and I wouldn't be able to see his face anyway.

* * *

I look up *Lake Whitney* on my cell while I drive, and follow the directions to a misty flat park surrounded by dense woods. I slow Charlie's truck as the road narrows and curves into the trees. The moon peeks over the distant hills and reflects off the steely lake, turning the trees gray and silver through the fog.

Houses line the waterfront, and just as I start to worry that I'll never find Riley in time, the road curves again, ending in front of a private beach and a thick cove of fir trees. Beyond the tops of the trees, I see a dark, slate-colored roof and chimney. I shift the truck into park and push the door open, but I leave the engine running, like Charlie did. Riley and I might have to make a quick getaway. Shoving my hands in my sweatshirt pockets, I hurry down the rocky gravel driveway.

I immediately recognize Riley's family's lake house from the photograph. It's a low, sprawling cabin made of weathered gray wood. Floor-to-ceiling windows cover one entire side of the house, showing a darkened room filled with sleek, modern furniture. A narrow wooden dock stretches far out into the lake. I picture Riley and Alexis spreading their beach towels across the wood and slow to a walk. I'm sure this is the right place. But it looks empty.

Then something moves on the porch, and I turn, narrowing my eyes.

Riley's huddled beneath a blanket on one of the wooden chairs, holding a cup of tea. She flinches when she sees me walking toward her, then sets the teacup on the ground and stands. The blanket drops from her shoulders.

"Sofia." Her voice cracks when she says my name. "Oh my god. I thought . . ."

She lets the end of her sentence trail off, but I know what she was going to say. She thought I'd died in that house with Brooklyn. She thought the fire had killed me.

"We have to go." I don't mean for my voice to sound flat and angry, but it does. As relieved as I am that Riley's not hurt, I can't just forget what happened last night—the fact that she left me to burn, the things she did to Brooklyn and to me.

She studies my face, and something inside her cracks. Tears pour down her cheeks.

"Sofia, things got really out of control," she says. "I don't know what . . ."

The truck's engine sputters, interrupting her. I step forward and grab her arm.

"We can talk about all that later," I tell her, glancing nervously over my shoulder. "But right now we have to get out of here."

Riley frowns. "Why? What's wrong?"

"Grace," I say. "She's dead."

Riley's eyes widen in horror. She takes a step back. "No."

"It was Brooklyn," I continue. "You were right about her all along. She's evil. She killed Grace, and now she's coming after you."

Riley lifts a hand to her mouth. The quiet unnerves me, and goose bumps rise on the back of my neck. I wrap my arms around my chest.

That's when I realize—the car engine. I don't hear it anymore.

"Oh, god," I whisper. I turn around and take a few steps back over the rocky driveway. Riley's feet crunch over the gravel behind me. When I see the spot in front of the beach where Charlie's truck is still parked, I freeze.

Brooklyn leans against the hood, tossing the car keys from hand to hand. When she sees me, she smiles.

"Hey, Sofia," she says. "Catch."

And she throws the keys into the lake.

CHAPTER TWENTY-EIGHT

Brooklyn steps away from the truck. Her smile is all teeth, and the longer I stare at it, the more it looks like a grimace. Brooklyn ripped the skin off Riley's face with those teeth. My knees buckle, and I nearly fall to the ground right there.

"Oh, god." Riley releases her breathe in a hiss. "Brooklyn."

Brooklyn wrinkles her nose. Her feet crunch over the gravel. "Hey, lover. Miss me?"

"Brooklyn, think about this," I beg, but she steps past me like I'm not there. A hammer sticks out of the waistband of her jeans. My stomach turns. No one blocks my path to the dirt road now. I could run to the main street and flag down a car. It was what Riley did to me in that burning house. It would be poetic, almost. The muscles in my legs tense to run.

Flames crackle beneath Brooklyn's toes. With every step she takes, she leaves a curl of fire behind her. It burns blue at first, but then the fire crawls over the white gravel in the driveway and its edges burn orange and red.

Any hope I had of running vanishes with the growing flames. I had to know, on some level, that Brooklyn was capable of this. I saw what she did with the candle in the attic, but I let myself believe it was coincidence, luck. Now I stare at the fire, watching it curl into the air and lick the ground. It's evil—she's evil. There's nowhere I can run to escape her. No matter where I go, Brooklyn will find me.

"You like?" Brooklyn asks. Riley opens her mouth, then closes it again. Brooklyn frowns. "What's the matter? Aren't you impressed?"

"I—" Riley's body flies backward, and the words are ripped from her throat. She slams against the lake house wall. The gray siding shudders as she slides to the ground. She looks dead, but then she lifts a trembling hand to her face to push her hair out of her eyes.

Brooklyn stops a few yards away from the house.

Flames lick at her toes and feet, but she doesn't seem to feel them.

She lifts her arms, holding them out to her sides like a cross. In the dim light her skin looks ghostly white, and the injuries from Riley's knife and the matches stand out in stark contrast. The red cuts and clotted blood seem almost fake, like they were drawn on using that cheap, oily paint that comes with Halloween costumes.

Before my eyes, blood moves back into the wounds and disappears, and the skin stitches itself together, leaving behind only faded pink lines. The stub of her pinkie stretches and grows, becoming whole again. It's like watching one of those nature shows where time speeds up and a flower blooms in seconds. The evil hovers around us, thick and suffocating. I couldn't run now, not even if I wanted to. The air weighs down my limbs like mud, holding me in place.

Brooklyn's scars grow fainter, then disappear completely. She rubs her hands over her arms, grinning. "That was fun," she says.

Riley releases a choked sob. She lowers her head again, and her hair swings over her tear-stained face. She clenches her hands in front of her.

"Hail Mary," she whispers. "Mother of God . . ."

"Your God doesn't care what you have to say," Brooklyn snarls. "Now, do you want to see a real crucifixion?"

Brooklyn throws Riley's body backward, slamming it against the side of the house again. Riley's arms shoot out from her sides—forming a cross. She groans, struggling against some invisible barrier holding her in place. She releases a choked, terrified scream.

Brooklyn stands directly in front of Riley. Fire eats the earth behind her, crackling and spitting in the wind. Smoke turns the air hazy. It looks like a mirage.

Brooklyn glances at me and winks, like we're sharing a joke. She tugs the hammer out of the back of her jeans.

"Sofia, help me!" Riley screams. She throws her head against the wall behind her, making the wood crack. "Help me, help me, please!"

I want to look away, but I don't. It feels cowardly, like if I can't save Riley, the least I can do is watch her die. Maybe that's Brooklyn's joke. Once again I'm forced to watch something terrible happen, helpless to do anything to stop it.

Brooklyn's lips curl into a wicked smile. She pulls a long silver nail out of her pocket.

"Hold still." She positions the nail directly in front of Riley's palm. "This is going to hurt. A lot."

She swings the hammer, driving the nail deep into Riley's hand and pinning it to the house behind her. Riley screams. Brooklyn swings again and again. I imagine the nail piercing skin and bone and muscle. Bile rises in my throat. I scream, too. The sound rips from my body and echoes until my chest burns and my throat goes raw and my head aches.

I don't scream for Riley. I scream because I'm next.

"Now, *this* is a crucifixion," Brooklyn says. I wrench my head up in time to see Brooklyn position a nail over Riley's other hand and swing her hammer. I throw my hands over my face, clenching my eyes shut. I don't want to watch anymore, but my eyes flicker open and I stare at Riley and Brooklyn through the spaces in my fingers.

Riley's body slumps and her weight pulls against the nails in her hands. The fire has reached the house now. It spreads over the grass below and climbs the walls. Gray paint bubbles up beneath the flames.

"H . . . hail Mary . . ." I try to pray. But the words get stuck in my throat. I squeeze my eyes shut, trying to picture the statuette of the Virgin on my grandmother's windowsill. But I can't hold her in my head. It's like she's deserted me.

Brooklyn flips the hammer in her hand and digs the clawed edge deep into Riley's chest. Riley opens her mouth, but instead of speaking, she releases a wet, gurgling sound. Blood bubbles around her teeth. Brooklyn yanks the hammer through her ribs, ripping her thin white T-shirt to shreds. She relaxes her grip on the hammer, and it clatters to the driveway. Her arm shoots forward and she pulls something from Riley's chest.

A heart. Riley's heart.

Riley's head slumps forward. Still holding her heart, Brooklyn turns to face me.

My legs tense, but I don't run. There's not a place on earth I could run where Brooklyn wouldn't find me. I know what's going to happen next. If I stand here and face it, then at least I won't die a coward.

Brooklyn steps toward me. I try to be brave, but the sound of nails crunching through Riley's skin echoes in my head. When I close my eyes I see Grace strung up on the shed, her blood dripping onto the driveway. Brooklyn's not a fan of quick, easy deaths.

"Why so glum?" Brooklyn says. She drops Riley's heart, and it hits the ground with a heavy, wet thud. I stare at Brooklyn's shoulder, at the feathered tail of her Quetzalcoatl tattoo as she walks toward me. I focus on the tattoo to keep from picturing blood blossoming on Riley's T-shirt, or the half-circle gash on Grace's neck, or the way Alexis's fingers curled toward her palm. Still, my hands tremble. I don't want to die.

"Haven't you figured it out yet?" Brooklyn asks. She tucks a spiky strand of hair behind her ear. Blood coats her hand like a glove, and she leaves a line of red along her cheek.

"Figured what out?" I whisper. All around us the cicadas buzz.

Brooklyn pulls me close to her. She whispers into my ear, "The evil lives inside you already."

The buzzing insects become a train's whistle. I squeeze my eyes shut, trying to push the memory away. But I can't help it. Images of that night on the tracks flicker behind my closed eyes. I see the headlight in the distance. I hear Karen screaming.

"Sofia, get off the tracks!" Karen drops her beer and grabs my arm, trying to pull me away. I don't move. The train honks again. I blink into the headlight. It's close enough now that I can't look at it directly.

"Oh my god!" Karen says. "Sofia, come on. This isn't funny!"

She tries to pull again, but this time I wrap my fingers around her wrist and tug her forward. She's so surprised that she stumbles onto the tracks next to me.

"Does it look like I'm fucking laughing?" I hiss at her, and I dive out of the way as the train crashes forward.

I open my eyes, and Brooklyn's watching me, grinning. Something stirs inside me, something thick and suffocating. *No.* I scratch at my skin, leaving red marks along my wrists. The evil is inside me. I feel it. I scratch harder to tear it out of my body, drawing blood. In my head,

I hear my grandmother's raspy voice. *Diablo, Diablo* . . .

But then the feeling stretches, spreading up my spine and into my arms and legs. It uncurls in my chest like an animal. It feels warm now, powerful. Like fire. Brooklyn grabs my wrist. I stare at the trail of blood around my arm and feel something new. Hunger.

"You're not going to kill me," I say. It's not a question. I already know the answer.

"Don't be silly, Sofia," Brooklyn says, dropping my hand. Her eyes glow red, like she's lit from within. "We don't kill our own."

ACKNOWLEDGMENTS

First of all, I'd like to thank one of my very favorite people, Rebecca Marsh, for having cool editor-like friends who don't seem to mind when you corner them at a birthday party and spend the entire night talking about how you really, really want to work with them. And, of course, and even bigger thanks to Emilia Rhodes, who didn't hold that against me, and who seemed to think that spending 45 minutes fan-girling over *Buffy the Vampire Slayer* qualified me to write a horror novel. To all of you wannabe writers out there who might be reading this, I really don't recommend this approach.

Next, I absolutely could not have written this book

without several hundred amazing people, most notably Josh Bank, Sara Shandler, and Katie Schwartz at Alloy, for being so supportive during the whole process, as well as Ben Schrank and Caroline Donofrio at Razorbill for some truly fantastic editorial notes and direction (also for the cookies. I feel like there have been a lot of cookies). Felicia Frazier, and the rest of Razorbill's sales, marketing and publicity team have also been amazingly supportive in ways I could not believe. After nearly five years working in children's book marketing, I know how many people it takes to make a book a book. Thank you all for helping me make mine!

I also have to thank my mother, who thought it was completely appropriate to let me watch Stephen King movies and read horror novels when I was still in grade school. Let's just chalk that up to research, okay? Thanks, also, to the rest of my fantastic friends and family, for letting me complain when things were hard and building me up when I got low. Seriously, I know the best people ever.

And, finally, I have to thank my husband, Ronald, for reading every pass, even though he hates horror. Prepare yourself, babe. The next one's going to be even scarier.

THE MERCILESS II
THE EXORCISM OF SOFIA FLORES

DAN|ELLE VEGA

RAZORBILL

RAZORBILL

An Imprint of Penguin Random House LLC
Penguin.com

RAZORBILL & colophon is a registered trademark of Penguin Random House LLC.

First published in the United States of America by Razorbill, an imprint of Penguin Random House LLC, 2014. This omnibus edition published by Razorbill, an imprint of Penguin Random House LLC, 2018

Copyright © 2016 Alloy Entertainment

Produced by Alloy Entertainment
1325 Avenue of the Americas
New York, NY 10019

ISBN: 9781595147264

This omnibus edition ISBN: 9781984836182

Design by Liz Dresner

Printed in the United States of America

1 3 5 7 9 10 8 6 4 2

THE EXORCISM OF SOFIA FLORES

CHAPTER ONE

I stand at the living room window, staring at the empty house across the street. A single strand of old Christmas lights dangles from the roof. Half the bulbs have burned out.

A woman and her son lived there until this morning. They didn't even say good-bye, just packed their things and disappeared, like everyone else in this neighborhood. I'm surprised it took them this long. After all, no one wants to live across the street from the murder house.

I exhale, fogging the glass. Rain lashes at the window and turns our yard into a swamp. A red Matchbox car floats down the driveway in a muddy river.

I stare at the churning water and try to breathe, but the air in the house feels thick. It's like inhaling sand. I cup my hands and place them over my mouth, forcing my lungs to draw in a ragged wheeze. I exhale through my fingers and choke down another gasp of air.

Breathe, I tell myself. My eyes flutter closed. *It's just a panic attack.* My chest unclenches, and I take a longer drag through my nose. The room stops spinning. I'm in control again.

I grab my phone off the coffee table. Mom is the first in my short list of favorites. The rest—Grace, Riley, and Alexis—are dead. I cast another glance out the window. Row after row of empty houses stare back at me, the tattered FOR SALE signs perched in their yards like warnings.

I hit Call and a photo of my mom, Sergeant Nina Flores, flashes across the screen. She glares at me over a bowl of cereal, a single Honey Nut Cheerio stuck to her cheek. Normally, her appearance is military-precise, but I caught her before her coffee.

The sight of Mom's face calms me a little.

"Chill, Sofia," I mutter to myself, lifting the phone to my ear.

Mom answers her phone mid-ring. "Sofia?"

"Mom?" Relief seeps through me. "Where are you?"

"I'm still at work, Sof. Is everything okay?"

I clutch the phone with both hands, shooting another look out the window. "I thought you were coming home early today."

"I told Jodi that I'd cover for everyone who took off early for Thanksgiving . . . Why? Did something happen?"

"No, I just—" I glance at the empty house across the street. It was different when I knew there was someone living there, even if she kept her curtains closed and averted her eyes whenever she saw me. "I just don't want to be alone."

Mom is silent for a beat. "Did you have another attack?" she asks, her voice gentle. When I don't answer, she sighs. "Honey, did you try the breathing exercises Dr. Keller taught you?"

I drop onto the couch and take another pull of air. Dr. Keller is the therapist who helped me realize that what happened last summer was a mental breakdown. In other words: *not real*. Because of him, I could finally accept that Brooklyn didn't make blood rain from Riley's ceiling, she didn't set fires with her mind, and she definitely didn't pull out Riley's heart with her bare hands.

He told me that I don't have evil inside of me. Just guilt.

He said that witnessing Riley's murder traumatized me, and I made up a story to cope. And I want to believe

Dr. Keller. But sometimes I can still hear the sound of Riley's heart falling to the ground. I still feel Brooklyn's lips on my cheek.

We don't kill our own was the last thing she said to me before disappearing into the woods. The police never found her.

"The exercises helped, I guess," I mumble into the phone.

Mom exhales. "See? It's like he said after your last session: the most important thing is to learn how to control your fear so it can't control you."

I pick at the skin next to my thumbnail. Brooklyn could be outside my house right now. My guilty conscience may have invented some of what happened over the summer. But Brooklyn was real, and she killed my three best friends.

Dr. Keller can prescribe all the breathing exercises he wants, but even he can't keep me from being afraid.

"How's *Abuela?*" Mom asks.

I shift my eyes to the staircase at the edge of the living room. Grandmother's rosary beads click against her table upstairs like a metronome, slowly counting the seconds. Yesterday, she woke up coughing and gasping in the middle of the night. She had a slight fever and her skin was clammy, but her temperature came down this morning, so we decided not to take her to the emergency room. "She's okay. She's breathing normally and her temp was at ninety-eight point six degrees," I say. "I checked when I got home from school."

"Good. I'm glad she's feeling better." Mom clears her throat. "And how's the rest of your day been?" she asks.

I frown and tug at a thread coming loose from my jeans. "Fine. Boring."

"What, no big Thanksgiving break party?" She's trying to be funny, but her voice sounds strained. She knows I don't have any friends left in this town. Charlie is the only person I still know in Friend, Mississippi, and he hasn't spoken to me since the night I stole his truck and tried to save Riley. I've barely said a word to another classmate since I found Grace's dead body hanging from our shed. The thread unravels, leaving a tiny hole in my jeans. I press down on the fabric, but the hole won't magically knit itself back together. None of the holes in my life will.

"Mom," I whisper, the word cracking in my mouth. "Why do we have to stay here?"

A sigh echoes through the phone. "Sofia . . ."

I blink hard to keep from crying. "Dr. Keller says this environment is toxic for me, and everyone else has already moved away. We could go back to Arizona, or—"

"I'm stationed here, in Friend. I have another sixteen months before I can apply for reassignment."

"But—"

"It's my job, Sofia. You know how the army works. There's nothing I can do."

I lay back on the couch, swallowing the rest of my argument. We've talked about this before. A lot. Silence stretches between us. Wind presses against the glass of the windows, and thunder rumbles in the distance. It reminds me of a car engine, except cars don't drive down this street anymore.

"Sweetie," Mom says, her voice a bit softer, "sometimes I wish we could leave, too. Even I get jealous of how everyone else can pack up and go. Our life is just a little more complicated than that. What's that needlepoint your grandmother has on her wall? Jealousy is cancer, or—"

"Jealousy is like cancer in your bones," I correct her. "It's from the Bible."

Mom releases a small laugh. "Right. Jealousy will eat you up inside if you let it, so let's try to look for a silver lining. Do you think you can do that?"

I shrug, even though I know Mom can't see me. "I guess."

There's a pause. "Look, I might be able to convince Jodi to let me leave a few minutes early," Mom says. "Everyone's already left for the holiday, so there's not much to take care of. How about I swing by China

Garden to pick up some takeout, and we can watch *The Wizard of Oz?*"

A small smile tugs at the corner of my lips. *The Wizard of Oz* is my favorite movie. We watch it whenever I have a bad day. "That sounds okay," I say.

"I'll call ahead and order the usual. See you soon."

"Thanks, Mom. Love you."

"Love you. Now do your homework."

"Roger that," I say, and we both hang up.

Reluctantly, I flip through my dog-eared copy of Shakespeare's *The Tempest* and open up my laptop. My last three schools have all done a unit on *The Tempest*. I could probably recite the entire play from memory. I stifle a yawn and my eye twitches.

The cover of *The Tempest* shows a girl in a blue dress staring out over a stormy sea. She has her back to me, her tangled red hair blowing in the wind. Miranda has been stranded on a deserted island with a crazy magician for twelve years but I'd still trade places with her in a second. Deserted island beats murder house any day.

Just looking at her makes my eyelids feel heavy. I'm supposed to write an essay detailing the major themes and, even though I've read the play *three* times, I can't think of a single thing to write. I stare at the blank Word document on my laptop. The cursor blinks mockingly. The sound of my grandmother's rosary beads echoes down the stairs and, after a second, the blinking and the clicking match up.

Blink. *Click.* Blink. *Click.* Blink.

I tear my eyes away from the screen and pick up *The Tempest.*

The girl on the cover stares right at me, a terrible smile on her face.

I jump up, banging my knee—*hard*—on the coffee table. I wheeze in pain at the shock. The book goes flying and hits the wall with a smack and then drops to the carpet, faceup. My heart is pounding so hard that I want to throw up.

I don't want to look. But I *have* to look. I lift my head.

The cover of *The Tempest* is normal again. Miranda stares out over the sea, her hair teased out behind her. No demon smile. I unclench my fists and stop holding my breath. The nausea has passed.

I sink back onto the couch and pull my computer onto my lap. My knee pulses with pain. I'll have an ugly purple bruise tomorrow, but I won't be able to distinguish it from the others. I've been so jumpy lately that I'm covered in welts and marks.

I lower my fingers to the keyboard and type: *Power and enslavement, the favored and the forsaken, lovers and masters. These major themes of* The Tempest—

My screen freezes. I frown and tap on the keys. Nothing.

"Shit," I mutter. I slide a finger over the trackpad, but the cursor doesn't move. It's not even blinking. I groan and close my eyes, pinching the bridge of my nose with two fingers. This is just perfect. My knee aches, my brain feels mushy, and now my computer's not working. It's like the universe doesn't actually want me to get anything done.

I open my eyes and reach for the power button to restart. A blank window pops onto the screen.

"What the hell?" I whisper. A cursor appears. Someone starts to type.

Hello, Sofia.

Fear curdles in my stomach. This isn't happening. My eyes must be playing tricks on me.

A GIF of a skinned cat opens on the desktop. Flies crawl over its limp, pink tongue, and its cloudy eyes stare out at me from a raw, bloody face. Someone painted a pentagram on the dead grass, and dripping candles form a circle around its rotting body.

Every other sound in the house goes silent. I can't hear the rain or Grandmother's rosary, but my breathing magnifies in my ears until the ragged gasps overwhelm me. I remember the smell of that cat. Milk gone sour. Fish left in the heat. I press the computer's power button, hoping to erase the image that's already seared into my brain. It won't turn off.

Another photograph appears. It's Alexis's dead body, crumpled beneath the second-story window of the abandoned house. I still don't know if she jumped or was pushed. The curve of her twisted limbs is deeply unnatural. A beautiful broken doll. She stares up at the sky, a thin line of blood dribbling from her lips. Her fingers curl toward her palms, as though she's reaching for someone.

I jerk away from the sofa and stumble to my feet, the laptop tumbling to the ground.

"Stop it," I whisper. I back up against the wall as more pictures flash across the computer screen.

A girl holding a butcher knife. Bloody handprints. Cockroaches racing across the floor.

Then a video file pops up, blocking all the other images. A train races toward the screen, headlights flashing. A horn blares, followed by a high, piercing scream. I press myself into the wall behind me, my breath fast and ragged. I'd know that scream anywhere. Karen. The girl I killed.

I squeeze my eyes shut and throw my hands over my ears. "Stop it!" I shout. "Please!"

Laughter echoes through the house.

I open my eyes and spin around, certain I'm going to see Brooklyn standing behind me smiling her terrible demon smile. But I'm alone. The laughing grows louder.

"Please," I whisper. My hands start to shake. I curl them into fists and hug them to my chest. *Please* stop."

"So-fi-a," someone says in a singsong voice, making the hair on my arms stand up. The voice is coming from the laptop speakers.

"You're one of us, Sofia," Brooklyn says. "I'm coming for you."

"No!" I shout, and I jerk awake, gasping.

I'm lying on the couch, my computer still balanced on my lap. There's nothing on the screen except for a blank Word document and a blinking cursor. The storm beats against the windows and my grandmother's rosary beads click away upstairs. Otherwise, it's dead quiet. My chest rises and falls as I try to catch my breath. It was a nightmare. Just like all the other nightmares I've had since the day Brooklyn killed Riley and revealed my horrible secret. No one else knows that I dragged a girl onto the train tracks at my last school. Not Dr. Keller. Not even my mother.

Tears spill onto my cheeks. I try to wipe them away but they come too quickly, blurring my vision and making my breath hitch. I vowed that I would never think about that night again. It was an accident, a moment of insanity. And, after everything that happened with Brooklyn, I've more than paid for my crime.

I start to do my exercises, but my hands shake so

badly that I can't keep them cupped around my mouth. I grab my phone to call Mom again, then pause.

The time blinks at me from the home screen: 9:47. I click on my recent calls list. I talked to Mom at six fifty-two. Almost three hours ago.

"What the hell?" I murmur. I wipe the last of the tears from my eyes. "Mom?" I call, pushing myself to my feet. "Are you there?"

I listen for Mom's voice, or the sound of her footsteps. There's nothing.

The doorbell rings, making me jump.

Nerves crawl over my skin like spiders. We never get visitors. I take a step toward the door, thinking of vacant eyes and bloody footprints and tattered skin.

I don't want to answer it, but the doorbell rings again.

CHAPTER TWO

"**M**iss?" a man calls through the door. It's a deep, unfamiliar voice. I lower my hand to the knob and turn, holding my breath as I pull the door open.

A police officer in a stiff blue uniform stands on our porch, a squad car waiting at the curb. His partner sits in the passenger seat. She holds a walkie-talkie in one hand, barking orders that I can't hear.

Calling for backup, I think, and fear shoots up my spine.

"Are you Sofia Flores?" the officer asks. I nod, resisting the urge to slam the door in his face and turn the dead bolt. The last time the cops were here was the night we found Grace's body.

I listened for sirens for weeks afterward, certain Brooklyn would tell them the truth about the train accident. But the cops never found Brooklyn, and my secret remains safe. The manhunt for her continues.

I watched the rust-colored bloodstains on our driveway fade under the sun and rain until, finally, Mom scrubbed them away with a bucket of bleach and a thick, wiry brush.

That's it, I remember thinking. *It's over.*

"Miss?" The cop narrows his eyes. Rain drips from his uniform, leaving puddles on the porch. "Are you okay?"

"Fine," I say. I brace myself for the silver flash of handcuffs, for the officer to jerk my arms behind my back and tell me I have the right to remain silent. "What's wrong?"

"I'm afraid your mother, Nina Flores, was in a car accident."

The words fall flat. It takes me a long time to process what he's saying. "I . . . I don't understand."

"Sofia, your mother died in the ambulance on her way to the hospital. I'm so sorry."

I stare at the officer's mouth. His lips are chapped, and there's a tiny gap between his two front teeth. He's still speaking, but I can't hear him. The entire world has gone still. I tighten my fingers around the doorknob and focus all my attention on the way my skin feels against the brass. The sweat gathering between my fingers.

"Miss?" The officer's voice jars me back to the present. "Is there someone else here you'd like me to speak to?"

I shake my head. "I just spoke to my mother on the phone. She's fine."

Something passes through the officer's eyes. *Pity*. I curl my hand into a fist and bang it against the door. The wood rattles.

"I'm sorry—"

"You've made a mistake!" I shout. But the anger dies as soon as the words leave my mouth. I feel weak. Empty.

"Is your father home?" the officer asks.

"He died," I say in a hollow voice. "When I was little."

"What about an aunt or an uncle?" I shake my head, and the officer lifts his walkie-talkie to his mouth. "We're going to need CPS here right away," he says.

CPS—Child Protective Services.

"Roger that, over," comes crackling over the radio.

"That's okay. I'm okay, thank you." I close the door before he can say another word. I can still see his shadow through the cloudy glass panes on either side of the door. He stands on our porch for a moment; then I hear the sound of his shoes on the stairs, walking away. He'll be back. Along with a bunch of strangers who'll decide what to do with me.

I press my hand flat against the wall, steadying myself. *Your mother died in the ambulance on her way to the hospital.* I shake my head. It's not real. I just talked to her. We're going to eat Chinese food and watch *The Wizard of Oz.*

I grab my cell phone and I dial Mom's number. The silly Cheerios photo pops onto my screen. Something in my gut twists.

Mistake, I tell myself. *This is all a mistake.* Mom's fine. I lift the phone to my ear and hold my breath, waiting for her to pick up.

The phone rings. And rings. A hollow space opens inside my chest. It feels as if someone has tunneled through my internal organs, leaving a hole straight through the middle of my body. Mom always answers my calls, even when she's on duty.

I let my mind travel to the dark place. *Your mother died.* My hands start to tremble. *Car accident.*

A cruel voice echoes through my head. *And why was she in the car, Sofia?* it asks, sounding eerily like Brooklyn. I swallow, tasting something sour at the back of my throat. Mom was only driving because I begged her to come home early. Because I couldn't stand to be here alone.

The phone slips from my fingers, but I don't hear it hit the floor. The sound of static erupts in my ears.

This is my fault. And now I'm alone—an orphan.

I don't remember walking across the living room and climbing the stairs, but when I look up, I'm standing in front of Grandmother's room. Deep red light spills into the hall. It's the color of the wine they serve during communion. The color of blood. Rosary beads click against the table.

"*Abuela?*" I push the door all the way open. Grandmother is sitting upright in her narrow hospital bed, sliding the rosary beads through skeletally thin fingers. Several years ago, she had a stroke that left half her body paralyzed. She lost control of the muscles in her cheeks, making her face look like something melted. Skin drips from her face like candle wax, and one side of her mouth curves in a perpetual frown. I see her scalp through her wispy white hair.

I step inside the room, shifting around the cardboard boxes of Grandmother's things. Mom and I always said we'd unpack them, but we never found the time to do more than put away her clothes and lean a few of her pictures against the walls. Her favorite framed needlepoint sits on the table beside her bed.

A peaceful heart leads to a healthy body, it reads. *Jealousy is like a cancer in the bones*. Proverbs 14:30.

The pain hits all at once, like a blow to the chest.

Mom and I are never going to unpack the rest of Grandmother's room. She's never going to pick up my calls or eat Cheerios or watch that scene in *The Wizard of Oz* that she loves, the one where Dorothy falls asleep in the field of red poppies. She's gone. Forever. Because of me.

My legs crumple beneath me, and I sink to the floor, banging my hip against Grandmother's bedside table on my way down. The needlepoint falls over, sliding back behind the table. I'm shaking all over. I can't breathe. I cup my hands around my mouth and inhale, but my exhale explodes into a choked sob. I cover my face with my hands and cry.

I wish I could go back in time and tell her not to get in that car. I don't need Chinese food and movies. I'm not scared anymore. I can be brave, just like her.

Grandmother stares straight ahead, clutching the rosary to her chest. Her brittle nails curl over the tips of her fingers, all yellowed and cracked. I stare at them for a long time. Painful sobs rattle through me.

"*Abuela*," I manage to spit out. I wipe the tears from my cheeks with the back of my hand, but they refuse to stop pouring down my face. "Mom is . . . she's . . ."

Grandmother's neck muscles aren't strong enough to hold her head straight anymore, and it bobbles, slightly, as she turns. She looks at me with milky, unseeing eyes and I realize she understands. She's outlived her only daughter.

I crawl across the floor and rest my head against her mattress. Rain crashes against the window, pounding so hard that I worry the glass will shatter. I think of all the empty houses sprawled around us. Street after street of vacant rooms and overgrown lawns and muddy driveways. I'm suddenly aware that I'm about to get my wish—we can't stay in this house now that Mom isn't coming back. I'll finally get to leave this stupid town. Not that it matters anymore.

Grandmother touches my head. Her hand is nearly weightless, and her skin feels almost exactly like crumpled paper. She pats, absently, as if she's not entirely sure what she's doing.

The heavy grip on my heart loosens, just a little. I close my eyes and rest my head against her leg.

The muscles in Grandmother's hand tighten. She digs her long, cracked fingernails into my skin. Pain shoots through my neck and I jerk away, horrified.

"Diablo!" Grandmother says in a thin, raspy voice. She lifts a curved finger that looks like a claw and points at me.

"Don't," I whisper. "Please, *Abuela*."

"Diablo!" she says again. I slink away from her and sink back against the wall, shaking with sobs.

CHAPTER THREE

Two days later, I'm standing in a graveyard, staring at the flag-draped casket that holds my mother's decaying body.

A steely-gray sky stretches above me, heavy with storm clouds. The temperature has dropped below fifty degrees for the first time since I moved to Mississippi, and cool wind cuts through my dress. I shiver, clutching a bundle of poppies to my chest. A handful of petals flutter from their stems and scatter in the wind. The man who handled the flower arrangements said they're not good for bouquets, but they are—no, they *were*—my mother's favorite flowers, so I insisted he cut me a dozen. Half the petals have already blown away.

A military chaplain stands at the head of my mother's casket, white robes draped around his shoulders. His face is made up of hard lines and deep wrinkles, the collar of his jacket digging into his leathery neck.

"A reading from First Peter," he recites, starting down at a thick leather Bible. "'Dear friends, do not be surprised at the painful trial you are suffering . . .'"

I try to listen, but the wind snatches his voice before it reaches my ears. It's a small funeral, only a half-dozen soldiers from my mother's unit crowd around the coffin. Next to me Jodi Sorrenson, Mom's commanding officer, dabs her nose with a crumpled tissue.

"Your mother would have thought this was beautiful," she whispers, sniffling. A fat tear rolls down her cheek, but I don't have it in me to comfort her.

"I'm sure she would have," I say instead. Mom didn't provide specific instructions for the funeral, so Jodi did her best to guess at her wishes. The truth is, I know Mom would have hated all of this. She despised Bible quotes and graveyards. She wouldn't have wanted the military spending money and making a fuss over her. She called funerals "morbid spectacles" and always told me that, when she died, she wanted to be buried in the cheapest casket I could find and for people to donate to charity instead of buying flowers.

"Or donate my body to science," she added. "Then at least my death could help people."

She wanted everything to be quick and easy. Efficient—like she was.

I clutch the poppies in my hand. The bouquet was the one thing I chose myself. Another bright-red petal dances off into the wind. I watch the flowers scatter, and fight against the sob building in my throat. Now it's just a bundle of ugly stems.

The chaplain raises his hands. This is my signal. I'm supposed to be the first person to lay flowers on my mother's coffin. The soldiers turn to look at me, waiting, but I don't move. My feet feel as if they've frozen to the dead brown grass. Jodi nudges me with her elbow.

"Go on," she whispers.

I stare at my ruined bouquet. The stalks are skinny green things. They don't even have leaves. Tears prick my eyes but I blink, refusing to let them fall. I wanted to surround my mother with red poppies. Then, when she was underground with her tacky, overpriced coffin, she'd have at least one thing she loved to make her feel less alone.

I can't give her these ugly stems.

Jodi steps forward, placing a white rose on my mother's coffin. The others follow. Some leave flowers, others just bow their heads and move on. I stay rooted in place as the few guests pay their respects. The honor guards meticulously fold the flag draped over my mother's casket, and present it to me. I barely hear the words they say as I take the stiff fabric in my hands. Jodi glances at me when the guests start to leave, but I refuse to meet her eyes. She nods and pats me on the shoulder.

"I'll wait by the car," she says. "Take as much time as you need."

I listen to her heels crunch against the dead grass. When I'm sure she's gone, I step forward and sink to the ground next to my mother's coffin, the flag nestled on my lap. I lean my head against the shiny wood, a tear crawling down my cheek. I don't have the strength to wipe it away.

"Maybe this is just a dream," I say. I trace the whirls of wood with my finger. "Like in *The Wizard of Oz*. Maybe we just have to click our heels."

Mom used to joke that Dorothy's trick of clicking her heels together and saying, "There's no place like home," wouldn't have worked for us. We've had so many homes that the shoes wouldn't know where to send us. I always giggled with her when she said that but, secretly, I didn't agree. Home doesn't have to be a place. It can be a person. I'd always known where my home was. Until now.

"There's no place like home," I whisper. I wipe the

tears from my cheeks, and set the flower stems on the ground next to the coffin. The wind blows, spreading red petals over the dead grass. I shiver and wrap my arms around my chest, watching the petals dance across the crumbling stone angels and moss-covered tombstones. Almost like droplets of blood.

Almost like someone's trying to warn me.

* * *

Jodi drives me home after the service. She offers to come in but Wanda Garrity, my social worker, is supposed to be waiting for me, so I tell her she doesn't have to. I climb out of the car and head to the house. Jodi waves and then her car disappears down the street, taillights flashing red. I lift my hand, a second too late.

Jodi gave me her phone number and told me to call if I needed anything. The stiff paper presses through the pocket of my coat, the corners digging through the fabric.

The house feels different. I notice it as soon as I step through the front door. The air hangs heavier on my shoulders. It seems to vibrate.

"Wanda?" I call out, but no one responds. She must be running late.

I close the door behind me, and the walls inch closer. This is exactly where I was standing when I found out my mother was dead. I close my eyes and that moment replays on a loop, like a nightmare that won't end.

Wanda showed up about an hour after the police left. I was still in Grandmother's room, shaking and sobbing, when she found me. She told me to pack a bag, and she took me to a group home for the night. I'm not eighteen yet, so the state won't let me stay in the house alone.

No one knows what to do with me, but everyone seems to agree that I can't live here. Wanda offered to call family, but Mom didn't have any siblings or close friends. She and my dad never married, and besides, he died when I was little. Our only other family lives in Mexico, and they couldn't even afford plane tickets up for the funeral. They wouldn't be able to take me in.

"Wanda?" I shout again. My voice bounces off the walls, echoing back to me. Wanda told me she'd meet me here after the funeral so I could pack the rest of my things and we could "discuss my options." None of it sounded good.

A few key words repeat in my mind: *Foster care. Group Home. Adoption.*

I hurry up to my room. Jodi arranged for my grandmother to be sent to a nursing home, so there's no one else here. It's the first time I've been alone in days.

I pull a suitcase out of my closet and place it on my bed. Then I open the top drawer of my dresser and remove underwear and socks and my neatly folded T-shirts. The rest of the house has already been packed up, my mom's things either in storage or sold off. Jodi and her friends swept through here and, before I knew it, everything was gone. At least they let me do my room myself. The house is supposed to be rented again after I leave, but I can't imagine anyone wanting to live here. Our story was all over the news. Everyone in Friend knows about the "murder house."

I focus on the stitching unraveling from the hems of my favorite jeans, and the way my Converse sneakers fit perfectly into the shoe pouch in my suitcase. I've packed my things to move dozens of times before. The motions are methodical and familiar. I can almost pretend Mom is downstairs in the kitchen, covering dishes in Bubble Wrap and humming along with the radio. I start to hum but my voice sounds shaky, so I stop.

That's when I hear it. Whispering.

The hair rises on my arms. I stop folding, a flannel shirt still clutched in my hands. I drop the shirt and turn toward the sound. The window above my desk is open. The screen broke over the summer, leaving a space just large enough to climb through.

A chill curls around my spine. I stare at the window, trying to remember the last time I undid the latch and pushed it open. Wind makes the curtains dance. The whispering drones on.

I swallow. I'm being stupid. Someone probably left

their TV on, or started playing music. But no—nobody lives in this neighborhood anymore. The entire block is empty.

I take a step toward the window and the sound grows louder. It sounds like cicadas.

"Brooklyn?" I whisper. I picture her crouched on the roof just below my window, her hair spiked, smudged black liner circling her bloodshot eyes. She smiles, and dozens of black bugs scurry over her teeth and cling to her lips and cheeks, wings twitching.

I'm coming for you . . .

I slide a biology textbook off my desk. It's heavy, the faded cover slick beneath my fingers. I take one step toward the window, cringing as the floorboard creaks beneath my feet.

The whispering drills into my brain. I can't quite make out the words, but it sounds like someone saying my name.

Sofia. Sofia.

I take another step toward the open window and, this time, the floorboards stay silent. I lift the biology textbook over my head.

Sofia . . .

I take a deep breath, and then leap toward the window, heart hammering. I search the roof frantically, my muscles tightening, preparing to swing.

The roof is empty.

I glance across the street and notice a sprinkler jutting up from the lawn, squirting a steady stream of water over the muddy grass. It makes a buzzing sound. Like a whisper. Fear drains from my chest, leaving me deflated.

I lower the book and release a short, unamused laugh. The neighbors had an automatic system installed a few weeks before Mom and I moved here. I *knew* that. They must've forgotten to disable it before they left.

A knock comes from the other side of my bedroom door.

I scream and whirl around so fast that my textbook flies out of my hands. It hits the floor with a thud.

"Sofia?" a woman calls from the hall. The voice isn't Brooklyn's.

"Um, just a second," I say. I let my breathing steady, and then I cross the room and pull my bedroom door open.

A short, dark-haired woman stands in the hall. She wears a navy-colored suit and low heels. It's just Wanda, my caseworker.

"Is everything okay?" Wanda asks, blinking her insanely long lashes. Her huge doe eyes and downturned mouth always leave her looking depressed.

"Sorry, you scared me," I say.

"The door was unlocked. Didn't you hear me knocking?"

I shake my head and Wanda gives me a small, polite, smile. "It's nice to see you again, Sofia," she says. "Do you mind if I come in?"

I move aside and Wanda steps into my bedroom. She sits in the chair next to my desk while I perch at the edge of my bed, nervously tapping my foot.

"I'm sorry to do this today," she says. "I know you just got back from your mother's funeral."

I pick at a piece of dry skin next to my thumbnail, suddenly aware of the way my tights make the backs of my knees itch.

"Have you decided where you want to go? I know it's a big decision," she continues, trying to sound positive.

"Can't I just stay here?" I ask, even though I already know the answer. "I'm graduating next year, and then I'll go away to college . . ."

Wanda shakes her head. "You know we can't allow that. You're still under eighteen." She pauses. "I've done some digging, and I think I've found a loophole we can work with. In her will, your mother stipulated that you were to be left in your grandmother's care. Your grandmother isn't fit to be your legal guardian but, since she's been officially appointed, the state's at liberty to default to the arrangements she made in her own will."

"Did my grandmother even have a will?"

"She did. Unfortunately, it's a bit outdated. She wanted her daughter—or legal dependent, in this case—sent to a school run by the Catholic church."

"Catholic school?" I ask. The words sound strange to me, like I'm talking about someone else's life. I'm an army brat, not a Catholic schoolgirl.

"I went ahead and made some calls to schools in the area. Have you heard of St. Mary's Prep?" Wanda asks.

There's something off in her voice as she asks the question, like what she wants to say is, *Have you heard* what happened *at St. Mary's Prep?*

I shake my head. "Should I have?"

Wanda clasps her hands in front of her, considering me with those giant, sad eyes. "It's a Catholic boarding school in Hope Springs, Mississippi," she explains. "It's a few towns over, but it's the closest one and is very well regarded. There wouldn't usually be any openings, but I was informed that a student left very suddenly last week. You have a spot there, if you'd like it."

I don't know what to say. Everything is happening so fast.

"I know it's not a perfect solution," Wanda continues. "But St. Mary's has a scholarship program for students of . . . lesser means. It would cover tuition and board, as long as you kept up your grades and obeyed the school's morality code. Plus, there's a nursing home less than twenty minutes away by car. I called them this morning and they have space if you'd like to transfer your grandmother."

I stare at Wanda, unsure how to respond. Catholic school. I picture plaid skirts and stained glass and nuns in long black habits. And it's a *boarding* school, which means I wouldn't get to leave the mean girls behind at the end of the day. I'd have to live with them.

"If you decide to go with St. Mary's, you'd officially be a ward of the school," Wanda continues. "That means you wouldn't qualify for a more traditional adoption. I understand if you want to try your luck at that. I'm told that the group home in Friend fills up pretty fast, especially with the holidays coming up in just a few weeks. There aren't a lot of beds available, so we'll need to get you moved in as soon as possible, if you want to stay around here."

I swallow. *Group home.* I think of the stained mattress I slept on for two nights, the cold concrete floors, and girls with cruel smiles. I imagine eating Christmas dinner in that sterile cafeteria.

I push away my concerns about St. Mary's. I'm being stupid—just like a minute ago, with the sprinkler. I'm inventing things to be scared of.

"I'll go to the school," I say. Wanda smiles.

"Oh, Sofia, that's great. I really think it's the right choice. Listen, I have some brochures and things in my car. Let me grab them for you."

She slips out of my room, giving me one last grin before she pulls my bedroom door shut behind her. I stare at the door for a moment, listening to the sound of her footsteps on our stairs.

A strange emotion rushes through my body, and it takes me a long moment to recognize what it is. *Hope.* Since my mother died, I thought I'd never feel hopeful again, but there's no mistaking the fragile, feathery feeling in my stomach. St. Mary's Prep School. Maybe this is the sign I'd been hoping for.

Movement flickers at the corner of my eye. I jerk around, my hands groping for a weapon.

But it's just a cicada. The black bug crawls across my wall and disappears behind my dresser, wings twitching.

CHAPTER FOUR

Everything I own fits inside two olive-green military duffels and an oversized rolling suitcase covered in burgundy flowers. I packed the rest into cardboard boxes and sent them to our storage unit just outside Hope Springs. I'm giving the house one last walk-through when I spot my grandmother's needlepoint leaning against the wall in her now-empty room. *Jealousy is like a cancer*, it reads. Jodi and the others must not have seen it when they packed the rest of her things. I kneel on the floor and pick it up. The frame is smooth in my hands, the painted wood starting to chip. I think of my mom saying those words during our last phone call, and my chest twists.

I slide the picture into my suitcase. It fits perfectly in the front pocket.

A silver minivan pulls up as I'm lugging my bags to the side of the road. The words ST. MARY'S PREP stare out from the side door. A woman with a shaggy brown bob rolls down her window and sticks out her head.

"Sofia Flores, I hope?" she calls.

"That's me," I say, struggling to drag my bags across the muddy yard.

"Let me help you." The woman starts to open her door, but I pull my duffel over my shoulder, and shake my head. First rule of being the new girl—never show weakness.

"Nah. I got 'em."

The woman hops out of the van anyway. The top of her head barely clears my chin, but she tugs my over-stuffed duffel off my shoulder and hauls it to the back of the van. She unlatches the rear door with one hand and tosses the bag inside.

"I'm Sister Lauren," she says, reaching for my suitcase.

"Sister?" I glance down at her navy-blue St. Mary's sweatshirt and white sneakers. "You're a nun?"

She tosses her hair out of her eyes and shoots me a smile that wrinkles her nose. "Surprised?"

I shake my head—then cringe, wondering if God will smite me for lying to a nun. Sister Lauren just laughs.

"It's the clothes," she explains. "Usually, when people think of nuns, they think of the penguin suit and funny hat."

"You don't wear that?"

"Only during class and Mass." Sister Lauren brushes her hair behind one ear, a strand of chunky brown beads dangling from her wrist. She catches me looking at them and thrusts her arm forward.

"They're prayer beads. From Uganda," she explains. "I was a missionary there for a few years after divinity school."

"They're beautiful." I push the beads around her wrist, admiring the way the sunlight gleams against the wood.

"The women who made them were so inspiring. If you're interested in missionary work, let me know. We have some outstanding volunteer programs at St. Mary's."

I've never considered missionary work before, but I try to picture it. Flying to some faraway place with all my possessions packed away in a single suitcase. Helping out at an orphanage or school. I smile at the thought. It's the kind of thing that would have made my mother proud.

"I'll definitely think about it."

Sister Lauren loads my last duffel into the back of the van and slams the door closed. Her eyes flick to the house behind me. "Is there anyone you want to say good-bye to before we head out?"

I look over my shoulder at the last place I ever lived with my mother. The windows are dark and a FOR RENT sign stands in the yard, swaying in the wind.

I square my shoulders and take a deep breath.

"Nope," I say, blinking a tear away. "It's just me."

* * *

The minivan crawls through the streets toward West 72, the only highway that leads out of Friend. We're traveling at ten miles below the speed limit and stopping at every light. At this rate, it's going to take three hours to get to Hope Springs. Pastel-colored houses and depressing strip malls creep past my window, then slowly give way to stretches of flat, dusty land and spindly trees. A headache pounds at the back of my skull. My eyes droop . . .

I must have fallen asleep because, a second later, I'm blinking my eyes open and wiping the drool from my chin. We're not in Friend anymore. Tangled tree branches drip over the road above us, blocking out the sky. A thick layer of moss covers their trunks and knotted roots creep up from the ground like huge, muscular snakes. It's like we've driven into a Gothic fairy tale.

Sister Lauren has the radio turned to some Christian rock station and she's singing along under her breath. She turns the volume down when she notices me stir.

"You awake?" she asks.

"Yeah." I groan and roll my head, trying to stretch my sore muscles. The road has changed from paved cement to packed dirt, making the minivan rock. "How long was I out?"

"About an hour. We're getting close."

I nod and peer out the window. Sunlight trickles through the trees like gold dust. It feels different than the sun in Friend. Softer. Like someone's found the dimmer switch. Wind moves through the trees, making the branches sway lazily.

We roll past massive houses with peeling painted and shuttered windows, and weave through a small business district. It's the middle of the week, but most of the shops are dark, and CLOSED signs hang in their windows. I frown and glance behind us. No cars on the street and no people on the sidewalks. The whole town has a dreamy, unreal quality to it. It makes me think of *Sleeping Beauty*. Not the Disney movie, but this older fairy tale my mom used to read to me before bed. In that version, the whole town fell asleep when Beauty pricked her finger. They'd slept for a hundred years before the Prince rode in to rescue her.

"It's pretty here," I say. We pull off the main street and down another dirt road that's lined with twisted, dripping trees.

"Isn't it?" Sister Lauren says. "I'm still getting used to all the moss and weeping willows."

"You aren't from the South?"

"Nope. I'm a new girl, just like you. I started at St. Mary's this year, actually. I almost missed the deadline to get my resume in for the job, but I guess the Big Guy was on my side, because I made it in just under the wire."

Sister Lauren smiles and touches the tiny silver cross hanging from her neck.

"What do you teach?" I ask.

"English lit."

I twist toward her in my seat. "That's my favorite subject. Or it was at my old school."

"Yeah? What were you reading?"

"Lots of Shakespeare and Dickens. And we just finished a unit on *The Great Gatsby*."

Sister Lauren places a hand over her heart. "Oh, *Gatsby*," she says in a swoony voice, like she's talking about an ex-boyfriend. "That's one of my favorites. You're a junior, right? You're probably in Period 1 English with me on Mondays. I'll see you bright and early at seven thirty."

"Seven thirty in the *morning*?"

Sister Lauren laughs. "Intense, right? Father Marcus runs a tight ship."

"Sounds like it." I study Sister Lauren's face. She has big eyes, and the kind of friendly smile that's almost familiar. "Is Father Marcus the principal?"

"He's the dean," Sister Lauren explains. "He's been with St. Mary's longer than any other teacher. You'll meet him today."

I knot my hands in my lap, trying not to show my nerves. Sister Lauren pulls up to a stop sign and glances over at me.

"Don't look so terrified," she says. "None of the teachers at St. Mary's bite."

An anxious laugh escapes my lips, and the sound is so unexpected that I flinch. I haven't laughed since Mom died. Heat rises in my cheeks. I'm not sure if I should feel guilty or relieved. It feels wrong to laugh now that she's gone—but also good. Like taking a drink of water after a long, punishing run.

Sister Lauren slows the minivan to a crawl and turns onto a wide, tree-lined road. A black iron sign arches above us. It reads: ST. MARY'S PREP.

"Home sweet home," Sister Lauren says. My heart climbs into my throat. We crawl forward, and I scoot to the edge of my seat. Red brick and stained glass peek through the moss-covered trees. I spot circular windows that look like eyes, and tall stone pillars. An elaborate iron gate circles the school grounds.

To keep us from getting out. I bite my lip, pushing that thought out of my head. If Dr. Keller were here, he'd say I was letting paranoia control me, and he'd make me do my breathing exercises. But I don't want to seem like a freak in front of Sister Lauren, so I just stare straight ahead, studying my new home.

St. Mary's Preparatory Institute is three stories high, and shaped like a giant U. The bricks are discolored from years of exposure to the sun and wind, and a white cross peers down from the school's highest tower. Fear prickles along my spine as we drive beneath the dark shadow it casts over the road.

"It's . . . old," I say. A statue of the Virgin Mary stands in the courtyard between the school's two wings. Mary bows her head, her arms open and welcoming. Rust stains the white stone of her dress. It looks like blood winding down her legs and pooling at her feet.

"I know it's a bit spooky," Sister Lauren says, "but you'll get used to it. That's our chapel over there." She points to a small, whitewashed building to the left of the main school. "It's the only one on campus, which means the boys use it, too. But you go to Mass at different times, so you won't see them."

I nod. Ivy snakes over the chapel's white walls and stained glass, practically obscuring the colorful images of Jesus and the saints. A window on the highest floor is boarded up. It's like the building has turned wild. Like the woods are trying to reclaim it.

Sister Lauren pulls the minivan to a stop next to the tall iron fence surrounding the school. A priest in black robes waits at the front entrance. He climbs down the steps, his hem trailing in the dirt behind him. Metal clinks against metal as he unlocks the padlock and drags the gates open.

"Listen, Father Marcus can be . . . intense," Sister Lauren says. The quality of her voice has changed. She sounds younger, less sure of herself.

"Intense how?" I ask. Sister Lauren flashes a stiff smile.

"You'll see."

We drive through the gates and park the van near the steps. As I get out of the car, I study Father Marcus's deeply lined face and hooded eyes. He doesn't look mean, exactly. But he's not someone I'd want to cross.

"Thank you for your trouble, Sister." Father Marcus's voice is strong and deep, made for leading prayers and reciting announcements at the front of a packed auditorium. Wispy, dandelion puffs of hair form a halo around his bald head. "If you'll take the van back to the garage, I can handle Miss Flores from here."

"But the bags—"

Father Marcus raises a hand, cutting Sister Lauren

off. His eyes fall on me. The effect is similar to being hit with a spotlight. I feel exposed. Naked. I glance at my shoes, my cheeks growing hot.

"Miss Flores looks perfectly able-bodied. I'm certain she can manage them. You'll meet us at the entrance to the girls' dormitories so you can show Sofia to her room."

"Of course," Sister Lauren says. She climbs into the van while I wrestle my bags out of the back. The grounds are strangely silent. I can't even hear the distant drone of insects that I've grown accustomed to since moving to the South. I strain my ears, listening for voices, or a car engine, or wind rustling through the tree branches. There's nothing.

Sister Lauren whispers "good luck" as I walk past her window. She winks and drives away, the van's tires spitting up rocks and clouds of dirt behind her.

"I'm Father Marcus," the priest says once we're alone.

"Sofia," I say. I pull a duffel bag over my shoulder, trying not to grimace at its weight. "But I guess you knew that already."

"I'm the dean of St. Mary's Preparatory Institute," Father Marcus continues, as though I hadn't said anything. "Please, follow me."

He turns and starts down the path toward the school at a steady clip. I hurry to keep up with him, tugging my suitcase along behind me. One of the wheels gets caught on a rock and the duffle topples over, spilling its contents onto the ground. Father Marcus stops walking and waits for me to gather my things, but he doesn't offer to help.

"The boys' dormitories are located in the East Wing," he explains once I pull my suitcase upright. "You'll find the girls' dormitories located in the West. Girls are not allowed anywhere near the East Wing and vice versa."

I balance the duffel bag back on top of my rolling suitcase. "Yes, sir."

Father Marcus cocks an eyebrow, nose wrinkled in distaste. "The main building holds all classrooms, the school's auditorium, as well as my offices and your teachers' sleeping quarters. It also acts as a buffer between the two wings to prevent any . . . fraternization. You are not allowed in the main building outside of school hours without written permission from an instructor. Is that clear?"

Heat gathers in my face. "Yes, sir."

Father Marcus narrows his hooded eyes. "In this institution, we believe that unnecessary contact between the sexes prevents students from realizing their full relationship with the Lord." He pauses and presses his dry lips together. Then he turns, black robes billowing behind him. "This way, please."

I struggle up the stairs, following Father Marcus through heavy double doors that open onto a dimly lit hall. I stop in my tracks as soon as the door slams shut behind me. My other duffel bag slips from my shoulder.

An arched ceiling soars overhead, crisscrossed with ancient wooden beams. Chipped frames line the walls, each holding a faded oil painting of some long-dead saint. Their eyes stare out at me. Watching. Sunlight streams through the stained glass, painting the creaky wooden floorboards red and blue and gold. The school is somehow beautiful and terrible at the same time. Like an extravagant mansion left to decay.

"Sofia?" Father Marcus stands at the foot of a twisting staircase, one gnarled hand resting on the ornately carved handrail. A ring glitters from his index finger, a silver cross set against a shield.

"Sorry," I murmur, hurrying to catch up. I try not to groan as I hoist my luggage up the stairs.

"St. Mary's is one of the oldest Catholic schools in the country," Father Marcus explains as we climb. "We're second only to Ursuline Academy in New Orleans."

I stop on the second-floor landing, next to a marble statue of Jesus, to catch my breath. "I think I read that on your website," I say. Father Marcus curls his lip at the mention of their website, like the Internet is something unpleasant that he wishes would return to the hell it came from.

"Many of our works of art and furnishings date

back over two hundred years," he continues, "so we'd appreciate if you'd refrain from carving your initials into our walls, or sticking gum on the bottom of your bed."

"I wouldn't, I mean—"

"The grounds are off-limits after nine in the evening and before six," Father Marcus says, talking over me. "Anyone caught outdoors during those periods will be . . . punished."

The way he says "punished" sets my teeth on edge. We reach the top of the stairs and stop beside a thick wooden door. A smudged plaque next to the door reads LADIES' DORMITORIES.

"We are here to help save your soul, Miss Flores," Father Marcus continues. "I make that promise to every young person who walks through our gates. But it must be understood, we do not suffer"—his upper lip curls— "*defiance*. You will respect your instructors, and you will show up *daily* for Mass services. I expect to see you at confession."

He wets his lips, leaving beads of saliva in the corners of his mouth. "You are here on scholarship, are you not?"

I nod, not sure I trust myself to speak.

"Understand that your scholarship is contingent upon you keeping up your grades, participating in school activities, and respecting our morality code." Father Marcus lifts a thin, crooked finger. "One misstep and your scholarship privileges will be revoked. Is that clear, Miss Flores?"

I knew my scholarship could be revoked, but hearing Father Marcus say it makes it actually seem possible. My chest tightens. If St. Mary's doesn't work out, that leaves me back in a group home in Friend.

I swallow. "Yes, sir."

Footsteps thud on the steps below me. I flinch, but it's just Sister Lauren. She hurries up the staircase, her face slightly red.

"How was the tour?" she asks.

"Informative," Father Marcus says. He studies me for another long moment. "Sister Lauren will show you to your room from here. Good luck, Miss Flores."

He nods at me and then heads back to the first floor. Sister Lauren peers down the staircase after him.

"I think he likes you," she says when she's certain he's out of earshot. She takes my duffel bag off my shoulder.

I stare at her, incredulous. "Why would you think that?"

"I've never heard him wish anyone luck before."

"Maybe he just thinks I'll need it."

Sister Lauren flashes me a kind smile. She pulls a heavy brass key out of her pocket and unlocks the door to the dormitories.

"You'll feel better once you've met your new roomies,"

she says, leading me down a much more modern-looking hallway. Wipe boards and photographs hang from the doors, and I hear the faint sound of talking and giggling behind the walls. Everything seems so normal, so nice, but I've been the new girl more times than I can count and I'm not fooled. High school is hell. It doesn't matter how many cute photos these girls tape to their doors, or goofy messages they write. They're screwed-up underneath. Just like we all are.

But this time, Mom's not waiting at home to ask me about my day. I'm all on my own here. It suddenly feels as if someone's wrapped a meaty hand around my windpipe.

"Breathe," I mutter to myself.

"Did you say something?" Sister Lauren asks, glancing over her shoulder. I shake my head.

"No, I . . . I'm fine."

Sister Lauren stops at a door marked 23 and knocks twice before pushing it open.

"Ladies, I'd like you all to meet your new roommate," she says. I take one last deep breath, and tug my bags through the door.

"Hi—" My suitcase handle slips from my fingers and slams to the floor.

Brooklyn lies on her stomach on the floor, playing with a pair of oversized black glasses. Bright-red lipstick stains her mouth. Riley leans against the far window, her tanned arms crossed over her chest. She cocks one eyebrow, a grin twisting her lips.

"Sofia?" Sister Lauren touches my arm. A shiver skips over my skin. The room comes into focus, and I realize I'm mistaken. The girl I'd thought was Riley is actually Asian. Freckles cover her round face and big cheeks, and there's a cherry-red knit hat topped with a silver pom-pom pulled low over her glossy black hair. Riley wouldn't be caught dead in that hat.

The other girl sits up, the black glasses still dangling from her fingers. Her red lipstick reminds me of Brooklyn, but otherwise she looks completely different. She's tiny, for one thing. I'd mistake her for a little girl if I saw her from behind. Tangled blonde hair hangs almost to her hips. She smiles at me, and I notice a gap between her two front teeth.

I crouch to pick up my suitcase, worried that I've already killed my reputation.

"Hi," I say, straightening. "I'm Sofia."

The Asian girl steps forward. The pom-pom on her hat bobbles as she walks. Her smile gets wider. It's so genuine and sincere that it catches me off guard.

"I'm Leena," she says, sticking out a hand to help me with my suitcase. "Welcome to St. Mary's."

CHAPTER FIVE

As soon as Sister Lauren pulls the door closed, Leena pushes the fuzzy red hat off her forehead and presses an ear to the door, screwing up her freckled face in concentration. "You think she suspected anything?" she whispers.

"Not a chance in hell," my other roommate drawls from her spot on the floor. She pulls down the front of her T-shirt to reveal a candy necklace that stains the skin on her neck pink and green.

"They don't allow candy here," she explains, tossing the oversized glasses she'd been playing with onto a pillow next to her knee. "Pretend they're . . . vitamins."

"Um, sure," I say. That's another new-girl rule—agree with everything, even if you don't mean it. I drop my duffel bags at the foot of the only unoccupied bed and look around. The dorm is tiny. Twin-sized beds crowd three of its four walls, two narrow dressers wedged between them. I guess we're supposed to share. Bedspreads and pillows spill onto the floor, and bookshelves stuffed with paperbacks and framed photographs of baby animals line the walls.

"What didn't Sister Lauren suspect?" I ask, glancing up at the ceiling. Someone started to paint a mural of the moon and stars across it but stopped midway through, leaving the rest of the space white.

"Our secret," Leena says in a conspiratorial voice. The word *secret* turns my stomach. Secrets only lead to trouble.

Leena plucks the black-framed glasses off the pillow and pushes them up her nose. She blinks, like she's seeing my face clearly for the first time. "What do you think, Sutton?" she asks the other girl. "Should we tell?"

Sutton has gotten up from the floor to study her reflection in the mirror on the back of the closet door, but she turns at the sound of Leena's voice. She flips her long, messy hair over her shoulder. "I don't know, Leenie-bean. You think we can trust her?"

"Look," I cut in, "whatever it is, I don't—"

But Leena is already crossing the room. She yanks a yellow-and-pink-striped pillow off her bed and tosses it to the floor.

"Ta-da!" she announces, motioning to a shivering ball of white fluff with bloodshot eyes.

"It's a bunny." I drop onto my bed, staring. The fluff ball looks at me, its pink nose twitching. It hops forward and sniffs Leena's pillow. Sutton releases a peal of laughter as Leena scoops the bunny off the bed.

"Ooh, he's the *best* bunny," Leena coos, making a kissy face. "Aren't you just the best bun-bun?"

"You look surprised," Sutton adds, nodding at me. She digs under her bed, and produces a warm can of Diet Dr Pepper. "Did you think we were gonna pull out a baggie of cocaine?"

"No," I say, but the doubt in my voice gives me away.

Sutton grins and hands me the soda. "Soda is against the rules, too," she says when I take the can from her. "Pretend it's . . . mineral water."

"Thanks," I say. I crack open the can and take a long drink. So far, this place doesn't seem terrible. I'm not sleeping on a concrete floor, and the girls are actually talking to me like they want to be friends.

"No problem," Sutton says. "And just so you know, neither of us is in here for drugs. No judgment if that's your deal. Pot just turns me into a space cadet."

"The boys giving you the pot turn you into a space cadet," Leena says. Sutton smirks.

"That, too." She sticks her candy necklace into her mouth and chews off one of the beads.

"I don't do drugs," I say, wiping a drop of Dr Pepper off my lower lip. Leena sits down next to me on the bed, and plops her bunny in my lap. I flinch, nearly dropping my soda.

"Meet Heathcliff. He's our fourth roomie."

"He lives in our closet," Sutton explains. "Don't worry, you won't even know he's here."

I stare down at the bunny, trying not to let my distaste show on my face. I've never been an animal person. When I was eight years old, I accidentally sat on my pet hamster, Mr. Whiskers (I wasn't a very creative child). Poor Mr. Whiskers barely survived. After that, Mom decided he'd be safer with our neighbors across the street.

Secretly, I was glad. I hated the way his cage smelled, and the twitchy, ratlike look of his little face. I could always hear him moving around in the dark while I slept. It gave me the creeps.

Leena frowns. "He isn't bothering you, is he?"

"Of course not! He's . . . sweet," I say, absently stroking Heathcliff's fur. I expect her to take him back, but she just leaves him in my lap, letting him gnaw on the edge of my jeans.

"Can you believe I found this cutie outside the chapel?" Leena asks, wrinkling her nose at Heathcliff. "His poor little leg was broken and he could barely hop."

"Leena made him a cast out of toothpicks and Band-Aids." Sutton rolls her eyes, but she leans forward and scratches Heathcliff behind his ears. The bunny hops toward the end of my bed and pushes his wet pink nose into her hand like he's looking for a treat. I try not to seem too relieved. That rabbit was starting to smell.

"Okay, time to spill," Sutton says. She pushes Heathcliff away and wipes her hand on her jean shorts. As she leans back against the bedframe, her skinny legs stretch out across the floor. "What are you in for?"

I frown and take another sip of soda. "What do you mean?"

"What horrible thing did you do to get sent here?" Leena asks. "It's already December and St. Mary's doesn't usually take new students midyear, so Sutton and I figured it had to be really bad."

"Stealing?" Sutton guesses. She pulls her legs to her chest and wraps her arms around them, resting her chin on her knees. "Drinking? Sleeping with your high school guidance counselor? If it's the last one, I'm going to need pics."

"Gross, Sutton," Leena cuts in, giggling. Sutton makes a face at her. Her front teeth are stained pink from the candy necklace.

"Wait." I hold up my hands to get them to stop talking. "What do you mean what did I do to get *sent* here?"

Leena stares at me. Her glasses magnify her dark eyes, making them look a little unsettling. "Didn't you know? This is where they send bad kids."

"Everyone here has gotten caught shooting heroin or sexting her English teacher or painting lewd graffiti on playground equipment," Sutton adds.

"Or, if you're me, your super-strict mother caught you trying a beer *for the first time ever* and flipped out," Leena mutters.

Sutton turns to her and smirks. "When you told me that story it was *four* beers, and you were sneaking into your bio classroom to set all the frogs free."

"They were going to dissect them!" Leena says. She throws a pillow at Sutton, but Sutton catches it before it hits her in the face. "It's not my fault there was an *alarm* on the freaking door." Leena shakes her head, exasperated, and turns back to me. "My mom completely freaked out at me. I have to call her every single day just to check in and, I swear, she thinks she'll be able to smell the beer on my breath through the phone. She's the worst—you have no idea."

Mom. Mother. She. I try to count how many times Leena has casually mentioned her mom already. My mom's cell phone photo flashes into my head: hair sticking out of her short ponytail, the Cheerio stuck to her cheek. I feel a needle prick of pain just below my left eye and blink until it goes away. I never realized how lucky I was to be annoyed by my mom.

"So, being sent here is, like, a punishment?" I ask, trying to keep my voice casual.

Sutton flashes me a sympathetic look. "No one told you, huh?"

I shake my head, remembering the way Wanda studied my face when she asked me whether I'd ever heard of St. Mary's. She had to have known the truth and she sent me here, anyway.

Does that mean she thinks I'm a bad kid? She's a social worker. Maybe she can tell that I'm rotten just by looking at me.

"So what did you do?" Leena scoots to the end of my bed and leans back against my pillow. "Was it really bad?"

My chest tightens, and I consider making something up. I could say I got sent here for shoplifting. I could even pretend to call my mom every day to check in, just like Leena.

The lie sounds so good that I want it to be true. But I have to keep telling myself that Mom is never going to pick up her phone again.

"My, um, mom was in an accident," I say. The words

feel strange in my mouth. I don't think I'll ever get used to saying them. "She died."

The color drains from Sutton's tanned face. "Shit, Sofia," she says. "That's awful."

"I'm so sorry we asked," Leena adds. She scoots closer to me and squeezes my arm. "It's got to be so awful to lose a parent. Sutton's dad—"

"He died, too," Sutton finishes, cutting Leena off. "It happened when I was really little, though, so I barely remember him. It's not the same."

I nod, and stare down at the bunny hopping around my bed. His white fur clings to my jeans and sheets. "My caseworker found this place," I say. "She thought it would be a good option since I don't have any family nearby. She didn't mention the part about it being a punishment."

"It's really not so bad. Promise," Sutton says. "Sure, St. Mary's can be strict. But there are perks, too. I mean, the eye candy can't be beat."

Leena grins and nods at the window behind her. "She means that the boys' dorms are just across the courtyard. Father Marcus makes them run sprints from the courtyard to the creek every morning at six o'clock sharp."

"I don't think he realizes we can see them from our window," Sutton adds.

I smile, grateful to think about anything other than Mom. I roll the empty soda can between my fingers. "Better than an alarm clock, I guess?"

"All girls at St. Mary's wake to the sounds of grunting, sweaty young men," Sutton says.

"At least it gives me something to say at confession each week." Leena folds her hands together, pretending to pray. "Dear Father, forgive me for I have sinned. I've had impure thoughts about a boy. *Again*."

"You've got a thing for a St. Mary's boy?" I ask.

"She's got a thing for *Julian Sellito*." Sutton's tongue curls around the name, making it sound dirty. Leena groans and puts her head in her lap.

"He's my one weakness," she admits, hiding her face, her voice muffled. "He makes me want to do very bad things."

"But he barely knows she exists, because Leenie-bean is a total prude." Sutton flicks the pom-pom on Leena's fuzzy red hat, making it bob in place. Leena shoots her a look, then leans forward and scoops up Heathcliff.

"I'm not a prude." Leena strokes Heathcliff's back, blushing so hard that her freckles turn red. "Jude and I have just never had a chance to talk before. Now that we're both in the play, I'll finally get a shot."

"Maybe lose the hat first," Sutton suggests.

Leena's lips part in a wide grin. "You haven't even seen the best part." She pinches the folded edge of the hat, and tinny music echoes through the room.

"*Rocking around, the Christmas tree, have a happy holiday . . .*"

Leena wiggles her hips and bounces in place. I laugh at her ridiculous dance.

"It comes with Velcro antlers, too," she says, collapsing back onto my bunk. "You can stick 'em on the sides and pretend to be a reindeer."

Sutton scrunches up her face, laughing. "Stop! Put it out of its misery!"

"*Fine.*" Leena pulls the hat off. Her hair sticks straight up from her head. "Better?"

"Perfect," Sutton says. "He'll definitely fall in love with you now."

"Maybe." Leena shrugs, turning a little red. "Unless some other girl gets him first."

"Don't be crazy. Only a total bitch would go after Jude." Sutton's eyes flick over to me. "Leena's been in love with this guy since freshman year," she explains. "Everyone knows that."

"Right," I say, picking a piece of white fluff off my jeans. "What about you? Are you swooning over a St. Mary's boy, too?"

"Nah, my guy's a townie," Sutton says. She scrunches

her hair with one hand, making it look even more tousled. "I sneak out to see him sometimes, but, you know. It's tricky. St. Mary's has rules about dating."

I frown. "What kind of rules?"

"Don't," Leena says, and Sutton snickers. "That's their entire policy. Don't date, ever. It's evil. The Lord will smite you. Not that my mom would ever let me be alone with a guy anyway. I'm pretty sure she's hoping I'll let her pick the guy I marry."

I wince. There it is again—*mom*. I never realized before how often people mention their mothers.

Leena looks at me and her face falls. "Oh God, I didn't even think . . ." she says. "I shouldn't be complaining about my mom when . . ."

"She didn't mean anything by it, Sofia, really," Sutton adds.

"No—I know. I'm sorry, I didn't mean to react like that." If I don't get it together, I'm going to be known as the girl with the dead mom all year. I force my lips into a smile and try to think of something to change the subject. "So they're pretty strict here?"

Leena's shoulders unclench. Crisis averted. "It's not so bad. Kind of like going to school in the fifties," she explains.

Sutton snorts. "Yeah, the eighteen fifties," she says. She digs another can of soda out from under her bed, and cracks it open. I must have a worried expression on my face because she tilts her head, sympathetically. "Don't worry, Sofia," she says. "There are ways around all the rules. We'll help you navigate."

"I don't know. I'm here on scholarship," I say. "If I get expelled—"

"You won't get expelled," Leena cuts in. "They haven't expelled anyone in years."

"That's right," Sutton adds, flashing me a wolfish grin. She lowers her voice, making it sound creepy. "Once you're at St. Mary's, you *never* escape."

"Really?" I laugh nervously. Wind creeps in through the open window, raising goose bumps on my arms. I shiver and Sutton's smile softens.

"Sofia, I'm kidding," she says. "Seriously, don't look so freaked. This place is totally normal. No worse than any other crappy school I've been to."

"Of course." I force my lips into a smile, and push myself out of bed. "It's getting a little cold. Do you mind if I close this?"

I nod at the window. Sutton and Leena both shrug, so I cross the room and push aside the curtains. Something catches my eye.

Three long gouges claw across the windowsill. I frown and run a finger over them, feeling the grooves' sharp edges, the tiny splinters sticking out of the wood. They look like they were made by fingernails. Like someone tried to claw her way out of this place.

* * *

I lay awake that night, Sutton's words running through my head.

Once you're at St. Mary's, you never escape.

Goose bumps crawl up my skin. The claw marks on the windowsill flash through my head, and I roll onto my side, mattress springs creaking beneath me. If Mom were here, she'd tell me to stop obsessing. Sutton was joking. I'm letting fear control me.

A tear crawls down my cheek. I find my thumb in the dark and tug at a piece of skin near the nail. I can't keep doing this. I'll never fit in if my roommates wake up and hear me crying about my dead mom.

"Go to sleep," I whisper to myself. Heathcliff hops back and forth, paws crunching on the shredded newspaper lining the bottom of his cage. I pull my pillow over my head to block him out. The faint scent of rabbit piss hangs in the air, making me feel sick.

Leena shifts in bed. Sutton releases a light snore and mutters something under her breath. They've both been asleep for hours. It's like they don't hear the bunny rustling around in its cage. They don't see the way its red eyes seem to glow in the dark.

I stare at the back of Leena's head. If anyone should

be kept awake by the bunny, it should be her. He's her little bun-bun, after all. But Leena fell asleep almost as soon as she crawled into bed. Right after her nightly phone call with her mom.

Jealousy is like a cancer in your bones, I remind myself. I squeeze my eyes shut. Mom would tell me to find the silver lining. Don't let jealousy consume me.

A minute passes. Heathcliff starts drinking from his water dispenser. There's a tiny silver ball lodged in the spigot to keep the water from rushing out all at once. When Heathcliff licks it, the metal ball hits the side of the spigot, making a kind of wet, clicking sound.

Click click click. Pause. *Click click click.*

It reminds me, strangely, of my grandmother's rosary beads clicking against her table. I think of her sunken face, her bloodshot eyes, and raspy voice. *Diablo,* she called me. *Devil.* But I'm not evil. Dr. Keller told me I'm not. Brooklyn was wrong.

Click click click.

The sound haunts my dreams long after I drift off to sleep.

CHAPTER SIX

I wake the next morning to the sounds of someone shuffling around the room.

"Get up, sleepy," Leena says. I roll over, groaning. Heathcliff kept me up most of the night. I'd be surprised if I got more than an hour of sleep.

Leena's piled her black hair on top of her head in a messy bun. She pulls on a fuzzy robe covered in giant yellow lemons. I stare at it and instantly hear my mother's voice. *When life gives you lemons, make lemonade.* I smile sadly. I always hated when she said that, but I'd give anything to hear her say it again.

"Mass is in a half an hour," Leena says, filling Heathcliff's food bowl with tiny brown pellets.

"What time is it?" I mutter, pushing myself up. I didn't bother unpacking last night. I reach for the duffel bag and dig around for my toiletry case. Leena loads bottles of shampoo and body wash into a plastic shower caddy.

"Just after six," she says. She picks up a can of raspberry-scented shaving cream, shakes it, then tosses it into the trash can next to her dresser. "Sutton's already in line for the shower. I told her we'd meet her. Hurry, hurry!"

Make lemonade, I tell myself. I slip on a pair of brand-new flip-flops that I bought for the showers, grab my towel, and follow Leena out of our room. The line for the bathroom stretches all the way down the hall.

"You've got to get up early to get in a good shower," Leena says as we take our place next to Sutton at the end of the line. "But Sutton was too busy sexting her boyfriend this morning and forgot to wake me up." She shoots Sutton an annoyed look.

Sutton giggles. "What can I say? I've got to keep things interesting."

"You have a cell phone?" I ask. Wanda told me that they weren't allowed and made me put mine in storage. Sutton presses a finger to her lips.

"A *secret* cell phone," she whispers. "Shhh."

I glance around, but the other girls aren't paying attention to us. I expected to hear talking and giggling as we wait in line, but the St. Mary's girls seem different. Strange, even. They're quiet, and the circles under their eyes tell me I'm not the only one who didn't get much sleep last night.

Father Marcus's voice echoes through my head. *We do not suffer defiance.*

I turn back to Sutton, careful to keep my voice low. "What did you send him?" I ask.

Sutton tightens the belt on her bathrobe. "Nothing crazy," she says, eyes wide and innocent. "Just a shot of me and my two besties."

I frown. "Are you talking about us?" I ask. Leena groans and pulls me closer.

"She's talking about her *boobs*," she whispers into my ear.

Sutton bursts into laughter. "You're just jealous," she says, pushing her cleavage together.

We're running late by the time we finally leave the dormitories and head through the wooded grounds to the chapel. Every girl in St. Mary's has on the same uniform: blue jacket, plaid skirt, white polo, and stiff saddle shoes. Leena dresses her outfit up with dangly beaded earrings, and Sutton folds her waistband over twice, leaving two inches of skin between the bottom of her skirt and the top of her knees. As she races to the chapel, her skirt twists in the cool autumn wind and I notice that she has deep scratches crisscrossing her knees and thighs.

"It's not some crazy sex thing," she says when she catches me looking. "I'm on the varsity field hockey team this year." She winks. "Don't look so scandalized."

Leena and Sutton hurry ahead of me, easily picking their way past rocks and gnarled tree roots. I move slower, stumbling over twigs and catching my heavy skirt on the bushes and branches that line the path. The grounds are beautiful but overgrown, the dirt paths crowded with weeds and pebbles. St. Mary's girls flit through the trees around me like strange exotic birds. I see them from the corners of my eyes—a bare leg, a lock of blonde hair, or a spot of blue plaid—but they're gone by the time I turn my head.

Sutton grabs my arm and tugs. She's strong for someone so tiny, and I stumble forward a few feet. "Come *on*. If we're late, we miss the altar boys and they're the best part."

"You don't want to be late to your first Mass," Leena adds ominously. She shakes her head for emphasis, and her dangly earrings knock against the sides of her face.

I force my feet to move faster, ignoring the sharp pebbles piercing the soles of my shoes, and the whip-thin sticks slicing at my bare ankles. The chapel sits just ahead, its whitewashed walls slightly yellow in the early morning light. Church bells peal through the air. A crow leaps from a nearby tree, cawing.

Sutton, Leena, and I slip through the heavy doors. A second later, a cute guy wearing a white robe pulls the doors shut with a thud.

"Just made it," Sutton whispers, smiling at the altar boy. Leena pushes her forward.

"You have a boyfriend," she reminds her in a loud whisper.

"I might not be planning to buy, but that doesn't mean I can't check out the merchandise," Sutton says, glancing over her shoulder. The boy keeps his gaze focused dead ahead, like he's some handsome Roman statue.

Most of the pews are already full, so we head to the front of the chapel. Sutton and Leena kneel next to the very first pew, cross themselves, and then slide down the row to make room for me. I copy their movements, even though it feels strange to cross myself. I can't shake the feeling that everyone's watching me, waiting for me to mess up.

Leena and Sutton kneel on the floor of the pew, resting their clenched hands on the back of the row in front of us. They close their eyes and bow their heads. I mimic them, but I keep my eyes open a slit so I can see what's happening. I've never been to a service like this before—my mom hated church.

The room is small and bare. Wooden pews stretch across the floor, surrounded by empty white walls. A small oil painting of the Virgin Mary hangs from the wall behind the altar. The stained glass windows are the only other decorations.

An altar boy pulls the heavy curtains behind the altar open and ties them to the side with thick rope. Another boy wearing white robes walks into the chapel. He carries an ornate golden cross. Two more file in behind him, each holding a single lit candle. I study them until I notice that everyone else still has their eyes closed. I snap mine shut and clench my hands tighter.

I hear more movement at the front of the chapel, but I resist the urge to open my eyes. A heavy smell floats through the air, clouding my head with strange spices, vanilla, and smoke.

Silence fills the room. There must be a hundred other students in the chapel with us, but no one coughs or whispers or laughs. Beside me, Leena seems to be holding her breath.

"Peace be with you," Father Marcus says in a deep, gravelly voice.

"And also with you," the students around me recite, their voices merging into one.

Leena touches me on the shoulder and my eyes flicker open. Everyone else has already opened their eyes and taken their seats. Even Leena and Sutton have slid, silently, back into the pew. I'm the only one in the entire chapel still kneeling.

My palms sweaty, I take my seat on the pew next to Leena. It's like I'm in the middle of a complicated dance, only no one taught me the steps.

Father Marcus stands at the front of the room, surrounded by a small army of altar boys in white robes. Father Marcus wears a wine-colored robe, gold thread glinting from the hems of his sleeves. Another altar boy stands beside him, clutching a heavy, leather-bound Bible in his hands.

"And now, a reading," Father Marcus announces. The altar boy hands Father Marcus the Bible. He's taller than the priest and he has to bend over to hand him the Bible. I wonder if he's a student from the boys' school. Or maybe he's Father Marcus's apprentice—like a priest in training?

"Please turn your Bibles to John, chapter two, verse fifteen," Father Marcus says.

Everyone around me reaches for the Bibles hanging from the shelves on the back of the rows in front of us, but I'm distracted by the altar boy. He hovers just behind Father Marcus, his face all hard lines and sharp angles.

He looks like he was carved from stone. Shadows pool in the dips and curves of his skin, elongating his nose and chin, and making his eyes look deeper than they should. A small wooden cross hangs from a leather cord around his neck. He rubs it with his thumb while Father Marcus speaks.

"Sofia," Leena whispers, poking me in the ribs. She has her Bible spread out between us, offering to share. I tear my eyes away from the altar boy and try to follow along.

"For everything in the world, the lust of the flesh, the lust of the eyes, and the pride of life," Father Marcus reads, *"comes not from the Father, but from the world."*

Father Marcus looks up from his Bible and stares over our heads with a glassy, unfocused look. He lets the silence hang. Then he licks his thin lips and turns the page, the sound echoing off the walls.

"The lust of the eyes comes *not* from the Father, but from the *world*," he repeats, louder this time. "Here, John is warning you about beauty and lust and *sex*—"

Sutton giggles. She tries to cover it with a cough, but she's too late. Father Marcus fixes his gaze on her, fury etched across his ancient face. Sutton stares at her knees, her face going pale. The energy in the room changes. Students shift in their pews. No one dares to make a noise.

Father Marcus clears his throat and tears his eyes away from Sutton. "John is warning you that these things were created not by God, but by the world. To *tempt* you. Desire is a temptation. Want of any kind is a temptation. *Do not love the world, or anything in the world*, John writes. *If anyone loves the world, love for the Father is not in them.*"

I glance away from Father Marcus at the same moment that the altar boy turns toward the audience. His eyes lock on mine.

Shaggy black hair hangs over his forehead and ears, just past needing a haircut. Two thick eyebrows arc over his eyes, giving him the look of someone who's always on the verge of laughing.

I don't realize I've stopped breathing until the air around me turns hazy. Sutton was right. The altar boys here are *hot*. The boy cocks one of his amazing eyebrows. It changes his entire face. Now he looks boy-next-door cute. The kind of guy who teases you when he likes you.

"Leena," I whisper. She glances up from her Bible. I nod at the altar boy. "Who's that?"

"Oh." Leena reddens and glances down at her lap, a smile twisting her lips. "That's Jude, the guy I was telling you about. I think I just caught him looking at me. Did you see?"

CHAPTER SEVEN

*O*nly *a total bitch would go after Jude.*

Sutton's warning echoes in my head. I didn't even know who he was, I remind myself. I didn't mean to stare at him.

I make my way alone to my first class of the day. St. Mary's is a maze. The hallways twist around one another and dead-end at strange places. Stairways seem to appear out of nowhere, and the light is so dim that I can barely see two feet in front of me. I get the feeling that whoever built this school wanted the students to get lost.

Once you're at St. Mary's, you never escape . . .

"Stop it," I mutter to myself, pushing Sutton's creepy warning out of my head. A crow flies past the window, its shadow stretching long across the hall. A shrieking laugh booms from inside a classroom and then cuts off as a door slams.

I wander down wrong hallways twice before finally digging out the map Leena sketched for me. She went over my schedule after Mass and drew little stars on all my classes. I have a strange thought as I stare down at the paper—what if Leena intentionally drew the stars in the wrong places? What if she wanted me to get lost?

I shake my head, pushing the thought aside. I have no reason to mistrust Leena—she's been nothing but nice to me. I stop in the middle of the hallway and squint down at my map.

A girl rushes past me, knocking into my arm. My map and notebooks go flying.

"Sorry," she calls over her shoulder.

"Wait!" I yell after her. "Do you know where Sister Lauren's—"

But the girl disappears around the corner before I finish my question. I drop to my knees and gather my notebooks.

"Hey—" The voice sounds like a hiss, and it comes from right next to me. I jerk my head up, but there's no one there. I hug my books to my chest, and push myself to my feet.

"Hello?" I call.

Someone giggles. The sound rises, and then fades just as quickly. I hurry to the end of the hallway and peer around the corner just in time to see a door swing shut. The hallways are now completely empty. It's my first day and I'm late.

"Creepiest school ever," I mutter, glancing at Leena's map as I retrace my steps. My English class is room 108. It's just two hallways down, which is strange. I could've sworn I was just there. I follow the map and find room 108 hiding at the end of a hallway. Finally. I hover near the doorway, listening to the students talk and laugh and greet their friends. No one looks at me, but I still feel awkward.

"All right, everyone, settle down," Sister Lauren says, standing behind an old wooden desk. I didn't recognize her in her full nun's habit. Black robes rustle around her legs and a white headpiece obscures her short brown hair. A long gold cross hangs from her neck. I clear my throat to get her attention.

"Sofia! I didn't see you there," she says, smiling. "Welcome to Junior English. Let's see, there's a free desk in the corner, next to Mr. Sellito. Go ahead and take a seat."

Mr. Sellito. I turn and see Jude crouched over a desk near the wall. He glances up at the sound of his name, but doesn't look at me. He's dressed like all the other boys now, in creased navy pants and a stiff white shirt, a plaid tie knotted around his neck. A dark lock of hair falls over his forehead, blocking most of his face. I replay the moment where our eyes locked in the chapel, and heat rushes to my face.

Only a total bitch . . .

I grit my teeth, forcing the words out of my head. I *didn't* go after Jude, so I have no reason to feel guilty. Still, Sutton's warning is stuck in my head. She seems very protective of Leena, and I don't want to ruin the only two friendships I have at St. Mary's. I try to ask Sister Lauren if there's another desk, but she's already turned to write something on the chalkboard.

People are looking at me. Someone giggles in the back row. I stare down at my notebooks and hurry to my desk.

"Let's all turn to page thirteen," Sister Lauren says, dusting the chalk off her hands. She opens the top drawer of her desk and pulls out a paperback book. "Sofia, you're welcome to use my copy until we get you one of your own."

She drops the book onto my desk. I blink down at it and, for a second, I think I'm seeing things.

The Tempest. Of course that's what we're reading.

Sister Lauren's copy looks exactly like the one I have back in my dorm. A woman with wild red hair gazes out over an angry sea. I stare at the woman's back for a long moment, daring her to turn and look at me. To smile her horrible smile. All teeth and hair.

Jude shifts in the seat next to me. He still smells like the smoky vanilla incense that was burning in the chapel. I tilt my head to the side, pretending to stare at the crack running across the wall behind his shoulder so that I can study him from the corner of my eye. He's scribbling something in a battered notebook, but it doesn't look like notes. His handwriting is small and slanted and half the words are scribbled out.

He pushes his sleeves up to his elbows. He's wearing the same wooden cross he had on in the chapel, only he's knotted the leather around his wrist, like a bracelet. The cross is worn and shiny, as though it's been rubbed smooth by his hands.

"In this scene, Prospero and Miranda have just witnessed the shipwreck," Sister Lauren begins. I tear my eyes away from Jude and stare down at my book.

The class drags. I've read *The Tempest* so many times that it's hard to pay attention as Sister Lauren talks about themes and imagery. My eyes glaze over, and my stiff new shoes dig into the backs of my feet. I can practically feel the blisters forming on my skin.

"Sofia?" Sister Lauren says.

The sound of my name snaps me back to attention. I blink. "Um, yeah?"

"Can you tell me why you think this passage was so compelling?"

My palms are immediately sweaty as I start flipping through the yellowed pages. The words blur together. "Um . . ."

A second ticks past. I narrow my eyes, pretending to study a line of text. I have this play practically memorized, but I have no idea which passage she's talking about.

"Come *on* . . ." the girl behind me mutters. Another student laughs under his breath. I curl my fingers around the edges of the book. I want to sink down through the floor and disappear.

"*The isle is full of noises,*" Jude whispers. He tilts his head toward me, pretending to study the cross knotted at his wrist. "Caliban's speech. Act 3, scene 2."

I feel an instant gut punch of relief. I wrote a paper on Caliban's speech last year. "This passage is compelling because it's so different from anything Caliban has said before. It changes the way the audience views him. They know he's a tortured soul."

"Very good, Sofia," Sister Lauren says. She writes Caliban's name on the blackboard, the chalk sending a high-pitched screech through the room. "Now if you'll all—"

The bell rings, cutting her off. Students around me stand and gather their things. I twist around, hoping to catch Jude and thank him. But he's already hurrying toward the door.

"Sofia?" Sister Lauren calls from the front of the classroom. "Could I speak to you for a moment?"

I grab my notebooks and walk up to Sister Lauren's desk as she erases the chalkboard. "Listen, if this is about how I need to follow along better, I know—"

"What are you talking about?" Sister Lauren leans against the chalkboard. "I think you did a great job today."

"Oh. Thank you."

"I wanted to talk to you about the school play. I'm directing this year and I thought you might be interested in helping out. We're doing *The Tempest*," she says, nodding at the paperback in my hands.

I hesitate. Leena said she and Jude were in the play. I don't want her to think I'm interfering.

"I know it sounds like a lot of extra work, and you're probably already overwhelmed, but you should consider it. First impressions are important at St. Mary's, and Father Marcus looks more"—Sister Lauren hesitates, searching for the right word—"*favorably* on students who get involved in school activities. He thinks it keeps them from getting into trouble."

Sister Lauren smiles, but there's an edge to her voice. I don't want to ask what kind of trouble she's talking about.

"What would I have to do?" I ask.

"Well, the roles are cast, but you could help with set design. You look like you'd be good with a nail gun."

The blood drains from my face. The sound of metal shooting through skin and bone echoes in my head.

"Sofia?" The voice makes me flinch. Sister Lauren is staring at me, confused. "Are you okay?" she asks. "I'm sorry, I was joking."

"I'll do the play," I say, swallowing and trying to dig up a smile. "But only if I don't have to use a nail gun."

* * *

After classes are over, Sister Lauren puts me to work painting sets. I kneel next to a cardboard tree, adding some painted texture to the bark. Spotlights shine down from the rafters, their glare so hot that a tiny bead of sweat rolls down my neck and disappears beneath the collar of my school uniform.

A senior boy named Connor saws a two-by-four in half backstage, and two girls talk in low voices while sorting through a trunk of plastic props. One of the girls is named Alice—I recognize her from my history class—but I haven't met the other girl. Someone practices the cello in the music room next door. Haunting snatches of music drift through the walls.

"Try to find the rhythm of the language," Sister Lauren says to the crowd of actors gathered in a semicircle around her. Leena catches my eye and waves. During lunch, I told her I'd be doing set design and she squealed so loud that half the cafeteria turned and looked at us.

I lift my hand to wave back just as Father Marcus pushes through the heavy stage curtains, his dark robes nearly blending into the shadows. He fixes me with his pale blue eyes and frowns. The wrinkles in his forehead deepen.

I lower my hand, feeling as if I've just flashed a symbol of the Antichrist instead of waving to a friend. Leena mentioned that Father Marcus comes to every practice, probably to make sure that no one accidentally touches a member of the opposite sex.

"Careful. You're dripping."

I flinch and whirl around, practically flinging my paintbrush across the stage. Jude leans against the wall behind me. The top few buttons of his uniform hang open, revealing the white T-shirt beneath. His plaid tie dangles, undone, around his neck.

"Oh—hi," I say.

"You sit next to me in English, right?" he asks, his mouth twisting into a grin.

"Yes," I say, looking away from his full lips. "About that, I wanted to thank you for—"

Jude shakes his head. "Hey, it's no big deal." He snaps his fingers. "Didn't I see you during Mass, too? You were with Leena?"

Leena's name jars me out of my stupor. *Off-limits.* "Yup." I turn back around and dunk my brush into the can of green paint. "And you're Jude, right? Leena's mentioned you."

I put a little something extra into the word *mentioned* but if Jude notices, he doesn't show it.

"Hold up." He leans forward, swiping his thumb across my knee. I flinch, but he holds up his hand, showing me a smear of green on his fingertip. "Gotta be more careful with that thing," he says, nodding at my paintbrush.

The skin along my leg prickles. I adjust my plaid skirt over my knee, feeling suddenly exposed.

"Mr. Sellito!" Father Marcus's sharp voice cuts through the auditorium. He steps away from the curtain, the heavy cross swinging around his neck like a pendulum. Jude looks up and Father Marcus glares, pointedly, at Jude's undone tie. "Make yourself *presentable*."

Jude's lips curl into a smile. He pulls his tie into a clumsy knot and buttons the top of his shirt. One of the girls behind me starts to giggle, but Jude doesn't seem to notice.

"Of course, sir," Jude says, crossing the stage to where the other actors are standing. "Sorry, sir."

Sister Lauren clears her throat. "Now that Jude's here, let's start at the top of act 3."

The actors shuffle around to grab their scripts and move into place. Jude slides his own rolled-up pages from his back pocket. I turn back to my task, anxious to drown them out. I've seen more than my fair share of teenagers butchering Shakespeare.

"Jude, begin with 'Admired Miranda,' whenever you're ready," Sister Lauren says.

There's a beat of silence. And then, "Admired Miranda. Indeed the top of admiration, worth what's dearest to the world . . ."

Jude's voice rumbles across the stage and sends a shiver dancing up my spine. I tilt my head—just a little—so I can watch him from the corner of my eye.

"Full many a lady I have eyed with best regard . . ."

He even *looks* different. There's something about the way he squares his shoulders and thrusts his jaw forward. There's no mischievous tilt to his lips now. He gazes at Leena like she's something precious. My breath catches. Another drop of paint hits my knee, pulling me out of the moment.

I flinch and wipe at the paint splotch with my thumb, smearing it across my leg. I turn to see if anyone's caught me, but Jude has entranced everyone. Even I find it hard to look away.

Jude's eyes lock on mine, and he angles his body ever so slightly in my direction. I glance over my shoulder, convinced there's some other, prettier girl behind me. But there's no one. He's looking at *me*.

"The harmony of their tongues hath into bondage brought my too diligent ear," he says in that deep voice. Another drop of paint hits my leg. This time, I don't even look down. I've read this play three times, but this is the first time I've ever heard it performed out loud. It's beautiful. Like a love poem. I find myself wishing I'd gotten here early enough to audition for a part. I imagine myself standing across from Jude instead of Leena.

Jude smiles slightly—just a quirk of his lips—and something inside my chest flips. "O you, so perfect and so peerless," he says, "are created of every creature's best."

When he finishes, the whole theater is still, as if under a spell. I feel as if I've just woken from a deep sleep.

I glance around the room, only to see that Leena's also looking directly at me, frowning. Guilt twists my stomach, but I push it away. It's not my fault Jude was looking at me. Leena already has the lead role in the play—what more does she want?

"Leena?" Sister Lauren says. "It's your line."

"Right." Leena turns back to her script. "If you'll . . . um . . . sit down." She hesitates, then motions to a stool at the corner of the stage a beat too late. "I'll bear your logs a . . . logs? Is that right?"

"We're actually on the next page." Jude shifts forward to point at her script, and Leena flinches. The script slips from her fingers.

"Sorry," she mumbles, bending to pick it up. Her face has turned a deep shade of red.

I should feel sorry for her but, instead, I feel a tiny prick of victory. I'd have been a much better Miranda. I know the play by heart.

"Um, I am a fool?" Leena says. "To weep for—" She flips to the next page, frowning.

"Leena, I think you turned one page too far," Sister Lauren says, cutting her off. "Start with 'I do not know one of my sex.'"

"I do not know one of my sex," Leena repeats, her voice low. She swallows and glances at her script, flipping quickly through the pages. "As . . . as well as it does . . . ?"

The victory I felt a second ago fades. Leena looks miserable. I shift toward her, my head bowed.

"No woman's face remember," I whisper, just low enough for her to hear. "Save, from my glass, mine own."

Leena exhales, and some of the red fades from her cheeks. "No woman's face . . ." she repeats, louder.

"Thank you," she whispers a moment later, while Jude's reading his line.

"Anytime," I whisper back. The back of my head prickles, as if someone's watching me. I glance up.

Father Marcus stares out from the shadows of the stage curtains, a deep line creasing the skin between his eyes. The corners of his mouth curve into a permanent frown.

My skin buzzes under the intensity of his gaze. I'm suddenly filled with the urge to cover my face, worried he'll see my horrible thoughts reflected in my eyes. He'll know I wanted Leena to do badly. That I enjoyed watching her squirm.

Father Marcus touches the cross hanging from his neck, his lips moving silently.

It feels, strangely, as though he's praying for me.

CHAPTER EIGHT

I leave the auditorium hours later, long after the sun has set and the last bits of warmth have drained from the air. I shiver, tugging my coat tighter around my shoulders. It's not usually so cold this far south. Maybe we'll get a snowy Christmas.

I hurry across the grounds, anxious to be back in my dorm. The other actors and crew members had already left, and even Sister Lauren took off about half an hour ago, saying she had a stack of papers to grade. I thought about leaving, but Father Marcus's face flashed through my head every time I started packing up my things. I'd remember how he watched me from the shadows, lips moving silently, as though in prayer. *One misstep and your scholarship privileges will be revoked,* he warned me that first day. That was enough to keep me gluing ivy vines to cardboard tree trunks, and arranging tree branches around the edges of the stage. Maybe if I work hard enough, he'll decide I'm good enough to stay.

Dead grass crunches beneath my shoes and gas lamps flicker, casting eerie shadows across the frosted sidewalk. Sutton told me St. Mary's is a historic site, so the school has to keep the campus the same as it was in 1893. Tonight, the lamps seem fainter than usual. But maybe it's just my imagination.

A twig snaps behind me. I freeze, nerves crawling up my spine. I spin around, peering into the gloom of the lawn.

"Hello?" I call.

No one answers.

I listen for another sound—footsteps or breathing—but the harsh wind hides all other noises. My eyes start to separate the shapes from the darkness and the world pieces itself together again. I take a deep breath, trying to slow my rapidly beating heart. I'm being paranoid. There's no one else out here.

Someone grabs my arm.

I bite back a scream and whirl around.

Father Marcus stands behind me, a grave expression

on his face. He looks much more creased and wrinkled up close. He reminds me of the portraits of the dead saints in the main hall, cracks spiderwebbing across their painted faces.

"Miss Flores," he says in a voice like gravel on sandpaper. "What are you doing out so late?"

"I was, um, setting up for the play." Even though I was just doing schoolwork, I feel like I've done something wrong. "I must've lost track of time."

"I see." Father Marcus fixes his icy blue eyes on me, making me feel even colder than when I first stepped outside. I shift in place, unsure whether I should keep walking toward my dorm or wait to be dismissed.

"I'm concerned, Miss Flores," Father Marcus says after a long silence. "You didn't stay for confession after Mass this morning."

I knot my hands together. "I didn't know I was supposed to."

Father Marcus holds my gaze. I'm hit, again, with the fear that he knows what I'm thinking. I find a dry piece of skin next to my thumbnail and tug, focusing on the bright stab of pain. I fight the urge to keep walking back to my dorm.

"When I was a young man, I was sent to a small village in Colombia to act as a missionary," he says. He gestures toward the girls' dorm and we begin to walk down the path together. A strange scent clings to his robes—mothballs and incense. I try not to wrinkle my nose as I follow him. "The village was called La Cumbra. It was a superstitious place. The locals performed witchcraft and voodoo. Wicked things."

Father Marcus is quiet for a moment, his eyes unfocused. He presses his lips together, and then separates them with a soft smack, the cracks lining his mouth glistening with saliva.

"The people of La Cumbra were desperate for a relationship with God," he continues. "Can you imagine that, Miss Flores? To feel *desperate* to connect with the Lord?"

I don't realize that he expects me to answer until he stops speaking, and fixes me with those cold eyes. I clear my throat.

"Yes, Father," I say.

Father Marcus nods and slows his steps. "The people of the village would cover their bodies with black mud. They'd lie in the dirt, surrounded by a ring of fire, and they would pray to the Lord to make them clean. These rituals would take days sometimes. Weeks. I used to marvel at them. These people wanted nothing more than to know our God. This country doesn't seem to share that same devotion. They would never cover themselves with mud. They would never lie in the dirt."

Father Marcus stops walking and his eyes bore into me, waiting to see my reaction. I shift my eyes to the ground.

"What about you, Miss Flores?" Father Marcus asks. "Are you . . . devoted?"

"Yes, Father," I murmur.

"And yet . . . you do not feel the need to confess your sins. You are not willing to remain behind after Mass, your first Mass at this institution, and work on strengthening your relationship with the Lord."

Heat rises in my cheeks. *One misstep,* I think. It would be so easy for him to send me away.

"Sin never leaves us, child," Father Marcus continues. "It is only through asking the Lord for His forgiveness that we might hope for absolution."

"Of course, Father."

"Would you like to confess now?" he asks.

My voice freezes in my throat. "Here?" I manage to squeak out.

"*The Most High does not dwell in houses made by human hands. Acts 7:48.* The Lord sees us wherever we are, child. You may kneel."

What the hell? I think. But I'm too afraid to say no. I kneel in the grass, trying to ignore the way the rocks dig into my bare knees. Cold air creeps up my legs, making my plaid skirt flutter.

Father Marcus places a hand on my forehead. His skin is rough and damp. Wind howls through the trees around us, rattling the branches and blowing through the last of the dead leaves.

I've never confessed before. "I don't know the words," I say.

Father Marcus presses his palm against my forehead, tilting my head up toward his face.

"Now you say, *forgive me, Father, for I have sinned,*" he says. "And you tell me how long it's been since your last confession."

"Forgive me, Father," I repeat in a voice that sounds nothing like my own, "for I have sinned. It's been . . . this is my first confession."

He nods, his hand sweaty against my forehead. "May God, the Father of all mercies, help you make a good confession," he replies.

Silence stretches between us and I realize it's my turn again. I'm supposed to confess something. I open my mouth.

The train flashes into my head, its headlight flashing white in the trees. The horn blares, making me flinch under Father Marcus's hand.

Not that. I think. *Anything but that.* My chest tightens, but I force myself to breathe. I imagine Brooklyn holding my wrist, her fingernails cutting into my skin, her eyes glowing red. I can still hear her voice. *We don't kill our own.*

I grit my teeth. I made that up, I remind myself. Dr. Keller said it never happened. There's no evil in me. I have to concentrate. There has to be something I can tell Father Marcus. My brain flashes forward, to the police officer standing on my porch. *Your mother's been in an accident.*

I push the memory aside, tears stinging my eyes. I can't tell him that.

Father Marcus's hand feels heavy. Like it's pushing me into the ground. I close my eyes and think of . . . Jude. Jude watching me during Mass this morning, a slight curl to his lips. Jude seeming to recite his lines to me during the play. I think of the hurt expression etched across Leena's face, and how good it felt when she messed up her lines. Heat burns through my chest. I barely feel the wind whipping against my legs.

"I . . . covet," I say, repeating a word my grandmother once used. *Codiciar* in Spanish.

Father Marcus shifts, black robes swaying around his feet. "And what do you covet, child?"

The thought of describing my romantic fantasies to Father Marcus makes something in my stomach clench. But Jude's not the only thing I covet. My mouth feels suddenly dry.

"I'm jealous of my roommate," I explain. "She has this great life. She's the star of the play, and she has a family and friends. Sometimes I wish it was mine."

Father Marcus's hand curls. The edges of his long, yellow fingernails press into my scalp.

"In First Peter 2:1, the Lord commands us to rid ourselves of all malice and all deceit, hypocrisy, envy, and slander of every kind."

Father Marcus falls silent, his words still hanging in the air between us. A rock lodges itself painfully against my leg, but I don't squirm. Pain cuts into my knee and I feel something sudden and warm trickle down my shin. Blood. Still, I don't move. The muscles in my neck strain against the weight of Father Marcus's hand.

"As penance, you'll perform three Hail Marys and an act of contrition," Father Marcus says.

"Yes, Father," I say, automatically. Maybe Leena can tell me what that means.

"Very well. I absolve you from this sin, my child. In the name of the Father, the Son, and the Holy Spirit. Amen."

"Amen," I whisper.

Father Marcus removes his hand. I stumble to my feet, feeling strangely cold and achy. Father Marcus grabs my arm before I can take a single step away from him. His fingers tighten around my wrist.

I turn slowly. "What is it, Father?"

Father Marcus reaches for my face without a word. His breath smells sour, and it takes all my willpower not to recoil. He drags his thumb over my forehead, tracing a cross into my skin. It burns, even after he lowers his hand.

"Blessed be the name of the Lord," he says.

CHAPTER NINE

I take the stairs to my dorm two at a time. My forehead still feels branded with the cross Father Marcus traced on my skin with his sweaty, papery finger. I touch it lightly, wondering if it'll actually help. Maybe my sins will disappear, like magic.

Sutton's too-loud, too-sharp laugh booms down the hall as soon as I turn the corner. I pause, the laugh triggering something in my memory. It sounds wild. Unhinged. I frown and push open the door to our room.

"Hey, Sofia," Leena calls. She sits cross-legged on the floor, leaning back against our mirrored closet door. Heathcliff lies in her lap, leaving little white bunny hairs on her dark-wash jeans. Some pop song I don't recognize blares from the speakers on her bookshelf.

Sutton peels off her sweater and tosses it onto her bed. "I need the white one with the lacy things at the edges," she says, her voice half whine. She yanks a drawer open, pulling so hard it nearly falls out of the dresser. "He hasn't seen that one yet."

Leena picks up Heathcliff, and makes kissy faces at his little pink nose. "I think you wore it last week. It's dirty."

"Damn, you're right," Sutton mutters, pulling open another drawer.

I drop my bag next to my bed and shrug off my coat. "What's up?"

Sutton glances over her shoulder at me as she digs around for a top. She's wearing more makeup than usual. Thick eyeliner coats her lids, and rosy patches of blush cover her cheeks. She looks older, her eyes dark, her face thin and angular.

"Just getting ready to meet my man," she says, shoving the drawer back. The bottles on top of her dresser rock in place.

I glance at Leena. She cuts her eyes toward Sutton, and mimes taking a drink.

As though on cue, Sutton plucks a tiny bottle of Jim Beam off her dresser and pours it into a can of Diet Dr

Pepper. The pop song comes to an end. Sutton touches a button on her iPhone, and it starts over at the beginning. She hums along with the opening chords.

"Maybe I should just wear this?" she says, motioning to her bra. It's yellow and lacy, with tiny white daisies lining the straps. Sutton's heart-shaped silver locket hangs down between her breasts.

"You'll be cold if you go topless," Leena says, giggling. She leans forward and grabs a light-pink top from a pile on the floor. "What about this one?"

Sutton takes the top from Leena and tugs it over her head. "You're so smart, Leenie-bean," she says, her voice muffled by the fabric.

I collapse onto my bed, throwing an arm over my eyes. "You're sneaking out?" I ask.

"Shh!" Sutton pulls her head through the top's opening and brings a finger to her lips. She tries to keep her face serious, but a giggle escapes. "I'm meeting Dean."

"Sutton, come on, you've got to be cool." Leena plops Heathcliff onto the ground and stands, helping Sutton fix her top. "Remember what we talked about? If you get caught, we all get into trouble. You have to be sneaky."

"I know, I know. I'll be good." Sutton applies a thick layer of pink to her lips and smacks them together.

"Don't stay out too late," Leena adds. "We have that physics test tomorrow, remember?"

"Physics is easy, Leenie," Sutton says. "Sometimes objects move, and sometimes they don't."

"You're going to have to be more technical on the test," Leena says.

Sutton rolls her eyes. "I gotta go. I'm gonna be late."

She slips the lipstick into her jeans pocket and unlatches the window. Our room is on the second floor, but the grounds slope up at the edge of the courtyard, so our window is actually only a few feet above the grass. I'm still lying in bed, and I push myself up onto one elbow so I can see outside.

A guy who looks like he's about twenty hovers near the edge of the woods, leaning against a tree with his arms crossed over his chest. Fog creeps over his feet, making him look like he's standing in silver ankle-deep water. He has swimming-pool blue eyes and golden hair that sweeps away from his forehead.

I wave, but his eyes slide over me, as though I'm not even there.

"Don't be offended," Sutton says, pulling her purse strap over one shoulder. "He just got off work at the bar. He's probably still stressed from all the frat guys trying to get him to take their fake IDs."

She wiggles her fingers at Dean. He jerks his chin up in an almost nod.

"You guys are so cute," I deadpan. Leena snickers, then pretends to cough when Sutton glares at her.

"I'll see you guys later," Sutton says. She hoists herself through the window and drops, easily, onto the ground outside. I push the window shut. Sutton leans forward and presses her lips against the glass, leaving behind a smudged kiss mark. I watch her race off into the trees, and I'm hit, again, with the same déjà vu feeling I got when I heard her wild laughter from down the hall. She reminds me of someone.

I shiver and yank the curtains closed. "Isn't she worried she's going to get in trouble?"

"Sutton doesn't worry about that when Dean's involved," Leena says. "They're in *love*. You know she's been with him for almost a year?"

"That's a long time." I lean over the side of my bed and grab my schoolbag. I have a physics quiz tomorrow, too, and I'm not as confident as Sutton that I understand force and motion. I pull my textbook out and quickly flip to chapter three. "How'd they meet?" I ask.

Leena is quiet for a beat. I look up from my book and see her frowning down at Heathcliff.

"You're going to think it's weird," she says, finally.

"What? Was he her teacher or something?"

Leena shakes her head. "Worse."

"Well, now you *have* to tell me."

Leena's cheeks redden. "Dean is, um, Sutton's aunt's . . . son."

I look up from my book too quickly, and a tiny flare of pain shoots down my neck. "Her . . . cousin? Sutton is dating her *cousin?*"

"It's not as weird as it sounds! Sutton's dad has been in jail since she was five years old, and—"

"Wait," I cut in. "Her dad's in jail? I thought he'd died."

"Oh, shit—I wasn't supposed to tell you that." Leena bunches her hand in a fist and presses it against her mouth. "Sutton tells everyone he died because she thinks it makes her sound less trashy. You can't tell her I told you. She'll be *so* pissed."

"I won't," I promise. "So, her cousin?"

"She met Dean for the first time a couple of years ago. I guess they kind of . . . hit it off."

I press my lips together to keep from making a face. Leena looks up at me and sighs.

"Look, I know it's gross, okay! But they say they're in love." She shrugs and scratches Heathcliff between his ears. "Anyway, that's why Sutton got sent here. Her mom thought it'd be good for her to get away from Dean. But then Dean got a job at a bar in town and moved to Hope Springs. Sutton says he's saving for a ring."

"Wow," I murmur. Cousin or not, I've never heard of

a guy planning to propose so young. "I guess that's kind of sweet?"

Leena drops to her knees and peers under Sutton's bed. She digs around for a second, then grabs a box of S'mores Pop-Tarts and sits back up. "Want one?" she asks, leaning against the bed frame.

I nod, and Leena tosses me a foil-wrapped package. "Sutton always has the best junk food," she explains.

"And booze, apparently," I say, thinking of the bottle of Jim Beam.

"She keeps more in her dresser if you want some," Leena says.

I shake my head. "I don't drink anymore."

"Me either." Leena pops a piece of Pop-Tart into her mouth. "Don't you hate the way it makes you act? I'm not myself at all. After that thing with the frogs, I was like *no, thank you.* Never again."

"I know how you feel," I say, staring down at my Pop-Tart.

"Anyway, Dean buys all this stuff for her. If you want something, just tell her and she'll ask him to get it for you." Leena nods at the Pop-Tart box. "These were Abby's favorite."

I bite into the Pop-Tart. Gooey marshmallow and melted chocolate oozes onto my tongue. "Abby was your old roommate, right?"

Leena nods. "She was cool. She was, like, one of those girls all the guys fell in love with. She was going to help me come up with a plan to talk to Jude. But then she took off." Leena pushes her glasses up her nose, accidentally smearing chocolate across her lip.

I think of Jude's dark eyes and velvety voice. The Pop-Tart suddenly tastes stale. "Where'd she go?"

"Dunno. We've been texting her from Sutton's phone but she hasn't responded yet. We think she went to New York. Her sister lives there. She probably wants to settle in before letting us know what's up." Leena shrugs. "Or maybe she thinks we'll tell someone."

"I don't get it. Was she expelled?"

"Not exactly. She used to sneak out with Sutton sometimes and, about a month ago, I guess she hooked up with one of Dean's friends. Sutton thinks maybe she's, um, *pregnant*." Leena whispers the word, then glances around the room as if she's worried someone will overhear her. "We think she didn't want Father Marcus to find out and expel her, so she went to stay with her sister while she figured out how to deal with it."

I break off another piece of Pop-Tart. Graham cracker bits crumble from my fingers and settle between the pages of my physics book. "She'd get expelled just for getting pregnant?"

Leena nods. "Dating is against the morality code. You

could get expelled just for being alone in the same room with a boy."

I tilt my textbook, pouring the crumbs into a little pile on my bed. "That's *insane*."

"Tell me about it." Leena glances at the window. I follow her gaze, and notice that I can still see Sutton's pink lipstick smeared across the glass behind the gauzy curtains. "Do you think it's completely crazy to go after Jude when I *know* I'll get in trouble if I actually try to date him?"

Guilt curdles in my stomach like food gone rotten. I fold the wrapper over the rest of my Pop-Tart. I don't feel hungry anymore.

"I don't know," I say carefully. "I guess it depends on how much you like him."

Leena looks right into my eyes. I should tell her about the chocolate on her face. I don't, and I'm instantly hit with a dark, satisfied feeling. Apparently, confession didn't work after all.

Silence stretches between us and, suddenly, I know she's going to ask me about play practice. She's going to accuse me of flirting with Jude.

"I used to think it was just a stupid crush," Leena says, "But it's different now. I think I felt something during practice. It was like he was reciting his lines directly to me, not to my character. Did you notice?"

I wait for her to say something else, but she just tilts her head to the side and smiles at me innocently. She really didn't notice him flirting with me. Or maybe she just didn't want to notice.

"Yeah," I say, clearing my throat. "I think I know what you're talking about."

Leena smiles so wide it looks as if her face might split in half. She glances at the alarm clock on her bedside table and her smile fades. "Crap, is that what time it is? I completely forgot to call my mom."

I twist around to look at the clock. The red numbers read eight forty-five. "It's not even nine yet. She's probably still awake."

"Yeah, but she'll be pissed. She expects me to call every day at the exact same time and, if I'm even a few minutes late, there's hell to pay." Leena pushes herself to her feet, Heathcliff still nestled in the crook of her arm. She shoves her feet into her slippers. "She's a nightmare. You have no idea."

I press my lips together and stare down at my hands. My mom was like that, too. I used to get chewed out if I came home even a minute after curfew.

I smile at the bittersweet memory. Leena pauses next to Heathcliff's cage.

"I'm such an idiot!" she says, smacking herself on the forehead. "I keep complaining about my mom and you . . ."

"It's fine," I say quickly. "Go call your mom."

"Are you sure?" Leena looks down at Heathcliff, who's gnawing at the edge of her shirt. "I could stick around if you want to talk or something."

I shake my head. "That's okay. I don't really like to think about the past."

"Here, take Heathcliff. He'll cheer you up."

Leena dumps the bunny into my hands before I can say another word. His fur feels greasy. Like he needs to be washed. He stares up at me with one beady red eye.

I force the word "thanks" out of my mouth. Leena watches me for a moment.

"You're not really into animals, are you?" she asks. I stroke Heathcliff's dirty back with two fingers, trying to keep the disgust from my face.

"No, I am," I say. "He's . . . cute."

Leena grins and heads into the hall, leaving me alone with the bunny.

I stare at the door, wishing we could switch places. I want to be the one hurrying down the hall to call my mom. I wouldn't even care if she was mad, or if she yelled. Just that she picked up the phone.

Heathcliff smells even more like piss than he did the last time I held him. I try to breathe through my mouth. Leena's copy of *The Tempest* lies next to her bed, the pages dog-eared. I shift Heathcliff to one hand and reach for it. A piece of notebook paper flutters from the pages. I unfold it, and see that it's an essay Leena wrote comparing the character traits of Prospero and Caliban. She got an A.

I open the book to a love scene between Miranda and Ferdinand. All of Leena's lines are highlighted in yellow marker.

"Do you love me?" I whisper, reading Miranda's first line out loud. I imagine standing onstage across from Jude, and jealousy pierces my heart like a blade. Leena gets a mom, and Leena gets Jude, and Leena gets to be the lead in the play. Heathcliff squirms in my hand.

"Stop moving," I mutter, holding him tighter. Leena even gets a stupid bunny that she makes everyone else take care of.

Two tiny, sharp teeth drive into my finger. I curse loudly. The door swings open and Leena steps back into the dorm.

"I forgot my—" Leena starts. I stumble to my feet, and Heathcliff rolls out of my lap and onto my bed, then hops to the floor.

"Careful!" Leena says, scooping a shivering Heathcliff into her arms. She looks up and her expression softens. "Oh, Sof, are you okay? He didn't bite you, did he?"

"Yeah, he did," I say, staring down at my hand. Two crescent-shaped marks cut across the pad of my thumb.

Blood oozes up and spills over onto my finger. It comes fast and hot, winding into the cracks of my knuckles and trickling into the spaces between my skin and fingernail. I curl my thumb into my palm to control the bleeding. So much blood for such a tiny cut.

"He's never bitten anyone before," Leena says. She sets Heathcliff down on the floor and pushes herself to her feet. "Let me get you a Band-Aid."

"I'm sorry I dropped him." But even as I'm apologizing, I imagine grabbing that fluffy white head with one hand and twisting. I can practically feel his skinny bones breaking beneath my fingers.

I cringe at the image, disgusted with myself. That stupid needlepoint was right—jealousy is like a cancer. I need to get it under control before it turns me into someone I'm not.

I stick my thumb into my mouth while Leena digs around in her closet for a Band-Aid. The blood tastes metallic against my tongue.

CHAPTER TEN

Iopen my eyes, and I'm standing in the woods. Barefoot. I don't know how much time has passed, or how I got here. Dead grass crunches beneath my feet. My toes look almost blue, but I don't feel cold. I don't feel anything. Moonlight illuminates the trees, casting shadows across the ground. The shadows look like they're moving, reaching for me. I look up, but the trees are still. There's no wind.

A choked whimper breaks the quiet. It sounds like an injured animal. Goose bumps climb my legs. I cross my arms over my chest, and something warm and wet seeps through my nightgown. I look down.

Blood coats my arms. I jerk backward, horrified. It soaks into my nightgown, staining the lacy fabric red. It winds around my wrists and drips from my elbows. It feels warm. Sticky. I try to wipe it away, but there's too much. I smear it across my hands. It oozes between my fingers.

I hear the noise again. A small sound, barely a breath. I stare at my bloody arms, and I start to shake. This blood isn't mine.

What did I do?

I turn around. A pebble stabs my toe. An animal scurries through the brush, rustling the leaves before going still.

Leena kneels in the dirt, her hands tied behind her back, a piece of duct tape covering her mouth. Blood leaks from her nose and from the torn, ragged skin near her scalp. Sweaty strands of hair frame her face, and a purple bruise blooms beneath one swollen, bloodshot eye. Deep red slashes climb her thighs. A bloody butcher knife lies in the grass, inches from my toes.

Mine. I pick up the butcher knife. The wooden handle feels warm beneath my fingers. Like it belongs there. I step toward Leena, and she flinches, releasing a muffled sob. She is the animal—the prey.

I pull my arm back and slash—

I wake up, gasping. Sweat plasters my pajamas to my body. I can't move. The room slowly comes into focus.

Sutton snoring from the bunk across from me. Heathcliff licking his water dispenser. Dawn creeping through the window.

I roll onto my side and stare at Leena's bunk. Leena lies on her back, her eyes closed. There's no blood on her face, no swollen eye or torn skin. Her eyelids twitch as she dreams. I force myself to inhale and then breathe out again, slow. I didn't hurt anyone. It was a nightmare. Leena's safe.

I check the clock on my bedside table. It's five thirty-eight in the morning. My alarm isn't set to go off for another twenty minutes, but the nightmare is still fresh in my head. I feel blood coating my fingers, anger pounding at my skull.

I didn't just want to hurt Leena. I wanted to kill her.

I crawl out of bed and pull on a pair of jeans and sneakers. My fingers shake so badly I can barely tie the laces. Leena murmurs something in her sleep and rolls over. Her blankets rustle and the mattress springs creak.

I freeze. I don't want her to catch me. I remove my jacket from its hook on the back of the closet door and creep out of the dorm. Leena stays still.

I hurry down the stairs and out the dorm without thinking about where I'm going. I just want to put space between Leena and me. That nightmare felt so *real*. I could smell her blood. I could feel her fear.

My chest tightens and, for a long moment, I can't

manage to inhale. Leena's my friend. I would never hurt her. *Never.* The ground seems to lurch beneath me. I lean against the wall just outside the building and cup my hands around my mouth.

Breathe. I choke down a lungful of air. Cold nips at my nose and lips. I exhale, and a misty cloud of breath leaks through the cracks in my fingers.

The old chapel sits just ahead, half hidden by trees. Tangled ivy snakes over the walls, twisting into thick knots around the double doors and stained glass windows. The vaulted roof pierces the sky like a dagger. I'm not supposed to be out of my room before six am, but it's just the chapel. They can't expel me for praying.

I walk across the grounds, dry grass crunching beneath my sneakers. The chapel looks silver in the early morning light, and darkness obscures the stained glass windows. I push open the door. The hinges creak and echo off the walls of the empty room.

A heavy wooden cross stands at the front of the aisle. Votive candles cover the altar, half melted in red glass candleholders. They flicker in the gloom, sending shadows dancing across the marble floor. I frown, wondering if the altar boys have to keep them lit all the time.

I slide into a pew and pick up a Bible with a broken spine. I let it flop open on my lap, and read the first line that I see.

Lord, if you are willing, you can make me clean. The words ring through my head like a bell. That's all I want. For someone to wipe away my pettiness and jealousy. For someone to take away my nightmares. I want this so badly that it beats in my chest like a second heart.

"Sofia?"

I jerk around. Jude stands behind me, a faded leather jacket slung over his gym shorts and long-sleeved T-shirt. His hair's all rumpled, as if he just got out of bed.

My chest rises and falls rapidly. It takes me a moment to catch my breath. "What are you doing here?" I ask.

"The guys all run sprints at six am," he explains. "I like to come here first and say a quick prayer. The chapel's usually empty."

I start to stand. "I'm sorry, I'll—"

"No, don't go." Jude slides into the pew beside me, close enough that our shoulders almost brush against each other. He smiles, then ducks his head, embarrassed. "It's kind of nice to have company."

"Yeah," I say. A thin layer of stubble shadows the bottom of his face. I imagine running my fingers over it.

"What're you doing here?" Jude asks, shrugging off his jacket. He's rolled his shirtsleeves past his elbows, and I notice a strange mark in the crook of his arm. Almost like a burn.

"Did you hurt yourself?" I ask, nodding.

Jude slides his sleeve down over his arm. He's not smiling anymore. "No, it's nothing."

I frown, but then Jude turns so that his body faces me on the pew, and my curiosity slips away. Dark hair curls around his neck, and the candlelight makes his skin glow gold. He stares at me for a long moment without saying anything.

I blush and look down at my hands. "You keep doing that," I say.

"Doing what?"

"*Looking* at me. You did it during play rehearsal, too."

Jude blinks. "Wow. I'm sorry. I swear I'm not a total creep—you just remind me of this picture Father Marcus has in his office, that's all."

"What's it a picture of?"

Jude glances up at me, sheepish. "Um, the Virgin Mary?"

I glance at a painting of the Virgin on the wall behind the altar. She has pale skin and dark blue eyes. "But she's white."

Jude follows my gaze. "Well, yeah, in that painting she is. The picture in Father Marcus's office is actually of Our Lady of Guadalupe. It's from a basilica in Mexico City where he did some missionary work after divinity school. She's Latina, like you."

Our Lady of Guadalupe. The name tugs at something in

my head. I think of the religious postcards and pictures gathering dust in Grandmother's room. "It sounds familiar."

Jude frowns. "You're not Catholic, are you? How'd you end up at St. Mary's?"

"No, I'm not Catholic." I look back at the painting of the Virgin Mary, my neck stiff. I swallow and say, "Actually, my mom died a week ago. St. Mary's was the only place that would take me."

There's a beat of silence, and then Jude puts a hand on my shoulder. His touch vibrates through me. "I'm really sorry, Sofia. That's awful."

"Yeah." I feel a familiar sting at the corner of my eye and blink to keep myself from crying. "It's still pretty hard to talk about."

"Have you thought about praying?" he asks. "God can be a great help at times like this."

His eyes are like sparks in the candlelight, absorbing every flicker.

"I don't know," I say. "I've never prayed before."

"It's easy. I'll show you." Jude slides his hand from my shoulder to my wrist. He wraps his other arm around me, pressing his body against my back.

I hold my breath. I feel his heart beating against my spine. He exhales, and his chest rises and falls against me.

"Is this okay?" he asks. His voice sounds different. Huskier. I nod.

Jude lowers his chin to my shoulder, and his breath tickles the hair on the back of my neck. He folds his hands over mine. His palms are warm.

"I always start by saying *Dear Holy Father*," he says.

"Dear Holy Father," I repeat. Jude laughs. It vibrates through his body, and into mine.

"You don't have to speak out loud to pray," he says. "Just think it. Think of God, and all the things you want to say to Him or ask Him or thank Him for. God will hear you, but He may not answer right away. He'll answer in His own way, in His own time. Go ahead. Try it."

I close my eyes, but I don't think about God. I think about how I can feel the heat of Jude's body through my T-shirt, and how his skin smells like soap and leather. The rise and fall of his chest as it presses against my back.

"Amen," Jude whispers, moving his fingers away from mine.

"Amen," I repeat.

CHAPTER ELEVEN

I see Jude again at play rehearsal. He and Leena run lines onstage while Sister Lauren watches from the front row. I try not to stare as I walk backstage.

"Wherefore weep you?" Jude says. His deep voice resonates throughout the theater, sending a tremor through my stomach. My hands still tingle where Jude touched them.

I hesitate near the curtain. Jude catches my eye, and my heart leaps into my throat. I sneak a glance at Leena. She's frowning over her script.

"At mine unworthiness," she says. She clears her throat, and shifts her weight to her other foot. "That dare not offer . . . um . . ."

Feeling reckless, I lift my fingers in a small wave. Jude flashes me a half smile and turns back to his script. I can't help the warmth that spreads through my chest. "That dare not offer . . ." Leena repeats. She trips over the words, making me wince.

Only a total bitch would go after Jude, I say to myself. Sutton's warning is the verbal equivalent of a cold shower. I am not that kind of girl. I will not go after my friend's crush.

I slip backstage, where Alice Merle is ripping up old sheets to look like sails and Dale Buford is lugging buckets of sand to create a makeshift beach. No one's looking at me. I drop my bag next to my feet and slip off the Band-Aid wrapped around my thumb, exposing the spot where Heathcliff bit me. It's just a tiny, crescent-shaped cut. Barely even there.

Jealousy is like a cancer, I think, and I drive my sharpest fingernail into the cut. Pain flares through my skin. I gasp, and tears spring to the corners of my eyes. But I don't move my fingernail. The pain is good. I focus on it, letting it wash over me.

I will not go after Jude.

Blood oozes around the edges of my fingernail. It feels sticky and hot against my skin. I move my fingernail and the pain dulls. I take a deep breath and reposition the bandage over my reopened scab.

The curtain behind me twitches. I jerk away as Sister Lauren yanks it back.

"There you are!" she says, stepping backstage. "Didn't you hear me call your name?"

I shake my head, trying to hide my bleeding thumb in the folds of my skirt. "Sorry. I was distracted."

Sister Lauren adjusts her white headpiece. *She saw my fingernail,* I think. I curl my fingers around my bloody thumb. She won't understand why I had to do that. I search my head for an excuse.

"No worries—I appreciate your focus, Sofia. Speaking of which, would now be a good time to take a look at our trapdoor?" she asks.

I blink. "Excuse me?"

"Remember? We were having a problem with the mechanism and you told me your old school had one just like it." Sister Lauren pinches the bridge of her nose between two fingers. "I could've sworn we talked about this after class this morning."

"Oh, right!" My cheeks flare as the conversation comes rushing back to me. "Yeah, of course, I'll take a look."

"Great!" Sister Lauren turns, her black robes swishing around her ankles. She leads me onto the main stage, and motions for Leena and Jude to stop rehearsing.

"Would you all mind shifting stage left?" she calls.

The actors move out of my way. I crouch beside the trapdoor, careful not to look at Jude. My Band-Aid is already stained with blood.

Leena kneels next to me. "You missed it!" she whispers, glancing over her shoulder. Her eyes linger on Jude. "There was this part in the script where Ferdinand was supposed to kiss Miranda's hand. I thought we'd just skip it, but Jude actually took my hand and . . . and he kissed me! A *real* kiss."

Leena touches her hand as she says this. She can't stop smiling.

"That's . . . great, Leena," I say. My response sounds stilted, but Leena doesn't seem to notice. Anger curls around me. The air in the auditorium seems hotter all of a sudden. The moment in the chapel—the moment I'd been replaying over and over—seems stupid, and childish. I press my injured thumb into my forefinger. *I will not go after Jude.*

"I think they're waiting for you," I say, proud that I manage to keep my voice steady. I nod at the actors gathered on the other side of the stage. Leena pushes herself to her feet.

"I'll tell you all about it later," she says. I stare at her back as she walks away. Her long black hair. Her swinging plaid skirt. Today, she's rolled the waistband to make it shorter.

A drop of blood hits the scarred wooden floor next to my knee. I look down and realize I'm still pressing my fingers together. My Band-Aid's a bloody mess.

I swear under my breath and turn my attention to the trapdoor. My thumb is bleeding freely now. I'll need to fix the door quickly so I can run to the nurse's office for a new bandage. Sister Lauren said the door latch has been sticking during Caliban's entrance. I fumble with it, but my Band-Aid slips around on my thumb while I work, and I have to stop to shift it back into place. I grit my teeth and try the latch again, trying to tune out the actors on the other side of the stage. This time I leave a thick red smear of blood across the floor. It glistens under the bright stage lights.

I wrinkle my nose and try to wipe the blood away with my hand. Gross. I really need a new Band-Aid. I slide the trapdoor closed and hurry backstage. I might have an extra floating around the bottom of my bag.

Jude's deep voice booms through the stage curtain, followed by Leena's halting, nervous lines. I crouch next to my bag and fumble through homework assignments and broken pens, holding my injured thumb so I don't bleed anywhere.

I can't believe Jude kissed her, I think, pushing aside my English notebook. *I can't believe I'm not even allowed to flirt with him because she liked him first.* I yank my physics textbook out of the bag and drop it on the floor with a little more force than necessary. The angry, jealous thoughts keep popping into my head. I tell myself I don't mean them, but I can't stop thinking about how unfair this all is. Leena already has everything. She should know what it feels like to have something bad happen for once in her life.

My lips curve into a smile at the thought. I catch myself a second later, and force them back into a tight line. It's not as though I want something really bad to happen to Leena. Just a little setback, to balance out the scales.

A sharp crack, like wood slapping against wood, bangs through the auditorium. There's a scream, and then something heavy slams into the floor, cutting the scream short.

A sour taste hits the back of my throat. I drop my bag, and I'm instantly on my feet, racing across the stage.

"Call an ambulance," someone yells. Footsteps pound down the aisle and a door slams open. I push back the heavy curtain, my heart hammering in my chest.

No, I think. *Just don't let it be . . .*

All the actors have gathered around the trapdoor. The actor who plays Prospero has climbed inside, and is speaking in hushed tones to someone I can't see. Sister Lauren's face has gone white. Everyone's here.

Everyone except Leena.

"What happened?" I ask. Jude is kneeling next to the trapdoor, but he looks up at the sound of my voice. There's something dark and frightened reflected in his eyes.

"Leena fell," he says, but he sounds far away. I stare past him, down into the darkness beyond the edge of the trapdoor. It seems to pulse. I inch forward until I can see Leena's tangled hair spread across the ground below and, in the second before horror washes over me, a thought echoes through the back of my head:

She deserved it.

* * *

Sister Lauren insists that we all head back to our dorms but no one leaves the theater. We linger on the front steps until an ambulance speeds through campus, red and blue lights flashing through the trees. It slams to a stop in front of the auditorium, and two men in dark jumpsuits leap from the back, a stretcher balanced between them.

Sutton races across the grounds, but I can't face her. Disgust floods my stomach. I step into the woods, pressing my back against the cold, rough tree bark and letting the shadows hide me. Tears stream down Sutton's face. She looks around, maybe for me. Sister Lauren approaches and they talk in low voices that I can't overhear. The men hurry back down the steps, and this time there's a body on the stretcher: Leena's body.

She isn't moving. I curl my hand into a fist and bunch it near my mouth. *Oh God.* She isn't moving. No one speaks as they load her into the ambulance. A sob claws at my throat, but I can't let it out or people might see me. If they see me, they might ask questions.

Like, *Weren't you working on the trapdoor?*

And, *Why wasn't it locked? What did you do?*

I close my eyes. I hear the sharp crack of the trapdoor slamming open. Leena's scream rings through my ears— cut off, abruptly, when her body hit the floor. I wanted something bad to happen to her. Didn't I think that, seconds before she fell? Didn't I think that she *deserved* it? I was jealous, and I wanted Jude for myself. And then she fell through the trapdoor I'd been working on. What a nice coincidence.

Nausea curls inside of me. It rises in my throat like the tide. I turn and double over, vomiting on the packed dirt ground. I wipe my mouth with the back of my hand and force myself to walk away. My shoes smack against the ground, every step sounding like an accusation.

My fault, my fault, my fault.

I pull open the dormitory door and walk straight into a wall of people. My body feels as if it's on fire. I duck my head, trying not to meet anyone's eye. Voices buzz around me, high and jittery. Nervous. I pick out bits and pieces of conversations as I weave through the girls of St. Mary's.

"Did she . . . ?"

". . . accident?"

"But who . . . ?"

They know, I think. Somehow, they all know about the trapdoor. They know this was my fault. I walk faster. Eyes follow me down the hall and up the stairs. I feel them on my back, like pinpricks of heat burning through my skin.

"Sofia! Wait!"

Sutton's voice stops me cold. I hesitate outside our room, feeling unmoored, like someone snipped clean through the strings that kept me tied to the ground. Sutton races up behind me, panting.

"What are you doing? Leena was asking where you went."

"She's awake?" I swallow. It feels like there's something stuck in my throat. "Is she . . ."

"She's going to be okay," Sutton says before I can finish my sentence. "The ambulance guy said she hurt her leg pretty bad, but they can fix it. She'll need a cast."

I collapse against our door, relieved. "Thank God."

"Alice is giving me a ride to the hospital," Sutton says. "Do you want to come?"

I press my lips together. I don't want to tell her, but she's going to hear it from someone else, anyway. *"I'm the one who was working on the trapdoor, Sutton. I must've left it unlocked. It's my fault Leena fell."*

Sutton nods but, otherwise, her expression remains unchanged. She already knew, I realize. Someone already told her. It's my third day at this school and I already have a reputation. That's got to be some kind of record. "Leena doesn't blame you," Sutton says.

I shake my head, not sure I believe her. "You should go. Leena will want to see a friendly face."

For a second, it looks as if Sutton might say something else. But she turns and hurries down the hall without me.

I push our door open and step into the dorm, my eyes traveling over the room. Sutton's hairbrush and bobby pins tucked away in a wicker basket next to her bed. A stack of Leena's books on the floor, ragged notebook edges peeking out between the pages. A squeaky carrot toy forgotten in the corner.

I lift my hands to my mouth and start my breathing exercises. In and out, in and out. The whispers and stares fade away. My breathing steadies.

"Leena will be okay," I say out loud, testing the words. I wait for the lump to leave my throat. But it just sits there, like food I can't swallow. Leena might be okay, but that's just luck. I still hurt her.

We don't kill our own. The words float into my head. I trusted Dr. Keller when he told me I wasn't evil. But he wasn't with Brooklyn that night. *I* was. I remember the flash of red in her eyes, the evil moving inside of me when she grabbed my hand.

Brooklyn's voice whispers to me. *You're one of us, Sofia. I'm coming for you.*

I lift a hand to my chest and only then do I notice that my Band-Aid has fallen off my thumb. My fingers are sticky and wet. Blood coats my palm.

A shiny drop winds around my wrist and falls to the floor.

CHAPTER TWELVE

The rest of the day passes in a blur. All anyone can talk about is Leena and the accident.

I spot Sister Lauren waiting in front of the main building on my way to the dorms after dinner, the St. Mary's van parked at the curb behind her.

"Hey, Sofia, why don't you hop in?" she calls to me. She's dressed in her St. Mary's sweatshirt and jeans again, her hair a little flat from the habit she wore during classes.

"Are you going to the hospital?" I ask. Sister Lauren nods.

"I'm dropping off some extra clothes for Leena. The

doctor says she has to stay overnight. Want to come along?"

I open my mouth, an excuse already forming, when Brooklyn's voice floats through my head. *You're one of us.* I snap my mouth shut, shame warming my face. Only a terrible person wouldn't visit a friend in the hospital.

"Perfect," I say.

Leena's asleep when we get to her room, a thin blanket pulled up to her chest. I can't see her new cast, but there's a large lump under her blanket. The lights are off and the fluorescents in the hallway leave a green tint on her skin.

"Let's ask the nurse if it's okay to wake her up," Sister Lauren says.

I stop her before she gets to the door. "No, don't," I say. It's easier this way. I'm not quite ready to look Leena in the eyes. "She probably needs her rest."

"If that's what you want." Sister Lauren takes a stack of clothes out of a St. Mary's tote and places them on Leena's bedside table. "Are you feeling okay, Sofia? You seem a little off."

I shrug, staring down at Leena's sleeping form so I don't have to meet Sister Lauren's eyes. Leena moans in her sleep, a look of pain flashing over her face. I hug my arms to my chest, trying to come up with a reason to get the hell out of here. This is too much. Leena's my friend and she's in pain and it's because of me. Because I was jealous. Because I'm evil.

I squeeze my eyes shut, the old argument playing on a loop in my brain: *I'm not evil. Dr. Keller said it was guilt. What happened with Brooklyn didn't really happen.* For the first time, I realize how meaningless these words are. *Karen. Alexis. Grace. Riley. My mom.* They're all dead because they knew me. Because there's something wrong with me.

The low blare of a train's horn sounds in my ears. I flinch, my eyes shoot open. It takes a long moment for me to realize that the sound isn't a real train—just an alarm somewhere else in the hospital. It drones on for a moment, then dies.

"Sofia?" Sister Lauren touches my shoulder and I whirl around.

"Sorry," I say. I squeeze my hands into fists, forcing the train out of my mind. "The alarm surprised me."

"Are you feeling guilty about Leena? Because I promise you, it wasn't your fault. I'm the teacher," she says. "I should have been paying closer attention."

I nod, but I'm not really listening. My palms feel sweaty, even as the air-conditioning coaxes goose bumps from my arms. I glance back at Leena. The pain has faded from her face. She looks peaceful.

"Do you believe in demonic possession?" I ask, my

voice barely above a whisper. Sister Lauren tilts her head to the side, a frown twisting her mouth.

"Have you been watching too many scary movies?"

"So you don't think it's real?"

"I didn't say that." Sister Lauren sinks into a chair next to the hospital bed, studying Leena's pale face. "It's kind of a complicated question." She pauses, weighing her words. "I think it happens, but not like in the movies. Demons can't take over your body and make you do whatever they want. I think it's more like getting sick, if that makes sense."

"Like catching a cold?"

"Well, I don't think it's as easy as catching a cold. I believe that when someone does something unforgive-able, a demon . . . attaches itself to them."

The train's headlights flash in my head. I feel Karen's cold fingers wrapping around my wrist, her skin sticky with beer. She screams.

Sofia, get off the tracks!

I wrap my hands around my arms, shivering. I have done something unforgiveable. I've tried my best to forget about it, but Brooklyn knows my secret. And now she's never going to let me go.

"So that's it?" I ask. "You make one mistake and you have to live with the demon for the rest of your life?"

"Well, no, not exactly. I think that's just the first step.

The unforgiveable act allows the demon to find you, like sending a flare up into the sky. But true possession can only happen to a weak soul. The Devil can only take you if you give in to the evil."

"What do you mean give in to—" I stop, my grandmother's needlepoint flashing in my head. *Jealousy is a cancer.*

That's it. I lower myself into a chair, my knees trembling. I'm letting jealousy control me and it's making my soul weak. That's how Brooklyn is getting in.

Sister Lauren leans forward, taking Leena's hand in her own. I stare at the back of her head. "How do I make my soul strong?" I ask.

You're one of us.

"How do you get rid of the demon?" I ask.

"I'm not as much of an expert as Father Marcus," she says, "but anyone can save their soul if they develop a relationship with God. You have to free yourself of distractions and focus on Him. Don't let yourself be made weak with desire."

Free yourself. Distractions. Desire.

I think of Jude's hands on mine, and his hair and the smoky smell of his skin. My cheeks grow warm. "You make it sound easy."

"It's not. It's a lifelong journey." Sister Lauren twists around in her chair, her face drawn in concern. "I know sometimes it can feel like there's something wrong with you, Sofia, but the truth is we all have evil inside of us. It's only through seeking the Lord that we're made pure. You should come to Bible study sometime. We can work this through with prayer."

I smile halfheartedly, wanting to believe that's true.

"What if prayer doesn't work?" I ask, my voice cracking. I clear my throat. "What if I can't form a relationship with God?"

The frown on Sister Lauren's face deepens. A line appears between her eyebrows. "Then I guess the demons win," she says.

* * *

I head straight to the chapel after I get back from the hospital. It's after dark and cool moonlight streams in through the windows, the stained glass turning it red and gold and green. My footsteps echo off the marble floor, the sound magnified by the arched ceilings and stone walls.

Jude sits in the first pew. I freeze, all of the oxygen whooshing out of my body. I should come back later. Jude is a temptation. He's making me weak.

But I take one step forward, and then another. I can't seem to control myself. It's as though my feet aren't connected to my brain.

Jude's hunched over in prayer, the collar of his

St. Mary's uniform all rumpled and creased, the hair on the back of his neck coming to a familiar point.

I'm suddenly aware of a million tiny things. My skirt is too heavy, and my ankle itches, and the curls around my neck have started to frizz—the stray hairs tickle my ears. But it's too late to turn back now. I stop next to his pew, and clear my throat.

Jude flinches and his eyes widen.

"Hey," he says. His voice sounds thick, as if there's something caught in his throat. "I didn't hear you come in."

"Sorry," I say. "I can sit in the back if you want to be alone."

"No, please." Jude slides over to make room for me on his pew. *Leave*, my brain whispers, but I perch at the edge of the wooden seat, too nervous to move any closer.

"I was hoping to see you again," Jude says, staring down at his clenched fists. I bite back a smile.

"About that, I . . ."

Jude lets his hands fall open and I trail off. His wooden cross lies in his palm, the leather cord dangling between his fingers. "I was praying for Leena," he explains.

I shift uncomfortably. It feels hot in here even though the chapel is barely heated. It's stifling.

"That's nice of you," I say. Jude shakes his head and bends back over his cross, a lock of hair falling into his eyes.

"It's not *nice*," he spits out, squeezing his fingers around the cross. The muscles in his shoulders tighten. "This whole thing was my fault. I was right there when she fell. It was just like—"

Jude stops talking abruptly and slams his fist against the pew. The wood shudders beneath my legs. He clenches his eyes shut and a vein throbs near his temple.

But I stare at Jude without saying a word. How have I never noticed the pain on his face before? It's etched into every curve, every angle. Dark circles shadow the skin beneath his eyes and deep lines crease his forehead. Leena's voice echoes in my ear: *This is where they send the bad kids.*

For the first time, I wonder what Jude did to earn his spot at St. Mary's. What secret is he hiding?

Jude swallows and the muscles in his face relax. He rubs a hand over his chin and, just like that, the lines and shadows vanish. There's no pain anymore, no darkness. He's just Jude again.

"Sorry," he chokes out. "I've been working with Father Marcus to control my anger. I guess I'm still learning that I can't fix everything that goes wrong in the world."

I think of my mother's face, a Cheerio stuck to her cheek. "Me, too."

"Father Marcus says I need to learn to trust God. He says this is all part of His plan." Jude turns to me, his eyes narrowing. "Do you believe that?"

"No," I say without thinking. "This was the Devil's plan, not God's."

Jude nods, but I'm not sure he really heard me. He stares off at a spot in the distance, his eyes losing focus. "I think that, too, sometimes," he says, almost to himself. "I've been taking all these extra classes with Father Marcus, really pushing myself to get closer to God, but then something like this happens and it all seems meaningless."

Jude clenches his eyes shut and lowers his head to his hands. "I keep having doubts . . . about myself, about God. About everything."

I scoot closer to Jude, even as my brain screams at me to leave. But I can't go now. I can't let Jude blame himself when I know Leena fell because of me. Because I'm weak.

"This wasn't your fault," I say. "It's—" *mine*, I think but Jude shakes his head before I can get the word out.

"You don't know the whole story." Jude cuts his eyes toward me. "I was distracted today. If I'd been paying attention, Leena never would have gotten hurt."

Jude shifts his body closer and lowers his hand to mine. The temperature in the chapel seems to rise another ten degrees. My hair sticks to the back of my neck and sweat gathers between my thighs.

I close my eyes and for a long moment all I think

about is his skin pressed against my own. I feel the rough calluses on his fingers, his heart beating in his palm. I imagine turning my hand over and weaving my fingers through his.

Free yourself.

"I can't," I say, my eyes flickering open. Jude jerks his hand away from mine, as if he's been burned.

"I'm sorry," he murmurs. "I thought—"

"I like you," I say. "It's not that."

Jude searches my face, but I keep my eyes focused on the pew in front of me. I'm not strong. If I look at him, even for a second, I know I'll cave. "Then what is it?" he asks.

"I made a promise to a friend," I explain. "I've already hurt her a lot, and I'm trying to make up for it."

Jude is quiet for a long moment. I study the huge wooden cross looming over us, my eyes traveling over every crack in the ancient wood. I'm still not entirely sure how to pray, but I find myself making a wish, like when I toss a coin into a fountain, or find a stray eyelash on my cheek.

Please, I think. *Help me do the right thing.*

"This friend," Jude says finally. "She means a lot to you?"

"Yes."

"Then you shouldn't do anything to hurt her."

Jude stands. I shift my eyes down to my lap and pick at the skin around my thumbnail. The sudden burst of pain feels refreshing. Like taking a deep breath. Jude slips out of the pew, his legs brushing against my knees as he moves past me. He walks out of the chapel without another word, his footsteps echoing off the walls.

* * *

Sutton finds me after classes the next day. She's dressed in her blue-and-white field hockey uniform, hair pulled back in a tight ponytail. She tears the wrapper off a Snickers bar with her teeth.

"You're going to get in trouble," I say, glancing down the hallway.

"It's medicinal," Sutton says, eating half the bar in one bite. "I have a migraine. Did you hear? Leena's back."

"Really?" I stop in the middle of the hallway and some girl I don't recognize walks right into my back.

"Campaigning for class klutz, Ally?" Sutton shouts. The girl turns and sneers at us.

"Is Leena okay?" I ask. "How's her leg?"

Sutton crumples up her candy bar wrapper and shoves it in her backpack. "Her leg is fine. Her cast is covered in more dirty jokes than a toilet stall."

"*Leena* wrote dirty jokes on her cast?"

Sutton wrinkles her nose. "Okay, fine, the jokes were mine. You should sign it while there's still space."

She cocks an eyebrow and I hear what she's really saying. *Go talk to Leena.*

"Are you sure she—" I start.

Sutton shakes her head. "Stop. I'm not going to be your go-between. We've got that game tonight, and if I don't hurry, I'm going to miss the bus. Talk to Leena!" She slips past me before I can say another word. Tonight's game is in Jackson, which is three hours away, so the entire team will be staying at a motel. Leena and I have the dorm to ourselves until morning.

It's the perfect time to talk, but every time I imagine facing her, I see Jude's smile. Smell his shampoo. Feel the weight of his hand on mine.

I can't avoid our dorm forever. I take a deep breath and head down the hallway.

Leena lies on her bed, a tangle of yarn balanced on her lap. A white cast covered in stickers stretches from below her knee to down around her toes. She wears an oversized sweater, her glossy black hair hanging around her shoulders. She's piled blankets and pillows beneath her knee to keep her leg elevated.

"Oh my God," I murmur, pushing the door shut behind me. Leena straightens, and the yarn rolls off her lap and hits the floor.

"Crap," she mutters, watching the yarn roll across the floor. I lean down and pick it up.

"I'm sorry," I say, staring at the yarn. Saying that out loud is like opening a floodgate. Words pour from my mouth so fast I barely realize what I'm saying. "I'm so sorry, Leena. I've been a terrible friend. All of this is my fault."

"Your fault?" A blush creeps over Leena's cheeks. "Sister Lauren told everyone in the auditorium that the trapdoor was busted, but I was the only one dumb enough to fall through it." Leena stares at a spot on her leg. I follow her gaze and see Jude's name scrawled across her ankle.

"If you want the truth, I was too busy staring at Jude to look where I was going," she says. "Stupid, huh?"

I swallow, thinking of the gold glint in Jude's eyes. The way he always seems to smell like incense. "That's not stupid," I murmur.

Leena presses her hand flat against the cast, covering Jude's signature. "Anyway, that's why I got hurt. You didn't do anything wrong."

I turn the words around in my head. Dr. Keller said the same thing over and over during our first session. I'd been a wreck after my friends' deaths. I thought there was evil inside me, controlling me, but Dr. Keller convinced me it was just guilt. He told me that, if I wasn't careful, my mind would keep going back down that path. That I'd drive myself crazy thinking the Devil's out to get me.

I release a breath, realization dawning on me. That's exactly what happened. There was a terrible accident and I convinced myself it was my fault. But maybe this isn't a sign that I'm possessed. Maybe it really was just a freak thing.

For the first time since Leena fell, I actually allow myself to believe that's true.

Leena leans over and pulls open a drawer in her bedside table. She shuffles around for a moment before removing an orange Sharpie. "Sign my cast?" she asks.

I take the marker and uncap the top. "What should I write? Sutton told me you like dirty jokes."

"No more! Please!" Leena cringes, staring down at the stickers plastered over her cast. "I had to use all my stickers to cover them up before Sister Lauren saw."

"Okay, fine." I lean over her leg and sketch two floppy ears and a twitchy little nose.

"Is that Heathcliff?" Leena asks.

"Yup." I add a fluffy tail and two big feet.

"Wow, Sofia. It actually looks like him. You're good."

"I used to draw a lot," I explain. I sketch a little bubble coming out of the bunny's mouth and write *Get Well Soon* before capping the marker. "There. You're all done."

"You're so much more artistic than I am," Leena says. "Did Sutton tell you I started knitting? I'm making a scarf."

She pulls a tangled red-and-green yarn rectangle out of the basket next to her bed, the cast making her movements stiff and clumsy. She straightens with a grunt. "Ta-da!"

Only the very kindest person would call the thing she's holding a scarf. One end is nearly six inches narrower than the other, and it's way too short to wrap around her neck. Lumps of yarn jut out at weird angles, and the pattern—some sort of snowman wearing a top hat—stops in the middle of the scarf, as though she got tired of doing it.

"It's . . . good," I say.

"You're such a liar." Leena smirks at me and flips the scarf around, examining it through narrowed eyes. "This is the worst scarf ever knitted."

"You might want to stick to acting."

Leena drops the scarf in her lap. "Speaking of acting, this broken leg might be a blessing in disguise. Sister Lauren's worried I won't be ready for opening night, so she's making me do an extra rehearsal tonight." Leena's eyes flash. "A *private* rehearsal. With Jude."

"Just the two of you?" I ask.

Leena uncaps her marker and draws a tiny orange heart on her cast, not far from Jude's signature. "Sister Lauren's going to chaperone, but otherwise, yeah. Just the two of us."

CHAPTER THIRTEEN

Leena leaves for rehearsal a few minutes later, and Sutton's not going to be back from her hockey game until tomorrow morning, so I grab my history textbook and huddle down in bed, desperate to catch up on my reading from the past few days. I never realized how hard it would be to study when you share a room with two other girls.

I flip a page of my book and uncap a highlighter. For an hour or two, I lose myself in my homework. I haven't done a unit on the post Civil War era at any of my other schools and most of the names and dates are unfamiliar. If I still want to take the final at the end of the semester, I have a lot of catching up to do.

I raid Sutton's junk food stash for dinner and read until my eyes go blurry. My head pounds with new information. When I finally check the clock, it takes my brain a moment to make sense of the numbers. 7:45.

I rub my eyes with my palms and check the clock again, but the time stays the same. It's been three hours since Leena left for rehearsal. What could they be doing for three hours?

An image pops into my head: Leena and Jude standing shoulder to shoulder in an empty theater. Jude brushing Leena's hair aside, whispering something in her ear. Jude raising Leena's hand to his lips and . . .

I turn a page so hard that it rips away from the binding.

"Calm down," I say to myself. Jude likes *me*. He wouldn't kiss another girl.

But you rejected him, a little voice whispers at the back of my head.

I turn back to my book, desperate to focus on anything else. Heathcliff moves around in his cage. He gnaws at his carrot toy, making it squeak. And squeak. I flinch every time the noise splits the room's silence.

An hour passes. *Squeak squeak.*

"Stupid bunny," I mutter, shoving my book aside. I climb out of bed and grab the carrot from Heathcliff's cage. I'm surprised nobody's thrown the damn thing away. I toss the carrot into the corner and climb back into bed.

Silence. I roll onto my stomach and pull my book closer.

Heathcliff hops across his cage. His paws make a soft *thwomp thwomp thwomp* on the sawdust. I grit my teeth together, but it's fine. Much better than the damn carrot.

A minute passes. Heathcliff starts drinking from his water dispenser.

Click click click click. Pause. *Click click click click.*

I curl my toes into my bedspread. *It's fine,* I tell myself. But it's not fine. We're not even supposed to have pets in this place. Why did Leena have to rescue a damn bunny? It's stinky and loud and it's not even cute, for Christ's sake. It has these bright-red eyes that look like tiny drops of blood in the middle of all that white fur.

Click click click click.

I turn another page. Why would anyone name a damn rabbit "Heathcliff" in the first place? I mean, how pretentious can you get? If Jude knew, he'd probably laugh.

Click click click click.

Another hour or so passes this way until, finally, I groan, and check the clock on my side table. It's almost ten. Leena's been hanging out with Jude for five hours.

I roll onto my side and stare at the bunny's cage.

Heathcliff glares back at me with those beady little bloodshot eyes. I can't believe I have to hang out in a room reeking of rabbit piss while Leena gets to be with Jude. Heathcliff is *her* pet. She should have to deal with him.

Click click—

I throw my pillow at Heathcliff's cage. It hits the glass with a soft *thwack*. Heathcliff bounces to the far corner, shivering. I have a sudden, horrible thought: *Why couldn't he have just died when Leena tried to fix his stupid leg?*

It's a terrible thing to think. I push it to the very back of my head, but I can't help the tiny spark of glee I feel at the idea. Leena's little "bun-bun" is a menace. I'm sure Sutton kind of wishes he'd have a little accident, too.

Frustrated, I switch off the overhead light and climb into bed. It's officially time for this day to be over.

Heathcliff finds his water dispenser again. His tongue sends the metal ball spinning and clicking. I pull a pillow over my head to block out the sound, but I can't fall asleep. My mind plays images of Leena and Jude on a loop. Jude touching Leena's arm. Jude leaning toward her face. Jude lowering his lips to hers . . . Heathcliff returns to his water bottle and the clicking starts again. *Click click click. Click click click.* It reminds me of Grandmother's rosary beads hitting her hospital bed. I can't stop clenching my shoulders. Grinding my teeth. I lie like that for hours, begging my brain to calm down. Fall asleep.

Then the darkness around me moves, taking on mass and shape. Jude crouches in front of my bed. The smoky, vanilla smell of incense clings to his hair. I smile at him, groggily. I must've fallen asleep at some point because my eyes are heavy and fuzzy. The room loses focus at the edges, like in an old photograph. Jude lifts a finger to his lips.

"Quiet enough?" he whispers.

A scream rips through the stillness. Jude breaks apart, his body nothing more than shadows that flit to the corners of the room like bats. I jerk awake.

Leena flicks on the lights. The bright fluorescent glow assaults my eyes. I cringe, blinking.

"What's going on?"

"Where's Heathcliff?" Leena hobbles across the room, her crutches creaking beneath her weight. "Did you let him out of his cage?"

"What are you talking about?" I murmur, still half asleep. "He's in the closet."

"He's *not* in the closet."

"Maybe Sutton took him out?" I say, rubbing my eyes with my palms.

"Sutton's in Jackson for that stupid game. Remember?" There's an edge to Leena's voice that sends something jittery and cold shooting up my spine. I blink, and my eyes start to adjust to the light.

"We'll look for him, okay?" I say, crawling out of bed. Leena nods. A tear slides out from the corner of her eye and rolls down her cheek but she brushes it away, hard. I open the closet, checking behind boots and coats. "I swear, he was in the cage when I—"

Someone knocks on the door, then eases it open without waiting for an answer. Sister Lauren sticks her head into our dorm.

"I heard a scream." She tucks a short brown lock of hair behind one ear. "Is everything okay?"

"We lost—" I start, but Leena jerks her head to the side to shoot me an angry look. *Shit.* The bunny's a secret. My head spins, trying to come up with a good lie. "I mean, Leena lost her favorite earrings, and . . ."

"Could the thing you lost have anything to do with this room smelling like a zoo?" Sister Lauren asks, wrinkling her nose. I press my lips together, not sure what to say. I knew it reeked of piss in here.

Leena opens her mouth to answer, but her face crumples. She lowers her head to her hands, her shoulders shaking. Sister Lauren kneels next to her and slides an arm around her shoulder.

"I'm not going to bust you, okay? Now, what was it? A hamster?"

Leena lifts her face from her hands. "A bunny."

"Let's check the hall," Sister Lauren says, squeezing

Leena's shoulder. "Sofia, you want to give the dorm another look before you head to bed?"

"Of course. I'm sure he's around here somewhere, Leena."

Leena nods again. Sister Lauren helps her to her feet and leads her into the hall. Our dorm is tiny, and it doesn't take me very long to search every inch of carpet. Heathcliff isn't in the closet or hiding behind the dressers. He isn't under either bed. He's just *gone*.

I know the bunny isn't here, but I check the entire room again, and then a third time after that. Sister Lauren and Leena haven't come back yet, so I look inside dresser drawers, and behind the books in our bookcase, and on the higher shelves in the back of our wardrobe. I don't get it. Heathcliff was in a cage, on a table in the closet. He couldn't have just escaped.

Finally, I collapse back onto my bed, frustrated. The sheets are pleasantly cool to the touch. My eyes droop. According to my alarm clock, it's past midnight. I can't believe Sister Lauren and Leena are still out looking. They must be searching every inch of the school. I'm going to be a zombie tomorrow if I don't get some sleep, so I stretch out across the cold sheets, yawning.

My fingers brush against something soft. My entire body stiffens. I reach a little farther, fingers grasping. It feels like hair, or . . .

I jerk my hand out from under the pillow and sit up. Not hair.

Fur.

I half leap, half fall out of my bed. Blankets tangle around my legs, and I lose my balance, slamming to the floor. Dull pain spreads through my shoulder and down my arm, but I barely notice.

I reach forward, and I curl my fingers around the pale pink pillowcase. My hands tremble.

I rip the pillow away before I can change my mind, letting it drop to the floor next to me. Heathcliff lies on the white sheets, his red eyes staring up at the ceiling. Blood blossoms across his fur like roses. I curl my hand into a fist and press it against my mouth to keep from screaming out loud. I *smell* him, all sharp and metallic. Like pennies.

That bunny cannot be lying there. Someone would have had to sneak into my locked room, silently kill it, and slip it under my pillow without making any sound. It's not *possible*. It's another Brooklyn nightmare. I pinch myself on the shoulder and a bright burst of pain flutters through my skin.

Or . . . could *I* have done this?

I wished for something bad to happen to Leena. And then she fell through a trapdoor and broke her leg. And tonight, just before I went to sleep, I wished that

Heathcliff was dead. Sister Lauren said demons could attach themselves to you. She said it was just like getting sick . . .

My mind slams closed on that line of thinking. *No.* This wasn't me. I'm not possessed. I would have remembered killing a bunny.

Footsteps sound in the hall outside my dorm. I go rigid, waiting for the door to fly open. For Leena to burst inside and see what I've done. But the girl moves past my room, the sound of footsteps fading as she makes her way down the hall. I exhale, my chest tight with worry. It doesn't matter how this happened. I have to get rid of it.

I work quickly. I rip the sheets off my mattress, and wrap them around the bunny, so I don't have to look into the creature's dull red eyes. I ball the sheets together, tight, and then I tug the case off my pillow and shove them inside. There. It looks innocent now. Like laundry. I tug my comforter over my bed, then shove a pillow underneath at the last second. Leena will think I'm sleeping. I throw a coat over my nightgown and creep across the room, easing the door open , the pillowcase heavy in my hands.

Hallway's empty. Dozens of doors stretch between the stairs and me, each one closed, hiding God knows what behind its polished surface. I creep forward until I reach the staircase. Then I run.

Icy rain pounds at the ground outside, creating rivers

of mud through the grass. I slosh through it, cringing at the sudden cold on my feet. Sleet slithers under my collar and cuts down my back, instantly soaking my thin nightgown. Mud oozes through my toes and climbs up around my feet and ankles. I hobble toward a thick grove of trees near the front fence. I drop to my knees and thrust my hands into the mud.

No one can find this bag. *Ever.*

I dig. Mud creeps in between my fingers and gushes up past my elbows. It's slick and cold, and soon my skin's gone numb and I can barely move my fingers. The muscles in my arms scream with pain but still, I dig. Pebbles and twigs bite my fingers, and a sharp rock peels away the skin along my knuckles. Blood appears, dark as oil against my skin. I grit my teeth, working through the pain.

Thunder rumbles in the distance, and a flash of lightning cuts across the sky, illuminating my shallow hole and bloody pillowcase. I sit back on my feet, gasping. This will have to do. I shove the pillowcase into the hole, then cup my hands and shovel dirt and mud on top of it. Something inside of me loosens when the last bit of pink cloth disappears below the ground.

It's over. The bunny's gone for good. Beneath the panic and the horror, I actually feel sort of . . . *good.* Heathcliff's dead, but it's okay. I fixed it. No one will ever know what happened.

I catch my reflection in the front door as I limp back to the dormitory. Mud covers my body. It's caked in my hair and in the creases on my knees and elbows. Long brown fingers streak along my calves. My nightgown is ruined. It's plastered to my legs, the hem ragged and torn. A hole has opened up just below my hip and a tiny glimpse of brown skin peeks through.

I lift my eyes to my face and, for a second, I don't recognize myself. I'm *smiling*. The expression is grotesque, like someone else has arranged my features into what they think a human smile should look like. My eyes are wide and manic, my lips stretched tight over my small white teeth.

My expression instantly changes into one of horror. What is wrong with me?

I lift a hand to push the door open and my fingers are raw. Bloody.

I hurry into the hall, a plan forming in the back of my head. I can't go to my dorm like this. Leena will know something's up. They keep fresh towels in the laundry room. I'll just sneak down and steal one, then hit the shared bathrooms on our floor. There's nothing suspicious about needing a shower. I'll shove my nightgown into my laundry bag before Leena can see it and change into—

"Sofia?" Sister Lauren's voice cuts through my

thoughts. I freeze. Water drips from my coat, forming a puddle on the floor.

Footsteps pound against the hall behind me. I'm too terrified to turn. I rack my brain, trying to come up with some excuse for why I was outside. Why I'm bloody and muddy and wet. My head goes blank. I have the sudden, foolish urge to run.

"Sofia?" Sister Lauren says, again. She's right behind me now. I release the breath I'd been holding, and turn.

Sister Lauren's eyes widen at the sight of me. She frowns, and a crease wrinkles the skin between her eyebrows. She opens her mouth, and then closes it again. She tilts her head to the side and understanding crosses her face.

"Oh, Sofia. Were you outside looking for Leena's bunny?"

Her words fall into my hands. The perfect lie, fully formed and waiting. All I have to do is take it.

"Yes," I say, surprised by the confidence in my voice. Like this was planned.

Sister Lauren smiles and shakes her head. "You're such a good friend," she says. "Leena's lucky to have you. Now go back upstairs and get cleaned up before anyone else sees you."

She nods at the staircase behind me, winking.

CHAPTER FOURTEEN

I don't sleep for the rest of the night. I lie on my back in bed, staring at the twisted crack running across the ceiling. I didn't have time to find new sheets, and the rough fabric of the mattress chafes my skin. I roll onto my side. A tiny spider clings to the glass outside our window. He casts a shadow over my bedside table as he scurries away.

The red numbers on my alarm clock tick past.

3:01. 4:15. 5:07.

I close my eyes, but the numbers are seared into my lids. Only now they look like eyes. Heathcliff's beady red eyes.

At five forty-seven, I crawl out of bed and dress silently. Leena fell asleep crying hours ago, but I still check her face to make sure her eyes are tightly shut. A strand of hair sticks to her cheek, fluttering when she breathes.

I creep past her and ease the door open, holding the knob to close it without catching the latch. Then I hurry down the staircase, out the main door, and across the grounds to the chapel.

It's empty this time. Silent. I head to the first pew, cross myself, and kneel. First the trapdoor, then Leena's bunny. And what's worse—I *liked* it. Both times I felt a spark of happiness that something horrible had happened. Brooklyn said there was evil inside me. She said I was just like her. I close my eyes and clasp my hands in front of my chest, but I'm not quite sure how to form a prayer. One question circles my head, instead.

Is the evil taking over my soul?

I dig my teeth into my lower lip, focusing on the pain until the question fades to the back of my mind. I'm nothing like Brooklyn. An evil girl wouldn't be kneeling inside a chapel at six in the morning. Possessed girls would never try to pray.

I stay kneeling, my back and shoulders stiff, but it's not the Lord I think about. It's my mother. I can practically smell the soapy scent of her skin and hear her soothing me in her calm voice. She would know exactly what to say if she were here.

"Mom," I whisper. "Please tell me what to do."

Pain pounds through my knees. I clench my hands together so tightly that my fingernails leave tiny, crescent-shaped marks on the backs of my hands. But nothing happens. My mother doesn't speak to me.

Thwap!

The sound breaks the silence of the chapel. Chills dance up the backs of my arms. My eyes shoot open and I jerk around, expecting to see someone standing at the chapel door.

But there's no one. The door stays shut.

I take a deep breath and twist around, still balanced on my knees. Tiny white candles flicker from the altar at the front of the room, sending a kaleidoscope of light and shadow across the chapel's floor. Leena told me they're called prayer candles. Apparently, they stay lit day and night, until their tiny wicks finally burn out. I never found them creepy before but now I can't help noticing how the tiny spots of brightness leave the corners even darker. Anyone could be hiding there.

Thwap!

I stumble to my feet, hugging my arms to my chest. The darkness seems to pulse. I can practically see it pressing in against the tiny spots of light. Threatening to extinguish them.

Thwap!

Heavy velvet curtains cover the wall behind the altar. I can just make out their edges in the light of the prayer candles. I open my mouth to call out, but something stops me. Maybe it's the silence. The chapel is so quiet that I hear the flames flickering, the wind rubbing up against the glass in the windows. I move forward, my footsteps soundless on the marble.

Thwap!

The noise echoes from the other side of the curtains, making the velvet flutter. It sounds like something wet and heavy slapping against the floor. I lower my hand and push the curtains open. Just an inch.

Thwap!

Candlelight spills past the curtains, bathing my feet in gold. It takes a moment for my eyes to adjust to the sudden glow.

Jude kneels on the floor inside the small room. Naked. Sweat clings to his bare skin, and deep red welts crisscross his shoulders. Tangled flesh bubbles up around his spine and twists down his back and around his waist. Fresh cuts overlap the old ones, the skin raw and angry. He stares at the floor, his wooden cross clenched in his fist.

A shadow moves behind him. I recognize Father Marcus's dark robes and the silver ring glinting from his gnarled finger. A length of leather rope dangles from his hand. He raises it over his head and, for a second, he just holds it there, the tapered end hanging between his shoulders.

The muscles in Jude's jaw tighten. He squeezes his eyes shut.

Father Marcus lowers his arm in a smooth, quick arc, bringing the whip down across Jude's back.

Thwap!

Something wet hits my cheek. *Blood*. My mouth falls open and I want to scream, but my voice gets trapped in my throat. I take a step backward and the sole of my sneaker squeaks against the marble.

Jude's head jerks up. His eyes lock on mine. A hundred emotions flicker across his face, all of them ugly.

Jude says something but I don't stick around long enough to find out what it.

I just run.

* * *

Leena hobbles around backstage, leaning into the crutches wedged beneath her arms. She stumbles, her crutch snagging on the edge of her costume.

"This is a disaster," she mumbles, untangling her skirt. "I'm going to fall flat on my face."

It's the opening night of *The Tempest*, a week after I witnessed the unsettling scene with Jude. I've been avoiding him, trying to keep a low profile and comforting Leena over Heathcliff's disappearance. Thankfully, I've convinced her to give up the search and told her that I'd even help her sneak a new pet into our room. She wants a mouse named Rochester.

The air around us buzzes with voices and the occasional nervous giggle. Actors flit across the stage dressed in stiff costumes, their faces caked with makeup. I'm helping glue the last tattered sails into place while Sutton crouches on an overturned milk crate, studying an ugly cut that twists across her thigh.

"You'll be fine, Leenie-bean," she drawls, picking at the scab.

"You're going to make it bleed," I warn, watching her dig her nails around the edges of her skin.

"Ugh, I know." Sutton makes a face. "It's *so* gross. But I want it gone before I see Dean." She starts picking at the scab again. "Stupid field hockey."

Leena balances on her good leg and waves her crutch between us. "Guys, focus. This is an emergency. I'm supposed to be onstage in like ten minutes."

"Can't you go without the crutch?" Sutton asks.

"Not if I want to walk."

A wicked smile crosses Sutton's face. "All the more reason to lean on Jude's big, strong arms."

Hearing Jude's name makes me flinch. I absently wipe my cheek with the back of my hand. I can still feel his blood on my face.

"I'm going to see if there's something I can use in the prop closet," Leena says, pushing through the stage curtain.

Sutton waits until Leena's gone and then leans forward, the milk crate creaking beneath her weight. "What's up with you?"

I turn my attention back to the sails I'm supposed to be working on, my heart beating so loudly I'm sure Sutton can hear it. I haven't told anyone what I saw in the chapel. I'm not sure they would believe me. "What do you mean?"

"Every time someone says Jude's name, you make the same face my mom makes when I bring up my dad." Sutton screws her face up, demonstrating. "It's like someone walked across your grave."

I laugh but it sounds hollow, even to me. I keep seeing Father Marcus's silver ring glint in the darkness, blood arcing through the air. I tell myself there must be some reason, but what explanation could there be for *that*? It was sick. Twisted.

My hands start to tremble. I curl them tighter around the glue gun so I don't drop it.

"Damn, Sofia," Sutton says, touching my shoulder.

"You look like you're about to lose it. Are you still thinking about that bunny? I'm telling you, Leena must've forgotten to close his cage. He used to get out once a week."

If only—Heathcliff feels like the least of my problems now. "I think it's just stage fright," I manage.

"You're not even in the play," Sutton says.

The hall door slams open before I can answer. The sudden thud makes Sutton and me jump. Sister Lauren pokes her head backstage.

"Five minutes to curtain!" she calls. She glances at Sutton and raises an eyebrow. "Funny, Sutton, I don't remember casting you."

"I'm calming your crew with my witty commentary," Sutton says.

"Thanks for that. Now it's time to take your seat."

Sutton squeezes my arm and stands. "We'll talk later," she says. I nod and she follows Sister Lauren back into the hallway.

Band members tune their instruments in the pit below. The air fills with strings screeching and horns honking. I hear muffled footsteps on the other side of the curtain as the audience takes their seats. I shake my hand out to stop the trembling and put the final touches on the sail. It's almost showtime.

The stage curtain rustles. "Hey."

The muscles in my shoulders tighten at the sound of Jude's voice. I fumble with the glue gun, accidentally dropping a hot bead on my finger.

"Crap," I mutter. Jude kneels next to me. He's already dressed as Ferdinand, with an emerald-green tunic buttoned up to his chin and a gold sash knotted at his waist. His wooden cross hangs from a leather cord around his neck. It looks as though the makeup crew loaded his hair with some product to make it look windblown, and a few days' worth of stubble covers his cheeks and chin. Sister Lauren must've wanted him to look disheveled. His character has been shipwrecked, after all.

"Are you okay?" He reaches for my hand, but I jerk it back. Hurt flashes across his face.

"I'm fine," I say. Jude leans back on his heels, hands folded in his lap. He was sitting in the same position that morning in the chapel. I think of the sweat glistening from his bare skin. I hear the crack of the whip hitting his back.

"Sofia," he says. "I was hoping we could talk."

I squeeze my eyes shut, forcing the horrible memory away. "I'm sorry," I say. "I have a lot of stuff to get ready before you—"

Jude grabs my wrist. "*Listen*," he says in a low, urgent voice. "There are things about me that you don't know. Things about my past, and what I did to . . . it's complicated."

"Complicated?" I repeat. What I saw wasn't complicated. It was disturbing.

"Father Marcus is helping me work through some stuff," Jude explains. "What you saw . . . it's a really old Catholic tradition. It's supposed to bring you closer to God. We thought it might help."

"Help with *what*?" I ask.

Sister Lauren's voice blares over the loudspeaker. "Five minutes to curtain! Take your places."

Actors shuffle across the stage and duck into the wings. The stage manager hisses at me to get off the stage.

"I told you," Jude says, his voice low. "I have trouble sometimes, with anger and self-control. Father Marcus says I have a 'hero complex,' whatever that is. Like wanting to help people is supposed to be wrong. He thought this might help me give in to God."

Jude's eyes flicker over my face, concern etched into his features. For a second, I forget about what I saw in the chapel. I stare at the curls lying against his neck. The freckle next to his upper lip. A familiar mix of anxiety and want flares to life in my chest.

"Can I ask you a favor?" Jude stands, offering his hand to help me up. This time, I take it without flinching.

"What is it?"

Jude drops my hand to untie the wooden cross from his neck. "This was my father's," he explains. "I wear it every day, but Sister Lauren says it doesn't go with my costume. I was wondering . . . could you hold on to it for me?"

"Of course." My voice sounds thicker than usual. Like it belongs to someone else. The corner of Jude's mouth curls into a smile. He leans in close, lifting the leather cord to my neck. His fingers brush my skin, leaving trails of heat along my collarbone.

He finishes knotting the necklace, but he doesn't move his hand away. My throat goes dry.

"Sofia," he murmurs. His breath tickles the side of my face. He curls his hands around my shoulders, pulling me to his chest. "I can't stop thinking about you."

"We shouldn't." I feel his heart beating through the fabric of his tunic. He's close enough to kiss. All I have to do is lift my face. I lean in closer. "Jude . . ."

"Jude?" The curtains rustle, and Leena hobbles backstage, plastic vines wrapped around her crutches. "I thought I saw you . . ."

I jerk away from Jude, but it's too late. Leena freezes. Her eyes move from Jude to the wooden cross hanging around my neck.

She blinks, and in that instant it's like something in her breaks. Her mouth goes slack and all the color drains from her face. Her stage makeup looks heavy and garish against her pale skin.

"Leena," I start, but she stumbles away from me. She grips her crutches so tightly that her knuckles turn white.

"We're needed onstage, Jude," she mutters before pushing through the curtains. "We're starting."

CHAPTER FIFTEEN

I don't stick around to watch the play. I duck into one
of the dressing rooms and hunch down on a stool at
the makeup table, hiding like a coward. My reflection
stares out from the mirror. I shift my eyes to my knees.
I can't stand to look at myself.

Speakers hang from the ceiling, broadcasting
the play to the empty room. Leena's staticky voice
bounces off the walls around me. She recites every
line perfectly.

I hide there until the play is over, and then I busy
myself backstage, sweeping sand and gathering props
until I'm sure Leena has headed back to the dorm. I've

practiced my apology a dozen times by then, but it still sounds wrong. Forced. Leena will never forgive me.

Our dorm is empty when I get back, but there's a note waiting on my bed.

We're meeting up with Dean and his friend at the chapel to toast Leena's AMAZING performance. Come meet us (use the back door)!!! —Sutton

ps—destroy this message after you've read it. xoxoxo

Leena snuck out? I swear under my breath, crumpling the piece of paper in one hand. She'd never risk getting in trouble if she hadn't seen Jude and me backstage. I push myself to my feet and grab my coat.

* * *

Moonlight paints the chapel's whitewashed siding silver. It glints off the stained glass windows, making them wink in the darkness.

I stop at the gate. Something dashes through the brush, rustling the leaves before going still. I flinch and glance over my shoulder, certain I'm going to see Father Marcus step out of the trees, the word *expelled* already on his lips. But there's no one. Clouds drift over the moon, blocking the last tendrils of light.

Voices echo from inside the chapel. I shiver and slip through the gate, pushing it closed with a creak.

The chapel's back door opens into a narrow room. A small table leans against the wall to my left, holding a leather Bible and a heavy brass candleholder. I brush my fingertips lightly over the candleholder, looking around the space. The room feels familiar. I frown, studying the shadows gathering in the corners, the stained glass window, the paintings staring down from the walls—

I feel the hot splash of blood hitting my cheek. I hear the sound of leather slapping against skin. *Thwap!*

I jerk my hand away from the table, horror rushing over me. This room seems familiar to me because I've seen it before. Jude knelt naked on the floor just feet from where I'm standing, cringing as Father Marcus whipped him.

I hold my breath and hurry through the heavy velvet curtains hanging open on the far wall. I don't inhale again until I reach the main altar. The air in that tiny room felt *wrong*, somehow. Spoiled.

Prayer candles flicker from the altar, casting a dull golden glow over the rows of wooden pews. I spot Sutton sitting on a windowsill near the front entrance. Dean hovers over her, his mouth buried in her neck. She wraps her legs around his waist, pulling him closer. I blush and avert my eyes. A boy I don't recognize hunches down in the front pew a few feet away, holding a Budweiser bottle and studying something on his cell phone.

A shape separates from the shadows to my left. I stumble away from it, smacking my hip into the altar. The candles wobble, wicks flaring.

"Leena?" I groan, a dull pain spreading through my side. "Is that you?"

Leena is still wearing her stage makeup. Dark circles of blush cover her cheeks, and she's smudged her lipstick. Sweaty strands of black hair fall loose from her braid and stick to her neck and forehead. She's changed out of her costume, though. A thick sweater hangs from her shoulders, half covering a pair of ripped jeans. She had to cut one of the legs short to fit it over her chunky white cast.

"You came." Booze makes her voice thick and sloppy. She hobbles toward me, balancing on just one crutch. A bottle of coconut rum dangles from her free hand. "I didn't know if you would."

I stare at the bottle. "Are you drunk?"

Leena wrinkles her nose. Her breath smells sickly sweet. "Brian bet me I couldn't drink the whole bottle," she says. "If I win, he's going to show me his car."

"Brian?" I glance at the boy sitting in the front pew. He's older than Dean. Greasy black hair falls over his forehead, and the corner of a tattoo peeks out from beneath his T-shirt. It looks like a woman's leg.

"You're not going anywhere with that guy." I shoot a glance at Sutton, but she's too distracted by Dean to catch my dirty look. I can't believe she left Leena alone with some creep. I take a step away from the altar and Leena stumbles backward, swaying. I grab her crutch to steady her before she falls. "Maybe you should sit down. I can find you some water."

"Don't do that." Leena's words slur. "Don't pretend to be nice."

She pulls her crutch away from me and rocks back on her feet, nearly stumbling over own her cast. We're standing near the edge of the pulpit, just inches from the stairs leading down to the pews. There isn't far to fall, but if Leena hit the ground at the right angle, she could reinjure her leg.

She lifts the rum to her mouth and tips it back, leaving her lips wet and sticky. I need to take the bottle away from her. I edge forward, like she's an animal I don't want to spook.

"Why don't you give me that?" I say, reaching for the rum. "You're going to hurt yourself."

"You don't care if I get hurt." Leena hugs the bottle to her chest. A tear spills onto her cheek and she wipes it away angrily with the back of her hand. "You *want* me to get hurt."

She rocks backward another step, sliding the

rubber-tipped foot of her crutch an inch closer to the edge of the pulpit. I cringe. "Leena, come on, you're really close to the stairs—"

"All this time I thought you were my *friend*. And then, when I saw you with Jude, I realized you were just playing me." Leena motions to me with her arm, sending an arc of coconut rum splattering across the floor. "You want me to get hurt so you can have him all to yourself. That's why you left the trapdoor unlocked, and that's why . . ."

Leena blinks, and it takes a long moment for her eyes to flutter open again. Another tear runs down her face, tracing a pink line in her makeup.

"I know you did something to Heathcliff," she says, her voice cracking. I swallow. My mouth feels dry.

"I didn't, Leena. I swear."

"You didn't like him." Leena leans into her crutch. The wood creaks beneath her weight. "And then, all of a sudden, he was *gone*."

My skin pricks with nerves. "What are you talking about?"

"You do terrible things. If you want something, you just take it, even if someone else gets hurt. You're . . . you're evil."

Heat spreads through my chest. I stare into Leena's unfocused eyes and, for a second, I want to push her.

She doesn't deserve her perfect life any more than I deserve my shitty one. I can practically feel her body tipping backward beneath my hands. If she weren't here, Jude and I could be together, and I wouldn't have to feel guilty about that damn bunny or the trapdoor. I could wipe the past clean and start over.

"You should be careful what you wish for, Sofia," Leena says in a small, trembling voice. "Jude may have chosen you, but God punishes sinners. You'll see."

Candlelight wavers behind me, casting our shadows across the floor. I study Leena. She's drunk. I could make it to the back door before she does, easy. And then, *oops*, all I'd have to do is slam the door and twist the dead bolt. I could stand back and watch this place burn.

I hear Brooklyn's voice whispering in my ear: *The evil lives inside of you already . . .*

Shame washes over me, and I stumble away from the altar. What the hell is wrong with me? I would never think those things. *Never.*

The sound of metal clicking against metal cuts through the chapel. I flinch, and jerk my head toward the front entrance. *Keys.*

"Shit! Someone's here!" Sutton hisses. She grabs Dean by the collar of his shirt and drags him behind a pew.

"Come on." I take Leena's arm and pull her toward the back room. She murmurs something and tries to push me away, but I dig my fingers into her wrist, holding tight. She stumbles forward on her crutch.

The keys jangle, then go still. We don't have time to make it to the back room now. I pull Leena's crutch out from under her arm, and help her crouch down behind the altar. Someone swears, and I see movement from the corner of my eye as Brian ducks behind the pew with Sutton and Dean. Dean knocks over an empty beer can with his foot, but Brian grabs it before it rolls into the aisle.

A creak echoes through the chapel. Someone releases a deep, phlegmy cough.

"Who's there?" he asks. Cold fingers walk down my spine. It's Father Marcus.

"Dammit," Leena whispers, huddling closer to me. Her ragged breath hits the back of my neck. I motion for her to keep quiet.

Footsteps make their way down the aisle.

I hold my breath and edge forward. Leena digs her fingers into my shoulders and I freeze, my heart thudding.

Father Marcus stops walking. "I heard voices. I know someone's here."

I glance over my shoulder. Leena stares back at me, her eyes rimmed with red. Sweat glistens on her forehead. I lift a finger to my mouth, then turn back around. Slowly, I lean past the edge of the altar and peer into the darkness.

Father Marcus stands near the center of the chapel, head cocked—listening. Shadows obscure his face, but moonlight glints in from the stained glass windows, painting the top of his head silver. He drifts forward, the hem of his black robes dragging along the floor.

Three shadows rise, silently, from the pews behind him. Sutton, Dean, and Brian hurry for the front door, their footsteps soundless on the tile. Sutton stays behind for a second, looking for me and Leena. She raises her shoulders in a desperate shrug—*there's nothing I can do*—before hurrying after the boys.

I hold my breath as she eases the door open and slips outside. The door clicks shut and Father Marcus whirls around. But Sutton's gone.

Leena's fingernails pinch the skin on my shoulders. "We're going to be expelled," she whispers.

Quiet. I mouth the word rather than say it out loud. Leena presses her lips together. Nods.

There's about three feet of open space between the altar and the velvet curtains that lead to the back room. If Leena and I can make it through there, we can get to the door without Father Marcus seeing us. I shift my weight to my front leg, poised to run.

"I know there's someone here," Father Marcus calls. "Best to just come out from where you're hiding."

Three feet. Maybe less. I could be out the door before Father Marcus made it to the pulpit. Leena would never make it with her cast, but Father Marcus would probably follow me outside, giving her a chance to get away.

The legs in my muscles tighten, itching to move. I lean forward.

A spray of pebbles hits the window, rattling the glass in the pane. I hear laughter outside, then running. Father Marcus whirls around.

"Little punks," he mutters, sweeping back to the front door. I shoot forward, dragging Leena behind me. The booze has made her slow and clumsy. She stumbles, banging a shoulder into the altar and nearly fumbling her crutch. A candle topples off the side of the altar and smashes into the floor. A hairline crack shoots across the candleholder. The flame flickers and sparks, but stays lit.

I shoot a nervous glance at the front entrance, but Father Marcus has already left to chase down whoever threw the stones. We're alone. The candle rolls across the floor, coming to rest next to a curtain. The flame grows and leaps onto the fabric. Leena blinks at it, her eyes not quite focusing.

"Just *go*," I tell her.

Leena looks at me, then lurches through the curtains. The flame gently licks the edge of the velvet. Something dark and hungry rises in my chest. I could just let it burn. Leena stumbles into something in the back room and swears loudly. It would be so easy to push past her on that stupid crutch. I could lock the door behind me. No one would ever know.

My fingers fumble for the cross at my neck. Jude's cross. I stomp out the flame, disgusted with myself. I hurry through the small room. It's empty—Leena must've made a break for the woods. I push the door open and hurry outside, letting it slam shut behind me.

"Come on!" Sutton calls from the woods. I catch a glimpse of her blonde hair and tanned legs before she disappears into the gloom.

It's too dark to see where I'm going, so I rely on muscle memory to carry me across the grounds. Muffled sounds reach me: footsteps crashing through the brush, heavy breathing, Sutton shouting *"Hurry!"* They seem far away, as if I'm hearing them underwater. I want to call out to the others, but I'm afraid Father Marcus is hiding in the shadows. Waiting to catch me.

I'm relieved when the trees part, revealing redbrick walls and my room's familiar window. Wind moves the curtain—the window's still open.

"Sutton?" I whisper.

A slim hand pushes the curtain aside and Sutton's blonde head appears in the window.

"Did it work?" She reaches for me and her fingers close around my wrist. "The pebbles? It was Dean's idea. He said we had to distract Father Marcus so you guys could get out."

"It worked." I wedge a foot against the wall, grabbing the windowsill with my other hand. Sutton grunts, half dragging me into the room as I struggle to pull my weight through the window. I lose my balance and wobble forward, but Sutton catches me before I crash into anything.

"Thanks," I say, brushing the dirt off the back of my jeans. A muscle in my shoulder twinges. I grimace and try to stretch it out.

Sutton leans past me. "Where's Leena?"

"She left before I did." I glance around the room, half expecting Leena to materialize from the shadows in the corners. "She isn't back yet?"

"No." Sutton frowns. "I didn't see her in the woods, either. You're sure Father Marcus didn't—"

"He didn't catch her," I say before she can finish. "But, Sutton, she was so drunk. I don't know how she's going to make it back here on her own." I think of Leena stumbling around on her crutch, her eyes blurry, and feel a sliver of guilt. "You think she'd get lost? Or something happened with her leg?"

"Leena's been going to this school for three years. She's not lost."

A floorboard creaks in the hall just outside our door. Sutton swears. She quickly pulls the window closed.

"Bed," she whispers, pushing me across the room. "Pretend you're sleeping."

"What about Leena?"

"We can't risk looking for her now." Sutton peels off her jeans and digs her polka-dot pajama pants out of her dresser. She yanks them on and climbs into bed, tugging her comforter up to her chin. "She'll have to find her own way back."

CHAPTER SIXTEEN

"**D**id you hear that?"

Sutton's voice jars me awake. I blink, slowly letting my eyes adjust to the darkness of our room. Sutton lies on her side in the bed next to mine. The whites of her eyes flash in the shadows.

"Hear what?" I murmur, my brain thick and heavy. Sleep pulls at me, dragging me down. My eyes flicker closed.

Wind howls through the trees. Only it's not wind. I ease my eyes back open, frowning.

"*That.*" Sutton sits up, her shoulders rigid with fear. The sound loops back on itself, growing distant at first, and then louder. Closer. Recognition flutters through me.

"Is that a siren?" I ask.

Sutton kicks off her comforter and climbs out of bed. I sit up, but I can't quite remember how to make my legs work. It can't be a siren. We didn't do anything wrong. And, besides, Father Marcus didn't even see us. I stare, frozen, as Sutton crosses the room and throws back the curtains covering our windows. The muscles in her jaw go slack and her mouth falls open. She lifts a trembling finger.

"Fire," she whispers.

Nausea floods my stomach. "No," I say, climbing out of bed. I cross the room and crowd next to Sutton at the window.

Smoke hangs above the woods, dark and thick, like someone spilled oil across the sky. Red lights flash in the trees. Sirens howl.

"Oh God." Sutton bunches a hand near her mouth. "It's coming from the chapel."

A dark thought wraps around my brain. I glance at Leena's empty bed.

The blood drains from Sutton's face, leaving her skin ashen. "Sofia," she breathes. "What if . . ."

Doubt seeps through me. Leena never came home, and now there's a fire . . . "Leena left the chapel before I did," I say, trying to convince myself as much as Sutton. "I *heard* her."

But I didn't actually hear Leena get out. She was just gone.

"She could have circled back to the chapel after you left." Sutton lifts a hand to her mouth, lightly touching a finger to her lips. "She was so drunk. If she couldn't figure out how to get home, and it was too cold . . ."

"I locked the door." At least, I think I did. I close my eyes, rubbing my eyelids. I think of the moments right before I ran through the back door, trying to remember twisting the lock. I come up blank.

Static fills my ears, blocking out the sirens and Sutton's voice. I think of the candle toppling from the altar and rolling across the floor. The white flame leaping onto the curtain. Leena's expression as she watched it catch, light dancing in her unfocused eyes.

But I stomped the fire out. I stopped it. Didn't I?

A sharp knock raps on our door. "Roll call! Five minutes!" Sister Lauren shouts. There's an edge of panic in her tone.

Sutton grabs my arm and drags me into the hallway. Dazed students stumble past us. Winter coats cover their lacy nightgowns and striped pajamas, and they've shoved their feet into Converse sneakers and UGGs. A girl I recognize from geometry—Erika—wears reindeer slippers with tiny bells on the toes. They jingle as she shuffles toward the stairs.

"Single file," Sister Lauren calls. She stands at the other end of the hall, a rumpled pair of St. Mary's sweatpants hanging from her hips, her hair piled in a messy topknot. Short, spiky pieces stick out of the elastic and fall around her face. "Stay calm, everyone."

Her eyes flicker over to Sutton and me, and something in her expression sharpens. "Put your shoes on," she says to us. "We need everyone outside for roll call."

"Did someone get hurt?" Sutton asks. Her voice has a little-girl quality to it that I've never heard before.

"That's what we're trying to figure out," Sister Lauren says, counting off the other girls. "We all need to gather outside."

I grab my coat while Sutton yanks a pair of cowboy boots over her pajama pants. We hurry down the front stairs, taking the steps two at a time. I pause at the main doors, hit with a sudden memory of the first time I walked through them. I was on my way to meet my new roommates, feeling anxious and hopeful as I climbed the stairs behind Father Marcus.

It hasn't even been a month and already, everything's different. One of those girls might be—

I shudder and push through the doors. I can't even think it.

Cold hits me in the face. It snakes around my bare ankles and blows straight through my flannel pajama pants. We make our way over to the crowd of nuns and students already gathered on the lawn.

Two fire trucks race down the narrow, twisted road leading to the chapel, sirens blaring. Sutton huddles close to me, her icy fingers finding my hand.

"Oh God," she whispers. I barely hear her. I tug my hand away and turn, searching the faces of the girls around us. Leena has to be here. She *has* to be.

"Do you see her?" A note of panic has crept into Sutton's voice. I don't answer. My eyes dart over face after face, until I find every single girl who lives on our floor, and everyone I know from classes and play practice. Everyone except Leena.

Sutton seems to realize this at the same moment I do. "She isn't here. Oh God, Sofia . . ."

My mouth feels dry. "She . . . she must've passed out in the woods," I say. Fear leaves my voice high-pitched and weak. "That's why she's not back yet."

Sutton nods, but she doesn't seem to hear me. She stares at the smoke staining the sky, frowning. I spot a shadow moving through the trees and my heart leaps into my throat. I grab Sutton's arm, my knees buckling in relief.

"There!" I say, pointing. "That's her!"

The figure walks closer. My heart seems to go still inside of my chest and every muscle in my body tightens. Leena's coming. Leena's okay. I'm so busy searching for black hair and dark jeans that it takes a long moment for my brain to recognize Father Marcus's bald head and long black robes. Familiar panic fills my body. I twist my hands together, squeezing so hard the blood drains from my fingers.

"It's not her," Sutton whispers.

"Maybe he's coming to tell us he found her in the woods," I say, but a horrible thought creeps through my mind.

Leena's dead, just like you wanted. You killed her.

Father Marcus stops in front of Sister Lauren. He runs a hand over his head and says something in a low voice. I move to Sutton's other side, sliding an arm over her shoulders so it looks like I'm comforting her. Sutton flashes me a confused look. I lift a finger to my lips and flick my eyes toward Father Marcus. Sutton nods.

"Everyone's here except for Leena," Sister Lauren is saying. She tucks a strand of hair behind her ear and glances back at the burning chapel. "She must've snuck out."

"Are you sure the rest of your girls have been in their rooms all night?" Father Marcus asks. Sister Lauren turns, catching my eye. I quickly look down at my sneakers, pretending to study the pattern of dirt on my toe. The top of my head itches and I know, without looking up, that Sister Lauren's still watching me.

She knows, I realize. She knows we're listening. She knows we snuck out. It's like she can see through the layers of hair and skin and bone, down to all of the terrible things I'm hiding. I squeeze Sutton's shoulder, bracing myself.

"I checked the rest of the girls personally," Sister Lauren says. "They were in their beds all night. Father, did someone—"

Father Marcus lifts a hand. "Not here. Why don't you lead your girls back up to their dorms. I don't want them to see—"

A siren blares to life and, seconds later, an ambulance explodes from the trees. It zips down the road, red lights flashing in the darkness.

My heart slows until it feels as if I can count every beat. Shadows move in the ambulance's back windows. EMTs crouch over something. Someone.

That moment in the chapel plays on a loop in my mind. The candle lighting the curtain on fire. Leena staring down at the flames, then stumbling through the back room toward the door.

"Who's in there?" Sutton turns to Sister Lauren. "Is it Leena? Is it *her*?"

"Sutton . . ." Sister Lauren reaches for Sutton's arm,

but Sutton drops to her knees, lowering her face to her hands. A sob erupts from her lips, shaking her entire body.

I stand completely still. This isn't happening. But even as the words enter my head, I feel something stirring deep within my chest. *I wanted this.* I wanted Leena gone. I wanted her life. And, one way or another, I get what I want.

"No," I whisper, pushing the thoughts away. That's the jealousy talking. I will not be weak. I will not let the Devil in. Tears run down my cheeks, tracing cold lines on my face. I wipe them away with the sleeve of my jacket—then freeze.

The smell of smoke hangs in the air but it's faint. We're not downwind of the chapel, and the trees block most of the smoky haze from reaching the lawn. I see the smoke lifting high above the chapel, but I don't smell it. Not really. Except when I lift the sleeve of my coat to my nose.

My coat *reeks* of smoke.

CHAPTER SEVENTEEN

Father Marcus stands on the stage in front of the velvet curtains, flanked by two altar boys dressed all in white and gold. Lilies and tulips and roses crowd the stage around him, their ivory petals fading to brown around the edges. They'd be lovely, except for the stiff black ribbons tied to their vases. Reminders of why we're here.

Father Marcus clears his throat. The thick, phlegmy sound echoes off the walls. He leans over his Bible, bald head gleaming under the hot overhead lights. "We have come together," he says, "to remember before God the life of Leena Paeng."

It's two days before Christmas break, three since Leena died in the fire that burned down the chapel. I sit in the aisle seat nearest the back wall, wearing the same scratchy dress I wore the day of my mother's funeral.

I took the first seat I could find, not even bothering to see if Sutton saved me a spot. I'm not sure I could face her. Sniffling students and crying teachers fill the auditorium. They pass boxes of Kleenex down the aisles. Some hold skinny plastic candles with electric wicks. We're not allowed to have open flames in the school anymore.

Dried mud clings to the hem of my dress. I pick at it with my fingernail.

That's graveyard mud, I think. *It's mud from the ground where my mother was buried.*

"God alone is holy and just and good," Father Marcus continues. His voice is stiff and cold, like he's speaking about someone he's never met and not a student at his own school. "In that confidence, then, we commend young Leena to God's healing and mercy."

I pick and pick, until a crust of dirt lodges itself beneath my fingernail and a thread unravels from the black fabric, leaving a tiny hole at the edge of my dress. A girl in the seat in front of me reaches for a tissue and blows her nose. The sound rattles something deep within my chest. I'm not even crying. Leena was my roommate, and I can't muster a single tear.

Father Marcus clears his throat again. The sound is thicker this time. Wetter. "Leena was a child of God and, like all children, she stumbled . . ."

Stumbled. That one word sends me back to the chapel on the night of the fire. I see Leena struggling with her crutches, her eyes glassy with booze. I smell burning hair. Burning *skin*.

I shift in my uncomfortable dress. I shouldn't be here. I inhale, but my lungs feel like paper bags, like someone's blowing air into them, and then squeezing until they're small and crumpled and empty. The room tilts.

I stand and race for the door. People whisper and stare, but it doesn't matter. I have to get out of here. I can't *breathe*. I push the door open as quietly as I can, and then ease it closed behind me.

The air in the hallway tastes different. Fresher. I lean against the wall, sucking it into my lungs. The room stops spinning, but my legs still feel shaky. I sink to the floor, pulling my knees to my chest. I inhale, and then let it all out. I lower my forehead to my knees. A thin layer of sweat coats my face, making my skin feel clammy.

Just breathe, I tell myself. Don't worry about anything else.

I've seen a dead body before. I didn't stick around after the train accident to see Karen broken on the ground, but there have been others. Alexis was the worst. She'd been burned, just like Leena, and then arranged like a doll in Riley's bed. I'd pulled back the covers and there she was—wispy strands of hair trailing away from her bloody skull, blackened skin peeling off her cheeks. Fire ate her lips, leaving her mouth in a permanent snarl.

A strangled sob bubbles up my throat, breaking the silence of the hallway. My chest feels tight and I can't quite manage to catch my breath. Alexis's death was my fault, just like Leena's death, and Leena's accident, and Leena's bunny. Everything's always my fault.

I tug Jude's wooden cross out from under my shirt. I haven't had a chance to return it to him. Classes were canceled after Leena died, and we've been told to stay in our dormitories unless there's an emergency. I tell myself I'm only wearing it now so I can give it back when I see him, but if that were true, I probably wouldn't keep it hidden beneath my clothes. I press it between my hands and close my eyes.

"Please, God," I whisper. The idea of praying still feels strange, but at this point, I don't know who else to turn to. Jealousy has made my soul a weak, easy target for Brooklyn, and Sister Lauren said the only way to strengthen your soul is through a relationship with the Lord. I close my eyes, focusing all of my attention on God.

"Please," I whisper, my voice trembling. I picture a demon clinging to my back, digging long, pointed talons into my shoulders. Its horrible smile looks just like Brooklyn's.

"I'm begging you," I continue. "Help me get rid of this . . . *thing.* Help me be good—"

The door creaks open. "Sofia?"

Jude's voice makes me start. I drop the cross and wipe the tears from my cheeks with the back of my hand. He's in his altar boy outfit again, same as when I first met him. Between the white robes and the black curls, he looks almost angelic.

"You're missing the service." He sinks to the floor, robes pooling around him. He's shaved since the night of the play. His cheeks look smooth, and there's a tiny nick just below his chin. His skin smells like aftershave. Pine, and something else. Cloves, maybe.

I tear my eyes away from him and focus instead on a thin crack in the wall across from us. It stretches all the way from the floor to the ceiling. I try to keep my voice steady. "Believe me, Leena wouldn't want me in there."

Jude tips his head to the side. "You were one of her best friends," he says. "Of course she'd want you there."

The students inside the auditorium start to sing. I don't recognize the song, but the melody is low and lilting. Something sad. Jude and I listen for a moment in silence. I wipe my nose on the sleeve of my dress.

"You're wrong," I say once the singing stops. "She was mad at me. After she saw us . . ." My voice cracks. I swallow and try again, but a fresh sob lodges itself in my throat. I curl my hand into a fist and ball it next to my mouth to muffle the sound of my crying.

Jude squeezes my shoulder, as if he can read my mind. "Yeah. She seemed pretty upset."

"She *hated* me," I choke out. "And if we hadn't been in a fight, she never would have been drinking that night. She wouldn't have gone to the chapel, and she'd still be . . ."

"I know it feels that way, but it's not true. You can't know what would have happened that night if you weren't fighting, or if you didn't go out, or if you'd said the right thing, or done the right thing."

Jude's eyes lose focus. He swallows—hard—his Adam's apple jerking up and down in his throat. *"Believe me.* I know what it's like to relive one horrible moment over and over. I get it."

I stare at his face, wondering what memory tortures him. "How?"

He absently touches a spot on his arm. "It's complicated."

I'm suddenly aware of how close we're sitting. I think of Leena, and shrug his hand off my shoulder, my skin burning. This is why I didn't want to talk to him. I can't stand within five feet of Jude without completely losing track of what I'm doing. The unfocused, dreamy quality leaves Jude's face. He looks at me, eyes narrowing.

"Is that why you're avoiding me?" he asks. "Because you think it's your fault that Leena died?"

"I'm not avoiding you," I say. Jude lifts an eyebrow.

"Maybe a little," I admit.

"Leena was the friend you were talking about?" Jude asks. "The one you didn't want to hurt?"

I nod.

Jude exhales. "I'm really sorry she died. But I need you to know—I never had feelings for her. You didn't do anything wrong."

"She saw things differently," I say.

"She would have gotten over it after a while. People change. I've changed. It used to be that all I could think about was God. And now . . ."

Jude's voice trails off. I stare at him. "And now?" I press.

"And now all I can think about is you."

I open my mouth, then close it again. My mind has gone blank. I've wished that Jude would say those words to me from the moment I saw him. Now that Leena's gone, there's no reason for me to stay away from him. Everything I wanted is within my grasp.

Be careful what you wish for, Leena said. Those were some of the last words she ever said to me.

"Just be honest with me, Sofia," Jude says. "Do you have any interest in me at all? Or is this thing between us in my head?"

"It's not that easy," I mumble. I picture the demon clinging to my back again, its talons digging deeper and deeper into my shoulders.

Jude furrows his eyebrows. "Why not?"

"I kind of need to work on myself right now," I say, "but you make it so . . ."

I hesitate, struggling for the right word. Jude shifts closer. "I make it so what?"

"I can't think straight when you're around," I spit out.

Hurt flashes across Jude's face. I squeeze my eyes shut. Everything I say comes out wrong. "I didn't mean it like that," I say. "It's just . . . what if we're making a mistake? You said it yourself—you can't focus on your relationship with God when I'm around." Leena's unfocused eyes flash into my head. She whispers, her voice thick with booze. *God punishes sinners.* "What if what we're doing is a sin?"

"Do you really think that?" Jude asks, his voice quiet.

I stare down at my hands, unable to answer.

Jude stands and pushes the auditorium door open. Father Marcus is leading a prayer. His low, gravelly voice drifts into the hallway like smoke.

"At the moment of our death, make us ready to—"

The door swings shut behind Jude, cutting him off.

I sit in the hallway alone for a long moment, staring at the crack in the wall across from me, wondering if I made the right decision. The school loudspeaker crackles on, and then the sound of church bells fills the hall. They echo and clang, then fade to a soft rumble. I used to love the sound of church bells but there's something off about these. The real bells were destroyed when the chapel burned down. This recording is a pale imitation. Haunting and soulless.

I press my hands over my ears to block out the sound but, somehow, that just makes it worse. The bells blend together into one long, hollow ring. It doesn't sound like bells at all. It sounds like an engine. Like the blare of a horn.

Like a train racing toward me.

CHAPTER EIGHTEEN

I head to the dormitory kitchens as soon as I wake up on Christmas Eve. Students aren't technically allowed to cook here, but Sister Lauren snuck me the key so I could raid the pantry over the holiday break. I'm basically alone until after New Year's, but I didn't have anywhere else to go, so the school agreed to let me stay in the dorms. It's a relief to have the place to myself. There's no one around for me to hurt.

I dig through the cupboards until I find flour, baking chocolate, and a dusty bag of red-striped peppermint chips nearing their expiration date. My *abuelita* used to make the best cookies. On Christmas morning, she'd fill our kitchen with *biscochos* and *garabatos* and gingerbread men and—my favorite—double fudge cookies with peppermint chips. Mom and Grandmother didn't agree on a lot, but every year I'd find them standing shoulder to shoulder next to the oven, whipping up batter and dancing to old Christmas carols.

Mom and I started making the cookies together after Grandmother got sick. And now . . . my mother might be gone, but there's no way I'm giving up this tradition. It's part of my plan for redemption. I'm going to do exactly what Sister Lauren told me to—I've already freed myself of the distraction of Jude, and now I'm going to seek communion with other believers. My grandmother is the most religious person I've ever known. If she can't help me repair my relationship with God, no one can.

I gather my ingredients and pull up some of Grandmother's favorite Christmas carols on my phone. Then I get to work. I thought it would make me sad to do this alone, but instead it's the opposite. Music floats through the air around me, and it feels familiar to crack the eggs and stir up the batter. It's almost like being home.

Someone raps at the kitchen door after I've been working for an hour. I flinch, nearly knocking my mixing bowl off the counter.

"Sorry, Sofia." Sister Lauren steps into the kitchen,

holding both hands out in front of her. "I didn't mean to startle you."

"It's okay." I wipe my hands on my jeans without thinking, leaving two streaky white flour prints on the denim. "Crap," I mutter.

Sister Lauren grabs a towel off the counter, and tosses it to me. "Are you making Christmas cookies?"

"For my grandmother," I explain, wiping the flour from my jeans. "I'm going to go visit her at the retirement home today."

"That's so nice of you. Take a cab, though. There's a storm moving in—I don't want you on the roads when it starts to snow." Sister Lauren leans against the fridge, folding her arms across her chest. She's dressed in full habit, and her long black robes hide her feet.

"I thought you only wore your 'penguin suit' for Mass and class," I say. Sister Lauren grins.

"Father Marcus and I are visiting the children's hospital today," she explains. "We like to pray for the sick during the Christmas season. But we'll be back in time for Midnight Mass."

I wrinkle my nose. "Mass is at midnight? Why?"

"Tradition," Sister Lauren explains. "I wanted to invite you to attend. There aren't many students staying on campus over the holidays, but Father Marcus holds a full service, anyway. It's really quite beautiful. It'll be in the auditorium this year since the chapel's out of commission."

"Sure. I'll be there." I pull open the oven door to check my cookies, and a chocolatey, pepperminty smell wafts through the kitchen. Sister Lauren sighs.

"Those smell amazing. I'm sure your grandmother will love them." Sister Lauren starts back toward the door, then pauses, rapping her knuckles against the wooden frame. "And please be careful on the roads today. Mississippi never gets snow. They're closing half the town in preparation, so you should head back early."

"Thanks for the tip," I say.

"Have a good time. You deserve a merry Christmas."

"Thank you," I say.

Sister Lauren smiles and sweeps back out into the hall, her black robes billowing behind her.

* * *

It's raining and freezing cold when my cab arrives at Hope Springs Retirement Homes. I pay my driver, balancing the cookie plate in one hand as I push the door closed. Muddy water slushes around my heeled booties, making it difficult to walk without slipping. I teeter toward the front entrance. The automatic doors whoosh open, blasting me with hot, dry air.

Beige walls and thin, worn-down carpeting lead me through a narrow hall to an empty receptionist's desk.

Fluorescent lights flicker above me. I'm not really sure what the procedure is, so I poke my head down the hall twisting off to my left.

"Hello?" I call.

A beat of silence. Then a voice echoes back, "Hello?"

The voice wobbles, sounding weak and confused. I take a step back, suddenly uncomfortable. That clearly wasn't a receptionist. It sounded more like an old man who doesn't know where he is.

I swallow and try again. "Is anyone here?"

"Is anyone here?" the old man repeats back to me. The phone on the receptionist's desk starts to ring. The tinny sound echoes down the halls, but nobody comes to answer it. I shift my cookies from one hand to the other, and the cellophane crinkles beneath my fingers.

I play a quick game of eenie, meenie, miney, moe—landing on the hallway twisting off to my right. Framed pictures of leaves and flowers line the walls, all painted the same muted pinks and dull browns. I turn a corner and practically walk into a set of double doors. I think I hear voices coming from behind them. I lift a hand to knock, then change my mind and push the door open.

Little old ladies and tiny, wrinkled men crowd a large, L-shaped room. A group watches *Family Feud* from an ugly plaid sofa, while others slump around scattered folding tables covered in dominos and playing cards and puzzle pieces. They stare up at me with vacant, cloudy eyes. I step inside, letting the door swing shut behind me. A woman stands.

"Can I help you?" she asks, her voice tired. She's the only one under seventy-five in the entire room, so I assume she must be a nurse. She wears wrinkled khakis and a stained yellow polo that's several sizes too big.

"I'm here to see my grandmother," I say. "Roberta Flores?"

The nurse tilts her head, giving me a puzzled look. Deep wrinkles trace lines from the corners of her nose and down each side of her chin, making her jaw look hinged on—like a doll's. Her hair is exactly the color of used dishwater.

"I'm sorry," she says. "I didn't realize Roberta had any relatives."

I shift my weight from one foot to the other. "I've only been here once before, to help her get settled in. I wanted to come more often, but I have school . . ."

"Mmhmm," the nurse murmurs, pressing her thin lips together. "Well, come on. She's just over here."

I follow her through the folding tables, past the plaid sofa, and around the corner. Grandmother slouches in a faded green chair, the blanket my mother knit for her draped over her thin shoulders. She stares out the window, hypnotized by the water trickling down the glass. The familiar wooden rosary dangles from her trembling fingers.

"The rain has gotten them all worked up," the nurse explains. I frown and glance around the room. The man directly behind me has fallen asleep. A trail of drool stretches from his mouth to his chin. The woman across from him stares at her cupped hands, seemingly fascinated by the whirls and wrinkles on her palms. If this is what they look like worked up, I can't imagine how they act when they're bored.

"Roberta?" The nurse kneels next to my grandmother, gently touching her on the shoulder. "Your granddaughter is here to see you."

"It's Sofia." I take a tentative step forward. "*Hola, Abuela. Feliz Navidad.*"

Grandmother turns to look at me. She moves in slow motion. It takes her ages to twist around in her chair, a century to lift her head. Her neck is no longer strong enough to hold her head steady, so her head rocks back and forth on her shoulders, looking as if it could tumble off her body and roll away. Loose skin hangs from her cheekbones, giving her face a sunken, hollow look. Her bloodshot eyes stare out from beneath paper-thin eyelids.

"I made cookies." I place the cookies on the table next to Grandmother's chair. "They're double fudge with peppermint chips. Our favorite, remember?"

Grandmother swallows and smacks her dry lips together. Tiny cracks split the corners of her mouth. I kneel on the floor next to her chair, folding my hands over her armrest. Rain slaps against the window and rattles the trees outside. Grandmother stares straight ahead, as if she doesn't know I'm here.

"Abuela," I say, again. "Grandmother, can you—"

Something dark appears in her left nostril. It seems almost solid, like something reaching out from the depths of her brain. It balloons just below her nose, then pops, sprinkling her wrinkled skin with blood. A thicker trail oozes from behind it. It winds down her face and seeps into the cracks in her lips.

I flail backward, catching myself just before I slam into the stained linoleum.

"Oh no." The nurse stands, looking around for a box of tissues. "This has never happened before."

Blood streams down Grandmother's face. It looks thicker than it should, and almost black. Like tar. I dig my fingers into the cracks in the floor and pull myself away from her. I feel responsible, but that's impossible. I didn't even touch her! My arms tremble, barely holding my weight.

The nurse swears and hurries away, muttering something about finding a towel. Grandmother's cloudy eyes search the room for a long moment before finally focusing on me.

"*Diablo*," she croaks.

A hollow space opens up in my chest. "Grandmother, no. It's Sofia. It's *me*."

Her lips start to move. They twitch at the corners, and curl up over her teeth. At first I think she's trying to smile. But then her mouth twists into a horrible, animal grimace. Blood drips from her lips in a solid sheet, staining her teeth red.

"*Diablo*." Grandmother's low, scratchy voice rips through the room. The drooling old man jerks awake, and the woman across from him looks up from her hands, startled. The nurse stops right behind me.

"Roberta's never spoken before," she says, twisting the towel between her fingers. She seems to have forgotten about wiping the blood from Grandmother's face.

"She's confused." I push myself back up to my knees, and reach for Grandmother's hand. She reels away from me. Her rosary clatters to the floor.

She lowers her hands to the sides of her chair and tightens them around the armrests. The wood creaks beneath her gnarled fingers. She pushes herself to her feet, swaying on her skinny legs. I can't remember the last time she stood on her own. It's been years.

"*Diablo. Diablo!*" Her voice is a creaky rasp. Blood cascades over her chin and splatters the knit blanket draped around her shoulders. She lurches forward, arms outstretched. She claws at the air in front of her, her curled yellow fingernails flashing under the fluorescent overhead lights.

Grandmother takes another shaky step forward, and her leg gives out beneath her. She drops to her knees.

"*Abuela!*" I move forward, but the nurse's hand shoots out in front of me, holding me back.

"You should go," she says. Whispers erupt around me, and I know without turning around that they're all watching me. Staring. Heat rises in my cheeks.

"But she might be hurt!"

"*Please.* Just go."

A part of me wants to yell. I listened to her favorite Christmas songs all morning. I made cookies from scratch. I wore the ugly velvet dress she bought me three Christmases ago, even though it's too tight across the chest and the sleeves don't even go to my wrists.

The nurse hurries to my grandmother's side, and helps her back into her chair. The nurse lifts the towel to Grandmother's face to stop the relentless flow of blood. I nod at the cookies on the side table.

"Those are for her," I say. "For Christmas."

The nurse glances at them, almost suspiciously. "Thanks."

I'm suddenly sure no one will eat them. The nurse will throw them away the second I'm out the door. Anger flares inside of me. I want to throw the cookies against the wall, just to hear the glass plate shatter. But I don't. I walk past the nurse, leaving the sad, beige-colored room without another word.

"Diablo!" my grandmother shouts after me. The other residents join in, their voices merging together in a single, horrible chorus. *"Diablo! Diablo!"*

CHAPTER NINETEEN

"Just drop me off here," I say.

My cab rolls to a stop in front of St. Mary's main entrance. I hand the driver a crumpled twenty-dollar bill and climb out. The rain has thickened into slushy snow during the ride. The cabbie's radio was tuned to news of the upcoming blizzard. It's going to be the biggest snowstorm in history, the newscasters say. Half the streets in Hope Springs have already been shut down— it took us twice as long as it should have to get back to St. Mary's.

Frozen grass crunches beneath my boots and wet flakes catch on my scarf. The cab peels away as soon as

I step onto the curb, its tires spitting up an icy spray of water behind it.

My grandmother's voice echoes in the back of my head. *Diablo.* I shiver, and hurry across the grounds without stopping to think about where I'm going. Wind gusts around me, rustling my hair and the hem of my velvet dress. Darkness seeps into the sky like spilled ink.

I walk past trees with bare branches frosted with a thin layer of snow. I don't stop until I reach the burnt husk of the chapel.

Only the skeleton of the building remains. Snow floats through the blackened beams of the ceiling, and broken windows reveal bits of gray sky instead of walls. Soot sweeps across the white siding. I step forward. The chapel calls to me, whispering my name. I'm the one who destroyed it, after all. A criminal always returns to the scene of their crime.

The front door swings open, and then bangs closed in the wind. I hear my grandmother's scratchy voice: *Diablo. Diablo.*

I tug at the front door, and it falls open with a crash, raining ashes down on my feet. I step inside.

Fire burned through the pews, leaving piles of blackened wood and singed Bibles in its wake. The massive wooden cross still stands near where the altar once was, blackened but still intact. The smell of smoke hangs in the air like a memory. Colored glass shines amid the piles of burnt wood, and an empty bottle of coconut rum lies beside what's left of the altar.

I stare at the bottle and an image flashes through my head: Leena's mouth wet with rum. Candlelight reflecting in her glazed eyes. I drop to my knees in the middle of the wreckage, ignoring the glass and wood digging into my shins. My chest tightens. I take fast, shallow breaths just to get the oxygen to circulate to my brain.

I did this. I destroyed the chapel. I killed Leena. Even my own grandmother thinks I'm evil. I push the words to the darkest corners of my mind and try to focus on other things. Like the cold air hitting the back of my neck, and the recorded church bells chiming in the distance. Smoke tickles my throat and I start to cough.

"*Please*, God," I choke out. I fold my hands together, squeezing so tightly that the tips of my fingers start to turn blue. The coughing subsides, but I can't catch my breath. It feels like someone's gripping my lungs and squeezing. Darkness creeps in from the walls. The floor seems to lurch beneath me.

"Please," I whisper. I squeeze my eyes shut. Tears sting the corners of my eyes. "Please . . . just take me. I can't do this anymore."

I hear Brooklyn's voice in the silence that follows my clumsy prayer.

We don't kill our own.

A cold hand touches the back of my arm.

I jerk forward, falling to my hands. A shard of glass jabs at my palm, but it doesn't break the skin. I hear a shuffle of movement and a shadow falls over the floor.

"Sofia? *Dammit*, are you okay?"

I recognize Jude's voice and push myself back up to my knees, my arms trembling so badly I can barely hold my own weight. "I'm sorry . . ." I say. "I . . . What are you doing here?"

"I stay for every holiday." Jude kneels next to me and wipes the tears from my cheeks with his thumb. "Save your breath, okay?"

I nod, and focus on breathing. *Just breathe*. I close my eyes. *Breathe*.

My chest loosens. Air comes easily now. Things stop spinning and the darkness fades. Jude draws me into his arms. I stiffen automatically, my heart racing. *I can't . . . Leena . . .*

But all I can think about are Jude's strong arms wrapped around me, his shoulder beneath my cheek. I relax, letting myself lean into him. He holds me tighter. For the first time since my mother died, I don't feel alone. I feel wanted. I feel safe.

Jude brushes my hair over my shoulder and kisses my temple. A shiver shoots down my spine.

"Is that okay?" he asks.

"Yes," I whisper. He curls his hand around the back of my neck and pulls my face to his. Our lips touch. He tastes like spearmint and there's a musky smell to his hair. I wrap my arms around his shoulders, pressing my body against his chest.

Jude shrugs out of his jacket and starts working on the buttons of mine. He unfastens them quickly, and I peel my coat off and toss it aside. I slide my hands beneath his thick sweater, running my fingers over the muscles in his stomach and chest. He moans and tilts me back, pressing me into the floor. I pull him down with me. His skin is hot.

"Sofia," he murmurs, his voice muffled by my hair. Something in the back of my head tells me I shouldn't do this. It's wrong. I think of Jude kneeling in the back of the chapel, the whip cracking against his back. I hear Leena's voice: *Be careful what you wish for . . . God punishes sinners*. I'm supposed to free myself of distractions. Rid myself of the Devil.

But then Jude moves his hand up my leg and over my waist, his fingers brushing against the edges of my bra. My dress rides up around my hips. His kisses get harder. Hotter. Hungrier. My doubts fade. I wrap my legs around his legs and move my hands down to the button on his jeans. I feel the cool metal edges against my fingers. *This can't be wrong.* I don't want to be alone, and Jude cares about me. He might be the only person in the world who still does.

"Are you sure?" he asks, and I nod without thinking. I unhook the button and unzip his jeans. Jude kisses my cheeks and my neck and my shoulders.

Steel-gray ash separates from the burnt ceiling beams and flutters toward me, landing on my wrist. I jerk back as if I've been burned.

Jude stops kissing me. "Are you okay?"

"Of course." I pull away from him, and prop myself up with one elbow, brushing the ash away with my hand. It leaves a streaky black line across my skin. I lick my thumb and rub, but the mark only seems to seep deeper into my skin.

Fear lodges itself in my throat. I've read stories like this in English class. About birthmarks that symbolize mortality, skin deformities that mark someone as evil. I press my thumb into my hand and rub so hard that my skin burns. But the black mark doesn't go away.

Leena's doing this, I think. She's warning me. *God punishes sinners.*

"Sofia?" Jude touches my arm and I flinch.

"Sorry," I say in a voice that sounds nothing like my own. "I just . . . maybe we shouldn't." I move my hand to my side so I don't have to look at the ashes on my skin.

"We don't have to do anything you don't want to." Jude rolls off me, and pushes himself to his knees. He buttons his jeans. "Are you okay? Did I do something wrong?"

Jude lowers his hand to my back. The second he touches me, something inside snaps clean in half. Tears form at the corners of my eyes. I blink them away.

"Sofia, tell me."

"I *can't*," I whisper, and my voice cracks. I shudder so deeply that Jude has to wrap his arms around me to keep me from shaking. I can't stop replaying what happened with my grandmother, what happened with Leena.

Jude kisses the top of my head. "Hey, you're okay," he whispers. "Tell me what's wrong. You can tell me anything."

"Not this. It's too terrible. You'd . . ." *hate me*, I think. I press my lips together before I can say the words out loud.

"Anything you've done, I've done worse," Jude whispers into my ear. He strokes my arm until I stop shaking. "We're the *same*. God forgave me. He'll forgive you, too." I shift in Jude's arms, finally looking up at his face. A lock of dark hair falls over his forehead, and wrinkles the skin between his eyebrows. He looks so concerned. It loosens something inside me. I stop thinking about Leena and think, instead, of him. Us. I want to rub the lines from his face and make his worry disappear. I want to trust him.

"Bad things keep happening," I whisper. "I think there's something . . . *wrong* with me."

"Wrong how?"

"*Evil.*"

Jude squeezes my arm, pulling me closer. "I know what evil looks like. You're not evil."

"You don't understand." I shift my eyes to my lap. I can't look at Jude as I say this next part. I don't want to see his face twist in disgust when he realizes how awful I truly am. "I was talking to Sister Lauren and she said she thinks that demons can . . . attach themselves to people who've done something terrible. It's like being possessed."

Jude's arm stiffens, but he doesn't pull away. "But you haven't done something terrible."

"Yes. I have," I say in a quiet voice. Then, before I lose my nerve, I tell Jude what happened with Brooklyn and my friends last summer. I tell him about Leena and the bunny and the night the chapel burned down. I even admit what I did to Karen. How I lured her onto the train tracks. How I let her die.

"Brooklyn said I was like her," I finish, my voice shaking. "She said I was . . . *evil*. And then, today, my grandmother said the same thing." A sob escapes my lips. I curl my hand into a fist, bunching it next to my mouth. "What if they're right?"

Jude is quiet for a long moment. Shadows hide his face, making it impossible to see his expression. He suddenly seems very far away. Fear curdles in my gut. I feel as if the floor could crumble out from under me at any moment. This was a mistake. I shouldn't have told him any of this.

"I was lost when I came to St. Mary's, but Father Marcus saved me," Jude says, almost to himself. "I felt unredeemable, like you, but I was wrong. No one is ever lost to the Lord. There's hope for all of us."

"You think I'm redeemable?" I whisper.

"Of course I do." Jude brings my hand to his mouth and kisses my palm. Heat floods through me, erasing my fears. I squeeze his fingers.

"I . . . I think I love you, Sofia."

A smile spreads across my face, so wide it makes my cheeks hurt.

"And that's why I have to do this."

My smile freezes. "Do what?"

Jude doesn't answer. My chest feels weird. My heart's beating too fast, and my lungs seem tight, as though they're straining against the air inside of them. The skin along the back of my knees prickles.

"Jude . . ." A sour taste hits the back of my tongue.

I push myself to my knees. "What are you going to—"

Jude pulls his hand back and whips it across my face. His knuckles slam into my cheekbone. I fly backward, crashing into the floor. My head spins, pain blossoming just below my skin. I swallow, tasting blood and soot at the back of my throat, and try to force my eyes back open.

Jude stares down at me, a lock of dark hair falling across his forehead. He leans forward and touches my face.

"Don't be afraid," he whispers, stroking my cheek. Darkness flickers at the corners of my eyes. I start to lose consciousness.

"I'm going to get the evil out of you," Jude says before everything goes black.

CHAPTER TWENTY

I feel the ropes first. Their rough texture against my skin. The slick of sweat between my wrists, and the thick knots. I'm curled on my side, and the ropes bind my hands behind me, pinching my shoulders together and jerking my arms back at uncomfortable angles. I groan, and pain blisters through my chin and jawbone.

"Are you awake?" Jude asks. I open my eyes. Candlelight moves across the blackened walls like a predator, hiding blurry shapes in the darkness. I watch the shapes for a moment, dazed, trying to remember what they are. Where I am.

"Jude?" I croak.

"You passed out. Do you remember?" His voice is sweet, like he's telling me I fell asleep while watching a movie. But that's not what happened. I fight against the pain pounding at my skull, trying to remember.

I see Jude standing over me, a strange look on his face. He pulls his hand back, and then—I close my eyes against the memory. A tear drops down my cheek and rolls over my mouth, leaving a film of salt on my lips.

"I had to run out to grab some supplies, but I won't leave you again. Promise." Jude hauls something off the floor with a grunt. At first, I see a backpack. The same black backpack Alexis had with her that weekend in the abandoned house. But then he drops it on the pew and it transforms into a green army duffel bag smeared with dirt and ashes.

"I'm going to help you, Sofia. You won't have to do this alone."

"What's that?" I ask, my voice cracking. The bag is big and lumpy. I stare at the shapes beneath the green fabric, my mind turning them into tools. Duct tape. A butcher knife.

A nail gun.

Jude crouches beside me. "Don't worry about that yet."

"You . . . you *hit* me." I still can't believe the words. Jude brings his hand to my chin. His touch sends shivers through my skin.

"Sofia, I didn't hit *you*. I would never hit you. I hit the demon inside of you." Jude's voice is barely a whisper. "I'm doing it because I love you," he says. "You know that, right? This is for us. I'm going to get that evil thing out of you."

A sob rises in my throat. "Jude," I whisper, leaning into his hand. This has to be a mistake. Jude wouldn't hurt me. "Don't do this. Untie me."

Something flicks to life inside of Jude's eyes and, for a moment, I see a shadow of the boy I thought I loved. The creases around his mouth soften. The tension leaves his shoulders. "Think about it, Sofia," he says. "You said yourself that you've been asking the Lord for salvation, but He hasn't answered. Remember?"

I think of all the times I've knelt on the floor in this chapel, my hands clenched together, trying to reach God. My voice cracks. "I remember."

"I'm here to give it to you. We can't wait for God to make you clean. *We* have to do it. Like this. Together."

I think of all the terrible things that have happened this year—things I've caused, even if I didn't mean to. I see candlelight reflected in Leena's dazed eyes. I see the horror on Karen's face when I tightened my fingers around her wrist and dragged her onto the tracks.

There *is* something evil inside of me. But Jude thinks I can be redeemed.

"Is it going to hurt?" I ask. Jude smiles, almost sadly.

"I'd never hurt you, Sofia," he says. He unzips the bag, and stares down at what's inside. He swipes a hand over his forehead and wipes the sweat on the back of his jeans.

He pulls something out of the bag and places it on the pew beside him. It looks like a set of handcuffs, except they're not normal—the cuffs themselves are vises attached to a thin metal lever. I picture how they work in my head. Someone twists the lever and the vises slowly crush the bones in your wrists.

The fear I'd been fighting hits me in a wave. I try to breathe, but my throat closes up and the oxygen leaves my head, making me dizzy. I start to cry.

Jude's at my side again in an instant. "Shh, Sofia, it's okay. Those aren't for you." He pushes the hair back from my forehead, his hand cool against my skin. "Father Marcus collects tools like this for *his* exorcisms. But I'm not going to use any of it on you, okay?"

Tears cloud my eyes. Jude's holding something, but my eyes are too blurry and I can't see it. I blink, trying to focus on his hands.

It's a Bible. Just a normal black Bible.

He presses his hand against the cover. "I'm going to pray for you," he says. "That's it. Is that okay?"

I nod. "Okay."

Jude flips the Bible open and clears his throat.

"*Credo in Deum Patrem omnipotentem,*" The words flow from his tongue. I remember what it was like to watch him perform, his velvety voice filling every inch of the auditorium.

"*Creatorem caeli et terrae. Et in Iesum Christum, Filium eius unicum, Dominum nostrum, qui conceptus est de Spiritu Sancto, natus ex Maria Virgine, passus sub Pontio Pilato . . .*"

My breathing steadies. I need to forget about the handcuffs and whatever else Jude might have in that bag. Prayer and Bibles are okay. And I wanted this—I begged the Lord to save me from myself. Maybe this is His way of answering my prayer.

Be careful what you wish for. Leena's words make a lump form in my throat. It's like she knew.

Jude paces the length of the chapel while he reads, his footsteps crunching over broken glass and ashes. I study the swirls of soot staining the walls, losing track of time. The ropes that bind my hands behind my back are too tight. The arm I'm lying on falls asleep and a dull headache pounds at the back of my head. Pins and needles prickle down the length of my arm, and spread through my hips. I stare into the shadowy corners of the chapel until the darkness seems to pulse. A cockroach darts across the floor, antennae twitching, and disappears into a pile of rubble.

Jude's Latin blends together until I can't tell where one word ends and another begins. Darkness crowds in from the corners of my eyes, and the floor seems to tilt and sway. My eyes droop.

Something wet hits my cheek—my eyes fly open, and I reel backward, wrenching at the ropes binding my arms.

Jude kneels in front of me, holding a tiny glass bottle. "Holy water," he explains. He smiles sheepishly. "Sorry. I didn't mean to surprise you."

I blink, shaking the water from my eyelashes. "Are we done?" I whisper.

Jude stands and slides the bottle of holy water into his jeans pocket. "Soon, my love," he says. He walks to the pew and leans over the duffel bag. "But I have to follow protocol. It's the only way to drive out the demons. Prayer and holy water are just the first step."

A shiver shoots up my spine. "First step?" I ask. "What does that mean? What's next?"

The muscles in the back of Jude's neck tighten.

"What are you going to do next?" A tremor has crept into my voice. I sound unhinged—hysterical. *"Tell me."*

Jude turns, a leather whip curled around his fingers. It's the whip Father Marcus used on him that morning in the chapel. The leather is frayed and stained red with blood—Jude's blood.

Panic claws at my throat. "I don't want to do this anymore." I yank at the ropes binding my arms, fear making my movements jerky. I picture the whip slicing through my dress, biting into my skin. Bile rises in my throat. The bruise where Jude hit me suddenly feels like nothing. A bump. "Let me go."

"I've been through it, too, Sofia," Jude says. But he doesn't look at me, and his hands tremble. "I know you're scared, but you don't have to be. I'm going to be right here the entire time. I love you."

His words prick into me like thorns. "This isn't love," I say. I swallow, trying to stay strong. "Jude, please. You have to let me go."

"That's the demon talking." Jude holds up his fist, and the leather creaks beneath his tightening fingers. "And *this* is how we overcome demons."

Jude loosens his hand and the whip unfurls. The leather tip brushes against the floor, making tiny patterns in the layers of ash. Jude slips a hand beneath one arm and hauls me to my knees. I inhale, and my breath shudders down my throat like a sob. I wonder if I could pull my hands loose if I caught him off guard, if I jerked my body away fast enough. I twist, trying to jerk my wrists out of his sweaty grip. But Jude holds tight.

"Take it easy," he says, kissing the top of my head. "I don't want you to fall. You could hurt yourself."

"Don't do this," I say again. But Jude doesn't respond. Fear rises in my chest, making my hands and legs stiff. I can't feel my toes or my fingers, can't feel anything other than my own rapidly beating heart. "Jude, stop," I beg. "Think about this. You love me, remember? You don't want to hurt me."

Jude circles me, stopping when he's directly behind my back. A sob bubbles up my throat.

"Jude, *plea*—"

The whip cracks against the arcs of my bare feet. Pain zips up my legs. I gasp and bite down on my tongue. Blood fills my mouth and trickles out around my lips.

"Stop," I say, squeezing my eyes shut. "Please stop."

The whip slaps into my back without warning, ripping through the thin velvet of my dress. The leather tears into my skin like some wild animal's fangs. Vomit spills onto my tongue.

I double over, heaving and coughing. Something thick and brown spews from my mouth and splatters across the dirty chapel floor. It's swirled with red. *Blood,* I think. I cringe, imagining Jude's whip cutting deep under my skin, leaving welts inside my body. I feel the vomit rising in my throat and I try to choke it back down.

I arch forward, pulling against the ropes binding my hands. I retch until my stomach feels raw, and a veil of sweat clings to my forehead. I stare at the brown-and-red puke, my eyes blurry and bloodshot. I swallow, tasting mint.

It's not blood, I realize, panting. *It's peppermint.*

Jude kneels beside me and takes my face in his hands. "It's working, Sofia. See? Your body is rejecting the demon. You're fighting it off."

I release a choked whimper. My eyes feel wet, but I don't remember when I started crying. *It's not a demon,* I want to tell him. It's the peppermint cookies I made for my grandmother. This isn't working.

Every muscle in my body aches. Every inch of my flesh burns. I want to tell Jude that we've failed, that I can't be redeemed. But maybe he'll finish sooner if he thinks this is working. And then he'll let me go.

Jude whips me again. And again. My back screams, and pain like fire shoots through my feet. My head lolls forward. For a long moment, I can't tell if my eyes are open or closed.

And then all I see is black.

CHAPTER TWENTY-ONE

I open my eyes. It's either been hours or minutes since I passed out, but I'm not sure which. Pain zigzags up my spine. Blood and sweat pool between my cheek and the floor.

"Water." I swallow, and taste the sharp mint and acid bite of vomit on my tongue. I blink my eyes open, and the chapel shifts and moves around me. The walls keep switching places.

I can't see Jude from my angle on the floor. Hope blossoms in my chest and, for a second, I think he's left. He's given up on my soul and abandoned me to die.

Then the shadows move and Jude steps out of the

darkness. Flecks of blood glisten along the line of his jaw and sweat clings to his hair. He digs through the duffel bag and produces a plastic water bottle. He kneels in front of me and carefully lifts my head. I whimper. The blood on my cheek has grown sticky, and my skin stings as he unpeels my face from the floor.

"Easy," he says, tilting the bottle toward my mouth. The water is so cold it makes me shiver, but I suck it down, feverish with thirst. "There you go," he murmurs, stroking my hair. I close my eyes and drink. The layer of vomit leaves my tongue. The room stops spinning.

Too soon Jude pulls the bottle from my lips. "Feel better?" he asks. I open my mouth to answer and a sob escapes instead. The muscles in my face spasm. I can't get my mouth to work.

"*Cold*," I choke out. I press my lips together to stop their trembling. The cold stabs into my skin and my bones. I feel it like a dull ache in my muscles. Goose bumps crawl over my arms and legs.

Jude frowns and presses the back of his hand to my forehead. "You feel a little warm, actually."

"Something's wrong," I whisper. My throat feels dry again, despite all the water I just drank. I can't stop shivering. Chills jolt through me, making me twitch. "Jude . . . please. I think I have a fever."

"No, this is just your body rejecting the Devil," he

says, moving his hand to my cheek. His skin feels hot against my face. It practically burns. "It's a good thing, Sofia. It means we're making progress."

"I think I need to go to the hospital."

"You don't know what you're saying."

"This isn't working." I curl into a fetal position, bringing my knees to my chest. "You have to let me go."

"That's the Devil talking," he says. The heavy cross looms over him, its wood charred and blackened.

"This is almost over." Jude reaches forward and brushes the hair off my forehead, his fingers skimming my face. "And then we can be together."

I stare into the shadows, trying to separate Jude's eyes from the darkness. I don't know what to believe anymore. Jude said he'd never hurt me, but then he whipped me until I passed out.

"Don't touch me," I say, my voice low and angry. Jude pulls his hand away.

"I love you, Sofia," he says. "But you're evil."

He's not going to let me go, I realize. He doesn't care that I'm sick and hurt. It doesn't matter what he says. You don't do this to someone you love.

"You don't love me," I whimper. "You're *a liar.* Don't you *ever* touch me again."

I spit in Jude's face. He reels backward, saliva running down his cheek. His hand comes down hard and fast against my cheek, and my head snaps against the floor. The pain is like slamming into a wall. I release a choked gasp, lights dancing before my eyes.

"Dammit!" Jude stands and takes two quick steps away from me. I can barely see him through the fog covering my eyes. The room gets hazy.

"I shouldn't have lost my temper." Jude's voice draws me out of the fog. I open my eyes, then squeeze them shut again. The whole world is light and pain. I moan, wishing for unconsciousness. Every muscle in my body aches. Every inch of my flesh burns.

"Sofia? Did you hear me? I said I'm sorry. I know it's not you saying those things. It's the demon. I shouldn't listen."

I feel Jude's hand on my cheek, and a tear slips down my face. "The Devil inside of you is strong," he says. "We need to be stronger."

Jude pulls his sweater over his head and tosses it to the chapel floor. His bare skin gleams gold in the near darkness, muscles rippling across his chest and stomach. Pain twists through me. I just ran my hands over his warm body. I kissed his lips.

Jude leans over the duffel bag. Moonlight streams in through a broken window, and catches one of the scars twisting over his shoulder. The gnarled tissue glints, almost silver. I stare at it, and a sound like a scream fills my head. Jude didn't get those scars from a single morning of being whipped by Father Marcus. Scars like that could've only come from being whipped over and over again. I imagine the scars that will soon snake up my own back. I'll be marked, just like Jude.

"I was hoping we wouldn't have to use any of this," Jude mutters, sorting through the bag. I hear the metal clink of chains against something heavy and solid. I think of the handcuffs he dug out of that bag a few hours ago.

Father Marcus collects tools like this for his exorcisms.

I thought I'd reached my capacity for fear, but then I think of those cuffs clamped around my wrists, digging into my skin, crushing my bones. My insides feel loose all of a sudden. If I wasn't so dehydrated, I'd probably piss myself.

"Jude," I breathe, my voice shaking. "Please, I'll be good, I promise."

"That's the demon talking again. You don't know how hard this is for me, Sofia. You look like you, and you sound like you, but you're possessed by something terrible. I need to find a way to keep it quiet while I do my work." Jude kneels in front of me, holding a pear-shaped device attached to what looks like a long metal screw. "I'm afraid this is going to hurt," he says.

I arch away, but Jude clamps a hand against the side

of my face, pressing me against the floor. He forces my mouth open, and shoves the pear inside. I try to scream, but then Jude turns the screw, and the pear opens in my mouth like a flower. Metal blades crush my tongue and dig into the roof of my mouth. Their edges split my gums, and stretch the sides of my lips. Tears form in the corners of my eyes.

"We can't take the pear out of your mouth until you're ready to praise the name of the Lord," Jude says.

He grabs me by the shoulder and hauls me to my knees. I gather my breath and try to scream. Blades cut into my gums, and blood oozes down the back of my throat. I inhale—coughing on blood—and try again. The pear muffles my voice, making it impossible.

"You're only making it worse, Sofia," Jude says. He tips my body over his shoulder and stands, lifting me as easily as if I were a bag of flour.

Oh God. I picture Jude hauling me outside and dumping me, covering me with dirt, the horrible metal pear making it impossible for me to scream as I'm buried alive. Fear drops through me like a stone. I try to speak, but the pear keeps me from moving my tongue. Blood leaks from the corners of my mouth.

"Don't try to talk," Jude warns, carrying me across the chapel. "You'll hurt yourself."

I twist my rope-bound arms, wondering how difficult

it would be to pull my wrists free. The rough fibers chafe my skin like sandpaper. I tug—hard—on my wrists, and the ropes binding me roll down to my knuckles.

"Stop squirming," Jude mutters. "I'm going to drop you."

I tug again. The rope scoots down my fingers a little farther.

Jude stops in front of the huge wooden cross. He adjusts my body and his shoulder digs into my gut, making it hard to breathe. I twist my hands, and my thumb slips free. I close my eyes and pull—ignoring the pain blistering through my hand, and the blood leaking from my skin. With a sudden jolt, I pull one hand loose of the bindings.

"Hey—" Jude starts. I grab for his face and claw into the fleshiest part of his cheek. He screams and jerks, but I just dig my fingernails deeper into his skin. I feel blood pooling below my fingers and seeping into the cracks around my nails. Jude grabs my wrist, and yanks my hand back, losing his grip on my body. I pitch backward.

Jude releases an angry, animalistic yell. He shoves me into the wooden base of the cross to keep me from falling to the ground. I squirm, but he leans against me, pinning my wrist beneath his shoulder. He's taller than I am. I stretch out my toes to try and touch the floor, but I'm too high up. Jude grabs my other hand and presses it to one of the cross's short arms. I release a choked, desperate cry.

"Hold still," he whispers, grunting. He takes the rope still dangling from my wrist, and twists it around the cross, tying my arm in place. I scream and kick, but Jude doesn't seem to notice my struggles. He pulls my other arm straight and holds it in place against the cross. His broad hand is like a vise against my wrist. I grit my teeth against the cold metal pear, and try to push him away. But he's too damn strong. He leans down and pulls at the ropes binding my ankles with his free hand.

"Almost there," he mutters, tugging the knot free. My legs dangle below me, untied.

I kick at him, but he dodges to the side, easily. He uses the length of rope that had been binding my ankles to tie my other arm to the cross. When he finishes, he steps back, admiring his handiwork.

My head falls forward, sobs shaking my shoulders. Pain arcs up my back, holding me upright. I pull at my arms, and ropes dig into my wrists. I lift my head.

He's tied me to the cross in a perverse imitation of Christ's crucifixion. My arms stretch out to either side of my body, my wrists tightly knotted to the splintery wood. I'm dragged down by own weight, my body pulling at the bindings until my arms feel as if they're going to rip from their sockets. It takes all my strength to hold my head upright. I try, again, to scream, but the metal pear steals my voice.

CHAPTER TWENTY-TWO

"I'm doing this to help you," Jude says, but his voice is hollow. His eyes dart to the bindings around my wrists before moving back to my face. "Please, stop fighting. You'll be grateful when it's over. You'll *thank* me."

I nod, even though I can barely make sense of his words. Pain bites into every inch of my skin. It takes all of my energy not to scream or cry or throw up. It's all I can think about.

Jude digs something out of his jeans pocket. A blue plastic lighter.

The muscles in my shoulders tense. I shake my head, and the metal pear rattles against my teeth. Jude studies the lighter. He rolls his thumb over the switch and a red-orange flame dances to life between his fingers.

I imagine that flame licking my toes. My *fingers*. I can practically feel my skin growing red and itchy, my nerves flaring as the pain sears hotter. My breath comes hard and fast, and my skin suddenly feels too tight. I shrink back against the cross, trembling. Jude moves his finger from the lighter. The flame vanishes.

"Anything you've done, I've done worse," he whispers. "That's what I need you to understand, Sofia. We're the *same*. We belong together. God forgave me. He'll forgive you, too."

I want to tell him to stop. Don't do this. I'll be good, I swear. But the pear presses down against my tongue, making it impossible to speak. I plead with my eyes.

Stop, please, I can't take any more, I can't. Jude doesn't look at me. He flicks the lighter on. And then off again.

"Did I tell you my parents sent me here when I was thirteen? Technically, I was a year too young to start as a freshman, but Father Marcus made an exception. He's a great man, Father Marcus."

Flick. The flame jumps to life. *Flick.* It disappears.

"I'd been having a hard time at home since my sister, Chloe, died. She was only seven years old. We were out skating and I was supposed to be watching her, but my friends were hanging around in the woods, drinking and getting high." Jude swallows hard and closes his hand around the lighter. He finally meets my eyes. "I was stoned when Chloe fell through some thin ice.

"I was too high to save her, too high to run for help. *I'm* the reason she died. So, yeah, I understand what it's like to do something evil. I was just like you, Sofia. I didn't believe in God when I came here. Didn't think I could be saved. But Father Marcus wouldn't give up on me. Look."

Jude stretches out his arm, showing me the thick red burn in the crook of his elbow. It's the mark I noticed that morning in the chapel. I thought it was weird that he refused to tell me about it, but I was too distracted by his hair and his smile. *Stupid.*

Staring at it now, I see the faint outline of a shield emblazoned with a cross seared into his skin. Like a brand.

"It comes from this," Jude explains, curling his hand into a fist. He's wearing a thick silver ring. It's familiar, but I can't place why until he turns the ring so that I can see the design on the front—a silver cross, a shield. All at once, I remember where I've seen it before. It glittered from Father Marcus's hand the day I caught him whipping Jude.

Jude twists the ring around his finger absently. "Father Marcus knows true evil. He was a missionary for years and years. A *real* one. He didn't just go to the places everyone goes, like China and Haiti. He traveled to tiny little villages no one's ever even heard of. We're talking places with no electricity or running water. He's stayed in the jungle, living with the locals to better understand their customs."

Jude swallows. He twists the ring faster.

"Father Marcus has witnessed some of the most depraved demonic possessions imaginable. Things the Vatican would've scoffed at," Jude says, shaking his head. He sounds as if he's reading a script, as if he's memorized everything Father Marcus ever told him. "But that's only because they haven't seen what he's seen. There are children out there who cry tears of blood. Some of them even *levitate*, and their eyes roll back in their heads. He's seen grown men and women who speak in tongues and crave human flesh.

"In the face of evil like that, Father Marcus was forced to resort to more archaic forms of exorcism," Jude continues. He touches the burn on his skin with one finger, tracing the gruesome scar almost lovingly. "The day he branded this image into my flesh, he told me he claimed my body in the name of the Lord. After that, things were different for me. I started to grow closer to God. I started to *heal*."

Jude uncurls his fist and stares down at the plastic lighter on his palm. "You want to heal, don't you?"

I look from the lighter to Jude's twisted scar and, all at once, I smell burning skin, burning hair. He's going to brand me. He's going to light that ring on fire and press it into my skin. I shrink away from him, pressing my shredded back against the wood of the cross. I pull myself up by the bindings at my wrists, ignoring how my spine aches and my joints howl with pain. A scream wells inside of my chest. I choke it back, forcing myself to focus on the metal blades cutting into the insides of my cheeks. A scream will only hurt.

"Let me get that," Jude murmurs. He twists the lever attached the metal pear, and the blades peel away from the sides of my mouth. I inhale, and fresh, stinging air brushes up against the open wounds. The sharp, metallic taste of blood clings to my gums. Jude pulls the pear from my lips, and tosses it back into the duffel bag.

I blink, my eyelashes wet and heavy. Am I crying? Or is it sweat? Blood? I can't tell, can't feel anything but pain and fear. "Please," I beg. "Please don't do that."

"I don't want to hurt you," Jude whispers. His voice sounds so sincere. Like he really believes what he's saying. He flicks the lighter and fire appears, like magic.

"Then don't do this," I choke out. "Please stop. *Please.*"

Jude stares down at the flickering fire. The flame reflects in his dark eyes. "I begged Father Marcus to stop, too," he says. "But now I'm grateful for what he did. I was just like you, Sofia. I'd done an unforgiveable thing and I thought there was no hope for me, no chance of salvation."

Jude reaches out and strokes my arm. The feel of his skin against mine is somehow both comforting and disturbing.

"You said you felt possessed, like you had a demon clinging to your back. I've felt that way, too, Sofia. But Father Marcus saved me from the sins of the flesh. He made me clean."

Jude moves his finger in small circles over my skin, raising the hair on my arms. For a second, I want to trust him. Maybe this *is* the way to salvation, and all I have to do is survive the pain to be rid of the evil inside of me. It would be so easy to just . . . give up.

Then I hear my mother's voice in my ear. *Be strong, Sofia.* A single tear leaks out from the corner of my eye. Sergeant Nina Flores didn't teach her only daughter to trust lying boys with pretty smiles. She didn't teach me to give up.

My voice cracks in my throat. "Father Marcus was wrong, Jude. He didn't save you—he *tortured* you."

"He made me *whole*," Jude spits. He looks up at me and, for the first time, I see real anger in his eyes. "He exorcised the demons from my soul, and he presented my flesh to God for salvation. I'm free because of the things he did."

I swallow, disgust twisting my stomach.

"Father Marcus is a hero," Jude says, almost to himself. He lowers his ring to the flame. Fire curls around the silver shield. "People don't understand, but that's just because they haven't seen real evil. They don't know. Everything he's done, he's done for the Lord."

"Jude—"

Jude's arm shoots out so quickly that I don't have time to jerk away. He catches my chin in his hand and yanks my face forward roughly.

"I'm doing this for *us*, Sofia," he says. "I love you."

He presses the ring into my neck.

Blistering pain explodes through my head. Red and orange lights dance before my eyes and nausea floods my stomach. I feel the skin on my neck bubble and melt, and I thrash wildly against the cross. I don't care about the cuts on my back and my feet, or the welts inside my mouth, and the dull bruises on my cheeks. All I can think about is my neck, the burning ache searing through my body.

The entire room seems tinged with red, like my eyes themselves are bleeding. I don't realize I'm screaming until Jude covers my mouth with his hand. His fingers are chapped, and his skin smells like blood. I try to catch my breath, but sobs clog my throat. The pain is too much. I can't hold myself up anymore—the muscles in my arms go slack, and my body drops like a stone, yanking at the ropes twisted around my arms. My shoulders scream with pain and I wonder, dimly, if I pulled my arm from its socket.

Something tickles my neck and I flinch before realizing that it must be blood. The blood trickles down my skin and gathers in the space just above my collarbone, quickly soaking the fabric of my dress. I choke down another, shaking breath. I must look crazy, shaking and sobbing like this. I must look possessed.

Jude leans his forehead against mine.

"Shhh," he whispers into my hair. I choke my voice back, whimpering. All I can think about is pain and fear and heat.

"I claim this body in the name of the Lord," Jude says. He lowers his face to my forehead and presses his lips into my skin.

"Get off me." I moan, pulling my face away from him. The burn on my neck flares. "Don't touch me!"

"Sofia—"

The sound of church bells drifts in from outside, cutting Jude off. They're the same tinny, recorded church bells they played during Leena's funeral. Jude turns and stares at the chapel door.

"Christmas Mass," he murmurs. He runs a hand back through his hair. "Dammit."

I swallow and pain blisters through my neck. Jude rises up to his tiptoes and kisses my cheek.

"I've got to go, but I swear I'll be back soon," he says. His lips feel cold and clammy against my skin. Like something dead. I cringe.

He hurries to the front door. I let my head fall back against the cross. The door opens, and then thuds shut again, and I exhale, relieved.

The burnt wreckage of the roof stretches above me. I can see the night sky through the blackened ceiling beams, stars winking down from the dark, endless sky.

"God," I whisper. "*Help.*"

The word gets stuck in my throat. I squeeze my eyes shut. Tears stream down my cheeks. I can't think of anything to say to him, anything to ask. He won't answer anyway. He never does.

He's forsaken me.

CHAPTER TWENTY-THREE

A gust of wind blows in through the tattered walls of the chapel, bringing my mother's voice with it.

Go, Sofia. Go now.

I stare at the tightly knotted robes binding my wrists to the cross. It's impossible. There's not enough time.

In my head, I see Jude racing across the grounds, his boots kicking up fresh snow. He didn't say where he was going, but I bet he's headed to the auditorium to tell Father Marcus he won't be staying for Mass. It isn't far through the woods, but the snow's falling heavily now. It could slow him down. Still, it'll only take a couple of minutes to get to the auditorium. Five, if I'm lucky. Then, maybe, another five minutes to talk to Father Marcus. And five minutes to get back.

That's just fifteen minutes. Maybe ten. And then Jude will come back and finish what he started.

For the first time, it occurs to me that I might die tonight. I could see my mother again in just a few hours. How will I face her, knowing I didn't fight for my life? That I didn't even try?

I grit my teeth and tug at my wrist. The rope feels coarse against my skin, and slick with sweat and blood. The cross groans, and the rope creaks, but the knot stays tight.

I cry out in frustration, my ragged voice echoing off the blackened chapel walls. I yank my fist down, and then up again to loosen the binding. I twist my arm. It feels like rubbing gravel into an open wound, like scrubbing my bare skin with sandpaper. Fresh blood oozes from my reddened skin. I press my teeth into my lower lip and pull. But the knot doesn't budge.

"*Come on!*" I shout. I collapse against the cross, cringing as my back presses into the wood. The ropes have cut off circulation to my hand. There's no loosening them. It takes all my energy just to wiggle my fingers. I stretch my feet, but my toes barely brush against the cross's heavy wooden base.

"*Fuck!*" I scream. I jerk both hands at once, thrashing,

my head swinging wildly back and forth. I curl my knees toward my chest and hurl them backward, slamming my bare feet into the wood. Pain licks at the ragged skin peeling away from the soles of my feet, but I don't care. I kick the cross again and again and—

I freeze, gasping. The cross *moved*. It shifted backward. Like it was tilting.

I suck down a breath, my chest rising and falling rapidly beneath my ruined dress. My head feels dizzy, a low thud at the back of my skull telling me I must've slammed it against the wood. I thought the cross was affixed directly to the floor. It's huge, much larger than a person. It never occurred to me that you could shift it.

If you can shift it, you can get it to fall.

I rock against the cross, testing. The cuts along my back flare. But the cross doesn't move.

I squeeze my eyes shut, forcing myself to breathe. How much time has passed now? Three minutes? Four? I imagine Jude racing up the stairs to St. Mary's, taking the steps two at a time, maybe double-checking his appearance in the glass door to make sure my blood isn't smeared across his face. There isn't a clock in the chapel, but I swear I can hear the *tick tick tick* of a second hand.

I lean forward, my wrists pulling against the ropes binding me to the cross. The knots scrape against my skin. Fresh blood rolls down my arms and drips from my elbows. My feet fumble along the bottom of the cross. The ruined skin along my soles flares and spits, but I just press them harder into the wood, gritting my teeth against the pain. Spots of light flicker across my eyes. The world around me tilts.

"This is going to hurt," I whisper. My voice doesn't tremble this time. It sounds steady—strong, even. I focus on each individual word so I don't have to think about what I'm going to do. "Are you ready for that? This is going to really, really—"

I hurl my weight against the cross. My back crashes into the wood and every single cut the whip slashed into my skin turns bright-white and screams. It feels like electricity ripping through my body, like nails driving deep into my muscles. My teeth slam together and my head snaps to the side.

The cross scoots across the floor, and then rocks back on its base. I open my mouth in a silent scream. My head lolls forward and a choked whimper crawls from my lips. The room flickers, like a candle sputtering. I don't have time to pass out. If I pass out, I'm dead.

"Five minutes," I say. "You only have five minutes left. Come on."

I wrench my body up by the wrists—and then I slam myself against the cross again. This time, it tilts on the edge of its base before crashing back in place. I sway from my ropes like a rag doll. Pain howls through me. It wraps around my spine and makes my toes curl.

I want to give up. I'm not strong like my mother. She would never give up.

Vomit rises in my throat and I swallow it down. It takes all the strength I have left to drag my body up by the wrists, to press my feet into the cross, and fling my body backward.

And then—

The cross rocks, then tilts. The air around me shifts as I plummet toward the floor. I have only a second to feel the sudden whoosh of triumph before the cross crashes into the tile, snapping clear of its base. I barely notice the ache spreading through my body. I gasp, staring up through the blackened ceiling beams. The moon hangs in the darkened night sky, shining down on me like a quarter. A laugh bubbles up from my throat.

I did it. I'm free.

I try to roll over but the cross is too heavy, and the ropes still knotted around my wrists pull me down. I drag my feet across the floor and push. I rock to the side, catching myself with one hand before the cross's weight shifts to my shoulders. I inch my knee up to help deal with the bulk and ease my body forward in a half crawl. If I move too far to the left or the right, I'll slam back to the ground and have to start again. There's no time for that. I swallow, and then slowly rise to my knees. The cross shifts. I sway backward, but maintain my balance. I grit my teeth together and slide one knee forward—then totter onto my foot. I drag the other knee forward and attempt to stand, the bottoms of my feet flaring with pain. But it's nothing compared to the pain in my back. The cross digs into my body, chaffing against my tattered skin. Blood sticks to my shredded dress, plastering it to the blackened wood.

I lurch forward. The cross is larger than I am, and it drags on the floor behind me. Each step is punishment. The wood is too heavy for me to lift and I'm doubled over, my knees practically buckling from the weight. I want to stop and try to catch my breath, but I worry that I'll collapse if I don't keep moving. I focus, instead, on my legs. I lift one, inch forward, and lower it back to the ground. My footsteps are short, my feet barely shuffling off the ground with each step. But still. I'm moving.

I have no idea how much time has passed. I picture Jude standing with Father Marcus in the auditorium, smiling that charismatic smile of his as he explains why he can't stay. Maybe the priest won't believe him. Maybe he'll hand him a Bible and tell him to find a seat. But I doubt it. I'm not that lucky.

Jude's probably already on his way back.

I stumble and stagger, my eyes glued to the velvet

curtains blocking off the back room. They're only three feet away . . .

Now two . . .

One . . .

I pitch forward, slamming into the wall. My foot slips out from beneath me and I crash down to one knee, groaning in pain. I press my lips together and pull myself back to both feet, gasping. I made it. I stand as best I can, and push through the curtains. I start to move through the opening, when something thumps against the wall. Pain shudders through me, and my body jerks backward.

I shift my head to the side to see what's keeping me from moving forward. It's the cross—it's too wide to fit through the door. The heavy wood clanks against the frame, my hand dangling.

"Shit," I whisper. I try to force the cross through the door, but I'm bent too far over, and I can't get it to tilt at the right angle. Either the top of the cross or one of the sides keeps thudding against the blackened frame. I'm stuck.

Blood drips from my body and pools on the floor beneath my toes, mixing with the ash to form a dull gray paste. The only way through the door is to break the cross. Which wouldn't be a problem, except that my *arms* are tied to the cross.

"Broken bones heal," I whisper meekly.

The front door creaks. I freeze, waiting for the sound of footsteps or a groan as Jude pushes the door open. I can't look over my shoulder, not with the cross tied to my back. I listen for a long moment, but I hear nothing over my own ragged breath. He isn't here.

Yet. He isn't here *yet.* I swallow, and the acid taste of vomit hits the back of my throat. The chapel door could fly open any second now. And if Jude sees me here, like this . . .

I slam one arm against the doorframe, hoping the wood's been burnt enough that it'll just give way. The door holds, but the cross splinters, and thin shards of wood jam into my skin. Pain spreads through my wrist and up into my shoulder. It feels dull compared to the sharp jabs along my back, but deeper. The kind of pain that won't fade after a few hours. Sweat coats my forehead, and nausea swirls through my stomach. The room around me spins.

I throw myself into the doorframe again and this time the wood cracks beneath it. One side of the cross stays attached to my back while the other—the one bound to my wrist—breaks free. I sigh, relieved, and then get to work on the knot. My blood has slicked the ropes enough that they slide easily off the broken edge of the cross, finally releasing my hand. I pull myself loose and my arm flops to my side.

It looks wrong, like there are too many bones rattling around below the skin. I try to move it, and pain shoots through my muscles. It's broken.

I release a scream that's half sob and collapse onto the ground, the cross settling heavily against my shoulders. I reach for my opposite wrist with my broken arm. Pain knifes through me as my fingers slip over the bloody knot, struggling to grip it. I dig and pull but the knot holds tight.

"Come *on!*" I scream as finally my fingers sink into the knot. I grit my teeth and pull, and the bindings unravel. The rope falls to the floor.

I hear something just outside. A crunch, like boots on snow.

Time's up.

CHAPTER TWENTY-FOUR

He's coming.

I stumble into the narrow room beyond. I prop my uninjured hand against the wall and kneel, my broken arm still cradled at my chest. The soles of my feet sting and ache.

I try the back door first—locked, of course. There's a window next to the door, one of the few in the chapel with the glass still intact. I briefly consider going back through the chapel and climbing through an already broken window, but they're all much higher off the ground. I could break my leg or twist an ankle if I jumped from that height. I shift my weight away from the wall—biting my lip through the pain—and fumble for a brass candleholder sitting on the table. Sweat coats my palms and my fingers slip over the heavy metal.

I groan, lifting the candleholder in my uninjured hand. It's heavier than I thought it would be. Or maybe my arm is weaker, tired from bearing the weight of my body on the cross. I aim the candleholder at a crack cutting down the center of the stained glass window, narrow my eyes—and throw.

Glass shatters outward, raining red, green, and blue shards across the snow. Cold gusts in through the opening, making me shiver. I rip a silky cloth off the table, wrap it around my fist, my broken arm still clutched to my chest, and knock the remaining glass from the window frame. I think, briefly, of trying to find my shoes. But there isn't time. And I'll run faster barefoot than in heels, anyway.

The window isn't far from the ground. I wedge one hand against the frame, hug my broken arm close to my body, and shimmy through the opening. Broken glass dusts the ground below me. I grit my teeth together and pull my body outside.

The ground rushes toward me. I swing my uninjured arm around to brace for the impact. Pain slams into my palm and shudders through my elbow. Glass bites into my skin. I roll away from it, my chest heaving.

I'm free.

A dozen tiny cuts tingle across my face, and my broken arm is useless. I clutch it with my opposite hand and make myself stand, my legs wobbly beneath me. The snow soothes my shredded feet, numbing the pain enough that I can stagger forward without gasping.

"Okay, Mom," I whisper, my voice trembling. "What now?"

Find a phone. Call the police.

The answer comes to me instantly, like my mother really is standing beside me, guiding me to safety. I take one step, and then another, until I'm sure I won't collapse under my own weight. I think of the cell phone hidden under Sutton's mattress and lurch into an unsteady run. *Please let it still be there,* I pray to God or my mom or the Universe—anyone who might be listening.

My body isn't well enough to move quickly. My muscles and skin and bones scream with pain, and it takes all the strength I have to keep my bare feet moving over the icy ground. The bones in my broken arm jostle against one another with every step I take forward, sending waves of nausea rolling over me. Snow flurries through the air, covering the trees and bushes, crunching beneath my toes. It glows white in the darkness, transforming the grounds into someplace unfamiliar and strange. Cold ripples through my bare feet and up my legs, coaxing goose bumps from my skin. I tighten my jaw and focus only on putting one foot in front of the other, on moving faster, faster . . .

A voice weaves through the trees.

". . . please . . . Sofia . . . come back."

I freeze, horror wrapping around my chest. My breath claws out of my lungs and up my throat, upsetting the silence around me with deep, ragged gasps. I press a fist to my mouth to hold it back. I duck behind a tree and sink into the snow, trembling.

Cold hugs my body. It's moved past soothing and onto brutal. Icy wind snakes up my velvet skirt and down the back of collar. It freezes the tears leaking from my eyes. I curl my arms and knees close to my body.

I grit my teeth together to keep myself from shivering. Wind blows in my ears, making it impossible for me to hear anything else. But the noise means Jude can't hear me, either.

Footsteps crunch in the snow. Then the wind shifts, carrying the sound away. I press my lips together, breathing through my nose. Tiny silver clouds hover in the air before my face. Darkness around me. I listen so hard that my head aches and my ears buzz. I strain my eyes staring into the darkness, but I see only ice-coated trees, their bare branches clawing at the sky.

I exhale, and my muscles start to relax. He must have

passed me. The tension leaves my neck and shoulders. I stretch my legs out to keep them from cramping.

The wind shifts again. It tickles my arms and creeps into my ears. Then—

"I know you're out here."

The voice sounds close, maybe a yard or two away from where I'm hiding. A scream bubbles up my throat—I bunch my fist in front of my mouth to keep from letting it out.

A tiny, dancing flame appears in the darkness—Jude's lighter. He'll see me if he keeps moving forward.

"I'm sorry," Jude calls. His voice makes my stomach turn. I press my back against the icy bark behind me, holding my breath. "I didn't mean to scare you."

I hold my breath. My heart thuds in my chest, so loud that I'm certain Jude will hear it, even with the wind blowing in his ears. Jude walks behind a tree, his lighter flickering out as he disappears from view. My leg muscles contract, tensing to run. It takes me another moment to spot the tiny orange flame again and, when I do, it's smaller. Like a firefly in the darkness.

My muscles relax—he's walking away from me. Silently, I pull my legs closer to my body. Something catches my eye. I turn—then press my lips together to keep from gasping out loud.

A single, bloody footprint mars the virgin snow. I

shift my gaze farther down the path and there's another one. And another. They glare up at me, such a bright red against the white. I stare at them in horror, willing them to disappear.

They lead right to me.

Jude heads farther into the trees, the darkness swallowing his tiny lighter flame. I exhale, my heart still hammering in my chest. But he'll circle back this way eventually, and then he'll see the bloody footsteps and follow them to me. I can't just run. I need a plan.

I hear my mom's voice. *If you can't walk, then crawl.* It's something she used to tell me when I was frustrated. *Keep going,* it meant. Never give up.

I ease down onto my knees and one hand, still clutching my useless broken arm to my chest. Even though I'm not putting any pressure on it, my arm still feels numb and unsteady and *wrong*. I dig my teeth into my lower lip and force myself forward. *It's no worse than the cuts on my feet,* I tell myself. But that's not true. It feels like something isn't lining up right, like all my nerve endings are grinding against one another. I cringe against the pain and do an awkward three-legged crawl through the snow. After a few feet, I glance over my shoulder to see whether I'm trailing blood.

Nothing but pure, white snow stretches behind me. I exhale, relieved. My hands and knees leave pockmarks in the path, but the snow's still coming down hard. Soon, even that trail will be hidden.

I groan and stagger forward. A shallow creek runs through the woods ahead. I can't hear the sound of water but I know it's close; I can practically picture it weaving through the trees. It cuts across the grounds and flows up past the dormitories. I'll be able to run in the water without worrying about trailing blood. Then I'll get to the dormitories, to Sutton's phone under the mattress in our room. Maybe Sister Lauren's there, too—her room is on the ground floor. She'll help me.

I move my hand over the ground as I crawl, preparing for the earth to transform into wet, slimy rocks. Darkness presses in, thick and ominous. Even the moon has ducked behind a cloud. I watch for Jude's lighter, but see nothing. Snowflakes kiss the back of my neck. I shiver as the cold melts into my skin.

I crawl onward, dragging my knees through the snow, ignoring the pain stabbing into the bones of my injured arm. Cold air numbs my shins and nose and mouth. I lower my hand to the ground—

—and pitch forward. Hard. My palm slams into ice and slides out from beneath me.

"Dammit." I breathe, pushing myself back up. I run my hand over the water's frozen surface. It's solid, but thin. I lean forward and jam my elbow into the ice. It cracks beneath me, soaking my arm with freezing water. I push myself up to my feet and step in.

Cold like I've never felt before envelops my feet. I swear under my breath, and hug my broken arm closer to my chest. It's so cold it burns, so cold that the bottoms of my legs disappear. It feels like my body ends at my knees, like I'm tottering forward on bloody stumps. I force myself to move. To walk. Then run. I can barely feel the sharp rock bed beneath my feet, digging into my ragged skin. The icy fire licks at my legs, creeping up past my thighs. Broken ice floats through the water around me.

Jude's voice echoes through the woods. He must've realized he went the wrong way. He's circling back now. I release a choked sob, fear curling around my spine. I push my legs against the current. Faster, *faster*. A dim light flickers through the trees. I glance over my shoulder. Looks like his lighter, but I can't be sure. I turn back around and press onward.

The girls' dormitories materialize from the darkness, the moss-covered brick barely more than a shadow in the trees. I stumble out of the creek, my legs so numb they give way beneath me. I slam into the ground, ice tearing the skin along my knees. I gasp and shove myself back to my feet. My toes curl into the snow as I pitch forward. I sprint to the first-floor entrance, my fingers fumbling for the doorknob. For one horrible second I worry it'll be locked. But it turns, easily, beneath my hand.

"Sister Lauren!" I throw the door open and hurry inside. My voice echoes off the walls. I push the door closed behind me, taking a second to slide the dead bolt shut. There are at least three other entrances into the dorms, but the lock could hold Jude off for a few precious minutes.

"Sister Lauren!" I call again. Her room is at the end of the hall. I stagger forward, collapsing against her door. I beat my fists against the wood. *"Please,"* I whisper, closing my eyes. I lift my hand to knock again and that's when I remember—Midnight Mass. Sister Lauren isn't here. Nobody is.

I wipe a tear off my cheek and try the doorknob— locked. My heartbeat speeds up. I force myself to breathe. *In, and then out.* The auditorium is back toward the chapel—too far to run without Jude catching me. So what's next?

"Phone," I whisper out loud. Sutton's phone is one floor up, but I remember seeing a landline in the kitchen on this floor. I push myself off Sister Lauren's door and lurch down the hall.

My bare feet slap against the floor. The icy water numbed my wounds, and I barely even feel the sting of pain through my skin as I run. I glance behind me to see if I'm leaving behind bloody prints. The cold must've done something to the cuts because I spot only a few drops of blood glistening from the tile.

I push through the kitchen door, pausing for a moment to catch my breath. The phone hangs on the far wall, next to the fridge. It looks like something from the '70s—avocado green, with a curly cord dangling from one end. I dart toward it without bothering to turn on the lights, yanking the receiver from its cradle. I lift the phone to my ear and poise my finger to dial.

No dial tone.

"Shit!" I jab the dial pad with my finger, but nothing happens. The storm must've knocked out the phone lines. I push down the hook, then release. Silence.

A door creaks open. I freeze, the phone still at my ear. The door swings shut with a soft thud.

"It's Sister Lauren," I whisper to myself. Footsteps move down the hallway. Creaking. I sink back against the wall. The footsteps don't sound like Sister Lauren's. They're heavier. A boy's.

Fear creeps down through my arms and legs. I hug my broken arm to my body and curl my toes into the linoleum. My fingers dig into the sides of the phone so hard that the plastic creaks.

I place the phone back on the cradle. An axe hangs on the wall behind a pane of glass that reads BREAK IN

CASE OF FIRE. My eyes linger on the case, but I don't have time to break the glass—and, besides, Jude would hear it shatter. I lower my hand to the drawer nearest to me and pull it open gently. A two-pronged carving fork lies inside. I curl my fingers around the wooden handle. It feels good in my hand.

Someone moves down the hallway, his footsteps almost silent. I swallow, staring hard at the kitchen door. I won't be able to leave this room without him seeing me. I need to hide.

I sink down to the floor, carefully opening a cupboard door. There's a lot of space below the sink, as if it was made for trash cans and recycling containers. It's empty now, so I climb inside, leaving the cupboard door open a crack so I can see out into the kitchen. My broken arm screams with pain as I squeeze into the tight space, but I grit my teeth together, refusing to make a sound.

I watch the door, the carving fork clutched tightly in one hand. And wait.

CHAPTER TWENTY-FIVE

The kitchen door creaks open, and a shadow spills across the floor. I stare at the dark shape, willing it to go away.

"Sofia?" Jude steps into the kitchen, letting the door swing shut behind him. He flips the light switch, but nothing happens. The storm must've knocked out the electricity, too. Jude swears under his breath and rakes a hand back through his hair.

"I saw the blood in the hallway," he says. "I know you're in here."

Blood. My eyes dart across the kitchen floor. It's hard to make out anything in the dark, but the more I search, the more I see. There's a bloody toe print next to the phone, barely visible in the shadows, and a smudge across the drawer where I grabbed the carving fork. Tiny red drops glisten on the linoleum, stopping directly in front of the cupboard where I'm hiding.

I tighten my grip on the carving fork. Sweat gathers between my fingers and the wooden handle. It's only a matter of time before he sees all that blood. And then he'll know exactly where I am.

"I love you, Sofia," Jude says in a low voice. "Everything I did was for us."

His footsteps are silent, his movements careful, like a predator. He reminds me of videos I've seen online: jungle cats hiding in tall grass, coyotes stalking their prey.

I lean as close to the crack in the cupboard doors as I dare, wincing as I shift my broken arm to the side. Jude stops in front of the pantry, then leans close to press his ear to the door. He lowers his hand to the doorknob and turns it, slowly, so the latch doesn't click.

He waits a beat—then rips the pantry door open.

I feel a little flicker of triumph. *Not there, asshole.*

Jude pushes the door closed and lowers his forehead to the wood. "Please, Sofia. I only wanted to help you."

His voice sounds soft, almost sweet. But I see how the muscles in his shoulders have tightened, and how he's curled his hand into a fist. I'm not fooled. I squeeze the carving fork tighter.

"I was just trying to take care of you." He pulls the door to the walk-in freezer open, then swears under his breath when he finds it empty. He shakes his head, pushing the door shut again. "I want us to be *together*."

He practically spits the word *together*, giving it sharp edges. He's getting frustrated. He runs a hand through his hair again, and this time he leaves it mussed. It sticks out on his head in odd angles. He's running out of places to look. My eyes shift to the blood spots on the floor. In the darkness, they look black. Like drops of oil.

"It'll be better this time. I promise."

I curl my toes into the splintery cupboard floor. Blood pools beneath them. The skin along the bottoms of my feet stings.

I barely notice. I have a plan.

Jude moves away from the freezer. He takes a step closer to the sink. I can't see his face from this angle anymore, so I study the soles of his heavy leather boots. They're all water-stained and flecked with ashes and blood. My blood.

Something sour hits the back of my throat. I imagine jamming the carving fork through the leather, and down into his toenails. I imagine driving the forked prongs deep enough to pierce flesh. I tighten my grip on the weapon. It feels good. *Right.* As though the wood was designed to fit against my palm.

Jude steps closer. The glistening drops of blood I trailed along the linoleum are less than a foot away from his shoes. All he has to do is glance down at the floor and he'll see them. I swallow. My chest feels tight, my throat dry. It's now or never.

"Sofia—"

I push the cupboard door open. Jude takes a quick step backward, eyes going wide.

"Wait," I say. I'm kneeling on the kitchen floor, my broken arm curled against my chest like an injured bird. I use the cupboard door to help push myself to my feet, careful to keep my uninjured arm hidden in the folds of my dress. I lean against the door and wince at the sudden flare of pain through my broken arm. "I'm sorry. I shouldn't have hidden from you."

The surprise drains from Jude's face. He presses his lips together and the muscle in his jaw tightens. He's all control again.

"I was worried," he says. I tilt my head down, looking up at him through my eyelashes. Concern creases the skin between his eyebrows.

"Are you hurt?" he asks. "I know I went pretty hard on you."

"Nothing more than I deserved." I take a step toward

him, my uninjured arm still pressed to my side, hiding the carving fork in the tattered folds of my dress. Jude looks down at my feet, at the blood pooling on the linoleum beneath my dirty toes.

"The Lord will make you clean," he murmurs, almost to himself. He reaches for my shoulder, and it takes all of my willpower not to cringe away from his touch. He pulls me toward him, wrapping one arm around my back to hold me to his chest. My broken arm is pressed between us.

"I knew you'd understand," he whispers into my hair. "I'm doing this for you. For us—"

I whip my arm out from behind my skirt and drive the carving fork deep into his shoulder.

Jude's face crumples. His eyes lose focus. I wait until they flicker back to mine, until I'm certain he can see my face. I twist the fork. Jude opens his mouth to scream, but no sound comes out.

"Go to hell," I say.

Jude stumbles backward, smacking his hip against the side of the fridge. I shove past him, and scramble onto the counter. Pain flares through my broken arm and licks at my shredded feet. I barely notice. I reach for the window above the sink, grunting as I shove it open one-handed. Cold air gusts in, wrapping around my body and making my skirt flap up around my legs. I climb out, holding tight to the window ledge as I lower myself to the ground. Snow crunches beneath my bare feet.

Jude grabs my wrist before I let go of the window. He digs his fingers deep into my skin, cutting off the circulation to my fingers.

"*Devil*," he chokes out. I try to yank my arm away from him, but he holds tight. My other arm is useless— there's no way I'll be able to push him off me.

"Let me *go!*" I snarl. Jude cocks an eyebrow. He reaches for the carving fork still jutting out of his shoulder.

Brooklyn's voice echoes through my head.

You'll have to use your teeth.

I sink my teeth into Jude's hand, biting down until I taste blood. He screams and reels away from me. I can't seem to unclench my jaw. I dig into his skin until something tears, and flesh comes loose in my mouth. My weight shifts backward. I'm falling.

I slam into the frozen ground shoulder first. Pain rips through my broken arm. Everything feels white-hot and dazzlingly bright. Stars explode in front of my eyes. I clutch my arm, groaning. Blood coats my lips and teeth, filling my mouth with the taste of salt and pennies.

Jude's blood. That thought makes me grin. The pain in my arm doesn't seem so bad all of a sudden. It's just a dull, throbbing ache, like a muscle cramp. I push myself to my feet and stumble toward the driveway twisting past the dormitory. If I follow it for long enough, it'll lead to the main road, which runs all the way to Hope Springs. Someone there will help me.

Snow swirls around me, thick and cold. I can't hear Jude, but I know he's coming. I picture him pulling the carving fork out of his shoulder, climbing through the window after me. I shuffle through the snow, willing my legs to move faster. The pain is back. It doesn't feel dull anymore. It's bright and sharp. It burns through me like a fire. It's so all-consuming that I can't tell whether it's coming from my broken arm or my shredded feet or the whip marks across my back. My knees buckle. I stumble, and then collapse onto my knees.

Something moves through the trees. I stiffen and squint into the swirling snow. It's too big to be an animal, and it can't be Jude—Jude's still behind me.

"Help." I try to shout, but my voice is too weak. I crawl forward, every movement agony. I'm in the middle of the driveway, I think. I feel concrete beneath my knees.

"Help!" I call again, louder this time. The figure pauses, and then, slowly, turns toward me. I think I see a white coat. Dark hair.

Mom, I think, desperately. Tears clog my eyes. It can't be my mom. She's dead.

"Help," I call again. And then my arm trembles and gives out.

CHAPTER TWENTY-SIX

"**S**ofia? Oh my God." Rapid footsteps pound against the driveway. Sister Lauren kneels next to me. She touches my cheek, her hand warm against my skin. "What happened? Are you okay?"

I try to lift myself off the ground but my arm wobbles beneath my weight. "We have to get out of here," I say. "He's *coming*."

Sister Lauren frowns. "Who's coming? Who did this to you?"

"Jude! He's right—" I turn and look back at the dormitories.

The kitchen window is empty.

"No," I whisper. Cold sweat breaks out on the back of my neck. My eyes dart, wildly, around the grounds, but I can't see farther than three feet in any direction. Snow gusts around me, turning everything white. He could be here now, watching us. I picture him standing in the shadows between the trees, smiling that manic smile, the carving fork sticking out of his bloody shoulder. I have to choke back a scream.

He could be *anywhere*.

Sister Lauren pulls a cell phone out of her pocket and dials. "We have an emergency at St. Mary's," I hear her say into the receiver. "I have a student badly injured . . ."

She pauses, a frustrated look on her face. "Fine," she says after a moment. "Just please send someone as soon as you can.

"Come on." Sister Lauren tucks the phone back into her pocket and slides my arm around her shoulder to lift me up. I stand, gasping as the tattered soles of my feet press into the ground. Blood gathers between my toes.

"You need a hospital." Sister Lauren eases me forward, one arm wrapped tight around my waist. "But the roads are a mess because of the blizzard. The police are on their way, but we'll have to make do with what we have in the infirmary until an ambulance can get through."

"The infirmary?" I freeze. The thought of heading

back to the dark, empty dormitory fills me with dread. "No, we can't go back there—"

"You're losing too much blood, Sofia. You need a sling for your arm, and there's dirt in your wounds. You're going to get an infection if we don't clean you up."

"But—"

"There's a lock on the door. No one's going to hurt you."

Sister Lauren coaxes me forward, her forehead creased in concern. I take one step, and then another. The dormitory looms over us, windows dark and empty. I picture Jude hiding in the shadows beyond the glass. Waiting. Watching. Goose bumps climb my arms.

Something rustles through the bushes behind me. I flinch out of Sister Lauren's grip, stumbling backward. A scream claws at my throat. I whirl around.

Nothing there.

"It's okay," Sister Lauren says, her voice calm, like she's talking to a spooked animal. She approaches me slowly, her hands held in front of her. "The infirmary is right inside. You'll be safe."

"Yeah," I breathe. "Okay."

I let her lead me into the dormitory. I can barely feel my broken arm. I wonder if I'll ever be able to move it again. The door slams shut behind us. I jump, muscles going suddenly tense. But no one leaps out of the shadows. The hallway stretches before us, silent and empty. The infirmary is only three doors down. I spot the familiar sign, its black letters so badly peeled that they read FI MA Y instead of INFIRMARY. Sister Lauren fumbles for the right key and fits it into the lock. The door clicks open.

"Come on," she says. She ushers me inside and I collapse facedown onto the narrow hospital bed, my chest heaving with ragged, shallow breaths. Sister Lauren closes the door behind her and flips the dead bolt. It slides into place with a heavy thud.

We did it. We're safe.

It's dark in the infirmary. I can just make out a short row of carefully made beds, each separated by a thin, threadbare curtain. I lift my head and spot a metal cart next to the door, covered in rust stains that look almost like blood. A skeleton stands in the corner behind it, positioned with one arm lifted above its head. Like it's waving.

Sister Lauren hurries over to the sink on the far wall. She fumbles with a drawer, and then a match sparks to life, filling the tiny room with a warm orange glow. The flame illuminates a row of cupboards just above the sink. Dusty blue and green bottles wink from their shelves. Sister Lauren lights a candle and sets it on the counter.

"Emergency candles," she explains, shaking out the

match. "We have them in every room in case of a power outage."

She cringes, looking over my shoulder at my tattered, bloody back. "I'm going to see if I can find any bandages. And maybe a needle. You might need stitches."

I nod, barely lifting my head. The bed feels warm and soft beneath my cheek. I hear drawers slide open and closed. Cupboard doors creak.

Sister Lauren rushes back to my side, her arms filled with ointments and bandages. She drops them on the metal cart. Jars and bottles roll everywhere. A tube of Neosporin hits the floor.

"Sorry." Sister Lauren jerks a hand back through her hair and I realize, for the first time, that she's scared. "I didn't know what you'd need, so I figured I should just grab it all."

She deals with my broken arm first, disinfecting and bandaging the cuts, before carefully looping a sling around my shoulder. Then she takes a deep breath and picks up a bottle of disinfectant and a bag of cotton balls. She seems a little calmer now, her movements less erratic.

"I'm going to lift up the back of your dress so I can take a closer look at your injuries," she says. "Is that okay?"

I nod. A second later, I feel Sister Lauren's cool hands

on my back, peeling away the tattered remains of my dress. She lowers a cotton ball to my skin. I expect the disinfectant to sting, but it feels cool. Nice. My eyes flicker closed.

"Why don't you tell me what happened?" Sister Lauren says, dabbing my back with the cotton. "Start from the beginning."

"It was Jude," I say quietly. Sister Lauren spreads some disinfectant over one of my cuts, and I cringe. "He said he wanted to save me."

The rest of the story comes in a rush. I tell Sister Lauren about how Father Marcus performed an exorcism on Jude when he first came here. I tell her about the morning I saw him being whipped in the chapel, the horrible scars on his back, and how he tied me up. How he beat me. By the time I'm done talking, Sister Lauren has finished disinfecting my back and started on the cuts covering the bottoms of my feet. She wraps the wounds in thick cotton bandages.

"We need to get the police here," Sister Lauren says. She shuffles through the closet and the cupboards until she finds an old St. Mary's sweatshirt and a pair of scrubs. Her fingers tremble as she helps me slide my broken arm through a sleeve, and then gingerly places it back inside its sling. "*Immediately.* I don't care if there's a storm. That boy needs to be locked up."

Something bangs into the door, making the wood shudder and creak. I flinch.

Sister Lauren stiffens. "What was that?"

I curl my fingers into the stiff mattress, my heart beating so hard I'm worried it's going to rip out of my chest. Every nerve in my body flares to life. Every muscle tenses. I picture the axe in the kitchen, hidden beneath a layer of thin glass.

BREAK IN CASE OF FIRE.

The infirmary door groans and shudders. A blade slams through the wood, its edge sharp. Glinting.

CHAPTER TWENTY-SEVEN

"I t's him." I try to stand, but my legs are numb. I stumble backward, whacking my ankle against the cot leg.

"Sofia, calm down." Sister Lauren lowers a hand to my shoulder, her other hand fumbling for the silver cross hanging from her neck. "We must have faith."

I want to shake her. Doesn't she understand how serious this is? How dangerous?

The axe crashes into the door. The wall shudders. A long, narrow sliver separates from the wood with a crack and flutters to the floor. Jude wrestles the axe back. I catch a glimpse of his dark eyes through the hole in the door. They focus on me.

"Sofia, please. Just open the door," he says.

I shake my head, and he slams the axe into the door again. The blade tears into the narrow opening, widening it into a large hole. Jude lowers the axe, gasping, and reaches through the hole. His hand slides through easily, but he can't get his arm past the jagged wooden edges. He swears and pulls his arm back.

"The Lord will not forsake us," Sister Lauren says, her voice trembling. "The Lord will not forsake us. The Lord will not . . ."

She sounds as if she's in shock. Her hand tightens around my shoulder, and I think of Jude's thick fingers circling my wrists, holding me in place. Her fingers seem small and fragile in comparison.

I catch sight of Jude through the hole in the door. He hoists the axe back over one shoulder, preparing to swing. I glance around the small room, looking for a weapon. Bandages and bottles of ointment crowd the metal cart, and dusty bottles glint from the shelves above the sink, but there's nothing sharp. Nothing heavy. There isn't even a window in here. We're trapped.

Sister Lauren bows her head. "Pray with me, Sofia," she says, fumbling for my hand. "We will be saved if we pray."

Jude slams his axe into the door again. Splinters fly into my legs, wood pricks through the thin fabric of the scrubs and nips at my ankles. Sister Lauren weaves her fingers through mine, and pulls me down to the floor beside her. Fear makes me clumsy. My knees slam hard into the tile, and I wince at the sudden pain. Sister Lauren folds her hands around my trembling fist, and presses her forehead to mine, my slinged arm wedged between us. Sweat breaks out on my palms. The Lord has never listened to my prayers before. Why would He start now?

"Our Father, who art in heaven," she whispers urgently, "hallowed be thy name . . ."

It's a prayer I've heard before, but I still don't know all the words. I listen to Sister Lauren recite it once all the way through. Her voice steadies as she speaks.

"Thy kingdom come, thy will be done, on earth as it is in heaven." She sounds strong now. Brave. It gives me courage.

"Our Father, who art in heaven," I recite, joining in as Sister Lauren starts the prayer over. My voice shakes and I stutter once or twice, but I manage to follow along. My fear dulls, just a little, as the prayer flows through me. I feel like someone's lit a fire just below my collarbone. I'm speaking to God at last. He's actually listening—I know it. He hears me in my time of need.

The axe crashes into the door. Wood cracks, and then something heavy thuds to the floor. The sound raises the hair on the back of my neck. I clench my hands together, my fingernails digging into my skin. My arms shake so badly that I can barely hold them steady.

"Thy kingdom come . . ." I pray. "Thy will be done . . ."

There's a beat of quiet. Then a lock clicks. Fear rips through my body.

He's in.

"On earth as it is in heaven . . ."

The door creaks open. Jude steps into the room. Cold seeps up through the tile, chilling my knees. But I'm not trembling anymore. The prayer has done what I always wanted it to do. I feel like God is with me, like He's protecting me. I glance up, still whispering the prayer under my breath.

Jude stands in the hallway, the axe hanging at his side. Crusty brown blood stains his shoulder, and a bite mark mangles the back of his hand. The skin around it has swollen and turned a deep, ugly red.

Good, I think. Jude grunts, heaving the axe up so that he's holding it with two hands.

I sneak a look at Sister Lauren. Her head is still bowed, her lips moving silently. She looks . . . serene. Peaceful. Maybe it's my imagination, or maybe there's some light slanting in through the open door, but I swear I see a halo of white illuminating her body, turning her into something holy.

"Our Father, who art in heaven," she starts again. She squeezes my fist, and I whisper the next part along with her. Our voices weave together, sounding like one. "Hallowed be thy name . . ."

Jude steps toward us, lifting the axe above his head. He releases a deep, animalistic cry that echoes off the walls of the tiny infirmary. My voice falters. I let go of Sister Lauren and throw my arm over my head.

Sister Lauren lifts her head and raises one hand. "Stop," she says.

I expect Jude to drive the axe through her face. I brace myself to feel the warm spray of blood across my cheeks, to hear the wet thud of her body hitting the floor. I cover my mouth with one hand.

But Jude lurches to a stop, looking almost confused. His fingers spring open, and the axe crashes to the ground. Jude looks down at his hands and then back up at Sister Lauren.

"I told you to *stop*," she says. Her voice sounds different this time, like it's layered with the sounds of dozens of other voices. I turn to her, amazed. Her eyes have taken on a golden cast. She looks like she's glowing from within.

The confusion drains from Jude's face. His skin looks pallid. Sickly. Desperation fills his eyes.

"What are you?" he asks. Sister Lauren stands and

moves toward him, her hand still raised in front of her. Her skin seems to radiate some unearthly light. Jude flinches and stumbles backward, smacking his leg against the ruined door. It swings open, slapping against the wall.

Jude turns and tears down the hall.

Sister Lauren lowers her hand. She strolls into the hallway after Jude without another word.

I push myself off the floor with one hand, knees shaking. My chest heaves. I feel light-headed, as if everything inside my skull has been scooped out and replaced with helium. I allow myself one second to calm down. Then I stand and race into the hallway after them, my sling slapping against my chest as I run.

The dormitory is empty. I don't hear footsteps or voices. I jog down the hall and throw open the door to the quad. Icy wind and snow whirls around me, pushing me back inside. I lean forward, against the wind, and force my way out.

Jude kneels in the middle of the snowy field, head bowed, almost as if he's praying. I step outside, letting the dormitory door swing shut behind me. Snow soaks through the bandages covering my feet. Snowflakes kiss the tip of my nose.

Sister Lauren stands over him. She's saying something, but the wind carries her voice in the other direction. She lifts a hand and Jude's shoulders begin to shake.

He's not praying. He's sobbing.

I hobble toward them as fast as I can. The light that seemed to radiate from Sister Lauren's skin grows brighter. I stare, stunned. This isn't sunlight or a trick of my eyes. Sister Lauren is actually glowing. I stop in my tracks. I no longer feel the wind whipping at my back, or the icy snowflakes landing on my nose and forehead. I feel warm.

God hasn't forsaken me—he's been here all along.

Sister Lauren clenches her hand into a fist. Jude's face swells like a balloon. He lifts his hands to his throat and claws at his own skin, leaving deep red gashes on his neck. I watch, horrified, as blood seeps into his eyes and trickles from his nose. His cheeks grow redder and redder. Purple and blue veins stand out against his skin.

Jude's eyelids stop flickering. His pupils roll back in their sockets. He pitches forward and lands in the snow. Dead.

"He saved us," I murmur, dropping to my knees. A giddy laugh bubbles up from my throat. "God saved us."

Slushy snow wets the knees of my scrubs. It seems to be coming down faster now. Icy shards prick my hands and the back of my neck. Wind howls through the naked trees, making the branches tremble.

None of it bothers me. I press my uninjured hand to my chest above the sling, a smile spreading across my face. God didn't forsake me. Tears pool in my eyes, freezing before they can slide down my cheeks.

Footsteps crunch through the snow. Sister Lauren lowers her hand to my head, her palm warm on my cold skin.

"Why are you crying?" she asks, brushing a lock of hair away from my forehead.

"Because God answered our prayers." I wipe the icy tears from my cheeks. "I'm not evil. This proves I can be good. That God loves me."

Sister Lauren throws her head back and releases a deep, strange laugh that sounds nothing like her normal voice. There's an edge to it. It could cut you.

"What's funny?" I ask. Sister Lauren stops laughing.

"*You* are," she says, touching her hand to my cheek. "You're one of us, Sofia. God didn't save you."

A chill that has nothing to do with the weather sweeps through my body. I picture it like frost spreading across a lake in winter. It freezes my lungs and chest, then crawls up my throat, turning my breath to ice.

"What are you talking about?" I want to look up, to prove to myself that this isn't really happening. But the cold holds me in place.

Sister Lauren kneels in front of me. I know it's Sister Lauren because she's wearing Sister Lauren's clothes. She has Sister Lauren's short brown hair, pulled back in a messy ponytail. Sister Lauren's silver necklace glints from her collarbone.

But something isn't right. I watch, horrified, as the skin on Sister Lauren's forehead and around her eyes smoothens. Her cheeks grow fuller and her pupils darken. Her mouth looks too big, too full of teeth. She shakes her head and Sister Lauren's hair falls loose of its ponytail. It shortens before my eyes, transforming into Brooklyn's familiar spiky pixie cut. The color fades into an orangey bleached blonde.

"Hello, Sofia," Brooklyn says. Her smile widens and, all at once, I realize why it seemed familiar that day in the van. It's Brooklyn's smile staring out at me from a stranger's face. "Did you miss me?"

CHAPTER TWENTY-EIGHT

I fall back on my heels, my hand propped against the ground behind me. This can't be real. It's a dream. I dig my fingers into the icy dirt.

"You aren't here," I say.

"I've been here the whole time," Brooklyn says.

"You're not here." I close my eyes. *Wake up,* I tell myself. *Wake the fuck up!*

Brooklyn stands, brushing the snow off her jeans.

"I told you I was coming for you, Sofia." She takes a step toward me, and I shift back onto my hand and knees in an awkward, one-armed, crablike crawl. Brooklyn's smile sharpens, amused. "You shouldn't be so surprised."

I think of my computer freezing, horrible pictures flashing across the screen. And then Brooklyn's voice whispering through the speakers: *I'm coming for you.* I crawl backward clumsily. Dull pain thumps through the soles of my feet, but all I can think of is getting away. Brooklyn takes a slow step toward me.

"It took a lot of work to get you in here. You should be grateful that I was willing to go through the trouble. Do you have any idea how hard I had to work to get your mom to crash her car?"

I close my eyes, a tear sliding over my cheeks. "You killed my mother?"

"Not just her. I had to take care of Abby Owens, too. And she *scratches.*"

I think of the gauges on the windowsill back in my dorm, and understanding washes over me. Leena and Sutton's old roommate didn't get pregnant and run away like they thought. Brooklyn murdered her. A sob claws at my throat.

"Why are you doing this to me?" I choke out.

"Have you forgotten about our little talk in Leena's hospital room? *When someone does something unforgiveable, a demon attaches itself to them.* You did something unforgiveable, Sofia. You pulled a girl in front of a train and watched her die. And more than that, you want, you lust, you covet. You're weak. And I'm the price you have to pay for your sins."

I crawl farther backward, my broken arm swaying in the sling at my chest. "But *why*? Why bring me here?"

"You kept fighting your true nature, and I needed you alone and isolated. I needed to show you how good it feels to let the evil in. Admit it, Sofia. You've done some pretty twisted things but didn't you like it? Didn't it feel good?"

"No, it didn't." My voice cracks. Rocks and ice dig into my palm. "It felt terrible."

"Don't lie, Sofia. That's another sin." Brooklyn crouches in front of me. "You can't get away from me. You're mine. Pure *evil*. Like me."

"I'm not evil," I whisper. I keep crawling backward, the muscles in my arm and legs burning from the weight of my body. I should stand, *run*.

Brooklyn touches my chin with one finger. "And then you went and hooked up with the only guy on campus even more depraved than you are."

Brooklyn glances over her shoulder. Jude's body is still slumped in the snow a few yards away from us. "He had bad boy written all over him," she says. "I get why you liked him, though. You really are just like me."

A tree trunk slams into my back and I groan. I move my hand behind me, dragging my fingers over the cold bark. I'm blocked in. The only way out is through Brooklyn.

Brooklyn cocks her head. "Do you recognize where we are?"

I take in my surroundings, but I don't see anything familiar. Everything is white. The snow has become an icy sleet. It comes down at an angle, biting into my face and hands. Ice clings to my cheeks and eyelashes and hair.

"Let me help you remember," Brooklyn says. She stares at a spot in the snow, and the ground begins to tremble, as if there's something drilling up from below the earth. I push back up against the tree, hugging my knees to my chest.

"What is that?" I ask, staring hard at the snow. It shudders and tumbles away to reveal frozen dirt. A memory surfaces in my brain:

I'm crouching in the mud, digging a shallow hole while rain falls all around me. I clutch a bloody pillowcase in one hand.

"No," I breathe as it dawns on me that I'm sitting at the exact same spot where I buried Leena's bunny.

My pillowcase lurches out of the ground, crusty brown blood blossoming across the fabric like an ugly flower. It hovers in the air two feet above the snow, turning in a slow circle. Something inside it wriggles.

I swallow, tasting vomit on my tongue. "Don't," I say. "Please."

The pillowcase falls away, revealing Heathcliff's

frozen, bloody body. Skinny pink maggots burrow into his fur and writhe from his nose. They crowd around his eye sockets, eating the last of his rotten, bloodshot eyes.

"Do you know how good it feels to snap a bunny's neck?" Brooklyn asks, staring at the dead animal. She flicks her hand, and his body jerks violently, sending a few maggots flying to the snow. I scream, then curl my hand into a fist in front of my mouth. The bunny drops to the ground just inches from my foot. His back leg twitches, then goes still.

"It's like breaking a stick in half," Brooklyn says. "And then all the light drains out of the little fucker's eyes just like"—she snaps her fingers—"*that*. I think you'd enjoy it, Sofia. It makes you feel powerful. Like God."

"You're *sick*," I whisper, tearing my eyes away from the maggots eating Heathcliff's face.

"The trapdoor was trickier," Brooklyn says, her face twisting. "I thought I was going to have to make up some excuse to get Leena to walk across it at just the right moment, but I lucked out. She's clumsier than I expected."

Leena's scream echoes through my head. I shudder and squeeze my eyes shut. "Stop it," I say. "I don't want to hear any more."

"And then there was the night of the fire. Do you know Leena passed out in the trees just a few feet away from the chapel? You ran right past her, Sofia. You almost tripped on her crutch. If you had thought of someone other than yourself for a single second, you would have found her. If you'd have looked down even once, you would have seen her lying on the ground and she never would have had to die."

"You killed her, too," I say. A tear oozes out of the corner of my eye.

"I might have set the pieces, but it was the evil inside of you that sealed her fate. You coveted her life. You let your jealousy consume you. Leena was drunk, and she had a broken leg, and you left her alone in the woods. A good person wouldn't do that. A *good* person would have tried to help her. I dragged her back to the chapel, dumped her body, and knocked over a candle. But you watched the place burn." Brooklyn's smile quirks. "It was a beautiful fire, don't you think?"

Brooklyn's words wash over me. I don't want her to be right. I don't want to have evil inside of me. I feel my body shutting down, ready to give up.

"I tried to be good," I choke out. "I prayed. I asked God to help me."

"But he didn't come for you, did he? I did." Brooklyn says. "I did all of this for you, because you wanted it. You say you wanted to be a good girl, but that's not how you felt in your soul. You liked how it felt to hurt other people. *You are evil.* Admit it. I may have broken that bunny's neck and locked the chapel door, but you were the one who *liked* it."

Something inside of me releases. I didn't murder Heathcliff or Leena. Brooklyn set me up. She preyed on my jealousy and weakness.

I push myself away from the tree. All along I thought I was making these things happen myself. But it was just Brooklyn trying to break me. I feel stronger all of a sudden. As though the exhaustion and pain from this night has drained out of my body, leaving me whole again.

I'm not evil. Not yet, at least.

I push myself into a crouch, the muscles in my leg tingling. Brooklyn turns back around, frowning.

"What are you—"

I slap her across the face, relishing the sharp tingle of pain that shoots through my palm. "You're wrong," I spit. "I'm *nothing* like you."

And then I leap to my feet and run.

CHAPTER TWENTY-NINE

Icy grass crunches beneath my feet. My pant legs bunch around my ankles, the soggy fabric dragging in the snow. I tear across the quad, heading for the boys' dorms. Or where I think the dorms should be. Sister Lauren said a couple of other students stayed behind over the holidays—the girls' dorms were empty, but maybe one of the boys can help me.

Snow swirls around me. Frozen curls hang over my forehead, making it impossible for me to see even two feet in front of me. I brush them back but they just fall forward, blocking my vision again. Bandages peel away from the bottoms of my feet, and I feel a sharp sting of pain as my cuts burst open.

The dorms can't be far now. I take another step and my foot hits a patch of ice. It slides out from under me and I fall—*hard*—on my back. My head whacks against the frozen ground. A deep ache spreads across my shoulders and down my spine.

I lie there, watching the ice and snow swirl through the velvety black sky. Cold seeps through my sweatshirt and the seat of my pants. Misty gray puffs of breath hover above my mouth, and my heart beats against my ribs like an animal. The world around me seems to spin. I close my eyes, waiting for it to stop.

I could stay here, I think. I could just let her catch me.

But I open my eyes and drag myself up to my hands and feet, pausing to catch my breath before I stand. I take a tentative step to my left. I can't remember which direction I was running away from, or where I was headed. The snow is too thick. Everything looks the same.

I barely make it two steps into the blizzard before slamming into something solid. A *wall.* I slide my hand over icy brick, so relieved I could cry. I did it. I found the dorm. I follow the wall until the bricks give way to a door, and then I run my fingers along the wood, silently cheering when they brush against the cold brass doorknob. I twist, but the knob won't turn.

"Help me!" I curl my uninjured hand into a fist and beat against the door. The wood trembles and shakes in its frame. "Help me! Somebody! Help me, please!"

Nobody answers. I beat at the door until the skin peels away from my knuckles, and my voice goes hoarse from screaming. My broken arm lies limp and unresponsive in its sling. Tears leak from my eyes. I glance behind me, expecting to see Brooklyn barreling through the snow, her lips spread in a manic smile, fingers curled toward me like claws.

But there's no one. Only ice and trees and swirling darkness.

Two hands clamp down on my shoulders and spin me back around. I try to scream, but my voice gets lodged in my chest and I only manage a whimper. It takes me a long moment to recognize Father Marcus's icy blue eyes and the white tufts of hair sticking out from his balding head. He stands at the door I was just pounding against, squinting into the snowy darkness, a threadbare robe hanging from his shoulders.

"*You*," I breathe. I don't know whether to be relieved or terrified. Father Marcus beat Jude. He made him into the monster that tied me up in the chapel and tortured me.

But there's no one else.

"Miss Flores?" Father Marcus's voice sounds thin and scratchy, like he just woke up. He swallows, his Adam's apple bobbing up and down in his throat. "You shouldn't be out of your dormitory. There's a storm—"

"*Please*," I cut in, gasping. "You have to help me. I'm being chased by the Devil."

The word *Devil* falls from my mouth unplanned. I cringe, certain I've lost my chance at getting help. He'll think I'm crazy.

But Father Marcus steps outside, his bare feet crunching in the snow. He crosses himself and something desperate flashes across his face. Something frightened.

"Where?" he asks.

"I don't know." I wipe the sopping, wet hair from my eyes and look back over my shoulder. "Close, I think. She was right behind—"

Brooklyn emerges from the darkness, smiling. Her skin looks almost blue, but she doesn't shiver. I shrink away from her, and Father Marcus moves in front of me, pushing me behind him with a sweep of his arm.

"I see you've gone for help," Brooklyn says, her smile twisting into something cruel and ugly. She hoists Jude's axe onto her shoulder. She must've stopped to collect it before coming after me. "Does this make you nervous?" she asks. She strokes the wooden handle, almost lovingly.

I swallow, tasting something sour and thick at the back of my throat. I stare at the axe's sharp blade, my stomach turning. I can practically feel it cutting open my skin, cracking my head like an egg.

I glance at Father Marcus's face. In the darkness, it's hard to see the lines on his skin, or the thin red cuts along his lips. He looks younger. He fumbles for something below his robe and brings out a heavy golden cross inlaid with red and green jewels. Brooklyn stares at the cross, her eyes narrowing into catlike slits.

"This one is beyond salvation, Father," she says, taking another slow step forward. "Her soul is weak. One more sin and she's ours forever."

"Back, demon!" Father Marcus holds the cross before him like a weapon.

Brooklyn stops walking. "You can't save her," she says.

"*Credo in Deum Patrem omnipotentem.*" It's the same prayer Jude recited while I lay crying on the floor, my wrists tied behind my back. But coming from Father Marcus, it sounds different. Stronger. He moves closer to Brooklyn. *"Creatorem caeli et terrae. Et in Iesum Christum, Filium eius unicum . . ."*

The smile fades from Brooklyn's lips. She stumbles backward.

"Dominum nostrum, qui conceptus est de Spiritu Sancto, natus ex Maria Virgine . . ."

The axe slips from Brooklyn's hand. She swears.

"Passus sub Pontio Pilato, crucifixus, mortuus, et sepultus,"

Father Marcus shouts. A zealous light fills his eyes. He grins wildly. It's pure, unfiltered joy—the kind of smile you see only on little kids and the mentally unstable. "Tremble before me, demon! You are nothing compared to the glory of God."

I turn back to Brooklyn. I want to see the look of fear in her eyes when she realizes she's lost. I want to see her desperate and trembling and afraid.

But Brooklyn isn't there anymore. All I see is swirling snow and the dark shadows of trees.

Cold fear seeps into my chest. "Where'd she go?"

"We've defeated her, child." Father Marcus's smile widens. He lifts his arms toward the sky in triumph. "Blessed be the name of the Lord," he booms.

I look around, but Brooklyn really is gone. I smile, tentatively, then wince as Father Marcus grabs me by the shoulder and pulls me into an awkward half hug, jostling my broken arm.

"You really think she's—" I stare at Farther Marcus, instantly forgetting the end of my sentence. His smile seems wrong, somehow. His mouth looks strained. Like the skin could rip apart.

Two tiny cuts slash past the corners of his lips. They're thin, almost like paper cuts.

"Father . . ." I whisper. The cuts lengthen, traveling up the sides of Father Marcus's cheeks. He makes a kind of gurgling, coughing sound deep in his throat. He drops his cross, and both of his hands reach for his face. His fingers tremble.

I should run, but I can't drag my eyes away from Father Marcus's grotesque face. The cuts grow deeper, wider. It looks as if someone is carving through the skin and muscle on his cheeks with a sharp, invisible knife. They reach past his cheekbones and up to the corners of his eyes. Blood trickles from his warped smile. It runs down his cheeks in a smooth red sheet, coating first his lips, and then his chin and neck. It stains his undershirt, and trickles from his shoulders and arms, sprinkling the snowy ground. It doesn't look red anymore. Now it's black and lumpy. Like tar.

Father Marcus tries to scream, but his mouth stays frozen in that horrible, morbid smile. The sound gets mangled in his throat, becoming something guttural and animalistic. He drops to his knees in the snow, still clawing at his face like he might, somehow, be able to push his skin back together. The manic gleam fades from his eyes. His pupils grow dull.

He falls over backward.

I stare at his limp body, frozen in horror. Memories play on a loop in my mind. I hear the echo of Riley's voice, screaming for me to help her, and then Brooklyn's hammer driving into her chest, the wet slap of her heart hitting the ground. I did nothing then. I stood by and let it all happen. Now it's happening again.

Town isn't far from here. If I run, and I don't look back, I could still get away. I stumble around the priest's body, trying to remember how to get to the main road.

Brooklyn's axe whips up from the ground and flies past me, sweeping straight through Father Marcus's neck. His head jerks away from his body. It rolls through the snow, leaving a trail of blood behind it. I stagger backward, gripping my chest with one hand. I don't realize I'm falling until I feel my knees slam into the hard, frozen ground.

Father Marcus's head rolls to a stop just a foot away from me. His dull eyes stare out at me, wide-open and shocked. His cracked blue lips are slightly parted. Lumpy black blood oozes from the stump where his head separated from his body. It doesn't look real.

I spot a twitch of movement in the blood. It's thin and black. Like an eyelash. My stomach turns. Another twitch, and then something scurries away from Father Marcus's head. A spider. It darts through the pool of his blood and disappears into the snow, leaving a trail of black behind it.

I pull myself backward as another spider crawls out of the severed head, and then another, and another. They swarm over one another, crawling through the blood and out into the snow. A spider crawls out of Father Marcus's nose and hurries across his face, its legs leaving tiny dots of blood on his skin. Another sticks a thin, spindly leg straight through his eyeball. I hear a kind of gushing, popping sound when it appears, and yellowish puss slithers down his face. I look away before the rest of the spider can crawl out.

I push myself back up to my feet. I can't stay here. I have to get away. My legs feel distant and weak, and I'm almost surprised when I'm able to lurch forward unsteadily. I take a wobbly step away from Father Marcus's body.

The smell of smoke drifts through the air. I freeze.

A tiny orange flame unfurls from the ground directly in front of my big toe. It twists and dances into the night. Smoke stings my eyes, and the heat presses against me, coaxing sweat from my skin. I stumble backward, coughing, and waving a hand in front of my face. The fire roars and curls and spreads through the snow as if it's gasoline.

A circle of flames grows around me, trapping me.

Something moves in the darkness beyond the circle of fire. I stare into the shadows, orange and red light searing my eyes. Sweat gathers in the small of my back, and heat presses into my neck and legs and hands. The circle closes in around me, flames reaching for my body like hands.

I catch a flicker of movement to my left. I whirl around, heart pounding. But it's just the fire.

"Where are you?" I shout. I tighten my hands into fists and turn around slowly. I can feel Brooklyn watching me beyond the flames, circling me like a predator. Wind howls through the trees, making the branches shiver and quake.

The sound sharpens into a low, cackling laugh. Brooklyn's laugh. A space opens in the flames, and she steps into the circle with me.

"Why are you doing this?" I ask. "What do you want?"

Her grin widens. I can see all her teeth.

"I want you to kill me," she says. She tilts her head and folds her hands together, like she's about to pray. Everything about it looks perverse. The Devil playing at being innocent. "Isn't that what you want? To be rid of me at last?"

Brooklyn flicks her wrist and the flames slither closed behind her. They grow taller and brighter, clawing at the night sky like fingers. Fire licks at my back and ankles. I smell something burning and dance forward, yelping. Brooklyn laughs.

"Or you could try to run. But I'll find you. I'll always find you, Sofia."

Fury flares through me. I can see the rest of my life

play out like a movie. Every few months, I'll head to a new city and try to start over. Brooklyn will leave me alone long enough to make a few friends. To feel safe. And then she'll destroy everything. She'll snap her fingers and burn it to the ground.

I won't live like this. I take a step forward. Brooklyn cocks an eyebrow.

"Come on, Sofia. You know you want to. Get your revenge. Make me suffer."

I press my lips together, tasting blood at the corners of my mouth. Father Marcus's body lies in the snow a few feet away, his ruined smile still leaking thick, tar-like blood. Jude's axe sits on the ground next to his lifeless hand.

Brooklyn's grin quirks even wider.

I know this is a trick. I feel the wrongness rushing through my veins like blood. *One more sin,* Brooklyn said.

But deeper than that, I feel something else. *Want.* It hums through me, making my bones tremble. I'm tired of being everyone else's punching bag. I want to destroy something.

I kneel in the snow and wrap my fingers around the axe's thick wooden handle. It's heavy and hard to lift with just one hand. The want buzzes louder. It fills my ears with static. It makes my skin purr.

"Give it to me," Brooklyn says, and this time she

isn't smiling. Her mouth is a snarl. A dare. "You know I deserve it. Prove to me that you're not weak."

Something inside me snaps. I lift the axe, barely noticing the weight pulling at my muscles, or my broken arm burning with pain in its sling. I swing, and the blade sinks into Brooklyn's chest. It rips through cloth and skin; it cracks ribs and tears muscle. Blood sprays my face and neck and hands. It smells coppery, like pennies, but below that is something else. The smell of something going rotten.

I yank the axe out of Brooklyn's chest. The blade makes a slurping sound as it leaves her body. Brooklyn glances at the wound casually, like she's examining a new tattoo or piercing. She drags her fingers through the blood, staining them red.

"Sofia—" Blood bubbles from her mouth and streams over her chin. It coats her teeth and lips.

I swing the axe again and Brooklyn flies backward. Her body smacks into the icy ground, arms flailing above her head like a rag doll. I climb on top of her and I bring the axe down, over and over. Her blood feels tacky and warm against my skin. Almost like candlewax. I feel it in my nostrils and in my ears and in the corners of my eyes. It sinks between my fingers and crusts up under my fingernails.

Brooklyn laughs. The sound is deep and unnerving.

It echoes in my ears. I bring the axe down again. My muscles burn, and my broken arm has gone numb, but I keep swinging. It's as if I'm being controlled by something else, something much stronger than my weak, ruined body.

The flames around me flicker, and then die, until all that's left is a black circle of soot. I pull the axe out of Brooklyn's body and swing it again, almost enjoying the low, meaty sound of the blade sinking through her organs. Brooklyn's eyes have rolled back in her head. Her chest is shredded and bloody. But, *still*, she laughs. The sound echoes through the air. It's like an air siren. Like an emergency alert, warning people of a flood or a tornado. Doesn't anyone else hear it?

Lights flash from in the trees. I notice voices, too, but they don't seem real. They're like something out of a dream. I should look up, but all I can think about is Brooklyn. I have to destroy her. I have to—

"Put down your weapon!"

The command cuts through me. I freeze, finally lifting my head. The sun has started to rise, and a silvery-white glow paints the horizon. The scene around me slams into focus.

Two police cruisers have pulled onto the quad, their thick tires crushing the dry, icy grass. The cops Sister Lauren called. They've parked a few yards away, doors thrown open to act as barricades. Police officers duck behind the doors, aiming silver-and-black guns through the open windows. Red and blue lights flash from the tops of the cruisers, and a siren howls through the air.

I glance around the quad, dazed. Father Marcus lies crumpled in the snow a few feet away. He's not just dead, he's been completely torn apart. The police officer closest to me levels his gun at my head. His hands tremble.

"I said *put down your weapon!*"

"It's okay," I shout. I stand, my legs wobbling beneath me. "I already—"

A half-dozen hammers click into place.

"Drop your weapon and put your hands on your head!"

Weapon? I glance at my hand and see that I'm still clutching the bloody axe. I look down at Brooklyn's body.

Brooklyn's bleached pixie cut has grown back into Sister Lauren's shaggy brown bob. The wrinkles have slithered back across her forehead and crinkled the skin around her eyes. Her cheeks have hollowed, making her look older. Sister Lauren's eyes stare up at me, cloudy and still.

I've killed an innocent person. Brooklyn is gone.

"No," I whisper. I lower my arm to my side, and the axe slips from my fingers, hitting the ground with a hollow thwack. Dimly, I notice a couple of police officers leap out from behind the cruiser and race toward me. Someone jerks my arm behind my back, and slides a cold, metal handcuff over my wrist. My broken arm is still in its sling, so he lets the other cuff dangle from my wrist, useless. Another officer has his gun aimed at my head. He's saying something I don't quite hear.

"You have the right to remain silent. Anything you . . ."

But all of this seems far away. Like it's happening to someone else, or like it's a story I heard once, but forgot the end of. I stare at Sister Lauren's face and horror lodges itself deep inside my gut. It seeps into my organs and my bones and my skin. It becomes a part of me at a cellular level.

"That's not her," I say, more to myself than to the officers leading me back to the police car. "You don't understand. She was a demon, but I killed her. We're safe now. We're finally safe."

CHAPTER THIRTY

I've been a patient at the Mississippi Hospital for the Criminally Insane for a month and two days when Nurse Simmons tells me I have a visitor. I curl my fingers into the sleeves of my straitjacket, digging my stumpy nails into the canvas. I'm not sure who it could be. Everyone I know is dead.

The visitor's room looks almost exactly like a suburban living room, except that bars cover the windows and all the paintings and furniture are bolted into place. Two men wait inside. One wears a stiff blue policeman's uniform. The other is dressed in a suit and tie, a wool coat hanging from his shoulders. They sit shoulder to shoulder on the white sofa, a manila folder on the coffee table in front of them.

I stiffen and Nurse Simmons places a hand on my elbow, gently nudging me forward. "It's okay, Sofia. The nice officers here just have a few questions for you."

She moves her hand to my back to steady me as I slide onto the hard plastic chair bolted to the ground. She's still holding the restraint chain attached to my straitjacket. When I'm seated, she kneels and fastens it to a metal ring protruding from the chair, then slides a heavy padlock through the links. The chain gives me a one-foot circle of freedom.

I lift my head, studying the men through my greasy curls.

"Thank you for speaking with us, Sofia," the man in the suit says. He's short, with broad arms and shoulders and skinny legs. He reminds me of a bulldog.

"It's nice to see you again, Sofia," the man in the police uniform says. He flashes me a nervous smile. There's a gap between his two front teeth.

"I know you." I sit up straight, shaking the hair out of my eyes. "You came to my house the night my mother had her accident. You're the officer who told me she was dead."

The officer's smile vanishes. He licks his chapped lips.

"I'm Detective Ramirez, and this is Officer Schultz,"

the man in the suit says. "We were hoping we could ask you a few questions."

I catch a whiff of musky-scented cologne as he flips the folder open and slides it toward me. I wrinkle my nose and lean closer, metal chains clinking like bells against my chair.

A photograph of a teenage girl lies inside the folder. She stares up at me, only she's not really staring because she's dead. Choppy, bleached-blond hair frames her hollow cheeks and vacant eyes. Skinny blue veins spiderweb across her skin. She lies on a metal table, a white sheet pulled up to her neck.

"This girl was found in the woods surrounding Riley Howard's family lake house," Officer Ramirez explains. "Can you tell us whether you recognize her as the girl you knew as Brooklyn Stephens?"

"This is highly inappropriate!" Nurse Simmons snaps. "Sofia is a very sick young woman." She tries to close the folder so I won't see the photograph, but Officer Schultz blocks her hand.

"Miss Flores is a key witness in an ongoing murder investigation," he explains. "We need her to identify the body."

Detective Ramirez brushes a piece of lint from the front of his coat. "You're welcome to wait outside if it'll make you more comfortable," he adds.

Nurse Simmons presses her lips into a thin line. "Very well," she says. But she doesn't leave the room. She stands against the wall, crossing her arms over her chest.

Officer Schultz turns back to me. "Sofia? Can you identify this girl?"

I study the photograph. The dead girl has Brooklyn's hair and Brooklyn's face. Brooklyn's black liner is smudged around her eyes. I've seen her lips twist into Brooklyn's half-crazed smile.

"I don't know," I mumble.

Officer Schultz and Detective Ramirez share a look. Officer Schultz leans forward.

"Don't get too close," Nurse Simmons warns, but Officer Schultz doesn't seem to hear her. He slides his elbows onto the coffee table.

"Sofia," he asks. "Help us out here. Is this the monster who murdered your friends?"

I feel my lips curve into a smile. *Monster.* I guess you could call the thing that killed Riley a monster. I prefer to call it *Diablo*, like my grandmother does. I glance down at the photograph. Brooklyn lies on the metal table, but she's hollow—a shell. There's no monster inside of her anymore. It's moved on, leaving her dead body behind.

I murmur something below my breath and Officer Schultz frowns, leaning closer. The wooden coffee table groans beneath his weight. "What was that, Sofia?"

"Officer, *please*," Nurse Simmons says, taking a quick step away from the wall. "Don't get too—"

I lunge forward, catching the fleshiest part of Officer Schultz's earlobe between my teeth. He screams and jerks away from me but I clamp down—tight. The salty bite of blood hits my tongue. A bit of warm flesh comes loose in my mouth.

Nurse Simmons digs a needle out of her pocket. It flashes under the fluorescent lights. She jabs it into my neck, and something cool and tranquil spreads through my body.

I pull away from the police officer and spit his skin onto the coffee table. It slides across the wood, leaving a trail of blood behind it. A hot, hungry feeling stirs inside of me. It's even stronger than the drugs coursing through my veins.

"That isn't the monster," I say, grinning. I feel Officer Schultz's blood on my lips. "You've got the wrong girl."

The demon isn't inside Brooklyn anymore. It's inside me.

ACKNOWLEDGMENTS

As always, I have a mountain of people to thank for bringing this book to life. First of all, a huge thank you to editor extraordinaire Hayley Wagreich, for reading this book a million times and helping me find the story at the center of all the gore. Hopefully, those yoga bells won't sound so creepy anymore! I couldn't have done this without the rest of my Alloy family there to support me—particularly Josh Bank and Sara Shandler, who never cease to be absolutely brilliant. Thank you to Heather David, for all your help on the social media front (particularly those amazing Twitter banners) and Annie Stone for that first brainstorming session. Thanks, also, to Theodora Guliadis for letting me take over the PLL Twitter for a day. I can't believe this is my job sometimes.

The team at Razorbill is the best in the business and I am so lucky to have them behind me. I couldn't have written this book without Jessica Almon's brilliant, insightful notes, or the nonstop support I received from Casey McIntyre and Ben Schrank. Sometimes I just sit and stare at this book's perfect cover, and I have Kristin Smith to thank for the eye-stopping design. Felicia Frazier, Rachel Lodi, Venessa Carson, Alexis Watts, and the rest of Razorbill's sales, marketing, and publicity team all worked so hard to help people discover my books. You guys are wonderful! In addition to the people named here, there are so many others working behind the scenes to make this book happen. I am grateful to all of you. I couldn't have done it without your support.

And finally, thanks to my fabulous, supportive family and friends. I'm consistently blown away by all of you. I couldn't have asked for better people in my life.

And, of course, thank you to Ron, who hasn't read this book yet but will, even though it'll give him nightmares.

HENDRICKS BECKER-O'MALLEY IS
ABOUT TO FIND OUT THAT HER FAMILY IS NOT
ALONE IN THEIR NEW HOME . . .

DON'T MISS

COMING SOON